Jimmy the Hand

Also by Raymond E. Feist

Magician
Silverthorn
A Darkness at Sethanon

Faerie Tale

Prince of the Blood
The King's Buccaneer

Shadow of a Dark Queen
Rise of a Merchant Prince
Rage of a Demon King
Shards of a Broken Crown

Krondor: The Betrayal
Krondor: The Assassins
Krondor: Tear of the Gods

With Janny Wurts:

Daughter of Empire
Servant of Empire
Mistress of Empire

Legends of the Riftwar

Honoured Enemy (with William R. Forstchen)
Murder in LaMut (with Joel Rosenberg)

Conclave of Shadows

Talon of the Silver Hawk

Voyager

RAYMOND E. FEIST
&
STEVE STIRLING

Jimmy the Hand

HarperCollins*Publishers*

Voyager
An Imprint of HarperCollins*Publishers*
77–85 Fulham Palace Road,
Hammersmith, London W6 8JB

www.voyager-books.com

Published by *Voyager* 2003
1 3 5 7 9 8 6 4 2

A catalogue record for this book
is available from the British Library

ISBN 0 00 224722 4

Typeset in Minion by Palimpsest Book Production Ltd,
Polmont, Stirlingshire

Printed and bound in Great Britain by
Clays Ltd, St Ives plc

ACKNOWLEDGEMENTS

As always, my first thanks must go to the mothers and fathers of Midkemia, who taught me the wisdom of listening to other voices.

To every fine writer who taught me how it should be done; I'm still trying.

To Jonathan Matson, again, and as always.

To Jane and Jennifer, two fine editors and better friends.

And to the usual suspects for all the love, support, humour and the richness of friendship.

And most of all, to my daughter Jessica and my son James for keeping it real.

To my readers:
Without your enthusiasm I'd be selling cars for a living.
Thank you from the bottom of my heart.

Raymond E. Feist

To Jan . . . and to Ray, Will, and Joel: the only guys who
could have brought this off.

S.M. Stirling

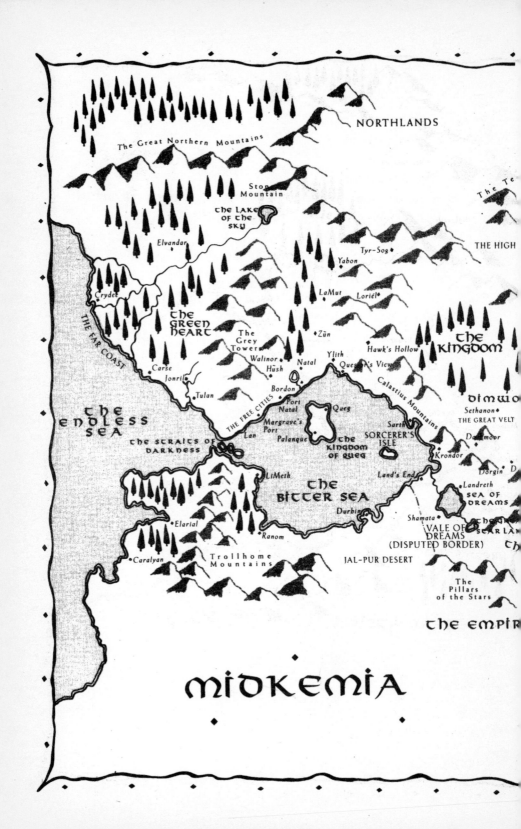

NORTHLANDS

The Great Northern Mountains

Stone Mountain

The Te

THE HIGH

The Lake of the Sky

Elvandar

Tyr-Sog

Yabon

Crydee

LaMut

Loriél

THE
GREEN
HEART

The Grey Tower

Zün

Hawk's Hollow

THE
KINGDOM

Walinor

Natal

Ylith

Húsh

Quesor's View

DIMWO

Carse

Bordon

Calastius Mountains

Jonril

Tulan

Sethanon

THE GREAT VELT

THE FREE CITIES

Port Natal

Ques

Sarth

THE
ENDLESS
SEA

Margrave's Port

Palanque

SORCERER'S
ISLE

Dawnoor

Lan

THE STRAITS OF
DARKNESS

THE
KINGDOM
OF QUEG

Krondor

LiMeth

Land's End

Dorgin

D

THE
BITTER SEA

Landreth

SEA OF
DREAMS

Durbin

Elarial

Shamata

SCARLAN

Ranom

VALE OF
DREAMS

Caralyan

(DISPUTED BORDER)

Trollhome
Mountains

JAL-PUR DESERT

The
Pillars
of the Stars

THE EMPIR

MIÐKEMIA

ONE

Escape

Men cursed as they grappled.

Jimmy the Hand slipped eel-like between knots of fighting men on the darkened quayside. Steel glittered in torch- and lantern-light, shining in ruddy-red arcs as horsemen slashed at the elusive Mockers who strove to hold them back. Only seconds more were needed for Prince Arutha and Princess Anita to make their escape, and the fight had reached the frenzied violence of desperation. Screams of rage and pain split the night, accompanied by the iron hammering of shod hooves throwing up sparks as they smashed down on stone, to the counterpoint of the clangour of steel on steel.

Bravos and street-toughs struggled against trained soldiers, but the soldiers' horses slipped and slithered on the slick boards and stones of the docks and the flickering light was even more uncertain than the footing. Knives stabbed upward and horses shied as hands gripped booted feet and heaved Bas-Tyran men-at-arms out of the saddle. The harsh iron-and-salt smell of blood was strong even against the garbage stink of the harbour, and a horse screamed piteously as it collapsed, hamstrung. The rider's leg was caught in the stirrup, crushed beneath his mount, and he screamed as the horse thrashed, then fell silent as ragged figures swarmed over him.

Jimmy fell flat under the slash of a sword, rolled unscathed between the flailing hooves of a war-horse scrabbling to find better footing, tripped one of the men-at-arms who was fighting dismounted against three Mockers, then dashed down the length of the dock, his feet light on the boards.

At the end of the quay he threw himself flat on the rough splintery wood to hail the longboat below:

'Farewell!' he called to the Princess Anita.

She turned toward his voice, her lovely face little more than a pale blur in the pre-dawn light. But he knew that her sea-green eyes would be wide with astonishment.

I'm glad I came to say goodbye, he thought, an unfamiliar sensation squeezing at his chest below the breastbone. *It's worth a little risk to life and limb.*

He grinned at her, but nervously; the fight with Jocko Radburn's men was heating up and his back felt very exposed. It wouldn't be long before the Mockers broke and ran; stand-up fights weren't their style.

Another, taller figure stood in the longboat. 'Here,' Prince Arutha called. 'Use it in good health!'

A rapier in its scabbard flew up to his hand. He snatched it out of the air and rolled over, just in time to avoid a kick from one of Radburn's bully-boys. Jimmy rolled again as the man pursued him, heavy-booted foot raised to stamp on him like an insect. Letting the sword go he reached up and grabbed toe and heel with crossed hands, giving it a vicious twist that set the bully roaring and twisting to keep it from being broken. That put him off-balance, and a kick placed with vicious precision toppled him screaming into the water. His gear dragged him under before the echoes of his scream could die.

'Time to go!' Jimmy panted.

Rolling up to his feet, Jimmy yanked the rapier from its scabbard and looked about for a worthy target – preferably one blocking the best escape route. Below, he could just make out the rhythmic splashing of the oars counterpoint the chaos of the battle all around him. Farewell, he said again in his heart. Then, as a pile of baled cloth blazed up: *Ooops!*

Lanterns began to appear on the boats around them, and watchmen from the surrounding warehouses came running, while from all around men called out: 'What passes?' and 'Who goes there?' And a growing shout: 'Fire! Fire!'

A man in the black and gold of Bas-Tyra snatched a lantern from one of the watchmen and marched toward the end of the dock, giving Jimmy an idea of whom to attack. The soldier grinned at the sight of the thin, ragged boy before him.

'Brought me a new sword, have you?' he said. 'Looks like a good one. Too good for gutter-scum whose whiskers haven't yet seen a razor. My thanks.'

He swung a backhand cut at Jimmy, a lazy stroke with more strength than style. No doubt he imagined that he could easily smash the rapier from the young thief's hand and then hack him down.

The finely-made blade was alive in Jimmy's hand; heavy, but perfectly balanced, limber as a striking snake. It flashed up almost of itself and turned the clumsy stroke away with a long *scringgg* of metal on metal. The guardsman grunted in astonishment as the redirected force of his own stroke spun him around, then shouted in pain as Jimmy danced nimbly aside and slashed at him.

More by luck than skill, the sharp steel caught the guardsman on the wrist, parting the tough leather of his gauntlet and cutting a shallow groove in the flesh beneath. With a gasp, the man shook his wrist and took a step back, disbelief visible on his coarse features even in the darkness.

Jimmy laughed in delighted surprise. Clearly not everyone had Arutha's skill with the blade. The hours he'd spent training with the Prince while waiting for Trevor Hull's smugglers to find a ship for Arutha and that old pirate, Amos Trask, to steal for their escape had paid off. Jimmy felt as if the soldier moved at half Prince Arutha's speed. He laughed again.

That laugh galvanized the soldier into action and he struck out at the young thief with blow after powerful blow.

Like a peasant threshing grain, Jimmy thought – he had little experience of matters rural, but a deep contempt for rubes.

The blows were hard and fast, but each was a copy of the one before. Instinct led him to raise the rapier, and the cuts flowed off steel blade and intricate swept guard; he had to put his left palm on his right wrist more than once, lest sheer force knock the weapon out of his hand. But he knew he was moments away from dodging to his left, thrusting hard and taking the soldier in the stomach. Arutha had always cautioned patience in judging an opponent.

An instant later Jimmy's back met the side of a bale; glancing to either side he realized he'd been neatly trapped in a short, dead-end passage of piled cargo. The man before him grinned and made teasing thrusts with his sword.

'Caught like the little sewer rat you are,' he growled.

The man raised his sword and Jimmy readied himself to execute his move, confident he would be through with the soldier in another moment. Then, suddenly, a pair of grappling bodies hurtled by, each man with a hand on the wrist of the other's knife-hand, stamping and cursing as they whirled in a circle like a fast and deadly country dance. They tumbled into the Bas-Tyran man-at-arms, throwing him forward with a cry of surprise. Jimmy didn't hesitate. He felt a mild instant of regret that he couldn't execute his fancy passing thrust, but he couldn't ignore such an easily acquired target. Jimmy stabbed out, and felt the needle point of the rapier sink through muscle and jar on bone, the strange sensation flowing up through the steel and hilt to shiver in his shoulder and lower back.

The man dropped his lantern with a cry that turned into a screamed curse as the glass shattered. The splattered oil blazed high, driving the wounded soldier back. He dropped his weapon and began to beat at spots of flame on his clothes, while Jimmy climbed the pile of bales like a monkey.

'You should know better than to corner a rat!' he called over his shoulder as he bounded down the back of the pile and struck the ground running.

He heard someone whistle the code to withdraw and saw Mockers streaming into alleys and side-streets like wisps of fog scattering before a high wind. Jimmy raced to join them, but before he ducked into an alley he turned to look out into the bay. Trevor Hull and his smugglers were diving into the water, some swimming under the docks while others made for long-boats standing by in the water. Beyond them, Jimmy could make out the form of the *Sea Swift* turning toward the broken blockade line, canvas fluttering free and catching the light like ghost-clouds in the dark; he raised his arm to wave. He knew it was useless; the Princess would have been hurried below to safety as soon as she'd been brought aboard. But he could no more have resisted that wave than he could have not spoken that one last word to her.

The young thief turned and ran down the alley, as light on his feet as a cat and almost as keenly aware of his surroundings. He might not be a great swordsman – yet – but fleeing through the darkened alleys of Krondor was a skill he'd mastered thoroughly long before he reached the ripe old age of thirteen.

As he dodged through the byways of the city, his thoughts turned to the time he had spent with the Princess and Prince during the last few weeks. The Princess Anita was what girls were supposed to be and in his experience never were. For a boy raised in the company of whores, barmaids and pickpockets, she was . . . something rare, something fine, a minstrel's tale come to breathing life. When he was near her he wanted to be better than he was.

It's well she's gone, then, he thought. A lad in his position couldn't afford such noble notions.

Besides, he thought with a wry grin, she would one day marry Prince Arutha – even though he didn't know it yet – so Jimmy had no business having such feelings for her. Not that having no business doing things had ever stopped him.

I suppose if she has to marry, and princesses do, he's the one I'd want her to.

Jimmy liked Arutha, but it was more than that. He respected him and . . . yes, trusted him. The Prince made him see why men would follow a leader, follow him to war on his bare word, something he'd never thought to understand. Jimmy's experience had been solely with men who commanded through fear or because they could deliver an advantage to those who followed. And Jimmy served at the pleasure of the Upright Man, who did both those things.

Jimmy ran his hand along the scabbard of Arutha's rapier, his now, and smiled. Then he grew suddenly solemn. Being with them had brought something special into his life, and now it was over. But then, how many people in the Kingdom got this close to princes and princesses? And of those, how many were thieves?

Jimmy grinned. He'd done better than well in his acquaintance with royalty: two hundred in gold, a fine sword, including lessons on how to use it, and a girl to dream about. And if he missed the Princess Anita, well, at least he'd got to know her.

He headed for Mother's with a jaunty step, ready for a light meal and a long sleep.

Best to sleep until Radburn cools off, he thought. Though that might mean he'd have to sleep until he was an old man.

Jimmy neared the large hall called Mother's, or Mocker's Rest, carved out among the tunnels of the sewers. To a citizen of the upper city it would have looked gloomy enough: the drip of water and the glisten of nitre on ancient stone. But it would have been little more than another junction of tunnels in the city's sewer system, a bit larger than usual, but nothing remarkable. To the average citizen of the upper city, the eyes watching Jimmy approach the entrance to Mother's would have gone unseen, and the daggers clutched in ready hands would have been undetected, unless at the last, fatal instant, they were driven home to protect the secret of Mocker's Rest.

To Jimmy it was home and safety and a chance to rest. He pushed on a stone, and a loud click preceded the appearance of a small opening, as a door fashioned of canvas and wood, cleverly painted to look like rock, swung wide. He was short enough that he could walk hunched over while a taller man would have to crawl, and he quickly traversed the short passage to enter the hidden basement. A Basher stood watch and as Jimmy appeared, nodded. Jimmy was thus spared a lethal welcome. Any unknown head coming through that passage had roughly a second to intone the password, 'There's a party tonight at Mother's' before finding his brains splattered all over the stone floor.

The room was huge, carved out of three basements, all with stairs leading up to three buildings owned by the Upright Man. A whorehouse, an inn and a merchant of cheap trade-goods provided a variety of escape routes, and Jimmy could find all of them blindfolded, as could every other Mocker. The light was kept dim at all hours of the day or night, so that a quick exit into the sewers wouldn't leave a Mocker without sight.

Jimmy nodded greetings to a few of the beggars and urchins

who were awake; most slept soundly, for there were still many hours until dawn. They would all be in the market minutes after sunrise on a normal day. But today would be anything but normal. With the Prince and Princess safely away, reprisals would be the first order of business. The City Constables and the Royal Household Guard had been easy enough to cope with over the years, but this secret police installed by Guy du Bas-Tyra since he took the office of Viceroy was another story. More than one Mocker had been turned snitch to them and the mood of the room reflected it. While there was a quiet sense of triumph at having aided Princess Anita's escape, the benefit was long-term; the Upright Man thought about things that way, Jimmy understood. Some day Princess Anita would return to Krondor – or at least Jimmy hoped so – and those who supported her and her father, Prince Erland, now had a debt to the Upright Man that he would contrive to collect in the most beneficial fashion.

But that was all for the future, for the Upright Man; for the common thief, pickpocket, or whore, there was no benefit this day. Instead, the city above would be crawling with angry spies and informants, looking to identify those who had embarrassed Jocko Radburn, head of the secret police. And he was not a man to embarrass without repercussions, Jimmy understood.

The escape of the Princess had been a secret undertaking, with only a few in the Mockers and among Trevor Hull's smugglers knowing who was being spirited out of the city. But once the fight erupted, more than one Mocker saw the Princess's face and her hallmark red hair and by sunrise the rumours of her escape would be making the rounds of the markets, inns and shops.

Most would feign ignorance of the deed, but everyone would know the reason for the sudden crackdown by Bas-Tyra's soldiers and secret police.

Jimmy moved to the far wall and picked up some rags, a whetstone and a small vial of oil from the storage box near the weapons lockers. Such thoughts made his head swim. He was a boy of unknown age – perhaps fourteen, perhaps sixteen, no one knew – and such considerations were intriguing to him, yet he knew he didn't fully understand all of it. Politics and intrigue were attractive, but in an alien way.

He made his way to a secluded corner to clean his rapier. *His* rapier, and a gift at that! There had been few of those in his life, making the fine weapon all the more precious. It would take the finest craftsman half a year to fashion such a thing of deadly beauty; it was as different from the crude, heavy weapons of ordinary soldiers as a war-horse was from a mule.

He pulled the blade from the scabbard again and realized to his dismay that he'd put it away bloody. He quirked his mouth wryly. Well, he'd never had such a thing before: he couldn't be expected to remember every detail of its care immediately. On closer inspection he realized that the scabbard was held together with ivory and brass pins, and could be taken apart for cleaning and oiling.

His pleasure in his gift went up a notch, if that was possible. This was a prize!

'Loot like that's to be turned in for sale, so's we can make proper shares,' Laughing Jack said. He reached for the sword and Jimmy slid it and himself away from Jack's hand with an eel-like motion.

'It's not loot,' he said. 'It's a gift. From Prince Arutha himself.'

'Oooh, you're getting gifts from princes these days are ye?' Jack had never actually been known to smile; his nickname had been bestowed on him by Jimmy as a joke.

But he sneers better than anyone else I've ever met, Jimmy thought.

The Nightwarden reached for the blade again, and again the young thief slid away. As senior lieutenant to the Nightmaster

9

he had a great deal of authority; most of the time, when appealed to, the Nightmaster would come down on Jack's side of an argument. But Jimmy knew he was in the right, and was sure that this time the Nightmaster would side with him.

Jimmy stood defiantly. More than one member of the Mockers had promised Jimmy someday Jack would kill him over the joke of a nickname he had given the glowering man. Now Jack appeared on the verge of making that prediction come true.

Jimmy stood a full two heads shorter than the Nightwarden. He was a slight boy, nimble and with a speed of hand and foot few in the Mockers could equal, and none could surpass. His own nickname was well-earned, for no Mocker was better able to lift a purse in a crowded market without being detected. He was a handsome boy, with curly brown hair cut tight against his head. His shoulders were just promising to broaden to a man's. His smile was infectious, and he had the knack of fun, but right now there was a hint of menace in his eyes as he stood with his hand on the pommel of the sword, ready to dispute Jack with blood if needed. His age was uncertain, perhaps thirteen years of age, perhaps fifteen, but he had already seen more danger and death in his life than most men twice his age. Softly he said, 'It's mine, Jack.'

'His. Saw,' Barmy Blake said in a voice like rock talking. The huge basher said no more, continuing on his way into the far recesses of the hall as though he'd never spoken at all.

Laughing Jack gave the basher's retreating back an uncertain look. Blake wasn't named Barmy for nothing; he was as unpredictable as a wild animal and capable of terrifying berserker rages. If Jack decided to make an issue of Jimmy's right to the sword after the basher had spoken up for him the Nightwarden might well find himself in a world of pain, senior lieutenant to the Nightmaster or no. Jack turned his sneer once again on Jimmy.

'Keep it then, but it's to be locked up.' He jerked his head toward the weapons lockers.

'Soon as it's cleaned,' Jimmy agreed. The rules allowed for that and they both knew it.

The Nightwarden turned away and stalked off. Jimmy turned his eyes to Blake who sat by himself at a table, a tankard in his beefy paw, gazing at nothing. He didn't bother to go and thank him; you didn't do that with Barmy. But he made a mental note of a favour owing, more honourable and more useful by far than any spoken thanks.

'Well, there's a pretty thing.'

Jimmy looked up and smiled at Hotfingers Flora, so named because of her early success in stealing pies that their owners mistakenly thought were too hot to handle. Unfortunately for Flora the insensitivity that allowed her to do so made her a very poor pickpocket despite Jimmy's best efforts. At sixteen, and pretty, she was turning to a different profession.

She sat beside him and twined her arms around his neck, slipping her legs onto his lap, and gave him a peck on the cheek.

'Hello, Jimmy,' she purred, fluttering her eyelashes at him, one chubby hand rubbing his chest.

He laughed. 'As if I'd keep anything valuable there,' he said.

Flora pouted, then smiled gamely. Pulling her legs off his lap she pointed at the sword. 'What are you going to do with that, eh?'

Jimmy gave it a swipe with the oiled cloth and held it up to glint in the torchlight. 'I'm going to keep it,' he said positively.

She looked at him speculatively, then glanced around the large hall. 'There was quite a fight out there tonight,' she said. 'Word's already spread the Princess and some other nobles escaped to the west.' She made a face and then added, 'Radburn and his bastards will be fit to be tied if that's the truth of it. When the Duke gets back . . .' She left the thought unfinished, but her expression showed a gleeful anticipation of what the Duke might do to the head of his secret police. 'The market'll be a quiet place with so many Mockers laying up licking their wounds.' Flora gave him a wicked look. 'Got any wounds you want licked, lovey?'

He laughed and gave her a friendly nudge. Inside he felt the slight tickle of excitement a rising flirtation often gave him, and flirtations with Flora often ended in bed. Flora hadn't been Jimmy's first, but not long after. He'd been around whores his entire life – his mother had been one – but Flora came from a better class than most; her father had been a baker before he died, so she had been raised a proper girl until she was ten. She could talk like a lady when she needed, which sometimes got her a better class of client. And she was prettier than most, with large expressive blue eyes and her light brown hair tending to curl around her face. She had a delicate chin and a nose that was 'just so'. She also had a lovely smile. It was a shame she had no skill with her fingers, thought Jimmy, more than once; she's just not suited to earn her living on the street.

Flora had said that she felt safe with him, and he assumed, without the slightest resentment, that it was because she was a foot taller than he was. As for himself, well, he liked Flora and he greatly enjoyed their private times together. He smiled at her blatant invitation and moved a bit closer. But then she gasped and her hand flew to her lips. 'Oh!' she said. 'I forgot, I, um, have to meet someone in an hour.' She snuggled against him. 'But I can be all yours until then.'

Jimmy thought it over; first they'd have to find somewhere private, which given the lack of time they had meant somewhere uncomfortable and smelly, and Flora would have to leave early to keep her appointment ... so that was far less than an hour, perhaps only a few minutes. Still, it wouldn't be the first time he and one of the girls had ripped off a quick bump in a dark corner while the others slept nearby. He'd been raised in a place where couples grabbed pleasure when and where they could all his life – but while Flora was one of his favourites, he didn't feel the usual hot rush, just a little tingle.

He was really tired. Besides, the Princess was travelling further and further away with every moment, and his heart sank. Suddenly a few minutes in Flora's arms was the last thing he wanted. He didn't like feeling this sadness . . .

Not that I'm certain just how I do feel. But it wouldn't be fair to inflict this strange mood on his friend.

'Sad to say I can't spare the time now, more's the pity,' he said with a grin as he put the pieces of the scabbard back together. 'Never thought I'd live to say that.' But now that he had said it he felt downright noble.

Flora giggled. 'Not to worry,' she whispered, 'there'll be other occasions.'

He gave her a one-armed hug and a kiss on the cheek. 'Oh, Flora, my flower, you are too good to me. Besides, I would probably disappoint you. All I have strength for is to look for a place to sleep tonight. I feel like I've been up and about since the day I was born.'

'You may have been about, but I haven't seen you,' Flora grumbled. 'Where've you been?'

'I was thinking the same thing about you,' Jimmy lied easily. 'I thought you'd been hired into someone's pleasure house.' If he wasn't going to take advantage of Flora's invitation he wouldn't suffer if she went off in a huff.

'No,' she said, looking away haughtily. 'I'm doing very well on my own.'

He looked at her; the new dress was pretty, but of cheap cloth, coarsely woven and coloured with dyes that would run and turn muddy soon: nobody had wasted good alum on fixing them. She wore a pair of dainty slippers on her feet, and a spangled scarf decorated her brown hair, more new things than she'd ever owned in her life. But she looked tired and not too clean.

The shine would be off her in six months, he knew, and in a year she'd look thirty. Life in the pleasure houses of the city was no holiday, but it was worlds better than the street. At least the girls had some hope of a future.

He couldn't forget what had happened to his mother. Murdered by a drunk just because she was on her own and so there was no one to stop him. He understood better than most that, for women, independence sometimes came at far too high a price.

'No you're not doing well,' he said quietly. 'You're risking life and limb every time you go with someone. Look, Flora, if this is what you really want to do I'm the last person to try and stand in your way. But listen to a little friendly advice. You're pretty enough that any house in this city would take you, and the better houses will take care of you. You speak well enough, almost like a lady, you could get hired at The White Wing, I'm thinking.'

Flora tossed her head with a 'tsk!', but he could tell she was listening.

'The pleasure houses will watch your customers for you, so you don't get sloppy drunks or bastards who'll beat you up for fun and not pay you. Better by far than the street.' He looked at her seriously. 'Better by far, of course, to do something else.'

She shrugged one shoulder. 'Like what? You know I'm a lousy thief. And I'm not about to pass for a beggar, now am I?'

He nudged her shoulder again and smiled. 'C'mon, you're a bright girl. I can get you some forged references. How do you think Carsten's sister got work at the palace?'

Flora looked thoughtful, then she gave him a sidelong glance. 'Does she like it?'

'Seems to,' Jimmy lied, having no idea himself. 'What wouldn't she like? She sleeps warm and in a bed of her own, with nobody else in it unless she wants him there, gets a new dress every year, good food, and paid in the bargain. Mind, she works hard, and the pay's no royal bequest, but all in all she seems to think it's worth it.'

His tongue itched to tell her, *and she helped to rescue the Princess Anita*, but he restrained himself. That would only lead to, *And so did I*, which wasn't something he wanted spread around. The last thing he needed was to be on Jocko Radburn's wanted list in a personal capacity.

Flora's mouth opened to speak when Laughing Jack stepped up onto a bench and thence to a table and called out,

'Listen up!' When the crowd had quieted and every face turned to him the Nightwarden continued. 'Word's down from the Upright Man, hisself! All Mockers are to lie low.' He raised his hands for silence as this announcement brought forth a torrent of muttered protest. 'That means out of sight, here, or if you got another flop, stay inside. And you beggars and younger thieves especially. Radburn seems to like to target your kind. No boosting, at all.' He paused and glared around the room: 'Not without special writ from the Day- or Nightmaster. We'll be getting some food in later, so you won't starve, until this business is over. Any questions,' again he passed a glare over the room, 'keep 'em to yourselves.' Laughing Jack stepped down and walked off to a rising chorus of speculation.

'What about the whores?' Flora asked, frowning.

'For Banath's sake, Flora,' Jimmy said, invoking the god of thieves, 'free food and a safe place to sleep! We're finally getting to see something for all those shares we pay out. Why work when we can laze about like –' he'd been about to say 'royalty', but changed it to, '– Bas-Tyra's bully-boys. Besides, it will give you a chance to think about your future.'

With a shy smile, she nodded, pleased at the attention. 'Oh, for . . .'

The Nightwarden took to the table again and said in exasperation: 'If you've got another flop, leave now! Those that don't can stay here.' He stepped down again and this time left the hall.

'Well,' Jimmy said, rising, 'I'm off to bed.'

He glanced at the rapier in his hand and decided after all to leave it in the weapons locker. A boy his age and station carrying a first-class sword down the street in what would soon be broad daylight was bound to receive unwelcome attention. The purchase price would be ten years' wages for a tailor or potmaker, much less a common labourer or child of the streets. He could scarcely assure the watch that, no, it wasn't stolen, a visiting prince had given it to him . . .

'What about you, Hotfingers?' he said. 'Do you need an escort?'

'Go on!' she said laughing. 'An escort!' She swatted him on the rump. 'Nah, I'm staying here to take advantage of the Upright Man's generosity.'

Jimmy looked around nervously; that was a somewhat over-bold statement, but no one had noticed.

'Good night then,' he said, and gave her a little salute with the hilt of the sword.

Flora broke into giggles at the sight. 'Escort!' he heard her say as he walked off.

TWO

Crackdown

Jimmy watched carefully.

Despite the early hour, the streets were rapidly filling with people. The scrawny street-sweepers with their brooms and pans were just clearing off; for a moment Jimmy thought it was a job should be paid for by the Crown. A bit of a tax on each business and all the streets would be fit for travellers rather than just some of the better boulevards in the merchants' and wealthy quarters where those who resided paid out of their own pockets. *If I was Duke of Krondor*, he thought idly, *that's how I'd do it.*

The sweepers were being replaced by cooks and their assistants returning from the farmers' markets with fresh produce, fruit and poultry. Butchers' apprentices hurried along carrying quarters of beef or sides of pork. Those tradespeople who didn't live over their businesses were off to open their shops in the next hour, and those whose work-day started a bit later were looking for their bite to eat at the start of the day.

Wood smoke curled from chimneys and he could smell porridge cooking, sometimes a fish or sausage frying – more odours to add their bit to the ghosts of ancient cabbage that haunted the city's poorer quarters. Wooden shoes clattered on the cobbles, bare feet slapped, hooves racketed.

The black and gold of Bas-Tyra wasn't as visible as it had been on other mornings lately, and Jimmy smirked to himself at the thought that they were still nursing their bruises. But the few members of the old Constable's company seemed on edge, as if trouble were coming and they didn't know which side of it they'd land. He passed a gate where four soldiers still wearing the Prince's tabards were huddled, talking with heads down rather than watching who passed through. Something was up and word was spreading. Jimmy knew every man on the docks the night before had been Bas-Tyra regulars or secret police.

For a moment he toyed with the idea of wandering over to the temporary barracks used by Bas-Tyra's soldiers and taking a look at the damage, but that notion was dispelled by a rare instant of common sense. Given how touchy the guards were no doubt feeling today, any number of poor boys were liable to be spending a few days in the city dungeon. But in his case it was liable to be more than a few days and a lot more painful.

Suddenly a sergeant of the Bas-Tyra guard appeared and the Prince's four sentries snapped lively and took their posts on either side of the gate. Jimmy watched from the sheltered vantage point of a deep doorway opposite the gate. The sergeant's mood was dark and dangerous and when he left, the four soldiers of the Prince were studying every face that passed, looking for something. As he was about to slip away, Jimmy saw them halt one ragged fellow and start questioning him. Jimmy knew the fellow: he was not a true Mocker, but one of the threadbare poor who flitted around the edges of crime from time to time. He was a labourer named Wilkins, and Jimmy had seen him unloading smugglers' cargo for Trevor Hull twice in the last year. One guard put the strong arm on him and marched him away.

Jimmy sank back into the doorway. If they were taking in

know-nothings like Wilkins, then he was certain to be nabbed if he showed his face. Although, if he could get into the dungeons he might be able to do something for Princess Anita's father.

If I could rescue Prince Erland, Anita would never forget me.

And it might be very profitable. He'd gained two hundred in gold for helping Prince Arutha and he'd only needed to guide him to safety. How much more could he make if it took actual effort?

The young thief stared into space for a moment, his fingers reaching out as if of their own volition to snatch up a bun from a passing vendor's tray as she edged close to the doorway to avoid a passing horse-drawn wagon. His hand moved in a swift unhurried arc that put the pastry beneath the tail of his jacket without any flash to attract the eye as he faded back into the shelter of the doorway. The stout woman continued on, ignorant of the theft, still calling her wares. Jimmy bit into the warm bun, considering possibilities and savouring the cinnamon and honey.

He'd need to speak to Mockers who'd been in the dungeon. That would lead him to the beggars, then. Thieves never made it out of the dungeons alive and bashers, who might be let go if they were thought to be innocent drunks who'd just got out of control, were people he tried to avoid. Especially when planning something the Upright Man might not endorse.

Well, definitely wouldn't endorse, he admitted to himself. *Definitely would reject with . . . oh . . . cold fury would be a good description.*

Laughing Jack's admonition to stay out of sight and out of action wafted through his mind to be dismissed. Being cautious never won the prize, at least not in his experience, and for thirteen or so he'd had a great deal of experience.

His jaws cracked in a massive yawn, so Jimmy decided to get some sleep before he did any more planning. He waited until the three remaining guards had their attention distracted away from him, then darted out of the shadow of the doorway. He turned a corner and headed off to one of his places, one he'd actually paid for. It was nothing more than a cupboard with a tiny window and just enough space for a pallet and a rickety table with a cheap candle stand. The old couple who owned the house believed that he was a caravan master's apprentice, which explained his frequent and sometimes lengthy absences. They charged only a few silvers a month and rarely climbed as high as his tiny room, providing him with both security and privacy. Even so, he only left a few rags of clothing there. Or, at least, that was all he left in his room so far. Up in the garret he'd found a few hiding places but had yet to use one. Now, with his gold heavy on his hip Jimmy resolved to try one out. He'd given some thought to a proper safe house, and decided for the time being poverty was his best cover; none of his fellow Mockers or any of the rare independent thieves who wandered into Krondor would suspect gold would be hidden in a hovel such as this.

He woke the old man up when he knocked and was greeted with a resentful grunt – since selling their businesses years before, the old couple slept in, often as late as seven or eight of the clock, and didn't relish having to admit Jimmy at dawn.

The old fellow locked the door behind the boy and headed back to his room, leaving Jimmy alone in the dim and dusty front hall. Jimmy started up the stairs, noting that the place smelled worse than it had the last time he was here. This was his only semi-decent roost. If it kept deteriorating like this he'd have to move.

'Listen to me,' he mumbled wearily, 'I'm starting to sound respectable myself.'

Baron Jose del Garza, acting governor of Krondor in the Duke's absence and now, temporarily, the head of the Duke du Bas-

Tyra's secret police, sat behind the desk of the commander of the palace guard, seething and staring at the narrow, pointed window in the stonework across from him. The room smelled of ink, musty parchment, cheap wine, tallow candles and old sweat.

Had it been his pleasure, he'd have been just about anywhere else in the Kingdom than in Krondor this morning. He'd have been far happier leading the charge against the Keshian raiders troubling the Southern Marches alongside the Duke of Bas-Tyra, rather than having to oversee the business before him today.

Del Garza was a man of modest ambitions. He served at the Duke's pleasure, and it had been Duke Guy's wish that he administer the city in his absence, seeing that bills were paid, taxes collected, crimes were punished, and overseeing the usual details of running the principality while the Prince languished in his private quarters. It would be easy to think of the Prince's confinement as being under arrest, but no guards were stationed outside his quarters; the man's poor health prevented any chance of his escaping the city, and whatever else he was, the Prince was obedient to his nephew, the King. When Guy had arrived in the city with the Writ of Viceroy signed by the King, Prince Erland had graciously stepped aside.

Now del Garza sat silently cursing the day he had left his native Rodez to seek service in Bas-Tyra. Duke Guy was a hard man, but a fair one, but since coming to Krondor, del Garza had been forced to suffer the companionship of Jocko Radburn. That murderous maniac had the face of a simple peasant, but the heart of a rabid wolf. And his inability to do something as simple as keep a sixteen-year-old girl under lock and key was now threatening to turn del Garza's life upside down.

Radburn had left del Garza in command of the secret police, and had commandeered one of the Duke's ships, the *Royal Griffin*, and set off in hot pursuit less than an hour after the girl and her companions had fled the city. Now del Garza was faced with cleaning up this mess and, more importantly, positioning himself so that if Radburn failed to recover the escaped Princess, as little blame attached itself to him as possible.

A knock came and he answered, 'Yes?'

A guard opened the door and looked through. 'He's coming, sir.'

Del Garza nodded, keeping his face calm as the door closed again. He had appropriated this office for a very specific interview, following which he would address his subordinates. But first, very much first, he would speak to the captain of the *Paragon*, a blockade ship that had just happened to drift off her position at a critical moment this morning.

He heard a man's voice approaching, clearly raised in anger. There were no answering voices as the one who shouted came closer. A knock sounded on the closed iron-strapped wooden door and del Garza contemplated it for a short interval. There had been a momentary silence after the knock, but it was soon broken again by the protesting, expostulating voice.

'Come,' the acting governor said quietly.

The door opened instantly and del Garza met the eye of his subordinate as he entered the office. He saw both amusement and exasperation there and not a little disgust. For an instant del Garza wondered if the thinly-veiled contempt was directed at him, but at the last, the man glanced to the side, and del Garza realized the scorn was directed at the man who followed close behind.

Though not a small man, the secret police operative was thrust aside by a very large, very self-important one wearing the salt-stained coat of a sea captain.

'What is the meaning of this?' the captain demanded. 'I must protest this treatment! I am a gentleman, sir, and I was brought here under protest! I was given a missive summoning me to a meeting with the acting governor, but no sooner did we make dock than this –' he sneered at the fellow he had shoved, '– *brigand* tells me that I am under arrest and seized my sword. My sword, sir! What possible excuse could there be for such an action?'

He stopped and stared at the man behind the desk. 'And *who*, if I may ask, are you, sir?'

Del Garza stared at him while the other two guards took up position behind the Captain. Captain Alan Leighton was indeed a gentleman, the third son of a very minor nobleman whose family were willing to pay to get him out of the ancestral home; in other words, someone of less real use than the average dock-walloper or ditch-digger. And he would have been dismissed from either position for incompetence within a week. His commission and his ship had been bought for him, not earned, while better men had to wait. The Baron knew his type and despised him. He was a man who was just important enough to be a nuisance, and not important enough to have any real value.

'I *am* the Governor,' he said, his voice as flat and cold as a window in midwinter.

The captain shifted his feet and looked at him uncertainly. Del Garza was an ordinary enough looking man; rat-faced, and his dress was of simple if expensive weave.

'Indeed?' the Captain said dubiously.

'Indeed,' del Garza confirmed quietly. 'Be seated, Captain Leighton.' His nod indicated a stool in front of the desk.

The Captain looked at it, then at the acting governor in disbelief. 'On *that*?' he sneered. 'The thing will collapse.' Leighton turned to one of the guards. 'You there, bring me a proper chair.'

Del Garza leaned forward. 'Sit,' he clipped out. 'Or *be* seated.'

The two guards moved a step closer to the blustering seaman, ready to reach out and slam him down. For the first time Leighton actually looked at their faces; he blinked, and slowly sat down, his gaze moving from each of the men in the room to the next. 'What is the meaning of this?' he asked. His voice tried to carry the bluster, but there was a quaver in it now.

In answer, del Garza rubbed one hand over the stubble on his jaw and gave him the glance that a tired man would give a buzzing fly. Every irritation and annoyance from the day he had set foot in Krondor until this morning rose up and seemed to resolve itself in the person of this pitiful excuse for a sea captain. Del Garza decided at that instant that Leighton needed to pay for them all. 'Can't you guess?' he asked through clenched teeth. 'Can't you even begin to guess?'

Leighton gazed at him like a mouse fascinated by a snake. 'No,' he said at last. He leaned back, remembered just in time that he was on a stool and frowned. Leaning forward, the Captain went on the attack. 'I say, is this some form of joke? If so it is in very poor taste and I assure you I shall complain of it to your superior.'

'Do I look as if I'm joking?' del Garza asked. 'Am I smiling? Am I, or my men, laughing? Does this seem to be an atmosphere of mirth and good-fellowship to you?'

Nervous perspiration dewed the Captain's broad brow, his eyes shifted left and right. 'No,' he said and shook his head. 'I suppose not.' He straightened. 'But I still do not know why I am here.'

'You have been arrested for treason.'

Leighton shot to his feet, ignoring the guards who moved yet another step closer. 'How dare you, sir? Do you know who I am?'

'You are the noxious toad who took a bribe to break the blockade,' del Garza said. 'During wartime such an act can be nothing less than treason.'

'I did no such thing!' the captain insisted.

The Baron smiled. 'Do you know how many fools have tried to lie to the Duke's agents?' he asked. He waved his hand casually at the two burly guards and at several other men whom he knew waited outside. 'Usually their next remark is something on the order of: *Stop! Gods, please stop!*'

'I admit that my ship floated off-station,' Leighton blustered. 'Such things happen occasionally, there's nothing deliberate in it. An anchor bolt rusted through and the tide caught our bow. It was merely misfortune that it happened at that particular moment. When I heard the commotion I rose from my bed, came topside and corrected the situation at once. At the very worst it was dereliction of duty, though even that would be coming it a bit high under the circumstances.'

Del Garza raised his brows and leant back in the commander's chair with his hands clasped over his lean stomach. 'Indeed?' he said.

'Of course,' Leighton said, allowing a touch of his former haughtiness to creep into his tone. 'I tell you these things happen, 'tis no one's fault, my good man. No one could have predicted that a ship would choose that particular moment to . . .'

'We know the Upright Man bribed you.' The acting governor waited for the explosion, but none came; the Captain merely stared at him, his mouth opening and closing like a gaffed fish. Not only guilty then, but the man had no spine. 'What was it, the gold? Or some misplaced sense of loyalty to Prince Erland's family?'

'We have known them a long time . . .' Leighton began.

Del Garza cut him off. 'You may as well admit it, you know. We have proof.'

The Captain shook his head silently.

'Oh, but we do,' del Garza insisted. 'We have our own sources inside the Mockers, you know.'

They didn't, of course, have either – proof, or sources. But it was obvious to the secret policeman that the Mockers had an interest in freeing the Princess Anita. It was certainly Mockers he and his men had been fighting this morning. Besides, every instinct he had told him that it was beyond unlikely that a ship would just 'happen' to drift off-station at precisely the wrong moment.

The lie came easily though, because if del Garza was going to have to answer for Anita's escape – and he was – then others would answer first and far more painfully.

Leighton licked his lips. 'You could hardly call it treason,' he said.

Del Garza leaned forward blinking rapidly, his brows raised incredulously. 'Oh, yes,' he said. 'Taking a bribe deliberately to disobey orders during wartime could never be anything else.'

'We are hardly at war with the Mockers,' the Captain argued.

'We are always at war with the Mockers,' del Garza corrected, his voice flat. 'That it has never been formally declared makes it no less a war. For if we were not at war with them, I assure you these thieves and murderers-for-hire are and have always been at war with the decent citizens of Krondor.'

'They are hardly worthy . . .' Leighton began.

'Opponents?' Del Garza sneered. 'If their money is good enough for you then why shouldn't they be considered . . . worthy?'

The Captain pressed his lips together and took a deep breath, then he straightened. 'I should like to see this "proof" you claim to have.'

Del Garza chuckled, an impulse he couldn't control. 'Are you now going to claim innocence, after all but admitting your guilt?'

'I have not admitted any guilt,' the Captain said. 'Come, come, you shall have to produce the proof at my trial.'

With a sad shake of his head the Baron asked: 'Would you really put your family through the shame of a trial when the conclusion is inevitable? Must we prove to them and all the world your villainy?'

The colour drained from Leighton's face. 'What are you suggesting?' he demanded, clearly shaken.

'You need do nothing radical,' del Garza said, suddenly all generosity. 'Naturally you cannot keep your commission.' He drew a document from a small pile and pushed it toward the captain along with a quill pen already resting in an ink stand. 'Herein you resign your commission; just sign at the bottom of the page, and the next page as well and then we'll send you home.' He lifted the pen from the inkwell and proffered it to Leighton with a slight smile. 'Your older brother wouldn't be the first nobleman who had to find a second career for a younger brother; much less a problem than shaming the family name.'

'That is all?' the Captain asked, taking the pen hesitantly.

Del Garza nodded. 'We will take care of everything else. All the arrangements,' he clarified. He pointed to the bottom of the page. 'If you would,' he invited.

As one hypnotized, Leighton signed. Del Garza lifted the corner of the page to expose the one beneath.

'Sign here as well, if you would be so kind.'

With a shaky hand the Captain signed the bottom page as well and the acting governor drew them back, sanded the signatures and shook them dry.

'Very good,' he said. 'But for one minor detail that concludes our business.'

Leighton mopped his brow with a handkerchief. 'What is that?' he asked.

At del Garza's nod the three guards stepped forward; two caught hold of the captain's arms while the third whipped a garrotte around his neck. The stool went over with a crash, and Leighton's legs became caught up in it so that he couldn't get his feet under him. Del Garza cocked his head, watching the consciousness of imminent death and agony flood into the man's eyes. Soon his heels beat a brief tattoo on the floor and after a very few moments he was dead.

The Baron neatly folded and sealed the two sheets of paper.

'Poor fellow,' del Garza said to the guards. 'Carry him to his quarters and arrange things there. Make sure the bracket he hangs himself from is stout; he was a fleshy sort.' He handed the papers to the chief guard. 'Don't forget to leave his resignation and most important, his confession, where they'll be easily found.'

The guard smiled as he took the papers. 'That was neatly done, sir,' he said. 'Makes me feel like we're getting a bit of our own back.'

Del Garza looked at him for long enough that the man knew the Baron wasn't amenable to flattery, then dismissed him.

Alone, del Garza considered his choices. Leighton had to die; there was no other option. Had he remained alive, word of the Duke's vulnerability would eventually spread. Loyalty to the Prince or avarice for Mockers' gold, the reason for Leighton's treason didn't matter. What mattered was who would be looked at when Duke Guy returned from dealing with the Keshians in the Vale of Dreams.

Del Garza could put a fair amount of responsibility on Radburn's shoulders, with justification. His iron grip on the city had bred discontent, and the way in which he ran roughshod over the Prince's own guards and the city's constables would be certain to drive some firmly into the Prince's camp.

The handwriting was on the wall, as they say; Erland was dying, no matter what the healing priests and chirurgeons did to hold death at bay. With no son to inherit, Anita would be a prize for any ambitious man. And with the King having no heirs, her husband was but one step from the throne in Rillanon. So, Guy would marry Anita, and some day, sooner rather than later, del Garza judged, Guy du Bas-Tyra would become King Guy the First.

Del Garza tapped his chin with a forefinger as he wondered where he might come out in all this. He was not by nature an ambitious man, but circumstances seemed to dictate that his choice was to rise or fall; there was no standing still. Hence, he would choose to rise. Who knew? An earldom in the east, perhaps near Rodez?

But to rise, he had to avoid falling, and to do that, he had to survive Guy's wrath when he returned and found the girl missing. He hoped Radburn would return soon with the girl in tow, or not return at all. If Jocko had the good grace to get himself killed in the attempt, everything would be his fault by the time del Garza got finished explaining things to the Duke. And that meant having lots of other guilty parties to parade before him.

'Cray!' he shouted, summoning the captain of the guard's secretary. When the man appeared he said, 'I want every commander of every unit involved with this morning's mission, from the sergeants up, in this office in one hour.'

'Yes, sir,' Cray said and sped off.

Del Garza sat back in the commander's chair, enjoying the way Cray had leapt to obey, enjoying the privilege of taking over the commander's office, enjoying the memory of the look on Leighton's face when he had realized del Garza held the power in Krondor for the moment.

He turned his mind away from feeling any pleasure at the prospect of authority. How could he enjoy anything when his lord had been humiliated this morning? How could that wicked girl abandon her father so? And why? So that she would not have to partake of the honour of wedding the Duke du Bas-Tyra; one of the greatest, one of the noblest men in the Kingdom! How dare the little baggage treat his lord so?

Poor Prince Erland, to have such an uncaring child. Not that he was much better, for he, too, had defied his lord's will. Well, he'd just have to suffer the fate to which his *own daughter* had condemned him. Del Garza considered: perhaps if the Prince was relocated to one of his draughtier dungeons, and word was leaked that he would remain there until his daughter returned . . .? He considered that a move to be made if Radburn didn't return with the girl soon. If the girl had been coerced into leaving the city, it might convince her to return of her own volition, and if the Prince didn't survive the ordeal, that was another problem that could be laid at Jocko's feet when the Duke again graced the city.

Del Garza sighed. So much to be done, and he so much preferred routine to the unexpected. But, at least he knew the task at hand.

These . . . *thieves*, these *nothings* must be brought to heel, whipped into place like the dogs they were. That they should dare to steal Guy du Bas-Tyra's rightful bride, interfering in matters they knew nothing about, and indeed *should* know nothing about . . .

With an effort del Garza calmed himself. He took deep breaths until his heart rate returned to normal. He shouldn't waste this anger; he should harbour his fury until the men came, and then release it. Things were going to change around here; soon and forever. By the time Guy du Bas-Tyra returned from the south, Krondor would be a city in order and under firm control. *Yes,* he thought, *in control.*

He called for a parchment and pen and set his mind to the list of things that would have to be done, and first on that list was to round up as many of the Mockers as could be ferreted out of whatever dark warren hid them.

THREE

Aftermath

The crossroads was crowded.

Hotfingers Flora was chatting and laughing with her friends while tossing saucy, flirtatious glances at every passing male when the wagon pulled up beside them. At first she didn't give it much of a glance; the streets were busy with men on foot, porters with heavy loads, handcarts full of golden loaves of bread, cloth, boxes and bales, a sedan-chair – she cast an envious glance at the court-esan lolling within it – and any number of farmers' wagons hauling in the city's food.

When it stopped in front of her, she realized that this one wagon was different. It was a curious sight, with high sides and hoops over the top as though it was meant to be covered by a canvas tilt. But there were crossbars tied onto the hoops with rawhide thongs, making it look like a cage. It was driven by a pair of Bas-Tyran guards and followed by four more on foot, their hobnails a counterpoint to the clangour of iron-rimmed wheels on stone and their halberds swaying as they marched in step.

Some of her friends moved away cautiously – anything out

of the ordinary was dangerous. But the majority of the girls watched with arms folded across their breasts and their eyes flicking toward the surrounding alleys, holding their ground despite their suspicion. After all, a lot of their business came from soldiers.

A sergeant descended from the wagon and approached the girls with the rolling swagger of a man who'd spent as much of his life on horseback as on foot. His corporal went to work lowering the tailgate and opening the cage door; the rest of the squad braced their polearms, the sharp hooks on the backs inter-linked, a bare upright tent.

The sergeant chucked Flora under the chin and turned to grin at his men who also moved in, smiling. He smelled of sweat, leather and sour wine; she was used to that, but this man was ranker than most, and she wrinkled her nose a little. Flora tossed her head and with a slightly nervous smile asked, 'Anything I can do for you, soldier?'

'Yes,' the sergeant said, leaning in close, 'you can come with me, my little canker-blossom, you and all your friends. We're having a party for you back at the keep.' He took hold of her arm with a hard grip and a cruel, crook-toothed smile.

'Well, there's no need to be rough about it,' Flora snapped, trying to pull away.

'I suppose there isn't,' he agreed amiably. 'But, ye see, I want to be.'

With that, he picked her up by her hair and the waist of her skirt and tossed her into the cage in a squawking cartwheel of limbs and cloth. Her knee hit something hard enough to bring tears to her eyes. Before she could get to her feet, her friends were thrown in on top of her, driving the breath out of her lungs with a force that left her struggling for air. One of her teeth cut the inside of her lip with a little stab of pain, and the iron-salt-copper taste of blood filled her mouth.

'Wait!' she cried after an instant, sucking back her breath as she went scrambling backward out of the writhing heap. 'We haven't done nothing! What are you doing?'

The cries of the others were shrill around her: protests, sobs, curses and wordless shrieks of rage. She hauled herself up by the bars of the wagon in time to see two of her friends scurry down an alley with their skirts gathered up, and took heart from the sight. Word would get back to the Upright Man and something would be done about it. Flora rattled the wooden bars of the cage as hard as she could, glaring.

'You can't just throw us in jail for nothing!' she shouted.

The sergeant came up to her and smacked her fingers with a mailed fist; not hard enough to break anything, but more than hard enough to hurt. 'Oh, yes we can,' he said, with what might have been mistaken for good humour, if you weren't watching his eyes.

Those eyes had something in them that made her shiver and remember what Jimmy had said about the risks of freelancing.

The sergeant slapped his gloved hands together; the metal rings on their backs clinked dully. 'So says the acting governor. We can do anything we want to trash like you, and serves you right. Now shut up and settle down like a good, sensible girl or I'll knock your teeth out.'

Flora sucked her wounded knuckles and did as she was told. The pain was distant, less real than the way her heart pounded with fear, and her throat tried to squeeze itself shut beneath a mouth gone parchment-dry.

By the time they arrived at the keep, the cage was full to bursting and Flora was pressed tightly against the bars – which was still better than being in the middle, since at least there was open air on one side. The wagon was filled with whores and beggars and a very few of the younger pickpockets who had been doing absolutely nothing illegal when they were taken. The soldiers had even rounded up a few people who were simply poor, or who'd happened to be standing next to the wrong whore. But she'd noticed that most of those in the cage with her were Mockers. And that frightened her. Clearly Jocko Radburn was not taking the Mockers' adventure with the Princess Anita lightly.

The gates clashed shut behind them. More Bas-Tyra guardsmen hauled them out of the wagons to join a growing file of prisoners being herded to stairways that led downward. Boots and fists and the steel-shod butts of halberds and pikes thudded on flesh; almost all the cursing came from the guards, though.

Their prisoners were mostly silent, except for the occasional cry of pain.

Jimmy had slept for a whole day and night, waking at midmorning on the second day after the *Sea Swift*'s departure. He stretched luxuriously, rose and put on clean clothes – or rather, the well-aired rags he'd left in this room the last time he'd slept here – and descended the stairs. Instinct made him walk close to the wall, where the boards were less likely to creak. On the whole he liked growing up, but there was no denying it made you heavier, and he was conscientious about learning to make skill compensate for the additional poundage.

'If ye're lookin' for breakfast ye can look elsewhere,' said his landlady. She was a toothless beldame who glared at him with rheumy eyes. 'Ye know I've nothing for ye at this hour.'

'I wouldn't think of asking you to trouble yourself,' Jimmy said gallantly. He smiled. 'I needed the sleep more than the breakfast anyway.'

'At your age?' the old woman sneered.

'It was a long trip this time,' Jimmy said.

And indeed it was, into a whole other world in its way. But now it was time to get back to business. First he would stop at

Mocker's Rest and see what was happening. Then he could start the planning stages of something bigger than picking pockets.

He'd been apprenticed to Long Charlie for the last few months, though that apprenticeship had been suspended the night Jimmy had caught sight of Prince Arutha attempting to flee Jocko Radburn himself.

The Prince, his Huntmaster – Martin Longbow – and Amos Trask – the legendary Trenchard the Pirate – had come secretly into the city a few days earlier before Jimmy's encounter with the Prince. They had tried to hide their presence but from Jimmy's point of view they stood out like red bulls in a sheep fold. By the time Jimmy had chanced across Radburn pursuing Arutha, the Upright Man had put the word out to pick up these three newcomers.

Jimmy had known something was up between the smugglers and Mockers, something beyond their usual uneasy truce, for Trevor Hull's men had come and gone in areas of the sewer that were clearly Mockers' territory, but as he was only a boy, albeit a very talented one, he was not privy to the secret of the Princess's escape from the keep.

Finding Arutha had changed that, and had plunged Jimmy into the heart of a conspiracy that had ended the night before with Anita, Arutha, and his companions successfully making their escape. He had not only become a conspirator but had become a companion to both Prince Arutha and Princess Anita while they awaited their opportunity for escape. He had played his part, earned royal thanks, and found within himself a sense of something larger than himself for the first time in his young life.

Such triumphs left Jimmy in no mood to return to apprentice-ship, opening practice-locks while Long Charlie looked over his shoulder. Besides, he'd long since caught the knack of lock-picking and the samples he'd seen didn't look as if they'd offer any challenge. Frankly, the training he was getting was boring and Jimmy knew in his heart that he was meant for more exciting things. Sometimes it seemed that Charlie was just giving him tedious work to keep Jimmy out of his hair. Even before the adventure with Arutha and Anita, Jimmy had made up his mind to request a new mentor. *Life is too short to wait for what I'm entitled to*, he thought.

One thing he should do today was steal some more respectable-looking clothes. The ones he was wearing smelled bad, even to himself.

Or I could buy some, just for a change, he thought. But first, a money-changer.

The changer worked out of a narrow shop in an alley, denoted by a pair of scales on a sign above the door; the paint was so faded that only a hint of gold peeped through the grime. Jimmy hopped over the trickle of filth down the centre of the alley, nodded to the basher who stood just outside, polishing the brick-work with his shoulder, and pushed through the door. The basher would find a reason to delay any citizen from entering the shop whenever a Mocker was inside.

Ference, the money-changer, looked up and said, 'Ah, Jimmy! What can I do for you?'

Jimmy reached inside his tunic and pulled out his coin pouch, and with a quick flip of his wrist, rolled half a dozen coins on the counter. The others were safely hidden on top of a ceiling beam in his room.

'Gold?' Ference said, looking at the thumbnail-sized coins Jimmy shoved across the smooth wood of the table.

The money-changer was a middle-aged man with a thin, lined face and the sort of squint you got from fretting about your strongbox when you should be sleeping. He dressed with the sort of sombre respectability a prosperous storekeeper might affect.

'Getting ambitious, are you, Jimmy lad?'

'Honestly earned,' Jimmy said, 'for a change.' And it was even true, for once.

He kept a close eye on the scales as Prince Arutha's coins turned into a jingling heap of worn and much less conspicuous silver and copper. The Upright Man's regulations kept men like Ference moderately honest – broken arms were the usual first-time penalty for changers or fences shorting Mockers, and then it got really nasty – but it never hurt to be self-reliant.

'There,' the changer said at last. 'That'll attract a lot less attention.'

'Just what I thought,' Jimmy said, smiling a little to himself.

He bought a money-belt to hold it – too big a jingling purse was conspicuous too – and wandered out into the street.

'Pork pies! Pork pies!' he heard, and the words brought a flood of saliva into his mouth; he had missed breakfast. 'Two of your best, Mistress Pease,' he said grandly.

The pie-seller put down the handles of her pushcart and brought out two; they were still warm, and the smell made his nose twitch. What was more, Mistress Pease's pork pies were actually made from pork, not of rabbit, cat, or the even less savoury concoctions you got from some vendors. He bit into one.

'Feeling prosperous, I see,' she said, as he handed over four coppers.

'Hard work and clean living, Mistress,' he replied; she shook all over as she laughed.

Well, a thin cook wouldn't be much of an advertisement, would she? he thought.

He washed the pies down with a flagon of cider bought from a nearby vendor, and sat in the sun belching contentedly, his back against the stone-coping of a well.

He was just licking his fingers when a pebble hit the top of his head.

Ouch, he thought, and looked up.

Long Charlie's cadaverous face peered around a gable. His hands moved: *Report to Mocker's Rest*, he said in the signing cant. *Right now. No delay, no excuses.*

Jimmy swigged back the rest of the cider and hastily returned his flagon to the vendor with polite thanks. Then he headed for the nearest alley.

Once in the sewers he moved at a confident jog – even through the pitch-black places, of which there were many – and passed the guards the Mockers had stationed at various locations, who seemed unusually alert today. Not that they were ever less than wide-awake; sleeping or getting drunk on guard duty could get you badly hurt or seriously dead.

The smell was homelike, though ripe; Jimmy flicked his toe aside and sent a rat more belligerent than most flying through the air. Its squeal ended with a sodden thud – you had to be careful about the ones that didn't run away, chances were they were sick with something. Jimmy had seen a man foaming at the mouth from a rat bite and it wasn't a sight he would quickly forget.

The Rest was like a kicked anthill, all swarming movement – although ants didn't produce that sort of din, or wave their arms so that you nearly got clouted in the face walking through. Agitated people moved quickly from group to group; everyone seemed to be talking at once. He spied a boy he knew standing apart and went over to him. 'What's happening?' he asked.

The boy, dubbed Larry the Ear because his were enormous, stood tense as a bowstring watching the frantic activity. He spoke to Jimmy without taking his eyes from the scene before them. 'Bas-Tyra's men are arresting the girls and the beggars and anyone else they can get their damned paws on,' Larry growled. 'They took Gerald.'

Jimmy blinked. Gerald was Larry's younger brother, not much older than seven, if that. Jimmy had known Radburn was a vindictive swine, but arresting babies was beyond contempt.

He started to ask, 'Was he pick . . .?'

'No!' Larry snapped, turning to glare at Jimmy. 'He wasn't doing nothing. He was just playin', just bein' a kid!'

'Damn Radburn's bones,' Jimmy said quietly.

'Damn him right enough,' Larry said. 'But this was del Garza. Radburn's out of town – took ship not an hour after the Princess got away.' Jimmy blinked. If Larry knew the Princess had been the one fleeing last night, then everyone knew it. So much for secrets. 'Del Garza's in charge, and he's gone crazy mean.'

Crazy like a fox, Jimmy thought, motionless, as implications ran through his mind. *Princess gone, Radburn chasing her – del Garza will want lots of people to pin the blame on when the Duke gets back. Radburn can at least say he went after them right away. What was that old saying?* Victory has a thousand fathers, but defeat is an orphan. *Del Garza wants to have as many other candidates for the role of defeat's father as he can.*

'Del Garza's a snake from the same egg as Radburn,' Larry said passionately. 'He's up to something and even if it takes hurting a little boy, he'll do it!'

Jimmy nodded in agreement. 'Well, we won't let him,' he said quietly. 'Let's see what the Upright Man decides and if he doesn't make the right decision, well, we'll see.' He punched Larry's shoulder. 'You with me?'

The younger lad's eyes filled with hope and he nodded.

'Who else do you think will take our point of view?' Jimmy asked quietly.

'I'll find out,' Larry said, swiping his dirty sleeve over his eyes, leaving dark smears behind.

Jimmy nodded. 'Me too. But we'll not discuss this again until we've found out what action will be taken.' And he meant by del Garza as much as he did the Upright Man and his lieutenants. 'Let's move around, see what we can find out.'

Larry nodded and they both moved off.

'Have any of the houses been affected?' a fat man was asking a group of prostitutes. 'The ones we're behind, I mean.'

'Not yet,' one of the women answered, a needle-nosed woman who looked well over forty. 'But if this doesn't get old Jocko what he wants they'll be next. Sitting-ducks, so to speak, that's what they are.'

'A lot of the gentry go to those places,' said one of her friends. 'They wouldn't like having their pleasures interfered with.'

'Oh, that'll worry the secret police,' needle-nose sneered. 'They'd just love to have something like that on a gentleman of quality, or a rich merchant with a jealous wife. Mark my words, even if this does get the bastard the results he wants, that'll be their next step anyway.'

'True,' the fat man agreed. 'Once he's begun, why should he stop?'

Jimmy had to agree. He supposed it was more surprising that the secret police hadn't already made such a move – Radburn was clever enough to see it. For a power-mad, soulless bastard it seemed a logical step, much more so than picking up the street girls. You could learn a great deal if you had the power to squeeze the sporting houses; the walls there literally had ears – conveniently placed listening posts behind false walls in several of the richer brothels. More than one merchant gladly paid a madam a little extra every month to keep him current on what his drunken competitors said to impress their current favourite. It took nothing for Jimmy to imagine an agent of the Crown behind that listening post rather than the madam.

Even before the events of the last week, rumours were that Guy du Bas-Tyra had ambitions to be the next Prince of Krondor, and that Jocko Radburn had his cap set on being the next Duke of Krondor. Western nobles would certainly object openly in the Congress of Lords to such appointments, but western nobles with something to hide might be a great deal less vociferous in voicing those objections. Besides, the more useful results Radburn and del Garza could squeeze out of this mess, the more likely the Duke would be forgiving when he returned.

Jimmy spied Noxious Neville sitting in a corner by himself; not unusual given Neville's aroma, which started with old sweat and worked up from there. But the beggar had been a frequent guest in Krondor's dungeons and might have useful information. It just depended on how addled he was today.

Jimmy squatted down in front of the old beggar and waved a piece of silver back and forth, knowing it was the best way to get the old man's attention. Gradually Neville stopped his rocking and his eyes began to follow the coin; then his hand rose and tried to capture it. Jimmy snatched it back and closed it in his fist.

'Neville,' he said, 'I need some information.'

The old man stared at him. He was quite mad, but deep in his eyes a canny intelligence lurked. After all, he hadn't starved or frozen or been kicked to death by drunks yet.

'Whatcha wanta know?' he asked, slurring his words.

'Tell me about the keep's dungeons,' Jimmy said. 'I want to know everything you can remember.'

Neville started to chuckle until he choked, then he coughed until Jimmy expected him to spit out a lung at any moment. Annoyed, because he suspected that the coughing was a demand for liquid relief, Jimmy nevertheless rose and acquired a mug of ale for the old beggar.

As expected, as soon as the flagon was in Neville's gnarled hand the spasm ceased.

'Take more'n one silver to get that much,' the old man rasped, then took a sip.

'How much?' Jimmy asked.

The beggar shrugged with his whole body. 'Twenty,' he said, clearly knowing he'd never get it.

Jimmy got up and started to walk away.

'Hey!' Neville called, clearly irritated. 'Where ya goin'?'

'To talk to someone who isn't crazy,' Jimmy threw over his shoulder.

'C'm back here,' the beggar demanded. 'Don-cha know how to bargain? What'll ya give me? I'm crazy, not stupid.'

Jimmy held up the coin and Neville started rocking and grumbling inaudibly.

'Gimme three,' he demanded.

'I've already spent two coppers on your ale,' Jimmy said. 'I'm not throwing good money after bad. You give me something for that and if I think it's worth more, I'll pay more.'

'S'fair,' Neville said reluctantly. 'Whatcha want to know?'

Jimmy sat before him, breathing through his mouth to avoid the old man's prodigious stench, and asked him questions about the dungeons. How deep were they, how to get in, how many cells, how many guards, how often were the guards changed, how often were the prisoners fed, how often were the slops taken out, if they were? Noxious Neville answered every question with his eyes fixed keenly on the young thief's face and with every answer Jimmy's heart fell further.

'Is there any way to get out without the guards knowing it?' he asked finally.

Noxious Neville barked a laugh. 'By the goddess of luck, who hates me, how should I know that?' he demanded. 'I never tried to get out. More trouble'n it's worth. Four days's the longest I's ever there.'

Leaning closer, Jimmy asked, 'Did you ever hear of anyone escaping?'

The old beggar began to giggle and wag a filthy finger at him. 'Whatsa matta? Jocko steal yer sweetie?'

Jimmy made his eyes hard. 'You've only got three teeth left, Neville,' he pointed out. 'Do you want me to break 'em for you?'

Fast as a striking snake the old man's hand grabbed Jimmy's arm with shocking strength.

'Like to see you try it, I would,' he snarled. 'Little brat.' He flung the young thief's arm away from him. 'Think I stayed alive this long by accident? Maybe Lims-Kragma, the great goddess of death, forgot about me? That what ya think? Hah! Stupid brat.' He spat to the side.

Jimmy assumed from that that the old man was still willing to earn his silver. If he'd finished talking Neville probably would have spat on him. *And then I'd have had to kill the old bastard. Or himself.* The idea of being spat on by Noxious Neville was that revolting.

'Did you,' Jimmy repeated evenly, 'ever hear of anyone escaping?'

The old man looked aside, shaking his head and waving the question away.

'Is there any way in or out that the guards don't watch?' Jimmy asked desperately.

'Only thing I know about is the drain in the floor of the big cell.' He chuckled, giving Jimmy an evil look. 'But you wouldn't like that, it's the hole we pissed in.'

Jimmy just stared at him, thinking hard. No, he didn't like it, but it might have possibilities.

'This drain, it leads directly to the sewers?' he asked. 'Or does the keep have a separate outfall to the harbour?'

Neville laughed again and Jimmy reflected that the old coot was getting a lot more pleasure out of this conversation than he should be.

'How should I know?' Neville demanded. 'Ye think I follow me piss to see where it goes? The hole's only this big!' He held his hands up to indicate a circle the size of a dinner plate and Jimmy's heart sank again.

'Hey!' Neville said and gave the boy a poke. 'Maybe the Upright

43

Man knows a way out of the prison. Why don't ye ask him?' And he laughed wildly.

The young thief rose and started to walk away.

'Hey!' the beggar screeched. 'Where's my money?' He held out a skinny hand.

Jimmy flipped him the single silver he'd first offered.

'Hey!' Noxious Neville cried. 'Yer s'posed to gi' me more! That was the bargain.'

'The bargain,' Jimmy said coldly, 'was that if I thought your information was worth more, I'd give you more. Give me something I can use.'

The old man made grumbling noises and glared at him, but something made Jimmy wait. 'Leads to the sewers,' Neville finally conceded. 'But the tunnel's half caved in, ain't safe.'

'And the drain?' Jimmy asked. 'Can someone get down there?'

Neville turned his head this way and that, as though protesting the continued questioning, then he nodded. 'Drain used to be bigger,' he admitted. 'Filled it in a bit wi' bits of stone and mortar they did. Shaft's big enough for someone skinny. Give it a coupla good kicks and the drain'll fall open, big enough for someone to crawl down if'n he don't have too much girth.'

Light broke in Jimmy's mind and he stared at the old beggar. 'You've used it!' he accused. 'You used that shaft to escape!'

Neville broke out in a flurry of crazed motions meant to indicate *go away and leave me alone or there'll be trouble* – a move he'd perfected over a long career of dealing with the public.

Jimmy stabbed a finger at him, unimpressed. 'Stop it!' He glared until the old man settled down and glared back at him. 'Now,' he said evenly, 'tell me what I want to know and if it turns out to be the truth, I'll give you this.' He flashed a gold coin for a fraction of a second. 'If it turns out you're lying, you get nothing.'

A gold coin was a fortune to a man like Neville; it would get him fifty flagons of ale – a hundred if he stuck to the really vile stuff sold in the Poor Quarter. He sat sucking his gums and thinking it over.

'Why not?' he said at last. 'Not like's a secret worth keeping. I's a thief once, 'n young. They caught me, wasn't easy.'

Noxious Neville's face took on a slackly reminiscent grin and just when Jimmy thought he'd have to shake him to bring him back to the here and now he began speaking again.

'I was gonna hang.' Neville spat again. 'But I knew if I had time and patience I'd get out. There's a grille,' he said, pointing down with one dirty finger.

Jimmy glanced down automatically then grimaced and looked back at the old man.

'Not too big, mind, but me, I could.' Neville wriggled where he sat, arms working above his head as though squeezing through a tight space. 'M'shoulders come apart,' he said and gave a wheezing laugh at the young thief's look of doubt.

Not that Jimmy hadn't heard of such before, but it was hard to believe the human wreck before him would have such a useful attribute.

Neville slapped his knee, laughing and after a moment he went on. 'Those days the grille wasn't even mortared, they di'nt think anybody could get down that shaft.' He shook his head, grinning. 'Wished I coulda seen their faces wh'n they come fer me.' He chuckled.

Jimmy nodded. 'So where is it?' he asked.

Neville stared into space, one finger tracing the air as he tried to remember the route. 'Take the fourth shaft at Five Points,' he said uncertainly. 'No, no, take the second –' He went silent, gazing. Suddenly he was more animated. 'Go toward dockside, always go for the lower way . . . no, no, that leads to the fullers. Don't want to go there.' He huffed impatiently. 'I know how te get there,' he said impatiently, 'I jes' never had to tell anybody how to get there.'

45

Jimmy stood. 'Show me then. It'll be easier.'

The old beggar looked at him as though Jimmy had suggested he strip to his loin-cloth and dance on a table.

'Not fer me!' Neville said. He waved his flagon. 'I've got all my comforts here.' He looked around and waved a hand as though to indicate the cosiest surroundings in the city.

Leaning close enough to singe his nose hairs Jimmy said, 'Four silver above the gold if you show me.'

Neville chewed his gums, looking at nothing, and didn't answer.

Jimmy chewed his upper lip impatiently, aware that Neville held the upper hand. What he had to do now was get the upper hand back before the beggar bargained him to bankruptcy.

'I'll buy a half skin of wine for the trip,' Jimmy offered. 'You can keep what's left once we get there.'

'Full skin,' Neville countered.

'Half.'

'Full!' the old beggar snapped. 'S'a bit of a slog.'

'Done,' Jimmy said and somewhat reluctantly, held out his hand.

Neville spat on his and clapped hold of the boy's before Jimmy could draw away. Then laughed uproariously at the young thief's disgusted expression.

FOUR

Plotting

Jimmy slipped through the crowd.

'Larry,' Jimmy said.

The younger boy gave a well-concealed start and Jimmy felt a small spurt of pride. Sneaking up on guardsmen was easy, but the boy was a fellow professional.

'I've found something out,' Jimmy said, looking around the crowd to make sure they weren't overheard. 'A way into the dungeon.' He made a pressing gesture with his hand. 'But there's a problem.'

'What problem?'

'The only one who knows the way is Noxious Neville – so we have to take him along.'

Larry's face went from joyful to sour, as if he'd just bitten into something unpleasant.

'And I had to promise him a half skin of wine. Which means . . .'

Ol' Neville was the type to disappear in an instant for reasons of his own, yet come back demanding the promised reward. Rewards never slipped the old man's porous memory, even when his recall of deeds performed was vague.

They turned, watching as Neville conducted a conversation with someone who wasn't there. Jimmy interrupted the conversation and lured Neville out of the Rest by pouring out a stream of raw red wine that Neville hastened to catch in his mouth. When they were outside Jimmy stoppered the skin.

'Lead us,' he said.

The old beggar smacked his lips, then rubbed his hands over his face and neck and licked up the drops of wine he collected from his fingers.

Jimmy ostentatiously swung the skin over his shoulder.

'Whenever you're ready,' he said.

'That's it,' Neville said.

The three Mockers crouched, straddling the stream of foulness that ran down the centre of the sewer. Ahead, an oval opening in a wall poured its own tributary into the fetid stream; broad streaks of glistening nitre down the brick showed that the trickle had been larger once.

'Took long enough,' Larry said sourly.

Jimmy shrugged. Not all of Neville's madness was an act; they'd backtracked more times than Jimmy cared to remember with the old man whining about how thirsty he was. But the young thief had been adamant; no wine until they found the place.

If he's like this half sober, we'd never see daylight again if I'd let him get drunk.

'Are you sure this is it?' Jimmy asked dubiously.

As he'd said, the tunnel was partially collapsed. Rubble splayed out in an incline into the main sewer, giving them easy access, but the air that blew towards them from above was more foul than the beggar himself. Larry said, 'Something's died up there!'

Neville ignored the comment to answer Jimmy's question. 'Yes I'm sure,' he snapped; his lips worked angrily and one discoloured snag of a tooth showed. 'You'd been payin' attention you'd know it!'

The old coot's right, Jimmy acknowledged unhappily. They'd passed signs that warned they were approaching the underpinnings of the keep.

'Phew!' Larry said and choked as he stuck head and shoulders into the gap. 'You can't mean it! We can't go in there! A snake couldn't get in there!'

Jimmy was definitely in sympathy with Larry. He tossed the wineskin to the beggar who hurried off without demanding the rest of his pay. He grimaced as he watched Noxious Neville scurry into the darkness, then climbed the rubble and thrust the torch through a gap.

'Look, it gets broader past here,' he said. 'And this rubble's easy enough to move.' He levered a handful aside, then wiped his hand on his breeches. *Good thing I was going to buy new ones anyway.*

'We could clear enough to get through in less than an hour, even if we take care not to make any noise. After that it's easy enough, for folk our size. We're not looking to ride a horse through, after all.'

The torch flickered and dimmed in a slightly stronger gust of air and Jimmy pushed himself back and staggered, retching, away from the pile of rock and earth.

He shook his head, his eyes streaming. 'You're right, only sheer desperation would get me in there. And even then . . .'

Three extremely wealthy merchants sat across the desk from the acting governor of the city. The men were members of the powerful Merchants' Guild – a body that included the most wealthy men in the city, along with representatives of the other important guilds: tanners, smiths, shipwrights, carters and others. After the authority of the Prince's Court and the temples, the

Merchants' Guild was the most influential faction in the principality. Too many nobles in the Kingdom owed debts to or did business with the more powerful members of the Guild. Crops didn't come to market from outlying estate farms if the teamsters didn't drive wagons. Dock warehouses filled up with goods that were headed nowhere if the dockworkers refused to load them on the ships. Originally begun as a body to adjudicate disagreements between the different guilds and independent merchants, they had evolved over the years into a voice for the merchant class in the halls of power. The Guild's co-operation was vital to the success of del Garza's plans, or at the very least he needed to ensure they were not in opposition to him.

The three maintained equally supercilious expressions while their eyes, glittering in the candlelight, were fixed on del Garza's every move. They waited for his attention with dignified restraint, ignoring the draughts that moved the wall hangings, barely moving to draw their cloaks tighter around their shoulders.

Del Garza continued to write, scratching away at an only moderately important document, fully cognizant of how rarely these gentlemen displayed such patience. He was enjoying this little exercise of power. Indeed, this was for his pleasure; the next part of the evening's endeavours would be for his lord's advantage.

He finished writing, sanded the document and shook it, then laid it aside and turned to look at the men seated opposite him. 'Thank you for coming,' he said, his voice coldly insincere.

Marcellus Varney, a shipper of Quegan ancestry, raised an eyebrow. He was a bull-necked man who had obviously spent his youth in hard labour. Now, in his middle years, there was still muscle under the rich man's fat. 'We were not invited,' he said precisely. 'I was under the impression that we were arrested.' His entire attitude spoke of distaste.

'Nevertheless,' the acting governor said with great politeness, 'you could have resisted.' He tipped his head to the side and opened his hands. 'No, no, you must allow me to thank you for your co-operation.'

'Get on with it,' the shipper said, his tone flat, his eyes resentful.

Del Garza glanced at each of them, then made an acquiescent gesture.

'As you wish, gentlemen.' He sat back in his chair. 'You are, no doubt, aware of the special orders and state of emergency I am about to declare in Krondor. I've submitted a copy of the order to your guild and I expect you've had the day to ponder it.'

The three men shifted in their chairs. It amused him; they might almost have rehearsed it, the timing was so mutual.

'I invited you here tonight to see if there was anything I could do to gain your support. Times ahead will be difficult and I want to ensure that the most respected voices in the Merchants' Guild speak in favour of the necessity for these acts.' *That's got their attention*, he thought with an inner smile. A little flattery beside intimidation did wonders.

The gentlemen focused on him as though they believed he cared about their opinion. Which, of course, he did, as long as it was in agreement with his.

Rufus Tuney, a grain merchant with six critically located mills around the city, grimaced, then waved a hand somewhat languidly. He was a foppish man who tended to wear excessive amounts of lace and powder, and a cloying cloud of spices and lilac scent surrounded him wherever he went. 'The new regulations you have proposed are not without merit,' he commented. 'The trouble is they seem . . . somewhat excessive.' He looked at the acting governor with raised brows. 'Even if the three of us were wholeheartedly in support of your position –' he gave a delicate shrug, '– of what use are a mere three votes?'

'Do not allow *that* to be a consideration, gentlemen,' del Garza said, his voice hard and flat. 'What you must consider are your own advantages in the matter.'

Silence greeted his remark and del Garza could see them resisting the urge to glance at one another.

'Advantage?' Varney queried.

I expected him to be the one to ask that question.

The third merchant, a spice trader named Thaddius Fleet, shifted in his seat. He was a nondescript man, given to well-made but simple garments. 'See here, del Garza. What exactly are you proposing?'

And del Garza had expected him to try to lead the negotiations. Sometimes it was almost too easy. He sighed. 'Must I go into detail?' he asked wearily. 'Remember where you were, gentlemen, when my men requested your presence here.' He watched that sink in. This time glances were exchanged from the corners of their eyes.

What fools these men are! He held most of their breed in contempt, but the three sitting before him now were particularly noxious. Tuney and Fleet had indulgences of which they were ashamed, which made them vulnerable. Varney had a profitable sideline selling young women and boys as slaves to Kesh, drugging them and smuggling them out in secret compartments on his ships. Once his usefulness was at an end del Garza thought it would be a blessing to the Kingdom to end his business. Slavery, except for prisoners of the Crown, was outlawed in the Kingdom.

Perhaps I'll sell him to Great Kesh. That should certainly provide some amusement. As for the others, they were just shallow men with foolish peccadilloes. One liked to be spanked by pretty women, the other liked to pretend he was a pretty woman. They harmed no one but themselves. *I'm almost grateful to them, and to Radburn for keeping such conveniently complete files.* Seeing the key members of the Guild in twos and threes over the next few days would bring them nicely to heel.

'That certainly puts things in a new light,' Fleet said grimly. He glanced at his two companions; none needed to say anything; they all knew del Garza was in possession of information that would ruin them, and in Varney's case, send him to the gallows.

After a moment's silence del Garza said impatiently: 'And by this new light can you see your way clear to supporting my decrees? After all, Baron Radburn will be returning soon. I assure you he will be far less concerned with the Guild's position on these matters than I am.'

'I . . . believe so,' said Tuney.

'Good. Then I can count on all of your votes?' Del Garza stared at them until each one of them had nodded and mumbled an affirmative. 'Excellent! I won't keep you further, gentlemen.' He gave them a bland smile as he took a document from a pile to his left and placed it before him. 'Enjoy the rest of your evening.'

He rang a small hand-bell and the door to the office opened. A guard waited without. Del Garza turned his attention to the document, apparently unaware of their existence.

The three merchants looked at one another in disbelief. They were not accustomed to being dismissed like that. As they rose from their seats they dared to cast upon del Garza's down-turned head the kind of looks that promised evil reprisal.

The acting governor timed the scene, so that when he looked up he caught those expressions, and smiled. The threat in that smile was much more powerful, and they knew it.

'Oyez, oyez,' the crier intoned.

Jimmy the Hand stopped in the shadows of a doorway, carefully inconspicuous. A man-at-arms in black and gold accompanied the crier, and his eyes were objectionably active. Two days had passed since his trip to the sewers with Noxious Neville and

Larry the Ear, but he'd only just cast off the mild case of the runs that had followed, and he was in no mood to be chased.

'By the proclamation of the acting governor of the City of Krondor, the following changes have been made to current law: Street prostitution will now be considered a crime equal to robbery and burglary, and for which the same penalties will apply. All bawdy houses and brothels in the city must obtain Crown licence to operate. Begging has also been declared a crime and will now be punished with no less than fifty lashes.'

He went on to the formal conclusion of 'by my hand this day of' and so on, but Jimmy had ceased listening.

Licensing the brothels meant the Duke's agents and soldiers would be searching the buildings and registering the girls. That was not important.

But burglary and robbery were hanging offences and fifty lashes would kill any but the strongest of men. He drew back into the alley in a daze. That meant that everyone they'd already caught – Flora and Gerald and the rest – were doomed. He turned and hastened through the maze of alleys to the nearest sewer entrance. It was now just a matter of days before they died.

'The acting governor has had his proclamation,' he muttered to himself, swinging down on a grating and dropping soundlessly to the slimy brick. 'Let's see what the Upright Man has to say.'

Mocker's Rest was packed; Jimmy had never seen so many people there, and he could barely hear himself speak. The mood was frightened, but the faces around him were blank and hard. There wasn't a Mocker here who didn't have a friend or relative already in the cells. Jimmy wondered if the prisoners knew what awaited them.

He slipped between bodies and found that no one had any

news except that of the announcement. No one knew what the Upright Man intended to do about it, nor had anyone seen the Daymaster for hours, and it was two hours yet before the Nightmaster was due. Meanwhile, no one dared go out, especially not the women and the beggars.

Jimmy spied Larry the Ear clinging to the V of one of the ceiling braces, crouched like a gargoyle, and made his way toward him. When he finally stood below Larry's perch and their eyes met it was like the shaking of hands, sharing the same thought without speaking. The younger boy's jaw set hard and he swallowed nervously, then he looked up and saw something that caused him to stiffen.

'What is it?' Jimmy asked.

'Laughing Jack,' Larry called down.

Others heard and turned to where the boy was staring, silence spreading like ripples through the shadows as word spread of the Nightmaster's lieutenant's approach. By the time the Nightwarden took a stance upon a table, the big room was silent except for the occasional cough and the sound of dripping water. Laughing Jack turned in a circle looking at all of them, his expression even more grim than usual.

'You've all got word,' he bellowed. 'So I won't repeat the edict. Orders are to do nothing. Leave the matter to the Upright Man and lay low as much as possible. Understood?'

For a long moment the crowd was silent, resentment building like a wave.

'Well?' Jack demanded, glaring.

A few voices murmured here and there, but mostly the Mockers stared, expecting more, and with their silence demanding it.

'Well aren't you a fine bunch?' Laughing Jack sneered. 'No faith, at all?' he shouted. 'Where would most of you be without the Upright Man? Huh? I'll tell you, most of you would have been dead by now. It's easy to be loyal during the good times.

Easy to follow the rules and do what's expected when everything's running right. But when times are hard, that's when you especially got to follow orders. Loyalty will carry us all through the hard times.' He swept them all with a hard look. 'So what's it going to be? Follow orders, or get tossed out in the streets so the guards'll find you?'

Confused silence greeted this question. There was a roar of affirmation waiting to happen but the Mockers looked at one another uneasily, wondering how to avoid sounding as if being kicked into the streets was what they wanted.

'Well, when you put it like that,' Jimmy muttered. 'Upright Man!' he shouted, punching his fist in the air.

The crowd went wild and took up the cry, bellowing until mortar began to rain from the ceiling and Laughing Jack held up his hands for silence.

'Get to your roosts and your flops,' he commanded. 'Keep your heads low and wait for orders. One thing I can promise is that we won't take this lying down, but nobody does nothing until you hear otherwise.'

There was another burst of applause at that which quickly died when Laughing Jack stepped off his makeshift stage. Jimmy looked up at Larry and jerked his head toward the door then moved off, knowing the younger boy would follow as he could.

Jimmy led the way out of the sewers and through a maze of back alleys, most sodden, some clean, until he came to a fence of cedar posts set in stone. He climbed it and stepped briefly onto a window ledge, then grasped a hole left by a crumbling brick and hoisted himself up to where he could step onto the window's ledge. Balancing, he reached up to grasp the eaves. He chinned himself up, his toes finding the space in the brickwork that allowed him to push himself upward until he could wriggle onto the tiled roof.

Then he silently moved over so that Larry could climb up beside him; neither of them was breathing hard, since the sky-routes were as familiar to them as a staircase to the attic would be to a householder.

They were on the roof of a noisy dockside tavern – the tiles beneath them fairly vibrated, as sailors the worse for wine made an attempt at song – but they still made as little noise as possible, moving into the dark shadow of a dormer window. Jimmy risked a quick glance in the window and found the room unoccupied. He lay down on his back looking up at the stars and listening for any sounds of pursuit. Larry sat quietly beside him, apparently doing the same.

'I think,' Larry whispered at last, sounding very unhappy, 'that the Upright Man will call del Garza's bluff.'

Jimmy nodded, then realizing it was too dark to be seen grunted in agreement.

'The only trouble is,' the younger boy continued fiercely, 'he isn't bluffing. Why should he? Nobody's going to complain if he hangs a dozen Mockers. A hundred even!'

Jimmy shushed him, for he'd nearly shouted that last. Larry muttered an apology and Jimmy gave the boy's arm a brief, sympathetic punch. But he agreed with Larry's sentiments. The acting governor would put the Upright Man in the worst position possible before he consented to negotiate, if he ever did.

In the history of the Thieves' Guild, the Mockers and Crown had never sat down across a table, but over the decades since the Guild had been founded, the Mockers had reached accommodations with the Prince of Krondor on several occasions. A word dropped by a merchant with connections in court, a trader having business on both sides of the law carrying a message, and from time to time a difficult situation might be avoided. The Mockers gave up their own when caught dead to rights; that was understood by every thief, basher and beggar. But occasionally an overzealous constable had the wrong lad scheduled for the gallows, or a harmless working girl or beggar arrested for a more serious crime, and from time to time trades were arranged. More than one Mocker was tossed out of gaol suddenly after the Sheriff of Krondor got clear proof of innocence – usually the location of the true malefactor, sometimes in hiding, at other times dead. On other occasions a gang without the Upright Man's sanction was turned over to the Sheriff's men, saving them the trouble of arresting them.

Larry said, 'The Upright Man's not going to do anything, is he?'

'Being in the position he was in, I don't think he can risk aggravating the situation further. I think we've got nothing to offer del Garza,' said Jimmy. 'As I see it, the only thing that could make him happy would be to see Radburn return with the Princess in tow. And as she's halfway to Crydee with Prince Arutha by now, I don't imagine that's going to happen. So, if he hangs a lot of us, at least he can say he tried to do something when Black Guy comes back. And if Radburn gets himself killed along the way, then del Garza can put all the blame on him and make himself look like he was trying. Our lads and lasses are in a bad position, no doubt.'

Jimmy fell silent for a moment: he knew it wasn't just a bad position, but a fatal one. Finally, he said, 'It's up to us.'

He heard a stifled sob and saw the glitter of Larry's eyes as the boy turned toward him. 'They might kill us,' he warned.

Jimmy chuckled. 'Del Garza's men will definitely kill us if we don't do something. As for the Upright Man . . .' He paused to watch a star shoot across the sky and to consider what the Upright Man might do. 'We won't be rewarded, that's certain, we'll probably have to take a beating for disobeying orders. But if we succeed in getting everybody out . . .'

'Everybody!' Larry's voice squeaked.

'Well, yeah. Why not?'

'I just want to get my brother out.'

'No, that's not enough!' Jimmy said, sitting up. 'You want to get your brother out; I understand that, but if we can get the others out safely, too, that would be great. Wouldn't it?'

There was silence for a moment, then, 'Ye-ah?'

'And it would make us heroes to everyone in the Guild. We'd be too popular to have our throats cut.'

'Well, I guess.'

Not the rousing confirmation Jimmy had been hoping for, but it would do. He stood up.

'First, let's go and look over that place Noxious Neville showed us. Once we know what we're dealing with we can make plans. Then we'll see.' He started off, followed by a reluctant Larry the Ear.

'See what?' the boy asked.

'See whether the Upright Man will kill us or not,' Jimmy said cheerfully.

Jimmy wore a vinegar-soaked rag tied over his nose and mouth and was still fighting the urge to gag from the stench. They'd removed a lot of the rubble from the blockage, but not all of it; the people they were to rescue were mostly small and certainly thinner than when they'd been arrested. The two boys laboured quietly and quickly, and then it was time for one of them to climb up the vertical shaft that Neville had told them about. Jimmy glanced at Larry, who was nervous, green, and on the verge of being sick, and didn't even think of suggesting the younger boy go. Jimmy took a deep breath through his mouth, as if he was about to plunge under water, and stuck his head into the opening. Then he pulled himself up.

It wasn't quite as tight as he'd expected from the old man's description, but then maybe the old beggar had worn some meat on his bones when he was young. And the walls were an easy climb, seeming to be a natural cleft in the rock below the keep, with plenty of nooks and crannies for fingers and toes. Even the girls would be able to manage it.

So far the only problem was that it was very slimy with things best not thought about and stank enough to shrivel the hairs in his nostrils, even through the sharp vinegar smell. He kept promising an offering to the Goddess Ruthia, Mistress of Luck, if she would let him get through this without anyone pissing on him. The higher he climbed the more extravagant the offerings became.

He heard a voice above his head and froze, but whoever it was passed by. He thanked the Lady of Luck and glanced up. He wouldn't have been able to go any further anyway. Just above him they had mortared small stones to the side of the shaft for a depth of about four feet from the top, narrowing it to just the size of his head.

Jimmy climbed down rapidly, his heart sinking. He'd imagined chipping away the extra stones around the grate, and had worried about how they'd cover the sound. He'd never imagined them continuing for four feet! Maybe ol' Neville hadn't known about it, maybe he didn't think it mattered, but it was certainly a big complication.

Jimmy imagined the wrath visited upon the gaoler when the escape of a prisoner – maybe it was Noxious Neville back-in-the-day – had been discovered. So either the heavily chastened gaoler or his newly-appointed successor had seen fit to ensure it didn't happen again. For a giddy moment he wondered how the current gaoler was going to tell del Garza and the Sheriff that dozens of Mockers had fled in one night. Then he put aside the amusing fantasy and returned to the problem at hand: how to get rid of a lot of brick and mortar in a hurry.

Larry was waiting down below the partially-collapsed tunnel.
'Well?' he asked in a whisper.

'I need a bath,' Jimmy said. It wasn't something he said very often and he'd never said it so sincerely.

'Me, too,' Larry agreed. Then asked, 'So?'

'There's a problem,' Jimmy said. 'A collar of stonework that narrows the opening so you couldn't pass a cat through it. It's pretty deep, too. Let me think about it.'

'We can't go in here!' Larry the Ear hissed in Jimmy's ear. 'This place is too respectable!'

It was; a two-storey building with more chimneys than a house, the sort of place where people respectable enough to want to wash regularly came, but who were not well-to-do enough to afford the equipment. It had a doorwarden; a thick-set man with a grey beard and a knotted club of vinestock beside it, who looked like a retired trooper.

Jimmy grabbed Larry and pulled him close so he couldn't be overheard. 'We need to get clean. Del Garza's men are out looking for sewer rats. Right now, we not only look like them, but we smell like them. We have to get clean, and it would help if we didn't look like Mockers for a little while. That's why we're here, instead of trying to get clean using someone's rain barrel or washing off in the Old Square Fountain.' He turned to look at the doorwarden. 'Just pretend you're someone and keep quiet.'

Jimmy walked up to the man. The doorwarden's nose wrinkled – *Well, I can't blame him*, thought Jimmy – and his eyes narrowed; a thick-knuckled hand went to the vinewood club.

Wordlessly, Jimmy held up a silver coin the size of his thumbnail. *I've known this sort of thing to work*, he thought, schooling his face to look embarrassed and supercilious at the same time. *I've just never been able to afford bathing in a proper bathhouse, before.*

He'd never been much of one for bathing in general, either; but associating with lords and princesses, even for a short while, tended to alter your standards. He discovered that enduring a bucket of cold water and some soap every day or two earned him approval from the Princess Anita, and that had been worth it. He had also discovered he itched a lot less and felt better afterwards.

'My good man, we need to bathe,' he said, shaping the tones of an upper-class accent. 'And to buy fresh clothing.'

'Ye certainly need the bath,' the man grumbled. 'Lousy too, no doubt.'

'Not in the least. We've been out on a . . .' Jimmy let his expression grow sheepish. 'Well, we'd rather our parents didn't find out, and . . .' He finished in a rush: 'You can have this yourself?'

Suspicion gave way to contempt as Jimmy handed over the coin; which was fine with him.

'We were attacked by street boys,' Jimmy chattered on – over-explaining made guilt look more plausible. 'They stole our clothes and pushed us in a sty. The maid at home gave us some coins to get cleaned up. Please, sir, my mother is very strict and she'll be very, very angry if we go home in this condition.' Jimmy had always been good at mimicry, and the time spent with Prince Arutha and Princess Anita had given him a wealth of new ways to speak when he needed. He sounded plausible in the role of the son of a minor noble or rich merchant. As long as Larry remembered to keep his mouth shut.

He and Larry had more than enough scrapes and bruises to make their story seem authentic. Knocking about in dark sewers and climbing walls and houses had added a good share of cuts as well.

'Go on through,' the doorwarden said. 'You can use the baths, but rinse off good first. You'll have to find your own clothes – this isn't a tailor's shop, lads.'

They went through; the doorwarden spoke a few words in the ear of the woman who sat by bathers' clothes so they wouldn't be lifted, and her scowl cleared a bit.

Raymond E. Feist & Steve Stirling

'I'll not put those wipe-rags near honest folk's clothing,' she said.

'Take them away and burn them,' Jimmy instructed, as he and Larry stripped. That was in character; even rags were worth something, and the woman would undoubtedly get a few coppers for them. She nodded and smiled, and Jimmy knew that later that night she would be boiling them clean and selling them to a rag peddler by this time tomorrow.

'You, boy,' Jimmy said, beginning to enjoy himself. One of the attendants put down his broom and came over.

'My brother and I will require new garments,' Jimmy said loftily. He looked at the boy before him and estimated that he was just between his and Larry's size. 'I need you to buy us some new things. Trousers, shirts and linen,' he instructed. 'Something just too large to fit you for me, and something just too small to fit you for my brother. We'll have to do without shoes and stockings, I suppose.' He glanced at Larry who nodded, a supercilious expression on his face. 'The colours should be muted,' he went on, sighing at the confused expression on the boy's face. 'Nothing red or orange or patterned,' he explained.

He counted out five small silvers, more than enough for the items. 'You may keep the change,' Jimmy said, ensuring that it would be. 'And if you hurry back, you shall have this.' He held up two more silver coins.

'Thank you, sir,' the boy said, tugging his forelock, and rushed off.

'Shall we enjoy the steam room while we wait?'

Larry sniffed his arm and made a face. 'Yes!' he said fervently.

Clean and dressed, the two of them headed for the Poor Quarter. They looked respectable enough, like apprentices, perhaps, except for their lack of shoes, so it was reasonable to think themselves fairly safe in the respectable parts of town. But under the circumstances they couldn't make themselves feel safe, a fact never far from their minds.

In the Poor Quarter their new clothes might raise a passing eyebrow, but it would be obvious from their attitude that they belonged and that the first glance wouldn't be followed by a second.

Ordinarily, that is. But then, under ordinary circumstances there would be street children and beggars everywhere, and not a few whores plying their trade. Now, as the two boys walked along they found the streets nearly deserted. The few people walking about were mostly grown men, their eyes constantly moving, and from them Jimmy and Larry received a great deal of attention. It felt as if they were surrounded by the secret police.

'I can't take this,' Larry said. 'I keep expectin' someone to grab my neck. I'm goin' to the Rest.'

Jimmy shook his head. 'Not me. I've had enough of sewers for one day. I'm for a drink.'

The younger boy shook his head. 'Not tonight.' He looked at Jimmy for a moment. 'Tomorrow,' he said, and it was almost a question.

Jimmy nodded. 'Tomorrow.' He made it sound like a promise.

They separated then, without so much as a backward glance; Larry disappearing into the gloom of an alleyway, Jimmy walking along the street.

As he walked, Jimmy thought.

The mortared collar needs to go, and we've got to do it some way that won't draw the guards. That was easier said than done. *Drugs?* he wondered. It would have to be something potent, to make them oblivious to the noise of stonework.

But there was no way to get to the guards without going to gaol, wherein getting at the guards was problematic at best.

Deep down an idea stirred. Too formless yet to grasp, Jimmy

let it go and simply followed his feet, trying not to think at all. He'd found that sometimes ideas were like that, they'd flee if you pursued them, but they just might come to you if you just left them be.

He walked along, hands in his pockets, eyes on his bare toes, listening to the sounds around him for quite a while, and quite a way. Finally he stopped and looked up to find himself before a tavern. There wasn't a sign, unless you counted the anatomically-based scratchings on the once-plastered wall, but there was a withered bunch of branches pinned above the door. That let out the noise of voices, the smell of rushes not changed in a long time, and much spilled beer.

Ah, yes, he grinned, and went in. *Where else? My feet are smarter than my head tonight; they've led me straight to the place I want.* It wasn't until this moment that Jimmy realized that what he really needed was magic. How else were they going to do it? And where else in Krondor would he find a magician willing to help him? Nowhere else.

And there was only one magician within a week's travel who wouldn't ask too many questions first, or tell someone else: Asher.

The few magicians in the principality with enough power or wealth to avoid being hunted down by locals for perceived curses – dead calves, curdled milk, crops to fail – all tended to keep to themselves. There was a three-storey stone house with a court-yard, near the southeastern gate to the city, that was reputed to be the occasional home of a powerful mage, but each time Jimmy had passed it, he could detect no signs of life. From time to time word would spread through the city that a travelling magician was stopping at this or that inn, and whether they were willing to trade services or magical goods for gold, but that was a rare event.

No, Asher was unique: a magician and a drunk. And from what was rumoured, one who also liked to gamble and enjoy the company of women less than half his age. So he kept permanent residence in the part of the city where no one had calves to stillbirth, milk to curdle, or crops to fail. With so few prosperous undertakings in the Poor Quarter, there was scarcely any reason to seek someone else to blame for failure. Failure was a daily fact of life here.

The tavern had seen better days; the booth-like 'snugs' tucked into the corner were too fancy for its present clientele, most of whom sat on their knife scabbards as they threw dice, to keep themselves conscious of where the hilts were.

Jimmy looked into the farthest corner in the place and his grin grew wider. But then finding Alban Asher in this tavern was as reliable as finding bad ale in a dirty mug. Jimmy had never seen him anywhere but in his cobwebbed corner. For all the young thief knew he'd grown roots there. But then, Asher didn't need to go anywhere. The world came to him. Despite being an old sot, compulsive gambler and womanizer, if he was sober enough, the spells he sold worked very well indeed. Jimmy had heard of a few failures, but they were more a disappointment than a disaster. Certainly not enough to put off any potential business. Besides, where else would one go in the principality to find a magician willing to sell magic for enough gold to get drunk on, sit down at a card game, or convince a young girl to bed someone her grandfather's age?

Jimmy got himself a mug of ale and acquired a cup of the tavern's best wine. Which smelled raw enough to strip tar, and though he wasn't the most fastidious fellow in the city, he had no intention of actually drinking the ale he'd bought. Going over to the magician's table Jimmy placed the wine before him and sat in the other seat, watching the formless heap of black robes across from him.

It took a moment for the man to come to life, but the scent of the wine eventually evoked a response. A clawlike hand reached out of a sleeve and lifted the cup; the magician took a sip and made a guttural, approving sound. Jimmy's throat closed when he thought of what the man must usually imbibe. The magician hiccupped and then gave a powerful belch, chuckling evilly at Jimmy's expression when the vapours hit him.

Jimmy sat, waiting.

It was impossible to guess Asher's age. For one thing, the tavern was dark, and this corner of it darker still; for another, the magician's head was surrounded by a bush of sandy hair. His beard, moustache, eyebrows and head-hair were all as thick and impenetrable as a bramble bush. As for his face, all that could be seen were a bulbous nose almost the same shade as the wine and the gleam of his eyes beneath his shaggy brows. It was suspected he might be as young as sixty summers, but then again, some suggested he was ninety and being kept alive by dark spells. All Jimmy knew from rumours was that the magician existed in a state of seeming indifference to the world around him unless he was drinking, gambling or whoring. And by all reports when the drinking wasn't excessive, he was fairly successful with the gambling and whoring.

'Ye want somethin', Alban Asher the magician said in a matter-of-fact tone. His voice was deep and raspy. Even sitting down he was weaving, indicating that he was already well into the bottle.

'Yessir,' Jimmy confirmed cheerfully. 'I'll pay extra for secrecy.'

After a moment Asher chuckled in a way that spoke of pure greed. With a gesture he encouraged Jimmy to continue.

'I need one or two spells that I can carry away with me and set off where and when I want,' the young thief said.

'Love spells,' Asher said, nodding sagely. 'Boys yer age're all after love spells.' He chuckled salaciously and touched one grubby finger to his nose.

Jimmy supposed that he winked, but couldn't tell. 'No,' he said quickly, 'not a love spell.'

'Boys yer age . . .' the magician began, sounding annoyed.

'Definitely not a love spell,' Jimmy repeated.

I prefer my girls to have a choice in the matter, he thought. *It's a matter of pride.* Not that there was any point in trying to explain that to someone oblivious to the concept.

'I've got a mortared wall I need to take down but I don't want to break my back. Have you got anything for that?'

Asher stabbed a finger at him. 'Yer a thief!' he snarled in a rather loud whisper.

Jimmy rolled his eyes. 'Thieves don't knock down walls,' he pointed out.

The mass of hair bunched around the magician's nose in what Jimmy assumed was a frown. 'Mmm, true,' Asher agreed, blinking like an owl suddenly confronting a lantern light. 'Got somethin' might work.' He rubbed his chin ruminatively. 'Somethin' about it though . . .'

'I'll take it,' Jimmy said quickly, sure now that the magician was drunk. 'I also need something to knock people out.'

'Ah!' Asher said and chuckled. 'Girls! I knew it!' Then he chuckled some more.

Jimmy had noticed that Asher had the most nuanced chuckle he'd ever heard. In this case it indicated that the magician's relations with women when he hadn't enough gold for whores wouldn't bear close scrutiny.

'No, no girls,' Jimmy said. 'Men, big, heavy men, so if size is an issue you should plan for that.'

'Men?' the magician said as though he'd never heard of them before. After a moment he shrugged. 'Ah, well, takes all kinds. I've got somethin' – I c'n make it stronger. It's that wall spell . . .'

His voice faded off and he looked over Jimmy's head so steadily the boy thief turned around to look. There was no one there but the tavern keeper, dozing behind the bar, and a man weeping into his beer. That would normally have attracted derisive attention had anyone else been present, except that the man looked to weigh about half what a heavy cavalryman's horse did, and had a scar like a young gully from the point of his jaw up over one empty eye-socket, not to mention layers of slick tissue half an inch thick over the knuckles of both hands.

Jimmy looked at the magician out of the corner of his eye, then back at the bar. If Asher wanted more wine he'd have to wait until they'd finished their negotiations and the goods had changed hands.

'What's wrong with the wall spell?' Jimmy asked. 'Doesn't it work?'

'Oh, aye, it works,' Asher said slowly. He shook his head as though that might dislodge something in his mind. 'There's jist, somethin' . . .' He reached out with thumb and forefinger, as if to grasp something.

'Is it dangerous?' Jimmy asked, his voice sounding as though he could be.

The magician blew out his cheeks. 'Only if ye're not supposed to use it!' he said. 'It works! It works very well, I tell ye.'

'What about the knock-out spell?' Jimmy asked.

With a dismissive wave of his hand Asher plopped a small bag onto the table. 'Hardly magic at all,' he said. 'But you want it for big strapping fellows, instead of skinny little girls . . .' He paused, looked at Jimmy for a moment as if trying to understand something totally alien to his imagination, then said, 'Never mind. Give me a moment.' He closed his eyes, waved his hand over the bag and muttered for a few minutes.

The hair on the back of Jimmy's neck rose. What he called his 'bump of trouble' let him know that Asher was indeed using magic. Since he could remember, Jimmy possessed a near supernatural ability to sense approaching danger or the presence of magic being used.

Asher finished, and said, 'Now it's stronger.' He pushed the pouch toward Jimmy. 'Take a pinch and blow it into the face o' the one ye're tryin' to knock down and down he'll go!'

'And the wall?'

The magician grunted. Turning, he grabbed a sack behind his chair and hoisted it onto the filthy table. He opened it and began to rummage around inside, digging deeper and deeper until he was halfway into the bag. Things rattled and clinked as Asher sorted through them, occasionally chuckling, as though being reminded of some nasty trick he intended to play as soon as he got the time. 'Ah!' he said at last and withdrew his head; he slung the sack back behind his chair and put a tiny bottle sealed with lead on the table between them. 'There ye are,' he said proudly.

Jimmy peered at it. It was only as big as the first joint of his little finger and as far as he could tell in the dim light it was completely empty. He reached out to take a closer look at it but the magician's hand came down over it before he could touch the bottle.

'Ah!' Asher said in warning. 'We an't discussed price yet.'

'There's nothing in that bottle,' Jimmy pointed out.

'Ah, but there is,' the magician whispered. 'One tiny drop. 'Tis all ye need to start the mortar turnin' to sand. Don't get it on yersel' whatever ye do,' he warned. 'Put it on yer wall and the job is done! Doesn't matter where – top, bottom, middle – because as long as stone and mortar are connected, it'll do the job.' He sat back. Judging from the position of his whiskers, he was smiling.

'How much?' Jimmy wasn't absolutely certain about any of this, but it was still the best idea he'd had.

Really the only idea beside a hammer and chisel and a lot of prayers to Ruthia that the guards go deaf. Still, he wasn't about to take the magician's first price.

'What's it worth to ye?' Asher demanded.

With a cheerful smile Jimmy suggested, 'Let's have another

drop to ease our bargaining. Innkeeper!' he shouted, waking the man. 'Two more of the same!'

It was closing in on dawn when Jimmy left the tavern with his prizes. He held the bottle up and squinted at it against the light of a flickering lantern; the air was chilly and damp, and smelled the way it usually did in the blighted gap between night and morning, as discouraged as the young thief felt.

Still looks like nothing. But, the old man doesn't have that sort of reputation. Asher was a lot of things, but in the years he had been plying his trade in Krondor, no one had accused him of cheating on a deal, which in the Poor Quarter was the next best thing to a Royal Death Warrant.

He hadn't got a bargain by any means. Though even making painful inroads into Prince Arutha's gold, he would never have been able to afford this much magic if the man hadn't been a complete sot. *Not my problem, not my fault.* But the price was fair, so he shouldn't have to worry about waking up covered in boils anytime soon. At least, the price was fair if there was actually something inside the bottle.

Something I mustn't get on myself, he thought. A worrying idea if you thought it through. How did you pour out something that didn't appear to exist? Very carefully, he supposed.

Think positively, he told himself. *I've got the means to save Larry's brother and Flora and the rest of them. Probably. Which means we're all better off than we were before.*

Now all they had to do was do it.

FIVE

Rescue

Larry's eyes grew wide.

'Alban Asher is a drunk!' His small face showed more panic than disapproval and his tone was more surprised than angry.

Just think how you'd react if Larry had come to you with this stuff, Jimmy reminded himself. *He's not trying to hit you, and not even walking away.*

'You can't be serious!' the younger boy went on.

'We're desperate,' Jimmy pointed out, making a shushing gesture; the Rest wasn't as crowded as it had been after the new laws were announced, but it was still busier than usual: a lot of people, normally on the streets, were sleeping. 'Desperate times call for desperate measures,' he went on. Jimmy had heard that saying somewhere and liked the sound of it: he usually did, when something made for a good excuse.

'Desperate, not stupid!' Larry insisted.

'Desperate measures often look stupid before they're carried out,' Jimmy said. 'It's a historical fact, you can look it up in the royal archives.'

'I can't get into the royal archives, and besides I can't read!'

the younger boy shouted. His face was bright red and tears of frustration brightened his eyes. 'But if I could I bet I could prove you wrong!' He thumped his back against a wall and slid down to sit in a heap on the floor. 'What are we gonna do?' he wailed.

'First,' Jimmy said, leaning over him, 'you can stop shouting, people are starting to stare.'

Actually, no one was looking. But then Mockers, being thieves and scoundrels, rarely stared; but they always eavesdropped and he couldn't afford to be overheard. Nevertheless, saying so seemed to stiffen Larry's spine. Jimmy had often noticed that nonsense at the right moment could do wonders, if it was the right nonsense.

'Sorry,' the boy said gruffly. 'It's just . . .'

'Larry,' Jimmy said, leaning close, 'if you've got a better idea tell it to me. I want to hear it.'

His friend hung his head and slowly shook it.

'All right. Look, if we get no further by using this we're no further behind either. And even if Asher is a drunk he's got the reputation for knowing his craft.' He gave the boy a pat on the shoulder and a crooked grin. 'If he didn't someone from the Guild would have cut his throat by now. Which means he wouldn't be working for me.'

Larry gave him a weak smile.

'Have you got the rope?' Jimmy asked.

The boy nodded. 'Stowed it in the tunnel just behind the collapse and piled some rocks over it.'

'Good.' *It must be well hidden,* Jimmy thought. He had left a bunch of rags and a bottle of vinegar there before coming to Mocker's Rest and he hadn't seen it. 'Well, let's do it then,' he said and started off.

Larry's eyes nearly bulged out of his head and he caught up with the other thief quickly. 'Now?' he whispered.

'The sooner the better,' Jimmy said wisely. 'And why not?'

Larry shook his head. 'It's daytime!' he protested.

'So, they won't be expecting us,' Jimmy replied, with a wink.

'But there'll be more guards, won't there?'

'Why should there be? Are the iron bars less sturdy during the day?'

'No, I mean, they're awake, in the keep walking around and acting like guards.'

Jimmy stopped abruptly and glared down at the younger boy. 'You want to do this or not?'

'Do!' Larry said, nodding vigorously.

Looking him in the eye Jimmy said, 'Then let's do it!'

He strode off without looking back. After a brief silence, Jimmy smiled to hear Larry's footsteps following. This would work and then he'd be a legend among the Mockers forever after. He carefully kept himself from thinking of the alternative – most of them involved ropes, sharp things or red-hot things, or things that were sharp and red-hot and applied to the tender parts of his body.

Jimmy the Hand was still less than fourteen years, more or less, and like most youngsters he felt as if he'd live forever. But like most Mockers he'd seen a great deal of death during those years; not enough to grant him a sense of his own mortality, but enough to teach him caution.

It was all Jimmy could do to force himself back into the half-collapsed tunnel and up the shaft that led into the main cell of Krondor's dungeon. He'd spent most of his young life wandering reeking sewers and stinking alleyways so he was used to the stench and the velvet-deep darkness. But if a smell could be terrifying, this was. The stink seemed to creep up on him. It had hair and teeth and mean little eyes, it had a personality all of its own, a very bad personality that bore down on his spirit with an almost physical weight. But by telling himself that he'd never have to do this again Jimmy was able to meet the challenge. Tying the vinegar-soaked rag over his face, he put the bundle of rags and bottle of vinegar into his shirt for the others. He knew a fit of retching on the way down might land someone at the bottom of the shaft a lot faster and in much worse shape than they needed to be. Not that the vinegar smell helped a lot, but anything was better than a bare face here.

He pulled on some gloves, slung the knotted rope across his chest and began climbing.

It went faster this time because he knew what to expect, but his prayers to Ruthia were no less fervent. Once he reached the blockage he braced his feet and shoulders against the walls of the shaft, pulled off one glove, worked the tiny bottle from the pouch tied to his belt and broke the lead seal with his fingernail. Then he looked for a place to spill out the invisible drop.

The mortar just above him was quite smooth and Jimmy remembered Asher's warning not to get the stuff on himself. Higher up, as though the mason was getting bored with the job or finding it harder to reach with his trowel, the work was messier, with little shelves and projections of cement making a good spot for the spell to be poured. But that meant pushing his arm and shoulder up close against that slimy hole. The very idea sent a surge of nausea through him, so he took a few slow, deep breaths, forcing himself to ignore the Smell and focused his mind on the goal.

Free the Mockers. Become famous. All the girls will admire you . . . once you've taken a bath.

Gradually his stomach calmed itself.

Part of the problem was that he still hadn't been able to see anything in the bottle and his faith in the drunken magician wasn't all that strong, in spite of what he'd said to Larry. He was more afraid they might fail than that they'd be caught and hanged.

'Do it,' he grumbled, gritting his teeth. As he'd said himself, it wasn't as if there was anything better available.

Jimmy bit his lips and thrust his arm into the hole, aiming for a large projection he thought he could reach, but aiming blind since his arm cut off what little light filtered down from the cell above.

Dear Ruthia, he prayed, *please don't let me get this on myself.* He braced his shoulders hard against the wall, quickly pulled the tiny stopper from the small vial, and tilted it away from his left hand, pressing the open mouth of the container against the mortar. He held it motionless for a long count of seconds, wondering how he was supposed to tell when the vial was empty. Finally, he assumed it had to be.

It was done, except for the waiting to see if the spell would work. He held his breath, pressed himself against the sides of the shaft walls, wondering what to expect.

He missed the first few grains of falling mortar but then a stone fell, hitting him on the thigh. It hadn't occurred to him that there would be falling stones; then he remembered the iron grate above and hurriedly climbed back down again, some little part of him wailing in discontent. He'd have to go up again after all.

In less than a minute the heavy iron grate that had covered the shaft fell down with a crash on top of the dislodged stones and the heap of sand that had once been sturdy mortar.

Jimmy noted a cracked stone beneath it and blew out a relieved breath. Then he re-wet the rag he pulled over his mouth and nose with vinegar, rolled his shoulders to loosen the muscles and began climbing again. He found a ring of faces waiting for him when he got to the top and hands reached out to pull him up. He blinked for a moment; even the twilight dimness of the big cell seemed bright, after the passageways below. Feet rustled in the damp straw that covered the floor, and he could feel more than see the inmates gathering around him.

'Jimmy!'

That was Flora's voice; she elbowed her way through the crush and embraced him, recoiling instantly, her eyes wide, her pretty mouth contorted into a rictus of disgust. Considering the condition of the dungeon and its inhabitants, that said a great deal.

'I know,' he apologized quietly. 'Quiet, unless you want the guards here! The smell can't be helped.' He pulled out the bundle of rags and the vinegar. 'This will cut the smell, but it's the only way out we could find.'

'I can't get down there,' a legless beggar said.

'Get down where?' asked one of the blind ones.

'Anyone who needs help getting down we can lower them with this rope,' Jimmy said.

He slung it off and looked around for something to anchor it to, settling on the bars of the cell. He glanced anxiously out into the dim corridor but saw no one.

Good. If the excitement caused by his arrival hadn't brought the guards running they were probably safe. At least for now. But then, why pay attention to a dungeon with no exit?

'Why are you doing this?' Flora asked him in a whisper. She smiled and shook her head, clearly embarrassed for him. 'They aren't going to keep us in here forever, you know.'

'No they're not,' Jimmy said grimly. 'Tomorrow or the next day they're planning to hang the lot of you girls, and the beggars get fifty lashes apiece.'

Flora stared at him in horror. 'What for?' she asked. 'What are we supposed to have done?'

'Only what you've always done,' he told her. 'It's just they changed the law.'

She closed her mouth and her eyes grew cool. 'Because of the Princess,' she said.

'Or just because del Garza's crazy,' Jimmy said with a grin. 'Doesn't matter. In a few minutes there'll be nobody left for him to hang. Unless he wants to hang his own guards for letting you go.'

She returned his smile slowly, a wicked glint growing in her eyes.

'Well, then. Let's get to work, shall we?'

Once they heard the news, the other Mockers and even the few strangers pitched in eagerly. When the rope was tied firmly, Jimmy said, 'As soon as you get to the sewers, scatter. Don't wait around, unless you're helping those who can't get away alone. By the time I get down last, I want you all gone. Make your way as best you can to your flops or back to Mocker's Rest, but be careful. Once they find you all gone, things in the city are going to get even worse for a while.' Jimmy sent Gerald, Larry the Ear's young brother, down first. Mostly to soothe Larry's fears, partly to show the girls and everyone else how easy the climb was. Except for the Smell. Wisely, he didn't dwell on that part. And once the escapees encountered it they certainly weren't going to climb back up, although if they'd known what was facing them some of them might have preferred hanging.

Finally it was just Jimmy and Flora. He turned to her with an excited grin.

'There's something I want to do before I go.' Flora looked puzzled, but nodded for him to go on. 'Rumours are flying that del Garza put Prince Erland in the dungeon. Do you have any idea where they'd keep him?' he asked.

'How would I know?'

'But he must be somewhere near here, right?' Jimmy asked.

Crossing her arms, she stared at him for a long moment. 'I suppose so. If the rumours said he was in the dungeons, that would be here.' She cocked her head. 'Are you thinking what I think you're thinking?'

He nodded eagerly, his grin growing wider, if that was possible. 'I'm going to get him out.'

Flora's eyes widened. 'Are you crazy?' she hissed, shaking her head as though trying to dislodge something. 'I can't even imagine what they'd do if you did that.' Her eyes widened further. 'The Upright Man!' Flora covered her mouth with her hand. 'Del Garza might not catch you, but the Upright Man certainly would!'

'He'd probably be very pleased indeed,' Jimmy said confidently. A lot more confidently than he actually felt. *The Upright Man doesn't confide in me, either.*

She lowered her hand and licked her lips. 'You really mean to do this, don't you?'

'Why not?' he countered, his eyes gleaming with excitement. 'What better chance will anyone have? What patriotic citizen of Krondor could pass it up?'

'All right,' she said breathlessly. 'I'll help you.'

That took him aback; he hadn't meant to convert her. 'I can handle it,' he said firmly. 'No need for you to risk getting caught again.'

'He's supposed to be ill, Jimmy. You may need some help with him.'

She gave him a steady look until he nodded reluctantly. Then he went to work on the cell's lock. It was tougher than he'd expected, but then, it was supposed to keep common prisoners in, not lock-crackers with a full set of picks. He worked the tumblers by feel, by the tension of the wire struts bending under his fingers, and for the first time blessed Long Charlie for all those tedious drills. Flora stood beside him, her body taut with fear, keeping an eye out for the guards. Then the last probe sprang back; there was a click sound from within the heavy lock-plate, and they both winced at the protesting squeal of the hinges.

'Which way?' he wondered aloud.

'They brought us in that way,' Flora said, nodding left down a corridor of mortared stone; what little light there was came from a round sun-well in the ceiling, no bigger than the diameter of a man's head.

'There were two large cells before this one, but little else. So

I think we should go this way.' She pointed to the right and then quickly moved off.

'Better let me go first,' Jimmy said. 'I've got something I can use in case we meet anyone.'

Flora raised an eyebrow, but didn't object.

Jimmy moved ahead of her, feeling awkward because while what he'd said was true the real reason he wanted to be first was, well . . .

Because I want to be first. And he suspected Flora knew it.

The corridor they followed was dark and narrow. Jimmy couldn't imagine why it was laid out this way, unless the proposed inhabitants were supposed to be owls and cats. He thought that it actually worked to their advantage though, providing them with cover when they needed to look around a corner, to see if the way was clear. So far, there was no one here to notice them. Every cell they'd checked on their way was empty.

Which surprised him; he'd been sure del Garza was jailing anyone he felt like throwing into the dungeon. And given Jocko Radburn's personality, Jimmy had been sure he'd find half the city behind bars. At least the official half.

He was getting impatient; they'd been walking so long it felt as if they must be all the way on the other side of the keep by now.

Then the flickering light of a torch outside a cell up ahead revealed the presence of a guard. A Bas-Tyran from his black and gold uniform and nearly asleep, even standing up and leaning on his halberd, judging from the way his helmeted head kept nodding off and then jerking up again. Sleeping standing up seemed to be one of the basic military skills.

Jimmy squatted, waving Flora down too; they were behind a quarter-turn in the passageway's meander. Then he dug the small bag he'd purchased from Asher out of his pouch and unknotted the string. That was when it occurred to him that he had no idea how much of the stuff to use. His mouth twisted in exasperation. He'd been thinking about the wrong thing; how much he'd pay, rather than how much to use and how long it would last. Too late now.

He decided to sneak up on the nodding guard and blow just a pinch into the man's face. He'd keep on doing that until the guard collapsed. Jimmy gave a mental shrug. It wasn't perfect, but it would have to do. After all, things had gone pretty well so far using trial and error.

He turned to Flora and silently cautioned her to stay put. She nodded and made a shooing gesture. When he'd turned away Jimmy crossed his eyes and stuck out his tongue, a gesture he'd never dream of making to her face; but he hated being told what to do. Especially when it was his idea to do it in the first place.

Focus, he told himself and did so.

He went forward swiftly but without hurry, moving on the balls of his bare feet like a cat. The guard was in the head-nodding phase of his waking doze: Jimmy took a pinch of the magician's powder and blew it into his face just as he jerked it up again. With a loud, pig-like snort, the guard dropped like a sack of potatoes and the young thief barely caught the man's polearm before it, too, crashed to the floor.

Flora moved up beside him and the two of them stared at the fallen soldier in astonishment.

'What did you use?' Flora whispered.

'Something I got from a magician,' Jimmy told her in a more normal voice. He snatched the keys from the guard's belt. 'Something I've got to get more of. Useful stuff!' He took the bag out of his tunic and handed it to her. 'Here, you keep it. If someone comes, blow a pinch into his face and make sure you don't breathe any of the powder yourself.' She nodded and put the small bag inside her bodice. 'Come on, let's open that door.'

* * *

The tiny cell was pitch-black, until they brought the torch in with them. It was colder than the corridor outside and smelled of mould and human waste.

On the floor was a thin pallet of filthy straw and on the pallet, beneath a single ragged blanket, lay a man. His face was waxen pale, eyes and cheeks deeply sunken and his breathing rasped and gurgled as if each one was a struggle.

Flora breathed an 'Ooooh' of sympathy and crouched by the man's side. She took one of his hands in hers and immediately began to chafe it. 'He's so cold, Jimmy.' She turned and looked up at him. 'Go and get that guard's cloak.'

Jimmy raised his brows; he hadn't expected her to start nursing anybody. But if this was the Prince he'd need to be a lot more active than he was if they were to get him out of here. He placed the torch in an iron bracket by the door and went to do as she'd asked.

When he returned she said, 'Let's get some of that under him. This straw's no protection at all from the floor.'

Jimmy nodded, but he was dismayed to find the man still unconscious. How were they going to know they had the right prisoner if he couldn't tell them? The young thief had only ever seen the Prince from a distance and he'd been healthier then, by far, than this man.

He slipped an arm under the prisoner's head and shoulders and heaved, almost sending him flying, for he weighed nothing at all, as if his body was made of sticks and air.

'Well, if we have to carry him we can,' he muttered.

'But, Jimmy, he's so ill,' Flora said. She tucked the cloak around her patient's emaciated body. Then she threw up her hands in despair. 'Just listen to his breathing, it's pneumonia, no doubt, and he's got a fever.'

'And we don't know if he's the Prince,' Jimmy said grimly.

'Who are you children?' the man whispered, and he opened his fever-bright eyes upon them.

Then he coughed, long and hard, curling into himself until the spasm passed, his face contorted with pain. When it was over he lay back with a careful sigh. His two would-be rescuers watched him with wincing sympathy that turned to solemn looks when he opened his eyes again.

'Well?'

'We're Mockers,' Jimmy said. 'Who are you?'

The man formed the word *Mockers* with his lips, but didn't say it. Then he grinned, a truly terrible expression on his pale and wasted features. 'I,' he said breathlessly, carefully separating his words, 'am Prince Erland of Krondor.'

They could see the pride in the man, even under these sordid conditions.

'Have you got anything to drink?' Flora asked. 'His lips are so dry.'

Jimmy shook his head. 'I'll check the guard.'

He was back in a moment and handing a flask to Flora.

'I think it's wine,' he said.

Flora lifted the Prince's head and brought the flask to his lips.

'Thank you,' Erland said after a long drink. He raised his brows. 'That was rather good, and I haven't had anything since they moved me down here this morning.'

It might have been his imagination but it seemed to Jimmy that the Prince's colour was better. Erland indicated that he would like more and Flora gave it to him.

'We've come to get you out of here, uh, your *highness*,' Jimmy said. At least he thought highness was the right thing to call him. He was pretty sure that your *majesty* was totally wrong.

But the Prince shook his head. 'There's little point.' He smiled at them. 'Not that I don't appreciate your efforts, young Mockers. But,' he paused to catch his breath, 'I will not live much longer.' He cleared his throat and the fear that he might cough was in his eyes. When no such fit took place he continued speaking. 'I have been ill for a long time, and I am tired. Putting me here will only hasten my death, but death is coming, no matter where I am.' He closed his eyes, shaking his head slightly. 'The priests and chirurgeons have done all they can, but there is a sickness inside my lungs that is slowly eating away at me.' His face was so drawn and pale, Jimmy would have thought him confined for years, not hours, so he judged the Prince a man very much close to death. 'Much too tired to make the effort to escape. But you should.' He smiled at them.

Jimmy knew the Prince was right for somehow he could see the man's death in his worn face.

'Your wife!' Flora said. 'We could help her escape.'

'She's under guard up in our apartment,' Erland said. 'You could never reach her.' He took a long, slow breath, trying to avoid another coughing fit. 'Del Garza ordered me put here when my daughter fled the castle. She's hiding somewhere in the city. He thinks that by threatening me with a cold death, she'll return without him tearing apart the city and starting a civil riot.'

'No, sir,' said Jimmy. 'She's not in the city. She's three days or more gone by ship to Crydee, with Prince Arutha.'

'Arutha!' said Erland, then he was racked by another coughing attack. When he could speak, he said, 'How is it the Prince of Crydee was here?'

Jimmy quickly recounted what he knew, that Arutha and his companions had come to Krondor to seek Erland's aid in the next spring campaign against the invading Tsurani, and had found the city under martial law and Guy du Bas-Tyra's rule. That they had tried to lie low while assessing what was in play in Krondor, and had come under observation of both Radburn's secret police and the Mockers; the Mockers had barely got to Arutha first.

He finished quickly by telling of the night fight at the docks and the successful departure of the *Sea Swift,* and the likelihood that Anita was safely away from Krondor if she hadn't been returned by now.

'Thank you for that,' said the Prince. 'That is comforting. If du Bas-Tyra returns to word my daughter is out of the city, he will almost certainly return me to the comfort of my apartments and the good ministry of my wife. I couldn't ask for better news than to know my daughter in safety with the son of Borric of Crydee.

'Now, you must go. The guard will rouse or another will come soon, and you must not be here. Return the wineskin and cloak as you found them. The guard must think he fell asleep. No matter what else, no one must know you saw me. If word reached the city I was near death, foolishly loyal men might seek to free me. Bloodshed on behalf of one already near death is pointless. Promise you'll not mention this visit to anyone?'

They both said they would keep silent.

With surprising strength, Prince Erland demanded, 'Not even to one another, lest someone overhear. Your oath!'

Jimmy blinked in surprise, but said, 'By Ruthia and Banath, my oath, highness.'

Flora repeated the same oath and the Prince relaxed somewhat. 'Good. Now go.'

Jimmy quickly returned the cloak and wineskin to the guard, taking a moment to pour a bit on the man's face and down his tunic so that his sergeant would be less inclined to believe any stories about unexplainable slumbers, and turned to look back before he closed the cell door. He saw the Prince seem to shrink, becoming even smaller as he lay back and closed his eyes, and something in his heart twinged.

The two Mockers moved swiftly back to the large cell, not meeting anyone on the way. Inside they found the floor covered with sand.

'Where did this come from?' Flora wondered. 'I swear it wasn't here before.'

Jimmy looked up at the ceiling nervously, but it seemed solid. Then he looked over at the hole in the centre of the cell and saw a flood of sand pouring down through it. *Oh*, he thought and his heart sank. Asher had kept mumbling about 'Something . . .' Apparently the 'something' he'd forgotten was how much of the potion to use. Maybe only a part of a drop, while Jimmy had dumped the entire contents! It looked as if the potion was far more powerful than Jimmy had anticipated.

Which might just mean that the ceiling would be coming down imminently.

'Let's go!' Jimmy said, giving Flora a shove.

She turned and gave him one back.

'Now, Flora! Before this whole place comes down on us!'

The girl stared at him, her eyes wide. 'Magic!' she said. 'You used magic!'

'What else?' he asked and thrust the rope into her hands. 'Now go!'

By the time she turned to him, she was up to her waist in falling sand. 'Don't tell me you went to Alban Asher.'

'At this point I'll say anything you want, Flora!' He waved her down. 'Go! So that I can go. Please!'

The last thing she said before she disappeared into the hole was, 'For the love of Banath, Jimmy, he's a drunk!'

'As if I didn't know it,' Jimmy muttered, taking hold of the rope.

This would be one of those times when the magician's spell didn't work as expected. Not exactly the way he'd planned for his name to pass into legend. But since, for the most part, this exploit had been a success Jimmy supposed he could accept this one little mishap. He pulled the cloth over his face, closed his eyes and went down the rancid shaft for the last time.

Laughing Jack smacked Jimmy hard enough to knock him down, then yanked him back up by his collar and shook him, hard.

'Enough,' the Nightmaster said.

Jack snapped a look at him, showing his teeth.

'I said, enough,' the Nightmaster repeated, quietly, but with an edge in his voice.

Laughing Jack let Jimmy go so suddenly the boy staggered. 'You can go.'

Jack nodded, his expression showing his disagreement. Then he glared at Jimmy and turned and left, closing the door behind him.

They were in the upper room of a supposedly abandoned house in the Poor Quarter, and they could hear the floor creaking with every step the Nightwarden took as he walked away.

The Nightmaster shook his head and tsked. 'You are too bold, Jimmy the Hand. Do you know that almost half a tower came down today? Straight down it fell, right into the west half of the dungeon. It's a miracle that no one was killed.'

The Nightmaster's face was bland, but Jimmy could hear a smile in his voice. It was all he could do not to smile in return.

'Word is you were at the bottom of this mess,' the Nightmaster went on. 'And the Upright Man is most upset that you have, once again, disobeyed direct orders. Do you know what those orders were?'

Jimmy thought it best to deny that he did, so he shook his head.

'Keep out of sight and do nothing. You don't remember hearing that? How odd, when I have witnesses that you were present at the time those orders were issued.' The Nightmaster sat forward and folded his hands before him on the desk.

'You've put the Upright Man in a difficult position, Jimmy the Hand. You've deliberately disobeyed orders, yet you've also rescued over thirty Mockers from certain death.' One corner of his mouth quirked upward. 'Not to mention that you've managed to hide their escape. It will be months, if ever, before del Garza discovers there are no bodies under all that stone. With those terrible rats down there gnawing on the corpses and the main sewers flooding with the spring rain, why even the bones will be washed out to sea before the workers get down there.' The Nightmaster fought to keep a smile from spreading too broadly as he added, 'Without his even knowing it, you've made our enemy look very foolish.'

The Nightmaster spread his hands. 'Yet, what can we do? The Upright Man's thankful you've saved thirty of your brethren, but he's still got to cut your throat and throw you in the bay. If such a breach of orders goes unpunished then others will believe that they, too, can do whatever the bloody hell they wish. Others far less clever, or lucky, than yourself. That way lies chaos and Old Night.' He rubbed his upper lip and stared at Jimmy. 'Of course, if you can't be found to be punished, then perhaps it will all blow over and nothing will need to be done at all. After all, every once in a while the Upright Man offers a general amnesty.' He leaned back, not taking his eyes from the boy.

Jimmy nodded. The amnesty was offered to all who came forward and confessed their transgressions. It usually required that any loot not shared out as it should be had to be offered along with the promise not to do it again. Jimmy thought it a good idea, as it made for a little extra something in the share out after the Upright Man and his crew took their cut, and it made it easier for the Daymaster and Nightmaster to know who to watch for double-dealing. It also kept the Upright Man from having to kill off all the members, as sooner or later every Mocker ended up breaking one rule or another. But, it would also apply to someone who disobeyed orders!

Jimmy said, 'Can't be found? As in can't be found, or can't be found because he was dropped into the harbour with heavy weights?'

'The first. If you were to leave Krondor, and travel around a bit . . . Travelling is said to be very educational, and in this case it would be very good for your health.'

Jimmy felt his gullet tighten and a heavy weight settle under his breastbone. He stammered: 'B-but I've never, n-never been out of Krondor before in my life!'

The Nightmaster leaned forward again. 'Let me put it to you this way – either take yourself off, or take what's coming to you. Am I clear?'

'Absolutely.' Jimmy forced calm on himself. How bad could it be? Other people managed to live beyond Krondor. There was a whole world out there to explore!

He was homesick already.

'Then you may go.' The Nightmaster looked at Jimmy from under his eyebrows. 'And when I say *go* I mean far away. Just in case you didn't understand the first time I said it.'

'Yes, sir.'

Jimmy darted out of the Nightwarden's room, past a snarling Laughing Jack, and headed quickly out of Mocker's Rest. He had to go fetch his gold before nightfall, then find a way safely to the caravanserai outside the eastern gate. He would somehow get past the guards – he had no doubt of his ability to do that – then either beg or buy his way onto the first caravan heading east or north. He might be told to go far, but he would stay in the Kingdom and not risk heading down into the deserts and Great Kesh beyond.

Feeling nervous and excited in equal measures, he hurried into the sewers one more time.

SIX

Journey

Jimmy raised his hand.

He held up two fingers, and the innkeeper filled two tarred leather mugs from the barrels that rested on trestles along one wall.

He was middle-aged and bald and fat; the barmaid was probably his wife, and looked the same, except for having hair. She waited expectantly until Jimmy fished in his pouch and brought out the coppers. The tavern wasn't much: a rush-strewn floor, brick walls with patches of what had once been plaster, and rough wooden tables and plank benches and stools. The smell wasn't too bad, though; mostly spilled beer, which was inevitable.

The place did have the advantage of not being a known Mocker hangout: most of the other customers right now were dockwallopers and labourers, nursing a mug of beer to make it last, with maybe bread and cheese and pickles on the side.

Not much of an advertisement for honest toil, Jimmy thought morosely, taking a mouthful and wiping the back of his hand across his mouth. *But then I was never tempted.*

The Sail and Anchor was as typical a sailors' dive as you could find in the dockside quarter of Krondor. Jimmy had scouted the caravanserai and had judged it unlikely he could slip out within a day or so, given the close scrutiny everyone was being subjected to as they tried to leave the city. The pulling down of the tower above the cells had saved over thirty Mockers, but it had driven del Garza into a frenzy of reprisals. A few Mockers too stupid to keep out of sight were already down in the Market Square Gaol – the Sheriff's Constables ran that lock-up – but they stood a fair chance of avoiding the gallows, for none had been collared for a hanging offence, unless del Garza changed the laws again. However, a few common workers and a couple of merchants' wives and daughters had also been rounded up, so now del Garza had the guilds and citizens in an uproar.

From what Jimmy could see in the falling darkness the previous evening, del Garza already had every engineer and mason in the Kingdom crawling over that tower – it looked as if he meant to have it back in place before Duke Guy returned from the Keshian border. Jimmy smiled. Toss in a magician or two and he might just pull that off.

'Thanks,' Flora said and took a sip, watching Jimmy over the rim of her mug. 'You're thinking. What about?'

He hunched over his own ale, blowing at the thin layer of froth and wondering if he looked as depressed as he felt. 'Just having to leave the city. And having to sneak aboard a ship. I don't care much for ships.'

'Have you ever been on one?' she asked, a little excitedly.

'No, but I know enough to know once you're on one, there's few places where you can bolt, unless you can swim like a fish. I'm good enough at hiding, but hiding out on a ship . . . they call it being a stowaway.'

'Well, don't. Go as a passenger.'

Jimmy sighed. 'Del Garza's checking passengers as close here as he is at the city gates.'

'Cheer up, Jimmy! It's not the end of the world,' she said softly, and grew thoughtful.

'No, the Upright Man just wants me to go to the end of the world,' he said. 'And drop off the edge for a while. Maybe he'd really like it if I managed to get kidnapped to Great Kesh, or that world the invaders come from.' Jimmy glanced up at her from under his brows; he wasn't even sure she was paying attention. *If I'm going to grumble and moan and pity myself, at least she could listen to the specifics,* he thought.

This was not the way he'd expected things to be tonight. Someone, many someones, should be buying him an ale and dinner besides, and singing his praises, and thumping his back until it hurt. Instead he couldn't go near Mocker's Rest or even the sewers: he had to be out of town, and soon. Even lingering this long was a bit of a risk.

Instead of being a hero, he was all alone in this working man's tavern, facing exile.

Well, all right, I'm not alone, but for all the attention Flora's paying me I might as well be. I'm a hero, gods take it. Girls, plural, should be all over me.

Now she was giving him a considering look. He knew that look. It was the look a woman gives you when she's going to ask for something. Jimmy raised a single brow, waiting for the shoe to drop.

Suddenly she gave him a brilliant smile. 'I know where we can go,' she said.

'We?' That was unexpected. 'What do you mean, we?'

'My mother told me that I have a grandfather and an aunt in Land's End. She said my grandfather didn't approve of my father.' Flora's eyes took on the far-away look of someone remembering. 'Not that my parents ever said so, but they'd look at one another and they'd have these odd smiles . . . sad like . . . Anyway,' she continued, 'we could go to Land's End and see if I still have family there. It would be like a quest! What d'ye think?'

Jimmy blinked. It was an idea, he supposed. Or a direction at least.

'Where is Land's End?' he asked. He'd heard of it, of course, but that didn't mean he knew where it was or anything else about it.

'I dunno. I never went there. But we can find out. What d'ye say? Shall we?'

He widened his eyes and tipped his head, shrugging. 'Why not? I've got to go somewhere, but . . . would we be welcome, just dropping in with no warning? I mean, if your grandfather didn't approve of your father . . .' He trailed off awkwardly.

Flora's lips thinned. 'Well, the way my Pa turned out after my mother died I could hardly blame him for that, now could I?'

Jimmy sidestepped the issue of how her father had become a brawling drunk by asking, 'Is that why you didn't go to Land's End after he died?'

With a grimace Flora shook her head. 'I was only nine years old, Jimmy. I had no money and no idea how to get there.' She shrugged, giving him a wry smile. 'And the only people I ever knew were here.'

'So you know how I feel,' he said.

Flora smiled at him. 'I know.' Then she put her hand over his and squeezed it. 'Maybe after supper I can make you feel better.'

Smiling wryly he raised his brows and sighed. At least someone was getting a free supper tonight.

Well, I do feel better, he thought, a few hours later, stretching and smiling smugly as his eyes opened again; the candle was guttering near its finish, casting patterns of shadow on the ceiling. *A lot better.*

He'd brought her to his best place; a half-ruined house with one very good room that he'd done up. Jimmy opened his eyes all the way, stretched again, yawned, and turned – only to find her gone. His sense of well-being undiminished, he crossed his arms beneath his head and remembered.

Just before they went to sleep she had thanked him.

He grinned. *I'm a hero and no mistake, by the gods*, he thought.

Suddenly the door opened and he jumped up, clutching the sheets.

'Good morning!' Flora sang.

'I thought you'd gone,' Jimmy said, one hand over his galloping heart and the other slipping a dagger back under the pillow.

'You're not going to get rid of me that easily,' she said, laughing.

She pulled off her shawl. Hidden within its folds was a loaf of raisin-studded bread. Saliva rushed into his mouth at the smell of it, sweet and yeasty at the same time. She extracted a pot of honey out of one pocket and a slab of butter, wrapped in a handkerchief, from the other.

'Where did you buy that?' Jimmy asked; there wasn't a market near this place, or a bakery.

'Buy?' she asked in astonishment. 'I'm not as good as you are, Jimmy the Hand, but I made my name stealing baked goods, I'll remind you!'

True, he thought.

Jimmy rose from the bed, wrapping a sheet around himself, smiling when Flora laughed at his sudden modesty. She sliced the bread while he poured out the rest of the wine they'd brought home the night before and they sat down to the important business of filling their stomachs.

After they'd eaten breakfast, things began to happen with the honey and the butter and they soon ended up in bed again.

As they lay quietly in one another's arms Flora said, 'I found out where Land's End is.'

Her words cut through him like a knot of buzzing insects

94

briefly invading his middle. He suddenly knew this wasn't going to turn out well.

'It's south,' she went on when he said nothing. 'Near the Vale of Dreams.'

Thank you, he thought a little sourly. *Here I'd just managed to pleasantly forget I'm leaving Krondor an exile, and you went and reminded me.*

When Flora spoke her voice held a little irritation; Jimmy felt a brief stab of guilt. *She's only trying to help, after all*, he thought.

'It takes five days to sail there,' she said, looking across at him. When he didn't answer and wouldn't meet her eyes she went on, 'The fare is four silvers, apiece, to go by ship if we sleep in the hold. They got cabins, but they're all full of people sailing past Land's End, on to Great Kesh.'

After a prolonged silence, during which he could feel her eyes giving him sunburn, Jimmy looked at her sidelong. 'How much by coach?' he mumbled grudgingly.

'There's a ship that sails today at high tide.'

'Four silvers is pretty steep,' he snarled. 'Didn't it occur to you to bargain?'

Flora turned a scalding glare on him. 'Yes, Jimmy, it did occur to me. That's why it's not six. All right?'

The way she was looking at him, it had better be all right. He changed the subject.

'When's high tide?' he asked. He should know: he'd lived in a seaport town all his life, but had only the vaguest notion, since the knowledge was of no great use to a thief who didn't work the docks.

Flora stretched luxuriously before answering – the sight of which improved his mood somewhat. 'In about three or four hours, I'd say,' she answered.

'Well if we're supposed to be on this ship we'd better get ourselves organized,' Jimmy said.

'I know you don't want to go,' Flora said suddenly, her eyes sympathetic.

He smiled at her, appreciating her understanding, and leaned over to give her a kiss. 'But I have to,' he said. 'Thank you for doing what I probably wouldn't have got around to until tomorrow.' He considered her. 'We should probably get you some new clothes, don't you think?'

She frowned. 'Why? Most of my things are spanking new.'

'Ah, true,' he said, somewhat taken aback.

It hadn't occurred to him that Flora would want to keep her new dresses. They were cheap and flashy and left the observer in no doubt at all as to what she did for a living. Yet, here she was talking about finding her lost family while wearing them. How should he phrase this?

'But, they, um, they're a bit, ah, fancy for a little place like Land's End. Don't you think? What's fashionable here in Krondor might be too daring for your grandfather. Especially if he's the disapproving type.'

Flora stared at him with her mouth open, then burst into delighted laughter, kicking her slim legs in the air, while he watched her in puzzled surprise. Every time she looked at his confused expression she went off again and it was a while before she stopped gasping and could say, 'Oh, Jimmy, you're such a dear!' She gave him a fierce kiss. 'There you are twisting yourself into knots to keep from saying, "But, Flora, you dress like a whore!" I can't remember when someone last took my feelings into consideration like that. You're a true friend.'

Greatly relieved, he smiled. 'I'm glad you approve.'

'I do,' she said, getting up. 'I hadn't even thought of it. But now I do think of it you're absolutely right. Only, what am I going to tell him about how I've been making my living the last few years?'

'Does he know your father is dead?' Jimmy asked.

'Well he certainly didn't hear it from me,' she said. 'But I can't take the chance that he doesn't know. That kind of news has a way of travelling.'

'Let's see . . .' He thought a moment. 'How about this? You lived with a neighbour family for a few years after your Pa died, working at chores for your keep. Then a kind old lady with a little gold took you in and you've been her companion the last few years – you still know how to talk like a swell, so if you don't fall into street cant, they'll never know it's a story.

'Anyway, now the old lady's died and her relatives wouldn't make a place for you. But they did pay your fare to Land's End so that you could find your mother's family. What about your father? Did he have family there?'

Flora shook her head as she did up her laces. 'If he did he never spoke of them. Come to think of it, he never spoke much at all, even when Ma was alive.'

Jimmy took a handful of silver and gave it to her. 'Go disguise yourself as a companion to a nice old lady,' he said. 'What ship is it that we'll be taking?'

'*Krondor's Lady*,' Flora said, counting with expert speed. 'Jimmy, I can't take all this!'

'Well, you don't have to spend it all. Don't worry about it. After all, I need you for my disguise, namely the younger brother of a nice girl who was companion to an old lady. I've got to get some newer clothing, and then I'll meet you on the docks,' he said and gave her a quick kiss. 'See you at high tide.'

She fled through the door, eager to be shopping, leaving Jimmy to finish dressing alone. As he pulled on his trousers, he thought he might find a tailor who could quickly provide him with a reputable-looking coat to wear over his second-newest shirt – the one he had purchased while he and Larry had bathed had to be burned after the second crawl through the sewer drain below the cell. He should also wear boots and a hat, he thought.

97

Yes, a young couple . . . no, he still looked too young. Flora was a few years older, so a grieving girl and her younger brother, yes, that would be it. On their way to Land's End because of a family loss.

Suddenly he was a great deal more sanguine about bringing Flora along than he had been a few minutes earlier. Silver was precious, but not as dear as his neck – which del Garza would happily stretch – or his head – which the Upright Man's bashers would happily club – so it wasn't a bad deal. Yes, brother and sister on their way to visit Grandpa. Besides, she filled his bed better than any girl he knew, and he thought that might be a welcome relief during exile. He was almost whistling when he left the flop. Then he stopped himself. *When did 'I' become 'we'?* he thought to himself. *I'm the one the Upright Man is running out of the city; Flora's free to stay here.* As he headed down the stairs he considered that he had never invited her to come with him and she had never asked his permission. It was just, somehow, done. Shaking his head in wonder, he realized he was now beginning to understand what some of the older men in the Mockers meant when they said they could bloody well do anything they pleased, so long as it was what their wives wanted them to do.

He turned his mind away from irritation and back to the soft feel of Flora's skin and her round rump and suddenly it didn't seem too big a price to pay, letting her have her way. He was back to almost whistling when he reached the street.

Krondor's Lady was old and small and tubby; about a hundred feet long and thirty wide amidships. The smell filtering up from the bilges made her more than a little homelike, to one who'd spent a lot of time in the sewers.

It had proven surprisingly easy to get aboard. While most of the guards on the docks were Bas-Tyra men, *Krondor's Lady* was under the watch of some of the Sheriff's Crushers, as the constables were known. A quick story about visiting grandpa, with Flora looking genuinely distressed – not entirely an act after her stint in the gaol – and they were allowed aboard. Jimmy was thankful for the change of clothing both had elected earlier that day. One glance at the sword at his hip and the constable had judged him a young man from a family of means.

Flora had gone below to see where they were being permitted to sleep, while Jimmy remained on deck to watch the departure.

'You make this run often?' Jimmy asked a sailor, dodging a group of others who went running by with a roll of canvas, obviously ready to kick the annoying deck passenger out of the way.

'Two, three times a year,' the sailor said, doing something nautical involving two pieces of rope and a knife, his fingers running on with an automatic nimbleness. 'Usually not so early. Storms, y'know.'

'Oh,' Jimmy said hollowly.

A last net of cargo – bales, boxes and sacks – swung off from the dock and down into the hold. Sailors hammered home the wedges that held a grating over the hatchway and did various mysterious things with the ropes and sails, mostly involving hauling or running up the ratlines while other sailors screamed at them. The captain was a short grizzled wiry man, with a gold hoop in his left ear and a missing little finger on his right hand.

'Loose sail!' he shouted from the rear of the ship. Canvas thundered down and bellied out into brown patched curves. 'Cast away fore, cast away aft, loose all, fend off! Fend off, don't tickle the dock, you bitches' brood!'

Sailors loosed ropes and pushed at the dock with long two-man oars. Jimmy swallowed and watched as the roofs of Krondor began to slip away, and the deck took on a slight rocking motion under his feet. A cold clammy feeling settled in his stomach.

Up on the sterncastle the harbour pilot directed the helmsman, while the captain kept shouting orders to his crew.

I'm leaving Krondor, he thought. It didn't seem quite real; it was as if he'd just said to himself *I'm going to the moon.* 'Leaving Krondor' was always something other people did.

Like the Prince and the Princess, he thought then, which cheered him a little. *Getting onto a bigger stage, that's what I'm doing!*

The pilot had the ship moving gracefully through other ships at anchor or coming in to the docks. They dodged freighters and long, sleek warships and fishing-boats and wherries and barges. At some point that was not significant to Jimmy, the pilot hurried down to the main deck, and with agility surprising in a man of middle years he swung a leg over the side and scampered down to a waiting rowboat.

The ship moved surprisingly slowly as it edged out of the harbour. Jimmy glanced back to the sterncastle and saw the captain keeping his own hand on the tiller as he barked orders.

'Ah, comin' on a bit fresher,' the sailor said.

The sky was growing clouds, cold and grey-looking. The water turned from blue to green-grey too, and began to crumple itself up into tall hills that moved toward him, topped with white foam. The ship's blunt bow rose to meet it, dug in and rose again with white foam coming across the forward railings and swirling ankle-deep across the deck. In what seemed to Jimmy to be unreasonable haste, the land fell off to nothing but a dark line to their left, and the rocking-horse motion of the ship acquired other twists, a curling roll, left forward to right back.

A sailor, some sort of officer, saw Jimmy the Hand's face turn pasty-white and how he clapped a hand to his mouth. 'The lee rail, you infernal lubber!' he snarled, then grabbed the boy by collar and belt and ran him over to it, getting his head over the side just as the first heave struck. 'Feed the fish, and don't foul our deck, damn your eyes!'

*   *   *

'I hate you,' Jimmy mumbled feebly, not sure whether he meant himself, Flora who'd got him into this, the ship, the crew, or all of them together.

His sides hurt, his head ached, his eyes felt as if they'd been rolled in hot sand. *Now I know what the word misery was invented for,* he thought, as he crawled hand-over-hand toward the rail and another spell of dry retching heaves until there was nothing left inside to come up.

And I stink.

So badly that he spent most of his time on deck letting the high winds blow his funk away. That meant he was mostly at the stern since the gale came from the south. He'd learned quickly that spitting wasn't the only thing you didn't do into the wind. The fresh air made it a little easier to live with himself. Even so, he avoided company.

Sometimes between bouts of retching he was tormented by memories of his original plans for this voyage. He'd imagined himself playing dice with the crew and cleaning them out easily. He'd done it often enough in Krondor, though most of the sailors were drunk at the time.

Instead, the crew were amusing themselves by sidling up to him and saying things like, 'Arrgh, sick are ye? Whatcha need laddie-boy is some nice ham floatin' in a bowl of warm cream! Or maybe you'd like some cold fish chowder?' Then laughing as he swore feebly, not realizing that he'd be cutting them down right then and there, if only he weren't so weak and if only moving didn't make him feel worse.

Or maybe they remember me from the dice and the taverns, and this is some sort of sick, twisted revenge.

Flora came staggering up bearing a mug of broth for him and hunched down beside him where he hid from the wet wind behind a crate secured to the deck.

'Flora,' he said, gasping and trying to drink the salty broth. It seemed to hurt less if you had something to give the sea. 'Do you think they recognize me? Could I have picked someone's pocket, or won too much at dice, d'ye think?' Then he shook his head. 'But there's no profit in it, so why bother?'

She shrugged. 'Well, my friend, if I thought someone who'd robbed or cheated me was nearby and the only revenge I was going to get was to make him throw up then I would, and gladly. And I'd consider that profit aplenty.' Flora smiled at his expression of abject horror. 'But I don't think they do recognize you, Jimmy. I hardly knew you myself when I first saw you waiting on the dock, you looked so respectable!'

She huddled deeper into her thick shawl and huddled closer to him, shivering with cold. He welcomed her warmth, and the fact that she blocked the wind on that side.

'Actually, it seems to be something they do whenever someone gets seasick; sailor or passenger,' Flora continued. 'I think it's mean and I've asked them not to do it any more. But I honestly don't think they can resist.'

He tried to dump the rest of the broth overboard – his shrunken stomach was starting to protest – but she pushed it right back at him.

So the crew didn't want revenge on him, they just wanted to torture him for the joy of it. That was nice.

It's a very good thing I can't put curses on people or by now the whole crew would be writhing in agony. Or dying horribly. And in the throes of violent sea-sickness a man can think up some very horrible things indeed.

He knew that if it weren't for Flora's influence the crew would be even worse. How she kept them off him he didn't know.

Perhaps he should.

'You're not giving them . . .' he hesitated.

'Giving them bribes to leave you alone?' Flora shook her head, smiling. 'If I were then I'd not be getting much in return for my efforts, now would I? But no, I'm not doing that any more. I'm going to be an honest girl if it kills me. At least until I find out if I do have a family.'

She watched him look miserably into the cup of cooling broth and gave his shoulder a pat. 'Just drink it, Jimmy. You've got to get something down you or you really will be sick.'

He gave her a piteous look, but all she did was nod encouragingly. He squeezed his eyes shut and drank the last, lukewarm half. He knew it would come up again, but at least now it was comfortably warm. Flora would have waited until he drank it even if the stuff grew a skim of ice.

Then he thought about what she'd said. 'I *am* sick,' he pointed out.

'You're not dying. But if you don't keep drinking water or broth, though, you actually might.'

Well, that was a pleasant thought.

Jimmy began to feel the broth dancing in his aching stomach and knew it wouldn't be long before the stuff made a break for it. He was too ashamed of his condition to encourage her presence at such times.

'Cook says if you can keep that down, and spend a while just looking at the horizon, so your senses can adjust, you just might get over this sickness. Some people do.' Then with a piteous look she added, 'And some people don't.'

'Maybe you should go below,' he suggested.

She looked at him askance, then nodded. 'It is getting cold out here.' Flora tucked a tendril of hair back under her enveloping shawl. 'I'll be back later with something else.'

'Oh, gods!' Jimmy groaned and rushed to the rail.

Flora hurried away; even then he managed to feel a mute animal gratitude.

Jimmy willed himself to hold the content of his stomach down. He did as suggested and watched the horizon and soon noticed that the rise and fall of the ship was less distressing on his stomach when he could see the motion as well as feel it. He took slow, deep breaths and attempted another sip of broth.

Gradually he became aware that one of the other passengers was watching him. The man was about thirty; of medium build, but standing with an easy balance that made some corner of Jimmy's mind say *swordsman* despite his dress; he was wearing dark clothes of good wool, but they'd seen hard use and were stained with salt. The sort of clothes might be worn by a travelling merchant in a small way of business, or by a ship's officer.

But that belt has wear on it, Jimmy thought, glad of something to distract him from his wet, chill misery. *Look at the way it's polished, and stretched a little. That's the attachment for a sword-sling.*

Like Jimmy, the man kept himself to himself, though probably for different reasons, lending the occasional, very competent, hand to the sailors when the seas became unusually rough. Otherwise he spent his time either gazing out to sea or staring at the young thief. Jimmy was beginning to find it very annoying.

It also worried him. After separating from Flora in Krondor he'd retrieved his gold and turned a fair bit of it into silver and copper, much of which he'd secreted about his person. There were times he thought the stranger somehow knew that he was carrying well over a hundred and fifty in silver and gold even though it shouldn't have been obvious to anyone.

Unless that someone had seen him changing his gold to silver.

Certainly Jimmy didn't look rich; Flora had outfitted him from a used-clothing store, one where respectable shopkeepers and craftsmen went. True, there were a large number of pockets, but that was something common to all the boys Jimmy knew, town or Mocker. And having a lot of pockets didn't necessarily mean that each one was full of money. Even if, in his case, it was.

The only bright spot is that if he wants to rob me he'll have to do it here on deck in front of the captain and the crew, and Flora, when she's here.

It would take a good long time, too, because as one of the best pickpockets in Krondor he'd long known the value of spreading your valuables around. And with no less than twelve pockets, not including the ones he'd sewn himself, he'd had plenty of places to put his gold. Of course, if he ever fell overboard he'd sink like a stone, but you couldn't have everything. Besides, the way he was feeling right now the idea actually had some appeal.

Jimmy clung to the rail and slanted his eyes toward the stranger where the man squatted with his back against the mainmast. The man caught his glance and rose in a single graceful movement. As he approached the stranger took something from his belt pouch.

Jimmy tensed.

The man held out a strap of leather. 'Let's put this on you.' Without waiting for an answer he grabbed Jimmy's left wrist and fastened it on, then positioned it just so. 'I couldn't bear to watch you suffer any more, lad,' the fellow said. His voice was deep and mild.

Jimmy could feel something like a pebble pressing lightly into his wrist. He looked suspiciously at the stranger.

'Keep it just there and in a few hours your problem should be solved.'

'Is it magic?' Jimmy asked.

The man snorted. 'I don't think so,' he said. 'The trick of it was shown to me by an old Keshian sailor, and I'd bet my last silver he had nothing magical about him.' He held out his hand. 'My name is Jarvis Coe.'

Jimmy shook his hand weakly. 'If this works, Master Coe, I'll be eternally in your debt.' At that moment the ship rose, then fell steeply and so did Jimmy's stomach. When he turned around again Jarvis Coe was gone. He looked goggle-eyed at the bracelet. *Doesn't seem to be working*, he thought miserably, as he turned his eyes back to the horizon and contemplated another sip of broth. Maybe between staring at the horizon and the pebble on his wrist he just might survive the journey . . .

But it does work! Jimmy thought exultantly, an hour later. 'Oh, gods, it works!' he mumbled aloud.

He looked down at his bowl. In it was some stew, the inevitable traveller's food, and there were beans and dried tomato and bits of salt fish floating around in it, and it didn't make him want to crawl groaning toward the leeward rail!

Even the wiggling thing that had dropped out of his hard biscuit when he tapped it on the table like everyone else didn't revolt him, and it would have back in Krondor. Now he just felt . . .

'Hungry,' he whispered to himself. 'It's been so long, I'd forgotten what it felt like!'

Flora was looking at him oddly. The passengers took their meals at a table set up in the passageway in front of the captain's cabin; he gave her a smile and saw her match it as he dipped his spoon into the bowl and methodically ate everything in it. That wasn't a big serving, and he felt stuffed – no wonder, after three days of nothing but water – but it stayed down.

Flora's hand jerked him awake just before he went face-down in the bowl.

'Come along, brother,' she said, helping him up.

When he came to under the coarse brown blankets that covered his bunk, an inner sense told him he'd more than slept the clock around. That was no wonder either, since he'd no more been able to sleep than to eat.

If that's what feeling old is like, I hope I die young, he thought, shuddering. His clothes were damp and clammy as he pulled them on in the little box miscalled a cabin, but he was no stranger to that, and his feet almost danced as he headed down the passageway and up the steep ladder-stairs to the deck, looking for his benefactor. He walked about watching the sailors work: it was always a pleasant activity watching someone else sweat.

Pleased as he was with the miracle of not being sea-sick, the whole world took on a rosier hue. The young thief decided that travel to Land's End just might be something to look forward to after all. He'd simply been startled by the Nightmaster's demand that he leave, that was it, and for a while he'd been worried because he wouldn't have anything or anybody familiar to fall back on. It wasn't fear he'd felt at all, he'd just been . . . taken by surprise.

Besides, he'd managed the rubes right handily when they'd made their way to Krondor; why would he have problems just because they'd stayed at home? *This is going to be an adventure, by Ruthia!* he thought. *I'll have some fine tales to tell when I get home.*

That he looked forward to getting home before he'd even reached his destination brought a wry smile to his face. Jimmy could fool most people, but he never could fool himself. *All right,* he thought, *so it's not something I would have chosen to do. But I've turned bad luck to good advantage before now. I don't see why this should be any different.*

He looked about: still no sign of Coe and he'd been on deck for most of the morning by now.

'Where's that fellow who was propping up the main mast yesterday?' he asked a passing sailor.

'In 'is cabin, I s'pose,' the man barked, brushing past. 'I'm not 'is nanny that I'd know.'

Guess I'm not as much fun to talk to now that you can't make me vomit, Jimmy thought snidely.

Even so, it was strange. One day the man was unavoidable, the next day he'd disappeared. Jimmy didn't like it, such behaviour was suspicious. It reminded him too much of Radburn's men.

His abused stomach lurched horribly and he thought, *Oh, gods! Not again, I thought I was cured.* But it wasn't sea-sickness that had caused the sensation. It was the idea that he might have been followed by one of Bas-Tyra's secret police that had given him such a qualm.

Jimmy knew many of Radburn's sneaking spies by sight, and usually, given time, could guess who was one by their behaviour. But did they know him?

He tried to dismiss the thought. At the moment he looked respectable, which was to say, not like himself. And when he spoke – which given his malady had been infrequently – he'd been careful to speak like a well-brought-up boy. There was absolutely no reason for anyone to suspect that he was a Mocker. Flora had had enough gentlemen of rank in her day to have some practice speaking like a girl of means, so she hadn't given him away with street cant; it'd been 'mister' and 'sir' not 'deary' and 'luv' – and not one obscenity had escaped her lips – since she'd traded in her whore's garb for a modest dress, shoulder-shawl, and hat. Besides, if Coe did know him, why hadn't he simply turned him in at the dock, or just chucked him overboard?

It would have been easy, Jimmy thought. Hells and demons, I would have thanked him for it!

And yet, having finally introduced himself, the mysterious stranger had disappeared. Was Coe just a concerned soul who'd been watching to make sure the young thief didn't fall overboard? Now that he'd given Jimmy the cure for his sea-sickness perhaps the man had decided to retire to the relative comfort of his cabin. Was that suspicious? Jimmy frowned. Actually, he did find generosity from strangers suspicious. Useful on occasion, he allowed. Especially if the giver was naïve and easy to manipulate. But Coe didn't seem the type one could use. In fact he seemed the type to ream you proper if you tried: Jimmy could smell that on a man. The young thief exhaled with a snort of frustration.

Focus, concentrate, he commanded himself.

If one of Radburn's spies had seen him and knew him for a Mocker, known what he'd done, which was unlikely – make that impossible – then without question he would have been arrested immediately. There was no reason for one of Radburn's boys to go following him to Land's End.

But what if one of Radburn's spies was going to Land's End anyway? Land's End was an outpost, near the Keshian border. More accurately, it was the domain of the Lord of the Southern Marches, Duke Sutherland, but that office had been vacant for years, due to some politics Jimmy didn't understand or care to understand. *Yes, maybe that's it,* he thought. Maybe it's just Guy du Bas-Tyra trying to extend his reach. Who knew how far the Duke wanted to extend his power? Jimmy watched the hills of water rise and fall, actually enjoying the clever motion of the ship as it followed their motion.

As far as he can, of course!

He wrestled with some more notions of what the Duke might be plotting, but grew bored with it. It was surprising enough as it was that he was interested in that question at all. Until meeting Prince Arutha he had no concept of what ruling must be like, but he had spent a fair number of evenings listening to Arutha, Martin Longbow and Amos Trask talking about affairs of state. He found it fascinating, and from time to time wondered if he could make the sorts of judgments they were forced to consider, decisions that would change the future of nations.

No, he reconsidered, he wasn't bored with the question; he was frustrated that he had no information upon which to base a reasonable guess as to what was happening. And that surprised him, as well. Grinning at a silly notion, he thought: *maybe some day I'll get to meet Prince Arutha again.* That would be interesting. He'd know what Duke Guy was up to and Jimmy could ask him questions about such things. But until that time, it was no business of Jimmy's what the Duke was plotting.

Meddling in the affairs of the mighty had only brought trouble on him and his kind. True, he was pleased to think of the Princess Anita as free and safe, but the cost to the Mockers had been high, perhaps too high. And while he was sorry for Prince Erland and his wife, saving them was well-nigh impossible, and even had that not been the case, to do so would very likely only have made things worse. For which the Upright Man would not have thanked him.

No, it was time to get back to looking after Jimmy the Hand, which was something he did very well. Let them plot and scheme among themselves; it had nothing to do with him.

Jimmy stopped to look around, as he and Flora stood on the dockside at Land's End, their scant baggage at their feet. The first street facing the harbour was broad and cobbled, but the cobbles were worn nearly flat by hooves and iron-rimmed wheels and sledges; the bowsprits of a row of ships ran over it, above the heads of stevedores, sailors and passengers. Teamsters moved wagons close to receive offloaded cargo and quickly transport it to shops or warehouses nearby, and the usual assortment of riff-raff lingered at the fringes. Jimmy instantly spotted two lads who were probably pickpockets and one who was the most obvious lookout Jimmy had ever seen – maybe looking to see if someone special came off the ship, or if a particular cargo was unloaded, ready to signal someone probably lingering half a block up the street or watching from an adjacent window. Jimmy kept his smile to himself; if this was the best Land's End had to offer, he might not return to Krondor, but rather stick around and take over.

Gulls made a storm overhead – always a sign of a thriving port, with plenty of offal. Green-blue water lapped at the sides of ships, at the black weed-and-barnacle-covered timbers and pilings of dock and seawall, a chuckling undertone to the clamour of voices and feet and iron on stone.

'Not nearly as big as Krondor,' Jimmy said stoutly. *I'm from the big city*, he thought. *This is the sticks.* 'Or as well-sheltered a harbour.'

The largest ships here weren't as big as those you saw in Krondor's harbour, either – the tubby *Krondor's Lady* was about as large as they came; more of them were Keshian, too. The dockside street was hedged on its landward side by warehouses, two or three storeys high, with A-frame timbers jutting out from their gables to help hoist freight. Some came down via block and tackle as he watched, a load of pungent raw hides. Streams of dockwallopers were trotting up and down gangplanks, with sacks and bales and boxes bending them double; cloth, thread, bundled raw flax, dried fruit, cheeses, blacksmith's iron, copper pots . . . Heavier cargo swung up on nets slung from the end of the yards that usually bore sails.

Beyond the warehouses, buildings rose up steep streets on the hills surrounding the harbour; they could get a few glimpses of the city walls, gates, and the pasture and forest beyond. Jimmy stared for a moment, realizing he could see farms up on the highest hillsides, tiny thatched houses with meadows and fields around them. He had never seen a farm before.

'It's bigger than I'd thought it would be,' Flora said, her voice sounding small.

Jimmy was glad she'd said it because it was exactly what he'd been thinking. He snorted. 'It's not a patch on Krondor,' he said. He straightened and threw back his shoulders. 'And we did just fine there.'

Flora touched his arm with a grateful smile. Then she looked out at the town, uncertain once more. She sighed. 'I have no idea where to begin.'

'Well, you know his name and what he does, or,' he shrugged, '*did* for a living, right?' He'd intended to talk with her about this on board, but he'd been too sick most of the way and too hungry for the rest of it.

'Yes,' Flora said. 'He was a solicitor and his name was Yardley Heywood.'

Oh, that's not good, Jimmy thought. If her grandfather was a court solicitor he had represented his fair share of criminals. Which meant he was all too likely to guess what his long-lost granddaughter had been doing to survive these last few years, no matter what she said. Worse, he'd be able to guess what Jimmy did.

'Yardley Heywood,' he said aloud. 'That sounds like a rich man's name.'

Flora laughed. 'It does, doesn't it?'

Picking up his bag decisively, and one of hers to maintain the illusion of his being well brought up, Jimmy gestured toward the town. 'First thing we should do is head for solid ground. I can feel this dock moving up and down and it's making me nervous.'

'It's not the dock, lad,' Jarvis Coe said with a smile.

Jimmy blinked in surprise. Twice: because he couldn't imagine how the man had managed to get that close without him noticing; and because of a subtle change. Coe's clothes were just a bit more prosperous than they'd seemed aboard ship, perhaps because he'd added a horseman's high boots and a long dark cloak with a hood, plus a flat cloth cap that sported a peacock feather. More probably because he wore the sword that Jimmy had suspected would be his to wear: a plain, narrow blade with a curled guard in a workmanlike leather sheath, matched with a dagger on the other side – a fighting dirk nine inches long, not the ordinary belt-knife people carried for everyday tasks like cutting bread or getting a stone out of a horse's shoe.

Coe still didn't look rich, or conspicuous; but he did look like a gentleman of sorts. He pulled off the cap and bowed slightly to Flora, who bobbed him a curtsey in reflex.

'It's the way everyone feels coming off a ship. In a day or so you'll get your land-legs back, as the sailors say. Where are you headed?'

Both the young Mockers frowned at him. *I don't like this,* Jimmy thought. *This man alters his appearance too easily, just by donning a new cloak and by changing the way he holds his head.*

Coe chuckled: 'I suppose it's none of my business,' he said. 'But if you're looking for a clean, cheap place to stay I can recommend a few.'

Jimmy and Flora looked at one another. Generosity from strangers, especially this close to Great Kesh and its slavers, was somewhat suspicious.

Coe looked at them and nodded thoughtfully. 'All right, then. I can see you'll be all right on your own. Just, if I may,' he nodded at a dockside inn, 'avoid The Cockerel.' He put a finger beside his nose and winked. 'Just a word to the wise.' Then he was gone with a swirl of his dark cape.

'Who's he?' Flora whispered. 'I never talked to him on board.'

'His name's Jarvis Coe,' Jimmy said. 'But who he is I don't know.'

He pulled at the bracelet on his wrist until the leather strap came undone. Then he studied it carefully. The slight pressure he'd felt against his wrist had been provided by a small pebble glued to the leather. The pebble looked ordinary enough, still . . . He tossed it into the water. Who could tell what might or might not be magic, or what that magic might do?

'What was that?' Flora asked.

'Something he gave me for the seasickness. It worked. It might be magic.'

'Well that was nice,' she said dubiously.

Jimmy glanced at her. Flora was looking into the water and frowning, then she stared down the dock. Following her example, Jimmy saw that Coe had vanished; not hurrying, just walking away and blending in like a wisp of mist. Something a Mocker knew the way of.

'Well,' he said, 'let's find a place to stay and stow our gear. Then we can start looking for your family.' He jerked a thumb over his shoulder with a grin. 'But what do we do about The Cockerel? It might turn out to be the safest place in town.'

Flora picked up her bag and started walking. 'That'd be a first for a dockside tavern,' she said.

Jimmy nodded, then stopped. 'Wait!' he said.

Flora looked at him enquiringly; he said nothing as he squatted beside their baggage, untying the cloth wrapped around a long narrow bundle.

The rapier came free, and Jimmy unwrapped the belt from the sheath and swung it around his hips. The tassets that the scabbard went through – a slanted row of loops on a triangular patch of leather sewn to the belt – kept the chafe – the metal reinforcement at the bottom of the scabbard – from tapping on the ground, if he walked with his left hand on the hilt. He wouldn't have to worry about that in a few years when he reached his adult growth, but right now he was a bit shorter than most swordsmen.

'Is that wise?' Flora said.

'It's a mark of respectability,' Jimmy said. 'Or at least that you're nobody to be trifled with!'

And there's no Upright Man in Land's End, the young thief thought. *Demons and gods, but I'm sick of being pushed around!*

They set out, walking slightly uphill along what Jimmy suspected would turn out to be the town's main thoroughfare to the docks. He assumed there would be a large town square somewhere up ahead, and near there a reputable inn. His eyes wandered and again he studied the distant farms and wondered what it must be like up there. From what townsfolk said about farmers, their lives were pretty boring.

SEVEN

Tragedy

The girl looked up as her mother spoke.

'When you've finished with that,' Melda Merford said to her daughter Lorrie, 'I want you to get the flax out of the pond.'

'Mother, please!' Lorrie protested.

She turned from where she'd been sweeping out the farmstead's kitchen-hearth, wiping at her eye where a drop of sweat stung. She used the back of her wrist because her hands were black, but still she got a smudge on her cheek. The fine flying ash drifted up her nose, smelling dusty, like old wood smoke, and she sneezed: cleaning the hearth wasn't a heavy chore, but it was disagreeable.

'I was going to hunt today.'

She certainly hadn't planned on pulling slimy bundles of flax out of the stagnant pond where it lay retting. Never a pleasant job, it would be more irksome still when her mind was fixed on a pleasant jaunt in the cool of the forest.

'No,' Melda said, not looking at her. She measured coarse flour out of a box into a wooden mixing bowl. 'I don't want you traipsing around those woods by yourself any more.'

Lorrie sat on her heels in astonishment. 'Why not?'

'You're getting too old to be running around like a hoyden,' her mother said calmly. 'Besides, we need to get that flax ready. If we can make enough linen and thread to take to the market fair we'll be able to pay our taxes.' She looked at Lorrie with a frown. 'We don't want to lose the farm like the Morrisons did.'

Lorrie looked away, her frown matching her mother's. The Morrisons losing their farm because they couldn't pay the taxes had sent a shock through the whole community. There had been a lot of people losing their farms lately, but none here until the Morrisons. Everyone had assumed it was because of all the sons going to the war, or perhaps those farmers were lazy, but you couldn't say that of the Morrisons; why, even the baby had chores. Taxes had gone up and up over the last few years, even before the war, and the smaller one's farm was the harder it had become to pay them. Now even a medium-sized holding like their own had to struggle to pay the debt.

Still, it wasn't exactly an emergency.

'But we have hardly any fresh meat in the larder,' Lorrie objected.

That wasn't an emergency either – they weren't nobles, or rich merchants, to eat fresh meat every day – but game helped stretch what they got out of the fields. The more they could sell rather than eat themselves, the better off they would be. The extra few coppers from grain sold rather than turned to bread could mean the difference between paying taxes and starving through the winter, or paying taxes and having enough put by to pay for fish from the town, and cheese from the dairy farmers.

Her mother bit her lip and raised her eyes to heaven. 'It's dangerous for a girl your age to go running around alone in the woods. Who knows who you might meet there with no one to help you.'

'So when Bram comes back from Land's End I can go with him?'

'No! Absolutely not!' Melda said firmly. 'If anything, that would be worse.'

Lorrie stood to confront her mother, hands on her hips. 'So I can't go alone because it's dangerous and I can't go with a friend I've known my whole life because that would be worse than dangerous?' she said, her voice ripe with sarcasm. 'This makes no sense at all, Mother.'

'Lorrie,' her mother said wearily, 'you're growing up. And there are certain things, unfortunately, a girl can do that a woman can't. One of which is keeping up with the boys she grew up with. You can do that as a child. But when you get older, some-times . . . those same boys, when *they* get older –' Melda sighed and looked her daughter in the eye, '– want things.'

Lorrie rolled her eyes. She was a farm girl and had seen animals mating since she could crawl. 'Mother, I know about those . . . things.'

'That's why it's dangerous! You think you know about the ways of men and women, but you don't, and it's not about watching a bull and cow or a cock and hen. It's about going all crazy inside when a lad smiles at you and forgetting what you think you know. You're a good girl from a good home, and some day when the right lad asks for your hand, you'll be glad for this. I'm your mother, and it's my duty and your father's duty to tell you what's right and what isn't. And until you're married and moved out, we'll keep that duty.' She took a deep breath, anticipating an explosion.

But Lorrie was icy in her response. 'So what you're saying is that from now on I can't go hunting, which I'm very good at and which I love, and which I've been doing since I was younger than Rip; but I can stay at home and do all the messy, smelly, dreary chores you can think of just because I'm a woman? Is that right?'

'You'll do the chores I tell you to do because you're my daughter and that's your place in this house. Your hands are needed here today and I don't want to hear another word about it. So finish that up and get going down to the pond.' Melda glared at Lorrie with her arms folded across her ample chest and hoped that she wouldn't hear any more argument. She probably should have dealt with this before; but Lorrie loved the woods so. As she had herself when she was a girl. Melda had never forgotten what a wrench it was to give that up. *All that freedom,* she thought wistfully. With an effort she suppressed a sigh. Well, she was dealing with it now.

With a long last glare and a pout Lorrie knelt down and went back to work, but with her stiff back, brusque movements and unnecessary clatter she let her mother know exactly how she felt. At last, with a last clunk of the wooden shovel, she stood up and silently bore the ash bucket from the kitchen.

No more hunting, hmm? she fumed to herself. *We'll see about that.*

The flax would be safe in the pond until tomorrow. Her mother would be angry with her she knew; very, very angry. But fresh meat, especially if she brought home some pheasant, would go a long way toward soothing her.

Lorrie dumped the ashes in the barrel where they waited to be leached and the potash used for soap, and brought the bucket back to the house. Then she marched to the barn and gathered the peg-toothed rake for mucking out the bundles of flax and the tarp for carrying them to the drying field. She also tucked her sling and bag of stones into her waistband under her apron, then headed for the retting pond.

The packed earth of the farmyard was littered with things – a broken plough-handle, an old wheel, foraging chickens that scattered clucking from around her feet, bundles of kindling – but she walked among them without needing to consciously use her eyes. They were as familiar to her as all the smells – smokehouse, the outhouse, the manure-heap. Too familiar; right now it all seemed like a prison.

Lorrie could sense her mother watching from the house through the warped boards of the closed shutter and knew her mood. Annoyed; that was how Mother felt. These days she and her mother struck sparks as often as not.

But how can I help it? Lorrie asked herself. *It's always, 'you're almost a woman' or, 'you're almost grown up'. Then they treat me more like a child than ever! Who wouldn't lose their temper? And now, suddenly, no more hunting! Not even, no, especially not with Bram! That just isn't right.*

As she walked along the hedge-bordered path, brooding, Lorrie slowly became aware of her younger brother's presence and sighed. This strong awareness of family was a gift inherited from her great-grandmother, who was secretly a witch, or so her mother said. She could always tell when her mother was thinking about her, or was nearby. But she was especially aware of her little brother, Rip. Right now Lorrie sensed he was as focused on her as an arrow speeding toward its target.

Wonderful, she thought, a wry twist to her mouth.

Her brother would be seven on the next Midsummer's Day but he'd already discovered the benefits of blackmail and he was disturbingly adept at it. She supposed she could work on the flax until he got bored or disgusted by the smell and went away.

But if I start then I might as well finish, she thought. Once you got that smell on you only soap would take it off. And the stink could drive off rougher creatures than the birds and hares she was after.

Maybe even the robbers and murderers her mother was so frightened of. So it wouldn't be worthwhile to go into the woods.

Rip was off to the right and a little ahead of her, uselessly creeping from bush to bush in the bit of scrubby pasture-cum-orchard to the right of the path. He knew she was aware of him.

He could sense her just as clearly as she could sense him. Sometimes she thought he was better at it. Lorrie didn't call out to him because she needed time to think of some way of getting rid of him.

At last the stand of currant bushes ended and he leapt out with a cry of, 'HAH!' His hands raised over his head and curved into claws.

Lorrie raised an eyebrow in his direction and marched on without comment.

After a short pause he skipped up beside her.

'Can I come?' he asked, bouncing up and down in excitement.

'You want to help me clean flax?' she asked dubiously.

Rip laughed and Lorrie frowned. He knew, he always knew when she was up to something.

'It's messy and smelly,' she warned.

'You're going hunting!' he accused, then covered his mouth to hide his grin.

'What makes you think that?'

Rip rolled his eyes at her elaborately casual attitude, put his hands on his hips and gave her a look of such adult conde-scension that she had to smile. 'You promised you'd teach me to hunt and track,' he said. 'You said you would.'

She nodded, feeling rather sad. 'I know. And if I can talk Daddy around I still mean to.' She stopped walking and looked at him. 'I really do mean to, Rip. Honest.'

Looking down, he scuffed the earth with his bare foot. 'I know,' he muttered. 'But if this is the last time you can go . . .' He looked up at her from under his eyelashes. For an instant she realized what a beautiful boy he was, and he knew it. He had used those long lashes more than once to wheedle his way with his father and mother.

She gave him a small smile. 'It's up to Daddy.' She shrugged. 'If I took you today then we'd both get punished.'

He considered that, still scuffing his foot back and forth.

Lorrie watched him sympathetically. 'When Bram gets back from his uncle's in Land's End I'll ask him to take you. Hey,' she gently punched his shoulder, 'maybe that way I'll be able to go, too.'

He rubbed his shoulder and smiled ruefully. 'That's all right,' he said.

'Then that's what we'll try to do,' Lorrie said positively. 'But it would be a bad idea today.'

Rip nodded wisely. 'Yeah. You're gonna get it.' He thought about this, then added, 'You're *really* gonna get it.' He looked at her, his expression somewhere between awe and doubt.

Lorrie saw the moment his mind turned to making the situation work for him by the slight change in his expression and headed him off. 'If you tell on me I'll tell Bram not to take you, ever. And you know he'll listen to me.'

Rip's brow furrowed and he gave her a considering look. Lorrie folded her arms and looked back, one eyebrow raised. He tried, unsuccessfully, to imitate that and gave up after a moment with a frustrated hiss.

'All right,' he muttered resentfully. 'But if Mummy asks me where you are I won't lie.'

'Of course not,' Lorrie said, picking up the rake and the tarp. 'Tell her the truth, tell her that you don't know where I am. Which you won't.' She grinned and ruffled her brother's hair to his considerable annoyance. 'You won't be sorry, Rip. I promise.'

He snorted and after a moment turned and walked away. Lorrie smiled at his back and headed off toward the pond and, just coincidentally, the beckoning woods beyond, humming a dancing tune.

Rip was confused and a little angry. Why couldn't Lorrie go hunting any more? And if she really couldn't, then why couldn't she wait to stop hunting until after she'd taught him everything she knew? And what was it that boys would want and make Lorrie give them? Her hunting knife? Rip craved Lorrie's hunting knife. It had a deerhorn haft and a seven-inch steel blade that took an edge so sharp there was nothing in the world it couldn't cut.

Some day it would probably be his, but not yet. If Lorrie was too old to do certain things then he was still 'too young'. He glanced over his shoulder in the direction his sister had been walking. He hoped she'd be all right. Mummy had sounded like she really was worried about her. Even about Bram.

Why would she worry about Bram? Rip wondered. Bram was the best person ever. And he liked Lorrie, you could tell. Rip shook his head. Grown-ups worried about all manner of things that he didn't understand. And asking questions just made things worse mostly.

With a sigh, Rip looked around. He'd done his morning chores so he was free to play until lunch time. *I'm a warrior!* he decided and galloped off on an imaginary horse to slay the invaders from the other world. He swept up a likely stick and waved it with a flourish.

'Ah ha! Villains! Attack my castle will you?'

And the battle to save the Kingdom began.

Come to Lorrie, the girl thought.

The coney was young, plump, and even by rabbit standards not too bright. Right now it was hopping slowly through the undergrowth along the forest edge, which was emerald and colourful with the first spring growth, stopping to nibble at berries or shoots now and then. And it was about to find Rabbit Paradise – a stretch of wild blackberry canes.

Now!

The coney's head was down and its ears forward, its full attention on what it was eating. The next generation would be more alert.

Lorrie had the sling ready, a rounded pebble in the cup, the inner thong gripped securely between thumb and forefinger, the outer pinned against her palm by the middle fingers. She came out of her crouch with a smooth steady motion, the sling beginning to move as she came erect. Then it blurred as she whipped arms and shoulders and torso into the movement, one full circle around her head. The coney rose on its hind legs, eyes and ears swivelling to find the sound, herbs dropping from its still-working jaws.

Whupp!

The stone went out in a long sweet curve, travelling almost too fast to see as more than a grey streak. It caught the rabbit on the side of the head just as it began its leap, striking with a flat smack sound that always made her wince. Still, food was food, and the rabbit died before it had more than a moment of fear – she hated pig-slaughter time far more, because the pigs were smart enough to know what the preparations meant.

The long furred shape was kicking its last as she loped over.

'Two or three pounds at least,' she said happily, picking it up by its hind legs. Good eating. Rabbit stew with potatoes and herbs, grilled rabbit leg, minced meat pie with onions and carrots . . . The guts wouldn't go to waste either: the dogs and pigs loved them, and the bones would be broken and thrown onto the compost heap.

A good day, she thought happily. Four pheasants and four fat little coneys. And since they wouldn't keep, dinner would be like a harvest festival all week.

The sun was low on the horizon as she lay at her ease beneath a great oak, daydreaming. Bram would be home from Land's End soon and she was imagining what it would be like when he came to see her. He might bring her a small gift, a hairpin, or some fine cloth for a shawl to wear at a dance. If he lacked the means for those tokens, he'd almost certainly bring her meadow flowers. He'd hand them to her with that charming smile of his and perhaps he'd kiss her. She felt her cheeks grow warm at the thought.

At fifteen Lorrie was more than ready to start thinking about who her husband would be and Bram was the best candidate in the neighbourhood. Handsome, skilled at everything a country-man needed to know, and heir to a good farm. He was hard-working, honest and sincere, but not without intelligence and humour, qualities the hard life of a farmer often beat out of a man even as young as Bram's seventeen years. And she was sure he felt the same way about her. With a contented sigh, Lorrie remembered his handsome face, his golden hair and the special smile he'd given her when he'd come to say goodbye.

Bram's mother, Allet, wanted him to concentrate his attentions on plump, spoiled Merrybet Glidden, whose father owned the grandest farm in the area, and who put on airs that she never had to turn her hand to honest work, what with three maids and a dozen farmhands. Lorrie smiled grimly; no doubt that stuck-up Merrybet would prefer it that way, too. Then she wrinkled her nose, and grinned, settling her shoulders deeper into the soft grass beneath her. Both Bram's mother and Merrybet were going to be disappointed – Bram was going to be hers. She just knew it.

Lorrie sighed. It was time she headed back, even though it was earlier than she'd intended. The plan had been to stay out until just after dark. If this was to be her last time hunting alone, or ever, and she was going to catch some punishment anyway, Lorrie hadn't felt obliged to be considerate. Let them worry, she'd told herself. She'd wanted to have as much time as possible in the cool, green solitude of the forest amongst the musty autumnal smell of mushrooms and fallen leaves – she was going to miss it so.

But guilt was calling her home. Lorrie hated the thought of worrying her mother, and her father. Daddy would patiently take the brunt of her mother's worried temper until she turned up, listening to threats that became more dire with each passing minute. But then they'd argue about her punishment, each claiming the other was being too harsh, until they settled on something that was hardly a punishment at all. Lorrie smiled: they were so predictable.

As she stood up to go a strange feeling began to grow in her, flowing down her neck to curdle in her stomach. At first she thought it was her imagination, but then she felt a flash of something that shrilled like fear. Or even more than fear, but it was gone almost instantly. Lorrie was so far away from home that the feeling had to have come from Rip. It shook her so that she started back at a jog, trying to think of every possible thing that could cause such a spurt of terror in a six-year-old boy.

Now, as she grew closer to home, her worry increased, until she was running flat-out, her long slim legs flashing like a deer's as she hurdled bushes and ran right through a sounder of half-wild swine grubbing for acorns.

She could sense Rip, but it was as though he was asleep, and with a stab of fear she suddenly realized that she couldn't sense her mother at all. All her life there had been that contact, the warmth of her mother's presence somewhere in a corner of her mind. Never had she felt an absence there, like the aching void left by a pulled tooth. The bag holding the string of coneys and pheasants banged against her leg, and then her lungs began to burn and her heart to hammer. She ignored it all.

Gradually she became aware that she was smelling smoke. *What's burning?* she wondered. Lorrie stopped and tried to tell where the smoke was coming from. If this had been midwinter she'd have thought her father was burning off a field. But it was far too late in the year for that: the new seed was already in and any pile of weeds being burned wouldn't put this much smoke in the air. Besides, it was too late in the day. Her mind jumped to the ashes she'd thrown out this morning. No, she thought. The barrel wasn't big enough to throw up this much smoke and it was right next to the watertub by the eaves which captured soft rainwater from the roof for the leaching process, and you could dump it right in with the pull of a rope.

A new thrill of horror ran through her stomach as she thought: *The house is on fire!*

People died in fires – there was a bad one in the district every couple of years . . . 'Mother! Father! Rip!'

Panic left her gasping. She threw down the game-bag and left the trail, vaulting over the snake-rail fence that separated the seven-acre field from the woods. The hay had been cut, stubble only calf-high, and she raced across it like the wind.

As she dodged around a huge and ancient oak, that her father had judged too much trouble to uproot – leaving it as a marker between fields, her foot caught on a gnarled root. Her arms windmilled for balance, but it was too late. The ground rose up and struck her as she landed full length with enough force to stun; she could taste blood in her mouth – iron and salt – where her teeth had grazed the inside of a cheek.

She lay panting for a moment and was about to rise and run again when she saw two strangers. Both male; they were a rough-looking pair and Lorrie dropped down again, frightened. The brown homespun and leather of her clothing would be hard to see against the earth and faded straw, and her hair was much the same colour. The late afternoon sun was throwing long shadows, and the landscape was now painted in bright edges around opaque darkness. In the shadow of the ancient oak she was invisible to the men. They would have had to have been looking straight at her as she ran down the hill to have seen her before the fall.

The men looked exactly like the kind of men who seemed to haunt her mother's nightmares, with their greasy hair and filthy clothes and faces that bore witness to a life lived hard. They were young and strong, though; she could see the corded muscle in their necks and forearms.

They were standing over something on the ground that she couldn't see from where she lay, and one drew a tool out of a stained burlap bag. It looked like the sort of long-handled pliers the blacksmith used, but with a broad front end.

One of the men worked the handles of the tool while the other bent over something on the ground. With a cry of disgust the man with the tool yanked and stepped back, something wet and floppy held in the grip of what looked like teeth.

Lorrie realized that it was blood and meat and her breath froze in horror. If they'd butchered a sheep, why tear it apart like this? Why not cut it up with the perfectly serviceable-looking knives they wore at their waists?

'Makes me want to puke!' the man with the pliers said. He dropped the torn meat into a sack and reached forward with the tool again. 'Why do we have to do it this way?' He dropped another strip of meat into the sack.

'We have to do it this way,' the other said, rising, 'because this is the way we're being paid to do it.' He gave a snaggle-toothed grin. 'And if I'd known you was a girl, I could have got more use out of you.'

The other man spat close by his companion's feet by way of comment, but not quite on them.

The second man studied what they'd been tearing at. 'Do you think that's enough?' he asked.

'It is for me,' the one with the pliers answered, dropping the tool into the sack. 'Let's get out of here.'

They moved away as Lorrie watched. She waited until they'd vanished behind a hedge and she scuttled over to see what they'd been doing, staying low. Glancing nervously in all directions Lorrie caught sight of one of the strangers disappearing over the hill toward her home and froze. She held her breath until she was sure they were gone, then cautiously moved forward again until she stood over what they'd been tearing apart.

For a moment Lorrie couldn't even breathe; was so shocked that all she knew was that this used to be a man. Suddenly something went snap behind her eyes, and she realized she knew him.

It was Emmet Congrove, the man of all work; she could tell by his clothes, and the thinning grey hair, and the wart on the back of his right hand, always inflamed where he picked at it.

He'd been with the family since just before Rip was born. How could they do that to him? How could anyone do such a thing?

Tearing her fascinated gaze from the terrible wounds on the body Lorrie turned aside, her hands covering her mouth. Falling to her knees she was instantly, helplessly sick; heaving and sobbing uncontrollably. Finally the nausea passed and Lorrie hugged her middle to ease the ache, spitting to clear her mouth.

A sudden stab of fear that was not her own sobered her. *Rip!* Lorrie leapt to her feet and ran toward home. Rip was in danger. *But where is Mother? Why can't I feel her?* In her heart Lorrie feared the answer, and she refused to believe it.

The smoke was growing thicker.

Coming over the hill that hid the house and barn from view she ran into a pall of black smoke so thick that she could see nothing. Lorrie stopped, choking. She heard hoofbeats and the neigh of a horse, but no longer felt the panicked fear that Rip had projected just moments before. A puff of wind parted the smoke and she could see that the barn was wreathed in orange-red flame, thundering where it had got to the packed hay in the loft and turning almost white along the rooftree. Beyond she thought she saw two figures on horseback riding fast down the road.

Thick sooty-black smoke poured out of every window of their house; wisps of it were coming out of the thatch too, and as she watched a few tentative tongues of flame. Lorrie let out a cry like the wordless shriek of a hawk and ran down the hill, careless of where her feet went, not minding the pounding shock as they hit the ridged furrows.

The wind shifted again, sending billows of smoke toward her, blinding her, blurring her eyes with tears. She coughed with a racking intensity, her lungs dry and burning with her effort and the harsh smoke. Then she tripped over something and fell forward with a thud. What had she tripped over? Slowly she turned, her heart hammering with dread, and looked behind her. It was her father, his throat torn out, his eyes staring sightlessly upward, his beard moving slightly in the wind that bore the smoke. His blood pooled out around him, so much blood that the ground was turning to mud beneath it. His wood-chopping axe lay not far from his outstretched hand, the edge still shiny.

She tried to scream, but her throat closed and all that came out was a pathetic squeak as she scuttled backwards across the dirt. Then with a choked sob, she forced herself to stand. For a long moment she looked down upon the grisly sight. Lorrie reached toward him, halted and drew her hand back, holding it against her chest, shaking her head in disbelief. Then she looked toward the house – her head moving in little jerks – and saw her mother, mercifully lying face down. There was blood pooled beneath her too, so much blood that Lorrie knew her mother could not possibly be alive.

Lorrie gave one sob and stopped herself. Rip was still alive! Rip had only her now, and only she could save him. Forcing herself to turn away from the horror, she wrenched her gaze away from her mother's body, turned and ran around the house, and down the road after the vanishing riders.

She ran until her lungs ached and she could taste blood in

the back of her throat. She raced up one hill and down another until she came to the top of a rise and saw them; two men, one of them struggling with a small boy.

Rip, she thought. One of the boy's shoes fell off, and the man holding him clouted him across the side of the head. In what seemed like a moment they were out of sight around a curve in the road and soon she couldn't even hear the hollow sound of the hooves on packed dirt.

Running full out Lorrie came to the place where her brother's shoe had fallen. She reached for it and fell to her knees, gasping as she was overcome with sobs and desperation. Finally, still weeping, she forced herself up and staggered down the road in the direction the kidnappers had gone. After a few steps she stopped.

I need a horse, she thought. The only one they had was Horace, their old plough horse. He was no champing stallion, but he was better than shanks's pony. The kidnappers couldn't keep galloping, they'd have to slow down sometime.

'Slow and steady gets the job done,' her father always said. 'And a man can walk further than he can run.'

Her breath caught in her throat as sharp as a fish bone when she remembered that she'd never hear him say such a thing again; the pain was physical, like needles stabbing into eyes and heart.

Turning toward home she saw flames flash through the smoke churning over the hilltop. Everything was burning. Lorrie thought of her mother and father lying in their blood . . .

They're dead, she forced her mind to say. Blackness threatened to rise up and overwhelm her. She wanted nothing so much as to awake from a horrible dream, or to discover this but a mad illusion from a fever. She kept looking around, expecting things to change. She knew that if she turned quickly, her father would be walking toward the house, or if she ran home fast, her mother would be standing in the kitchen doorway.

A great primal sob shook her, followed by a scream – more than a scream: a deep roar of rage, pain and defiance that caused her to clench fists and throw back her head and shriek until her throat was raw and there was no air left in her lungs.

Gasping for air, she forced herself to look clearly ahead. She had to put pain aside. Mourning would come later. *Rip's alive!* she thought again, and everything in her turned cold, her outrage and pain turning from fire to ice. *Rip must be saved!* Hysteria and confusion would serve only to put him at more risk. Obviously those who took him wanted him alive for a reason, otherwise he would be dead with his parents.

Rip might be facing slavery or worse. And there was nothing she could do for her parents. At least not now. She looked around once more, burning the images of this moment into her young memory. She would never forget.

With silent resolve, she set off toward her home.

EIGHT

Family

Lorrie ran.

She wasn't quite home yet when she saw Bram's father, Ossrey, coming across the fields. His wife, Allet, was with him, and a field hand; behind them more neighbours were coming, the whole valley turning out. The men carried shovels and axes and the women carried buckets. Lorrie ran to them, throwing herself into Ossrey's arms, weeping so hard she couldn't speak.

Ossrey held her for a moment, stroking her hair then, keeping one arm around her shoulders, he guided her toward the house and barn.

'Where are your ma and pa?' he asked gently. 'Did they send you for help?'

Shaking her head, utterly breathless from weeping, Lorrie couldn't answer him. Just then they came in sight of the house and barn and the bodies of her mother and father.

'Sung protect us,' Allet whispered in horror.

'Stay here, Lorrie,' Ossrey said, putting her gently aside.

But Lorrie grabbed hold of his sleeve and wouldn't let go as she struggled to get herself under control. Finally she was able to speak.

'Men who did this . . . took my brother,' she managed to gasp out. Pointing down the road, she said, 'Help me get him back.'

'First we must see if we can help your parents,' Ossrey said calmly.

Lorrie shook her head, tears flowing down her face. 'You can't, you can't,' she said plaintively. Then once more, 'You can't.'

'Oh, Lorrie,' Ossrey said, gathering her into his arms. Over her head he and Allet exchanged glances.

'Please,' Lorrie said, pushing herself away from his chest, 'help me find Rip.'

Just then a piece of the barn roof collapsed, sending up a storm of sparks, and Ossrey's head whipped round at the roar of the fire.

'We must take care of the fire, girl,' he told her. 'If it spreads to the crops, you'll not be the only one around here to lose your fields.'

By now other neighbours had come up and were staring in horror at the scene before them.

'What's happened?' someone asked in a dazed voice.

Lorrie looked from face to face and could see that they'd all be occupied with the fire in a moment and deaf to anything she said.

'Murderers have kidnapped my baby brother,' she said. 'Help me get him back!'

'Are you sure the boy is . . . wasn't in the house, girl?'

'No, men took him!' Lorrie said, her voice verging on the hysterical. Exhaustion and fear were driving her to the brink of collapse.

Ossrey asked, 'Any of you see any men riding along the road today?'

A murmur of voices answered in the negative. 'I saw them!' shouted Lorrie.

'Lorrie, girl, someone will go for the constable, he'll be the one to hunt these men down.' Ossrey nodded to several of the men who started to hurry to the other side of the barn, while others ran to the well to get water. They would see that any fire in the fields started by blowing embers was quickly quenched.

She looked up into Ossrey's kind face and knew that no one would follow the killers, at least not today. 'I'll go,' she said impulsively. 'I'll take Horace and ride to the constable. That will leave more men to fight the fire.'

But Ossrey was shaking his head. 'You go with my Allet,' he said. 'You've had a bad, bad shock, girl. Someone else will go for the constable. Try to rest,' he advised. 'We'll take care of everything.'

'These are teeth marks,' Farmer Roben said, looking down at her father's body. 'An animal did this.'

Lorrie looked at them in wonder, more and more of them were starting to fight the blaze. It was as though they hadn't heard her, or understood what she'd said.

'It wasn't,' she started to say.

Allet put her arm around Lorrie's shoulders. 'We'll leave it to the men, shall we?' She turned the girl toward her own farm and patted her. 'You could use a nice rest.'

Lorrie pulled away, or tried to. Allet took her arm in a strong grip.

'I need to find my brother!' Lorrie shouted. She waved her free arm frantically. 'Does anybody see him here? He's been carried off by murderers, not animals, and he needs our help! We have to follow them now or we'll lose them forever!'

'That's enough!' Allet snapped, shaking her arm. 'You leave it to the men and come with me right now! Don't you get hysterical on me, girl,' she warned.

Lorrie stared at her, open-mouthed. Then she looked around at the circle of her neighbours, those who weren't already fighting the fire. 'You don't believe me,' she said at last, her voice full of wonder.

One of the women stepped forward and put her hand to Lorrie's cheek. 'It's not about believing you, child. It's about doing what we can. You wouldn't catch anyone on your old Horace, and any of us would have to run all the way back to our farms to get horses not much better.' She sighed. 'Meanwhile that fire might get out of control – you've lost the house and barn, but there's still the crops, and if they go, the fire could spread to other farms. Besides, if we left now we'd be no closer to your brother. We'll send word to the constable; he'll know what to do about this. Try to have faith, dear.'

Lorrie started to weep again from sheer frustration, then began a keening that she was horrified to discover was beyond her control. Allet gave her arm another shake and a hard look. The other woman moved in to hold her gently but firmly. 'What can one girl do against grown men except get herself into trouble?' she asked quietly.

'You leave it to the men now,' Allet said, 'and trust them to do their best.'

Lorrie let them take her to Ossrey and Allet's farm knowing that wouldn't be enough.

How can I trust them to do their best for Rip when they've already given up?

Her mind stopped whirling, and a coldness came over her, like a wind cutting through smoke or fog. *If I make a fuss, they'll watch me close. Go along with it, and I can slip away,* she thought.

Allet put her to bed in Bram's room – it was a mark of a good farm and a small family that even the eldest son had a room to himself – and Lorrie felt a pang at being surrounded by his familiar, dearly-missed scent.

'Here's a posset for you,' Allet said: she was a notable herb-wife. 'Drink it right down, dear.'

Lorrie gagged a bit at the taste – sharp, musky, and too sweet at the same time. Then the world spun as she set her head back on the feather-filled pillows.

Waking was slow; her head was splitting with pain, and her chest burned, and she had aches and bruises all over.

Gods! Lorrie thought, as memory came back with a rush. *What's the hour?*

She started to cry and buried her head in Bram's pillow, forcing back her sobs by sheer will. There was no time for that now.

Rising quietly, she went to the door and found it barred – barred on the outside.

Stifling a hiss of anger, she moved to try the shutters. Mercifully they opened, letting in a flood of bright moonlight that revealed that her clothes were missing. Shaking her head and mentally cursing Allet's thoroughness Lorrie went to the chest at the foot of the bed. After a bit of rummaging she found some of Bram's outgrown clothes and shoes. They felt strange when she put them on, but she reckoned she'd get used to them quickly enough. She swung an old cloak over her shoulders and started out the window. Then stopped. Moving on instinct, Lorrie felt beneath the straw-stuffed mattress on Bram's bed. Her fingers touched soft leather: a purse, half the size of her fist, half-filled. The small, edged metal shapes of the coins inside were unmistakable under her fingertips.

She hesitated for an instant – it was probably the savings of years, from odd jobs he'd done off the farm – and then took it. Like any farm-child in the district she'd been raised to despise a thief even worse than a sluggard, and nearly as much as a coward, but her need was great.

It's like borrowing an axe or a bucket when there's no time to ask, she told herself; people did that as a matter of course.

Lorrie looked out both ways; Bram's family had the rarity of a second storey to their home, added in a prosperous year by his grandfather, and it was ten feet to the ground below. A quick look at moon and stars told her it was halfway between midnight and dawn; not a time anyone was likely to be stirring. There was a narrow strip of sheep-cropped grass beneath the window; she let herself out, hung by her fingertips and then let herself drop.

Thud.

Something stirred. She waited, then let out a gasp of relief when she saw it was only the family dogs, Grip and Holdfast, big mongrels who'd known her since they were pups. They were out at work, making sure no fox tried for the poultry or a lamb.

'Quiet,' she said, letting them sniff her hands – they were conscientious dogs, and wanted to be sure she wasn't a stranger violating their territory. 'Quiet!'

A glimpse around the rear corner of the farmhouse, her face pressed to the gritty, splintery logs. No lights, only silver moon-light across the yard, and the two barns, a shed, and a rail-fenced paddock where the working stock and the family's milch-cow were kept.

As she'd thought, they'd brought her family's stock home with them and she found Horace easily; he wouldn't be fast, but she'd ridden him now and then all of his life, taking him to be watered in ploughing season, or shod, or sometimes just for fun. He nuzzled and sniffed at her as though happy to see someone familiar and she rubbed his velvety nose. Lorrie bit her lip and thought about what she had to do. She needed a saddle and tack and some grain for the horse. It was stealing, plain and simple, and she knew that her mother and father would be disappointed in her.

Maybe not, she thought fiercely, *maybe they'd be more disappointed in their do-nothing neighbours.*

There was an old saddle just inside the smaller barn's door – a simple pad affair, for farmers didn't ride often.

If I don't do it, nobody will. Rip will die, or worse.

And that, she knew, would disappoint her parents even more.

She led Horace from the barn, slid the bridle over his head, arranged the blanket carefully, then slid the saddle on his back with a grunt of effort, for it weighed about a quarter of what she did, and tightened the girth. The horse gave a resigned sigh, knowing that meant work.

Back into the barn. She looked through a gap between the boards back toward the farmhouse, but there was no sign of life, only a drift of smoke from the banked fire through the chimney. That made her hands start to shake for a moment, but she forced herself to be calm, taking deep breaths.

Oats, she thought firmly. The sweetish smell led her to the bin, and there were always a few sackcloth bags near it. She filled two, then added a few horse-blankets to her loot for nights spent on the road.

Horace gave a whicker of interest as she threw the sacks over his withers; he knew what that smell was. 'Later,' she whispered to him, taking a moment to soothe him quiet before scrambling up on his back, for he was a tall mount for a fifteen-year-old girl, and tightened her thighs around his broad barrel of a body.

Obediently, the horse set out down the road which wound like a ribbon of moonlight to the south.

I'm coming, Rip! she thought.

Finding Flora's grandfather had been easy; there weren't more than a couple of law-speakers in a town this size. Getting up the nerve to see him had been harder.

'What if he hates me for my father's sake?' Flora asked anxiously and for the hundredth time, looking at the tall house of pale mortared stone, not far from the town's main square – it oozed respectability, right down to the costly diamond-pane glass windows.

'Then he's not much of a grandfather,' Jimmy said stoutly. 'And in that case, who needs him?'

His answer was the same one he'd given her almost as many times as she'd asked the question; by now it was automatic right down to the tone of his voice. Jimmy had pretty much stopped listening to her and was pretty sure she wasn't listening to him at all.

They were at the entrance to Legacy Lane, a prosperous-looking street. They were beautiful buildings, with large glass windows curtained in embroidered cloth, the red tile roofs making a pleasing contrast with the honey colour of the stone and each window bearing a flower box overflowing with brilliant blooms. There was even a sweeper, a ragged youth with broom and pan and box, to keep the cobbles free of horse-dung.

It was clean, it was neat.

It makes Jimmy the Hand's mouth water, Jimmy thought. *Oh, the silver services and candlesticks they'll have here, all put out for the guests to admire! The glassware, the little strongbox 'hidden' somewhere that a merchant thinks is safe, then . . . Stop that, man! You're the foster-brother of a respectable woman come to see her safe with her kin!*

Then a thought made him smile. *And if Flora's grandfather turns us off at the door, why, then I'm not a respectable woman's foster-brother any more; I'm Jimmy the Hand, and in need of funds!*

One way or another the old man would contribute to his grand-daughter's welfare. And Jimmy's as well if the haul was big enough.

At last a man came up to them and said, 'What is your business here?' He spoke with authority, but mildly, and he wore the badge of Land's End's Watch.

'We were looking for this young lady's grandfather, sir,' Jimmy said. He had put on his favourite lost waif expression, hoping he wasn't too old to use it effectively.

'And who might that be?' the man asked.

He didn't seem to be affected one way or the other by the lost waif expression, from which Jimmy concluded that it was no longer effective, but not completely ridiculous.

'Mr Yardley Heywood, sir,' Flora said softly.

'Ahhh, Mr Heywood, is it?' He turned and pointed with his club. 'Third house down, with the green door and pansies in the flower boxes.'

'Thank you, sir,' Flora said and bobbed a curtsey.

The watchman nodded affably and smiled.

Well, her waif-look still seems to be working, Jimmy thought. Guess it lasts longer for girls. Tucking one of the bundles under his arm he took Flora's hand and began walking toward the house the watchman had indicated. After a few steps she began to hang back, until she stopped completely and their arms were stretched out as if they were partners in a dance.

He turned impatiently. 'Flora, you've taken far greater risks for much less reward.'

She came up to him slowly, hardly taking her eyes from the fine house before them.

'It doesn't feel that way,' she said in a small voice.

'Then it's up to me.' Jimmy turned on his heel, marched up the steps and seized the brass door knocker. Before he could drop it a woman opened the door and started to step down.

'Oh, hello,' she said in cheerful surprise and stepped back. 'I didn't see you there.' She was dressed to go out, wearing a shawl and a hat with an empty market basket on her arm. 'May I help you?' she asked.

Then she glanced down at Flora and her face froze. 'Orletta?' she said in astonishment. Then immediately shook her head. 'But no, that's not possible, you're so young.' She swept by Jimmy as though he wasn't there and descended the steps to the street, walking right up to Flora. 'Who are you, my dear?'

Flora bobbed a curtsey, looking awkward for the first time since she'd begun dropping them. 'My name is Flora, ma'am, my father was Aymer the baker and my mother was Orletta Heywood.'

The woman cried, 'Oh!' and swept Flora into a warm embrace.

Jimmy grinned to see Flora's startled eyes over the woman's plump shoulder. Was this her grandmother? If so there wasn't going to be a problem.

'I'm your Aunt Cleora,' the woman said, holding Flora at arm's length. 'Oh, I thought I would never, ever see you, child.'

She swept Flora back into her arms and Jimmy had all he could do not to laugh at the expression on his friend's face; half thrilled, half horrified.

'Where have you come from?' Cleora cried.

'K-Krondor,' her niece stuttered, completely overwhelmed.

'Oh, you poor child! You must be exhausted! Come with me and we'll get you settled. Oh!' she said and turned with a smile to Jimmy. 'And who is this?'

'Jimmy is a friend,' Flora said nervously. 'Practically a brother, he's escorted me.'

'Then you must come, too! I'll find you something good to eat. Boys always like a little something to eat,' Cleora confided to her niece. She started off down the lane, her arm around Flora's thin shoulders. 'I think you might require some feeding up as well, my dear,' she said and laughed.

Jimmy blinked, startled, then picked up the bags at his feet and ran after then.

'Excuse me, ma'am,' he said. 'But isn't that where you live?' He pointed back at the house behind them.

'No, no, that's my dear papa's house. He's napping now, my dear. You'll meet him later. In any case, dear Flora, I want you all to myself for the time being. No, my dear husband and I live nearby. Our home is not quite so grand as my father's but it's more than large enough to fit us all quite comfortably. You'll see!'

With that she bustled off, a happily astonished Flora in tow, and an equally nonplussed Jimmy following with the baggage.

Jimmy lay upon the soft, clean bed he'd been assigned and contentedly patted his rounded stomach. Aunt Cleora's cook was wonderful, and her employer had hardly needed to press Jimmy to eat and eat; his only regret was that he'd had to stop. He looked about the room, it was small, but neat and in the main part of the house, with a small fireplace and patterns pressed into the cream-coloured plaster of the walls.

He'd expected to be relegated to the servants' quarters but it apparently hadn't even crossed Cleora's mind.

'It's a little one,' she'd said when she'd brought him up to show it to him. 'But boys don't mind such things, do they?' And she'd stood smiling at him, just a touch of anxiety in her kind brown eyes as though wondering what she'd do if he didn't like his accommodations.

'It's just fine!' he'd assured her.

And still thought so. This was, without doubt, the softest berth he'd ever known. If he didn't watch out, under Aunt Cleora's influence he'd soon be looking for honest work. He grimaced; that was a thought to give one the cold grue.

Uncle Karl, Cleora's husband, was a sea captain currently visiting Krondor. Flora's aunt had assured them both that he would be absolutely thrilled to have them here. Jimmy was going to have to take her word for it since Cleora had no idea when he'd be back. He frowned thoughtfully; if it was longer than two weeks Jimmy was pretty sure he would have moved on by then. By then, Flora would be completely settled in.

Yardley Heywood was no longer practising law. Flora's grandfather had fallen ill earlier in the year and was recovering slowly.

He convalesced at home, with Aunt Cleora looking in on him daily. She promised Flora she could come along in a day or two, after breaking the news to the old man the girl had returned to the family. Jimmy frowned. There was a great deal of bother with relations and keeping stories straight, he thought. Still, Flora seemed up for the job, and after only a few hours in this house it was hard to remember being on the streets of Krondor.

Still, Jimmy knew the role he played would come apart under close inspection. Flora had lived in a nice home for her first nine years, and many of her customers had been swells; she could talk like a proper girl, and Jimmy, while able to keep up appearances if he didn't have to talk too much, had only listened to people of rank for a few weeks, while with the Prince and Princess.

No, he'd keep his mouth shut and answer as few questions as he could get away with, and suffer a warm bed and good meals while he planned out what to do next in his exile. Land's End might not be Krondor, but it was a town of size, and there was booty to boost for a lad with nimble fingers.

Then his smile returned and he folded his arms beneath his head. This would be a fine place from which to work: no one would suspect sweet Aunt Cleora of harbouring a thief and there was no Night- or Daymaster to govern his movements. Poor old Land's End wasn't going to know what had hit it. He chuckled evilly.

'What are you laughing about?' Flora asked.

Jimmy nearly levitated off the mattress. 'Haven't you ever heard of knocking?' he demanded.

She frowned at him and came in, shutting the door behind her. 'Keep your voice down,' she whispered. 'I'm not supposed to be in here.'

'Did your aunt say that?' he asked, surprised. From the way Cleora had been behaving Jimmy had expected her to give Flora the key to the front door at any moment.

Flora gave him an exasperated look. 'No, of course not. She would expect me to know how a young lady should act.'

Jimmy raised his eyebrows as her face fell. Flora sat on the bed and slumped dejectedly. 'I have to tell her the truth, Jimmy,' she said.

He sat up and tipped his head toward her. 'Come again?'

'She deserves to know the truth.' Flora looked up at him from under her lashes and gestured toward herself awkwardly. 'About how I've . . . made my living.'

Jimmy swung his legs off the bed and put his hand on her shoulder, looking her earnestly in the eyes. *No wonder she made such a bad thief,* he thought, *she's bone-honest!*

'You can't do that, Flora.'

'I have to, Jimmy. She deserves the truth.'

'You can't be that selfish, Flora, I know you can't.'

Flora's mouth dropped open. 'What?'

'Think how hurt she'd be,' Jimmy pointed out. 'You've told her your father died when you were just a little girl. You saw her face. Then when you told her that you'd been living with an elderly lady as her companion she looked so relieved! If you tell her the truth she'll suffer agonies of guilt. You know she will! How could you put her through that?'

Flora still looked shocked, her mouth opened and closed but nothing came out and her eyes filled with tears.

'B-but how can I keep lying to her? She's so nice, Jimmy, I really like her. I don't want to build our lives on a lie.'

'Then maybe we should just go,' he said, standing up. 'If you haven't got the strength to protect your relatives from the truth, then,' he shook his head, 'just go. It's kinder.'

Flora started to cry and Jimmy rolled his eyes: now he was the villain. He looked down at her. *Well, maybe I am the villain.* The young thief sat down and put his arm around Flora's quaking shoulders. *And if you do the gods-cursed sensible thing and lie like a sailor, I get to stay in this pleasant room and eat Cleora's wonderful food.*

Maybe confessing everything right at the beginning was the best, most noble, most honest thing to do. But in his heart, Jimmy was convinced it was also the best way to get them kicked out of the house and out of the life that Flora so obviously was meant for. And it would break her aunt's heart. He shook his head. *I'm being totally selfish and totally helpful at the same time. Damn, there's no doubt about it: I was born for greatness.*

'Sometimes, Flora, the right thing isn't always the best thing to do. I see a lot more heartache and loss coming out of an honest confession of the hard facts than out of your very plausible fib. My advice is to sleep on it: things may be clearer in the morning. All I ask is that you tell me first if you're going to tell her about being a Mocker. All right?'

She sniffed and looked at him solemnly, then gave him a brief hug and rose. 'You're right,' she said and wiped at her eyes with the back of her hand. 'And I will think it over. I'll tell you my decision tomorrow, I promise.' Leaning down, she kissed him lightly on the cheek and then, in a swirl of skirts, she was gone.

Jimmy's mouth twisted wryly. Suddenly all that good cooking was sitting in his stomach like a lead weight. Why couldn't women think things through? It was always the emotional side of things with them, never the logical. He gave an exasperated sigh. He'd never sleep with his belly in this kind of torment; perhaps a nice evening stroll was in order.

NINE

Encounter

A lone figure trudged down the road.

Bram had left the merchant caravan – if that wasn't too grand a name for two wagons and two pack mules, where the road branched off toward the village of Relling – just before sunset the night before.

There was a good inn in Relling; they had a first-rate shepherd's pie, and they brewed a noble ale. Not as good as his mother's cooking or his father's home-brew, though. The young man had squared his shoulders, swung his pack over his shoulder on the tip of his bowstave, and set off down the road once he'd made his goodbyes.

By avoiding the loop in the King's Highway where the road headed off to Relling, and by walking most of the night – he usually slept for four hours – he would see his home just before sunrise, just in time for his mother's breakfast. There was little danger along the trail he hiked, few animals that would trouble a grown man, and no robber was likely to be lurking along such a byway in the dead of night.

Every hill that challenged his legs was a step nearer to home.

He recognized trees he'd climbed as a lad, fields he'd worked in or tended stock through, jumped over a creek that crossed the roadway and grinned at the memory of the first time he'd been able to do that dry-shod. He was already man-tall in his seventeenth year, with a little soft yellow fuzz on his cheeks and a shock of rough-cropped gold hair, broad-shouldered and long-legged, his open blue eyes friendly. A lifetime's hard work had put muscle on his shoulders and arms, but it was stalking deer that had given him grace, and made his soft boots fall lightly on the dirt of the road.

And thinking of which, he thought, his head coming up. Something fairly large crashed off through the roadside brush. *Pig?* he wondered, then stooped. The false dawn gave him light enough for tracking. No, deer, right enough. The cloven print was a little too big and a little too splayed for swine.

Bram chuckled. 'Run off and get chased by a nobleman,' he said.

Nobles hunted deer on horseback, with dogs; which was rather like killing chickens with a battle axe to his way of thinking – easily done and not much sport in it – but there was no accounting for tastes. The joy was in tracking and stalking, not the kill. After the kill came the hard part, dressing out the carcass and lugging it back home. But then nobles had servants to do the hard work, he conceded.

He took a deep breath of the musty-cool air and continued down the roadway, whistling. A brisk four-mile walk had brought him almost to his own door and he paused with a smile on his face to look at the old place.

The lane to the farmhouse looked so welcoming in the early morning that the sight of it lifted his heart. There were lanterns on the fence posts on the way up to the house and one beside the door, while the downstairs windows of the house were aglow with candlelight, the flame blurred to a warm yellow through the scraped sheep-gut or thin-sliced horn that made the panes. There was a lantern by the barn door as well, he saw.

That's a real welcome! he thought; beeswax candles were expensive, and tallow dips weren't free either.

Then he remembered that they would have had no way of knowing that today would be his homecoming. Which meant that all this extravagant light was for some other cause. A wedding? But there hadn't been any in prospect when he left. Besides, it wasn't Sixthday afternoon, when most weddings were held. That meant a wake was the mostly likely explanation, since nobody stinted in honouring the dead. And many of the men would drink through the night until their wives said *enough* and took them home.

Everyone had been healthy when he left, but that meant little: illness or accident could take a healthy man or woman suddenly enough, and farmers knew that as well as any.

Bram hastened up the drive, pausing when he noticed Farmer Glidden's wagon, which had been hidden by his mother's lilacs. Then he glanced into the barn, where another lantern was lit, and he noted several horses belonging to the neighbours and a few beasts that belonged to Lorrie Merford's family, including their dairy-cow Tessie.

Something was most definitely going on and it probably wasn't good. Why was the Merford stock in his father's barn? Bram knew that his family couldn't possibly afford to buy them; nor would the Merfords sell them.

Bram hurried to the house. Hearing voices raised inside, he entered quietly through the rear door, the better to hear the fast and furious discussion that was going on. The big, single room that held the main hearth was filled with neighbours, many seated on the benches around the kitchen table, others on stools around the room, the rest standing or squatting against the wall.

'It was animals! Wild dogs or something like that!' said Tucker

Holsworth, smacking the table for emphasis as he waved his pipe in the air. His face was black with soot and dirt.

'But what about what Lorrie said?' asked Bram's father.

'Y'mean about men doing it with some sort of tool?' Holsworth puffed on his pipe as he sought to keep it lit.

'Well, she was there. If that's what she said she saw should we be doubting her?'

'But those marks were made by some animal's teeth! No knife did that to them,' offered Rafe Kimble, who stood by the kitchen hearth. He was also black from soot.

'And little Rip? Where did he go to if someone didn't kidnap him, then?' asked his wife, Elma.

'He could have perished in the fire, and the girl just didn't see it,' insisted Allet.

'If the animal was big enough then it could have dragged him off to its den.' That came from Jacob Reese, who sat at the table with the other two men.

'But how could an animal like that or even a pack of animals, be in the area and us not notice?' asked Ossrey. 'Where have they gone then? I've heard no rumours of such as happened to the Merfords happening anywhere else.'

'What are you talking about?' Bram exclaimed. 'What's happened?'

'Bram!' his mother cried. Allet jumped up from her seat and made her way through the crowd to embrace him.

'Son!' Ossrey said. 'Good to see you, boy!' He offered his hand across the kitchen table and Bram leaned through the crowd of neighbours to take it with a brief smile. From the leftover food on the table and the open jugs, it was clear the women had been in the kitchen all night, cooking breakfast for the men, who had just finished eating.

'You must be starving,' Allet said. 'Sit down, Bram,' she pushed him toward her place at the table, 'and I'll get you something.'

'I'm fine, Mother,' Bram said, but he did take her seat after he'd unslung his bundle and propped the bow and quiver against the wall beside the door. 'What's happened? It sounds bad.' He looked around at his neighbours, then turned expectantly to his father.

Ossrey bowed his head and looked at Bram from under his shaggy eyebrows. He was a dark hairy man except for a thinning patch on top of his head, and broader-built than his son would ever be. 'I'm so sorry you've come home to such bad news, son,' he began. 'The Merfords have suffered a terrible tragedy.'

'Lorrie?' Bram asked immediately.

His mother's lips thinned and she frowned slightly, her eyes shifting to Farmer Glidden to see how he took Bram's singular interest in Lorrie Merford.

'She was fine the last time we saw her,' Allet said, crossing her arms.

'What do you mean the last time you saw her?' Bram demanded. When no answer was forthcoming, he gripped his mother by the arms and asked, 'Mother, what happened?'

'Lorrie's parents were both killed,' Farmer Glidden told him quickly. 'Their house and barn were burned down and we spent the night over there putting out fires in the fields. Just got back here an hour ago.' He was silent a moment, then added, 'Her brother's gone missing. I'm told Lorrie took her horse and rode out. Probably gone after the boy.'

There was a flurry of 'tsks!' both sympathetic and condemning, accompanied by nods and shaking heads.

Bram released his mother's arms. 'So Lorrie and Rip are *both* missing?'

'Didn't I just say so?' Glidden said.

'Has anyone gone after them?'

From the glances exchanged around the room, Bram could tell no one had.

'When did all this happen?' Bram ran a desperate hand through his hair, looking around in confusion.

'The marks on Melda and Sam's bodies looked like they'd been made by an animal of some kind,' Ossrey said. 'We think the boy must have been dragged away by whatever killed them.'

'Animals!' Bram said. 'Here?' He looked around again. 'Has anyone tracked the beasts? Are you saying they . . . had they eaten Melda and Sam?' Then it struck him. 'Do you mean to tell me that Lorrie has gone alone, tracking some animal big enough and dangerous enough to kill two adults? When did she go?'

'Lorrie said something about men doing it,' Dora Commer said, looking defiantly at Allet and Ossrey. 'Said they tore up the bodies with some sort of tool to make it look like a beast did it, then headed down the road toward Land's End. She wanted to follow them at once, but of course we couldn't let her do that. We thought she was in a panic.' The woman shrugged, looking guilty. 'And there was the fire, we had to take care of that. For all we knew the boy had been in the house or the barn and she just couldn't take the idea. Besides,' she continued into his silence, 'if there were men and they'd killed both her parents what could one girl do against them?'

'We brought her here and put her to bed,' his mother said. 'The men had to fight fires in the fields all night, and have been arguing this thing since they got here. When the Lormers were leaving, a little before you got here, they saw the Merfords' horse gone. I checked your room and it was empty. She'd gone out of the window, wearing some of your old clothing, and she stole your purse from under the bed!' She said the last as if it was more important than the other news.

'She's welcome to it,' said Bram, 'if she needs it to find Rip.'

'I checked her farm,' Long Paul, the foreman of Glidden's farm said. 'I took a lantern, rode out there and checked. No sign of her.'

'Well, there's nothing there for her now, is there?' Jacob Reese's wife asked, sniffing sadly.

'We're going to send word to the constable after sunup,' said Glidden officiously. 'It's their job to deal with things like this.'

Bram looked incredulous. 'The constable?'

Glidden looked displeased. 'Doubt much will come of it. No doubt they've much more important things to do than be after a girl looking for her brother.'

'But wasn't he right there on the minute when it came to evicting the Morrisons from the farm their family had worked forever?' Dora said indignantly. 'They jump right to it if you're a money-lender needing to foreclose.'

At this more arguments broke out and threatened to go on for some time.

Bram watched them in wonder then finally shouted over the uproar, 'What have you been doing to find Lorrie and Rip?'

'And what should we do?' his mother asked, sounding offended. 'We offered her our home and our comfort and she ran away, with your purse, without so much as a thank you or a farewell. If she doesn't want us we can't force ourselves on her.'

He looked at her, then turned to his father. 'And there's been no further sign of these so-called animals?' he asked.

'None,' Ossrey said. 'None before, and none since.'

'We didn't find any tracks to follow,' Long Paul told him.

Bram stared at him. Long Paul was the best hunter in the district; it was he who had taught Lorrie and Bram to hunt. If Long Paul couldn't find tracks then there were no tracks to find. 'Doesn't that strike anyone as odd?' he asked. 'The Merfords' farm is seven miles from any sizeable stands of woods. Any animal large enough to savage a full-grown man and woman would have been seen by someone if it was crossing the fields from the Old Forest or the Free Woods. Unless you think it just trotted down the King's Highway without a trader, traveller, or horseman noticing it, then it turned down the Old Mill Trail to Lorrie's farm.'

His neighbours looked at one another in confusion.

'Well, yes,' Long Paul said. 'Not that it signifies. Tracks I mean. Those marks on the bodies were definitely made by an animal's teeth, Bram. I'd swear to that. The fact that it's odd doesn't change the evidence. Could have been a flyer.' He shrugged.

'A flyer?' asked Bram.

'Well, never saw one, but heard tell of some things on the wing up in the mountains that are big enough to attack a man, wyverns and the like.' Then he cocked his head, frowning. 'What are you getting at?'

'That something's not right here,' Bram told him. 'Lorrie said she saw men taking her brother away, and you didn't believe her.' He glanced pointedly at his mother. Her face became more pinched. 'But the only evidence of animals is the marks on the bodies and she said that men did it with some sort of tool. Meanwhile Lorrie has run off alone and everyone's just sitting here talking about it.'

Ossrey looked shamefaced and he wasn't the only one, but no one spoke up and no one moved a muscle. Bram picked up his pack and rose.

'Where are you going?' Allet asked, alarmed.

'Mother, Lorrie is a neighbour, more, she's my friend and she's only fifteen. She's just lost everything in the world and she's out there on her own. Rip may be out there too or he may be as dead as his parents, that's something we don't know. But we do know about Lorrie. We have an obligation to help her.'

'No,' his mother said, thin-lipped. 'No, I don't see that. We tried and she spurned our help. As far as I'm concerned that ends our obligation. And as for her being fifteen, you're only seventeen yourself. So there's no reason to think that you'll do more going after her than she could do for herself.'

Bram was disappointed in her, but not surprised. As soon as he'd begun taking an interest in Lorrie his mother had turned against the girl: this was just more of the same. He looked at his father.

'Do what you think is right, son,' Ossrey rumbled.

Allet hit Ossrey's arm and glared at him.

'Would anyone else like to help me hunt for Lorrie?' Bram asked.

There was a certain amount of foot shuffling and mutterings about not liking to be away from their families while a threat lurked near. And the constable, they should wait on the constable.

'All right,' Bram said. It was what he'd expected. He kissed his mother's cheek and nodded to his father, then turned to go. 'I'll be back when I'm back, then.'

Allet reached out, her face a study in astonishment, but her husband held her back. He placed a large finger athwart her lips as Bram threw a few things into a haversack – a loaf of coarse brown bread, a lump of cheese and some smoked pork – and then took up his bow and quiver, nodding to the assembled company before he stepped back out into the night.

Lorrie drew rein half a mile from the gates of Land's End. The sun was burning down over her shoulder. It had taken old Horace longer to cover the distance than she had thought. Rather than reaching the city by early morning, the poor old creature had managed to get there by midday. She'd been to the city as a child, of course: it was the only market town for the area within two weeks' travel, and her father had let her come along to the Midsummer's festival once, but she hardly had any sense of the place.

And I've been all night on the road.

It hardly seemed possible that only one night had passed since her world had ended . . .

A mule-drawn wagon went past her, and pack-horses; folk were hurrying to get to town and settle their business before the market stalls emptied out. A half-day's commerce still waited those seeking to trade. She urged Horace into a fast walk, scanning ahead.

The town lay in the cup of the hills. Those immediately around it were too steep and rocky to be good farmland, but they'd been logged clear and a good deal of the traffic on the road was firewood from further away. Behind her rose hills dotted with lovely farms, many reminding her of her own, and but a day's ride away the smouldering ashes of that farm were all that was left.

There were some sheep about, but mostly dairy-cows, which surprised her, until she realized that a city would be a good place to sell fresh milk. Nearer to the town there were worksteads on both sides of the dusty white road: trades that weren't allowed in the city or needed more space – a big tannery whose stink made her blink and cough, a potter's kilns like big stumpy beehives sending off waves of heat she could feel a dozen yards away, some smithies, and . . . yes, a stock-dealer. Horses, mostly. She could see them milling about in the pens behind chest-high fieldstone walls. And a saddler's next door, with some of their own. Probably they both rented mounts or draught-animals, as well as dealing in them.

Lorrie felt her stomach rumble at the smell of cooking from a booth; she had had nothing to eat since the previous morning, the shock of the day's events having driven all hunger from her. Now, yesterday morning seemed a long time ago to her stomach.

She'd known that she couldn't keep Horace once she got to Land's End even though the thought broke her heart. There was no money to board and feed him and only the little in Bram's purse for herself.

I'll make the money up to Bram! she thought. *I'd better get the best deal I can.*

The saddler was sitting in his open-sided booth, packing his tools before shutting down for the day. He looked up as she swung down from the saddle, a man in his thirties in breeches and a sleeveless jerkin, his arms ropy with muscle and his hands big and battered, scarred by awl and knife and strong waxed thread. His eyes were green, and shrewd. 'Can I help you, lad?' he said.

She hesitated. It never occurred to her that wearing Bram's clothing, with her hair tied up under a hat, she looked like a boy. For a brief moment she considered that it would prove an advantage, for a young man would be far freer to move around than a farm girl would. Thought what would her mother think? That brought a thought of her mother, and she forced herself to answer before tears came: 'I'm looking to sell the horse,' she said.

'Come to town to make your fortune, eh?' the saddler said, sizing up the animal and the bridle. 'Well, that horse is past mark of mouth, and the bridle's no younger. Let's see them both.'

A few minutes later, the saddler sat back on his bench with a grimace. 'Five silvers for the lot, bridle, pad and girth, and no more,' he said. 'And I'm being generous, at that.'

'It's fair,' Lorrie said virtuously. *Country-folk aren't easy marks, whatever a city man might say,* she added to herself.

'I'll give you twenty-five for the horse,' the saddler said. 'That's a gift, mind you, a gift.'

Lorrie hesitated. The price was fair, but she didn't like the look of the stock behind the shop. *I don't think he feeds them well enough,* she thought.

There were men who'd buy horses cheap, work them to death and buy more; a fool's bargain, she thought, but perhaps worth while in a city, where fodder had to be cash-bought and was expensive. What she couldn't bear was the thought of Horace used so, wondering in bewilderment why he'd been abandoned.

157

'It's the first time in a long year that Swidin Betton's made a gift to anyone, kin, friend or stranger,' a voice said.

The man leaning over the fence was about the saddler's age, with curly reddish hair and a friendly smile.

'I'll take him off your hands, lad,' he said. 'And I'll match the price. He's a good horse, looks to me a draught beast mostly, though, eh?'

And your horses don't look underfed, she thought. The saddler shrugged and handed over the price for the bridle and pad; Lorrie led Horace to the stock-dealer's pen. There were some stables off to one side, and she checked them: the straw looked to have been changed fairly recently, and the hooves of the beasts there were in good shape and kept clean, none cracked, the shoes not worn too thin.

'He's like an old friend,' she said, handing over Horace's rein. 'I wasn't that old myself when my father brought him home.' She scratched Horace under his chin and the old gelding's eyes half closed with pleasure.

'There's always someone looking for a gentle, hard-working creature like this one,' the trader said. 'He's no colt, but he's got years left, no doubt. Don't you worry, he'll find a home.'

'He can plough the straightest furrow you ever saw,' Lorrie said stoutly.

The trader chuckled. 'Lad, you've already sold him. But I'll remember to tell that to prospective buyers.'

Lorrie smiled and nodded, then turned away, somehow managing not to look back, even when Horace gave an enquiring neigh. She came to the edge of the animal market and sighed. Before her was one of the city's gates and beyond, somewhere within the city, was her brother.

Lorrie wandered along the street, unsure of what to do next. She had some sense of Rip still being alive, but no sense of his proximity. Maybe she'd erred in coming here. She had found the constable's office, but the one fellow on duty was an old gaoler, and he said he could do nothing for her. Best to come back at the end of the day when the constable would be bringing in whoever he arrested. He'd be filling cells just before supper, the man had said.

Lorrie's mind turned to finding a place to sleep. Putting her hand in her pocket, she squeezed the purse she'd taken from under Bram's bed now fattened with the thirty silvers she'd got for Horace and the harnessing. She'd done well in her bargaining, but this was no fortune. How long it would keep her Lorrie had no idea: city prices were higher than country, she knew that much.

She felt herself start to go light-headed, and realized she still hadn't eaten. She had to find something decent to eat before she fell over.

Half an hour later Lorrie was licking the few remaining crumbs of a meat pie off her fingers and contemplating buying another one. Afternoon was fleeing, and the streets were crowded but already starting to thin out. The vendor had only one pie left and was moving away. If she wanted another, she had to decide now. She was just about to rush over to the pie-seller to see if she could get a bargain on the last sale of the day when a man walked up to her.

'Hey there, young fellow,' he said cheerily.

Lorrie looked at him. He was about her father's age and short, only a little taller than she was. He wasn't any too clean, though not beyond the bounds of respectability, and his clothing wasn't worn at the collar and cuffs. All in all he looked like a city man and probably a bachelor. He sported a wide black moustache and an even wider grin. Lorrie was certain from the lines in his face the man used dye to make his hair and moustache so absolutely black. She had heard of noblewomen colouring their hair with different things, but never heard of a man doing it. It struck her as odd, but he seemed friendly enough.

'Hello, sir,' she said cautiously.

'You seem a likely lad,' he said.

'Thank you, sir.'

'How would you like to earn two shiny silver pieces?' he asked.

'Very much, sir,' Lorrie said eagerly. That would help. Gods knew how long it would take to find Rip.

'Can you run, boy?'

'Oh, yes, sir,' Lorrie assured him, 'faster than anyone.'

The man laughed and pointed to an alley nearby. 'There's a fellow waiting there at the far end of the alley who needs someone to take a small package across the city for him. His name is Travers and he will give you your instructions. Tell him you're the lad Benton sent him. Now, go, let me see you run!'

She raced to the alley and down it to the corner where a man stood picking his teeth under the creaking sign of a tavern; it was a relief to get out of the narrow lane, where daylight hardly filtered through. The city looked to Lorrie to be worse than a forest at night, with houses that towered up three and even four storeys on either side. She wrinkled her nose: a farm-girl didn't grow up squeamish, but where she was raised dung went on the fields where it belonged, and people didn't piss up against buildings.

'Sir?' she said, 'would you go by the name of Travers?'

The man nodded and swept a glance over her from head to foot. 'Who're you?' he demanded.

'I'm the boy Benton sent you,' Lorrie told him.

'Ah.' He pulled out a purse from his pocket. 'I need ye to take this to The Firedrake, an inn near the north gate. There's a gentleman there named Coats who's waiting for it.' He handed it over. 'Go on, then. What're ye waiting for?'

'Um, Benton said that I would get two silvers for this errand,' she said.

'And so ye shall, when ye've done it,' Travers roared. 'The sooner ye do it, the sooner ye'll be paid. So get goin'!'

Lorrie took to her heels feeling foolish and just a little unnerved. Of course she wouldn't be paid until she'd delivered the package, no one would take your word on such a thing here. But she couldn't help reflecting that Travers was a very surly man, not nearly as nice as Benton.

The streets were far less crowded now as the day waned and she still had nowhere to spend the night. Perhaps if The Firedrake looked like a reasonable place she could stay there. Lorrie paused and looked around. Then she dashed down a short street toward the city wall, reasoning that following it would lead her to the north gate eventually.

Suddenly she went flying, knocking her forehead on the cobbled pavement with an oof! and a dizzying wave of pain. Blood trickled down into her eyebrows, warm and sticky. Through the buzzing in her ears she heard far in the background a cry of 'Stop! Thief!' and was glad she'd got past the place without trouble.

Lorrie started to push herself up when something hard struck her in the middle of her back and pushed her back down again.

'Stay where you are!' a familiar voice barked.

The girl turned her head and stared in astonishment at the cheerful Benton, looking far less than cheery at the moment.

'Ah ha!' Travers said, arriving in a hurry. 'Caught the little rat I see!'

'Then this is the thief?' Benton said.

'Indeed, sir! With my purse in his hand!' Travers said loudly.

Lorrie looked in disbelief from one to the other. The few people about were pausing to see what the excitement was about and she felt compelled to protest.

'But you gave it to me!' she cried. 'You told me . . .'

Benton smacked her with his cudgel on the back of the neck with precisely calculated force, and she fell back, dazed.

'None of that!' he cried. 'You can tell your lies to the judge and see what he thinks of them.'

Some of the people around them looked smug and nodded in agreement; a few were doubtful, but disinclined to interfere.

'I am Gerem Benton, an independent thief-taker, sir. I must ask you come with me, as witness,' Benton announced.

The doubtful among the onlookers now seemed satisfied. The thief-takers worked indirectly for the Baron, being paid a bounty for each thief caught and turned over to the city constabulary.

''Tis no less than my duty,' Travers agreed. He nudged Lorrie with his foot. 'Up with you, boy!'

Lorrie couldn't seem to co-ordinate her limbs and after a moment stopped trying.

'What a dainty head the creature has,' Benton said. 'If you'll take one arm, sir, then I'll take the other and we'll be on our way.'

They hoisted her up and everything went black for Lorrie. Throbbing pain spiked its way up both sides of her neck.

When she came around it was to find herself flat on the ground in a dark lane behind a building. Benton and Travers were having an argument with two other men.

'. . . is my territory, Gerem Benton, and well you know it!' growled a man with an eye-patch. He towered over Benton who was trying to reason with him.

'It all started over in the East Market,' Benton was saying. 'But we have to go through your territory to get to the gaol. Be reasonable, Jake.'

'I saw the whole thing!' Jake roared, by no means inclined to be reasonable. 'I don't care where you started, you carried out the business end of it in my territory!'

He pulled back his fist as if to strike and Travers caught his wrist. Then Jake's companion chose to interfere, giving Travers a hard shove.

'Ah, demons take it,' Benton cursed. 'You have the right of it, then, if it's your territory.'

He turned half away, and then shoved his club into Jake's middle just below the floating rib, a hard swift jab. 'But who says it's your territory, dog's-pizzle!' Benton grabbed the other man by the hair and yanked his head back. Cutting off the man's airway with the club he growled, 'Remember who's running things here, boyo. You and your little crew are free to boost and cut purses, but only because I keep the constables off your neck. I haven't had a thief to turn in for almost three weeks now, so if I have to, I'll turn some farm boy into a thief. But I'll hear no more about "your territory" and "my territory".' He let the man go and watched as he staggered back. 'When it comes to things dodgy, all of Land's End is *my* territory.'

Lorrie crab-walked away for a few paces, then turned over and scrambled to her feet. Before she'd taken two steps the four of them had grabbed hold of her and were cuffing her about the head and shoulders, shouting at her and each other and pulling her arms.

She sank to her knees with a keening sob. Someone had drawn a knife . . .

Something about having his rapier on his hip, even if it was carefully hidden by his cloak, gave Jimmy a sense of being taller – even full-grown. He could feel it in his walk, a new swagger – let him cross my path who dares! He shifted his slender shoulders and grinned.

He'd never dream of wearing the sword on the street in Krondor; the watch would have it off him and himself in a cell before he could begin to argue about it. As for the Mockers, well, unless you were a basher they didn't encourage the open wearing of weapons. It tended to lead to trouble.

Which it could in Land's End as well, I suppose.

But here he was dressed quite respectably, which he knew counted for a great deal and, even more importantly, had a very respectable address. Of course he hoped he wouldn't have to fall back on that. Flora would kill him – assuming she hadn't already revealed all to Aunt Cleora and wasn't sitting on the front steps weeping. In which case they were both likely to be arrested. But when he had last seen them, they had been sitting together while Aunt Cleora regaled Flora with family stories, holding the girl's hands as if they were gold. With no children of her own, it seemed Cleora had found a suitable object for all her maternal instincts. Sometime this evening, Jimmy assumed, they'd finally get around to visiting Grandfather.

Resisting the urge to throw back his cloak off his shoulder, showing the blade, Jimmy continued on. *No point in borrowing trouble,* he thought. *Must continue to look as respectable as possible,* he reminded himself. *And there are advantages to it. I can case any target I please, and the shopkeepers bow double and ask me to take their inventory, instead of calling for the watch or throwing horse-apples!*

So he strutted as he walked, enjoying the mild air as dusk fell and the way his cloak swung about his calves. He rather liked this town. It was so compact compared to Krondor, and so quiet.

'*Leave me alone!*'

Jimmy's head snapped toward the sound. Down a dim alley he saw four men fighting over a struggling shape. *See,* he thought smugly, *there's where an organization like the Mockers comes in handy.* In Krondor such an unseemly situation would never occur. Any freelance thief would know better than to contest a prize with a Mocker and two groups of Mockers would simply take the loot and let the Day- or Nightmaster sort it out. This was uncivilized. And it was not even dark yet!

For just an instant a last, golden ray of sunshine struck the face of the victim, turned toward the end of the alley where Jimmy was standing. His heart seemed to stop and his breath caught in his throat. Then she turned her head and the light was gone, leaving the alley darker than before and Jimmy in a state of paralysis.

It can't be! he thought.

It was impossible, yet . . . In that last flash of daylight he'd have sworn that he saw the face of the Princess Anita. But she was safely on her way to the far coast. What would she be doing, alone, here in Land's End?

The girl made a cry of pain, galvanizing the young thief into action.

He'd passed a box of ashes by the steps of a house just a step away; he grabbed a handful and rubbed it on his face, then pulled the hood of his cloak over his head as far as it would go and ran back to the alley. Jimmy yanked out his sword and with a blood-curdling yell rushed at the heaving, shoving group at the end of the alley.

'At 'em boys!' Jimmy bellowed. 'No quarter!'

Up to now it had been hard words and harder clubs, and one man waving a dirk without using it, but the introduction of an edged weapon and the possibility of more attackers threw the four thief-takers into confusion for a crucial moment. Jimmy slashed out at waist level and the men let go of the girl and jumped back.

Whereupon Jimmy grabbed her tunic and pulled. She was older than he was, he judged quickly, but no taller. And a game lass, he thought; on her feet in a second to follow him out of the alley. He let go of her and slid his rapier back into its sheath, leading her toward that box of ash.

It hadn't taken the four men long to recover from his

unplanned attack, or to realize that there were no 'boys' intent on giving 'no quarter', and they were soon hot on Jimmy's heels. He suspected that they might happily let the girl go free in order to pummel him into the cobbles. It was sad, but he often had that effect on people.

When they reached the house with the ashes Jimmy picked up the box, spun round and flung the contents into the air right in his pursuers' faces. They fell back, cursing and coughing. With dexterity bordering on the supernatural, he again drew his blade and delivered a few well-placed nicks and cuts to the four men, who tried to fend off the much longer blade with clubs and a single dirk. Jimmy had only a few weeks' practice with the blade, but his teacher had been Prince Arutha, and more, Jimmy was faster than most experienced swordsmen. The men tried to fan out and approach from two sides. For their efforts they received some nasty cuts on the arms and hands from Jimmy's much longer blade. Jimmy laid about, his blade hissing as it cut air, and each time it made contact, an attacker yelped in pain and fell back. Then the leader of the group, the man with the black moustache, tried to leap in, and Jimmy cut him deep across the shoulder. One of the men turned and fled, and in a moment, the rout was on, the attackers beating a hasty retreat; the price of the girl and the boy wasn't worth bleeding to death.

Jimmy grabbed the girl's hand and led her through the narrow space between two houses. It was barely wide enough for him and in a few steps his cloak was strangling him where it had caught on the rough surface somewhere behind him. He managed to get a hand up to release the clasp and with the girl's help dislodged it.

'They won't be able to follow us through here,' he said.

'What's to stop them from going back down the alley and coming around?' the girl asked. She had a low, husky voice, and she asked very sensible questions.

Jimmy liked that, but she didn't sound like the Princess, meaning he'd probably interfered with something that was none of his business. *Ah, well. Win some, lose some*, he thought philosophically. Perhaps there was something here he could turn to his advantage. And if it was a madness, it was a noble madness.

When they came out behind the house, Jimmy looked around and traced a path to the rooftops. The roofs were different here in Land's End, slightly steeper and mostly tiled, but not impassable; the walls had more stone and less brick and half-timbering, but his fingers were strong and his toes nimble.

'Can you climb?' he asked.

'Yes,' she said shortly.

'Then follow every move I make,' he ordered.

He unbuckled his belt and refastened it over one shoulder so that the hilt of his sword lay between his shoulder-blades.

Up the drainpipe, he thought: it was bored-out wood and quite strong enough, fastened to the stone with bolts. Onto the transom of a window, thence over the eaves and onto the roof. From there, it seemed to Jimmy, the city was theirs. The girl put a hand up and he took it, giving her a lift that helped her scramble up. Then he led her to the deepest shadow he could find, hoping they'd be invisible from the street below.

And not a moment too soon, as around the corner of the alley came four very angry men, now bearing swords or clubs. They looked up and down the street, then took a moment to argue, until the short one pointed one way and then the other, whereupon two men went up the street and two men went down. The man with the moustache shouted, 'Find them. They're worth three silvers each!' He headed up the street, while the other men took off in different directions.

'Three silvers!' the girl exclaimed. 'Those bastards!'

Definitely not the Princess, then.

'What was that?' asked Jimmy.

'That man said he was a thief catcher. They were going to turn me in for a bounty.'

Jimmy was silent for a moment, then said, 'It's an old grift. Two or three "citizens" testify you're a thief, and if you don't have no one from around here to vouch for you, you're off for the work gang or worse.' He paused. 'Did you happen to catch the name of that fellow with the moustache?'

'Yes,' Lorrie replied. 'He said his name was Gerem Benton.'

'Ah,' said Jimmy slowly.

'You know him?'

'I know him,' said Jimmy with a nod. 'Gerem the Snake. Used to run a confidence game up in Krondor. Thought he was dead.' He stood up. 'I'm Jimmy. If you like I'll escort you home.'

'I don't live here,' the girl said gruffly, then was quiet for a moment. 'Thank you. I don't know what would have happened if you hadn't interfered.'

'It depends,' Jimmy said. 'But nothing good, you can rely on that. So what's your name?'

'Uh, Jimmy,' she said.

The young thief laughed so hard he slipped a couple of yards down the roof. He elbowed his way back up and grinned at her.

'No, no, that's *my* name,' he said. 'You weren't paying attention.' He leaned a little closer and whispered, 'I know you're a girl.'

She looked startled, and her lips parted as though to deny it.

'I know you are,' he insisted.

'How? They certainly didn't!'

'Well, I'm more . . . alert, I suppose. Or maybe it's that you look amazingly like someone I know, and she's most definitely a girl.' He gave her shoulder a gentle poke. 'So, what's your name?'

'Lorrie,' she said, sounding discouraged. 'Lorrie Merford.'

'Nice to meet you, Lorrie,' Jimmy said at his most suave, managing to copy Prince Arutha's courtly bow in miniature, while lying on slippery red tiles.

She smiled at him. 'Nice to meet you, too, Jimmy,' she said.

The sun was now setting, and night was almost upon them. It would be getting harder to see in the gathering darkness, but the young thief crossed his ankles as though they had all the time in the world. Better to let their pursuers get farther away before they themselves moved on.

'So if you don't live in the city, where do you live?' he asked casually.

'Somewhere you've probably never heard of,' she said. 'The nearest village is a tiny place named Relling.'

Nope, never heard of it, he thought. *Sounds like an early-to-bed-early-to-rise land of honest toil and earthy, peasant virtue. Hope I never have to go there.*

'Were you going to go back there tonight?' he asked.

'Uh, no.' Lorrie shook her head. 'I've got something to do here.'

I'll bet you do, he thought. He'd also bet it was something her family wouldn't approve of. Why else would she be in disguise? 'So where are you staying?' he asked. 'As I said, I'll walk you home.'

With a short laugh she said, 'I'm not staying anywhere. I just got to Land's End today and almost the first thing I did was meet Benton and agree to run an errand for him.' Her voice was rich with self-contempt.

'Don't be too hard on yourself,' Jimmy advised. 'He's pretty slick. I'm a stranger here myself, so I don't know which inns might be good for you. Do you have any money?'

There was a long pause at that. 'A little,' she admitted cautiously.

Almost none, Jimmy thought. *Poor kid.*

'Well,' he said, rising, 'let's go exploring. Maybe we can find you somewhere really cheap to stay.' He helped her to her feet and led her back to a place where they could climb down.

*   *   *

Jarvis Coe sat in the darkest corner of The Cockerel and sipped his beer with his cloak wrapped about him. There was a tired-looking roast of pork turning on a spit over the fire; but he'd contented himself with a hunk of dark bread and some cheese and a few good apples, since they were less likely to lay him out with stomach cramps. One advantage of being out of Krondor was that market-food was fresher and less expensive.

He'd paid for the use of the table at the outset of the evening, since he didn't intend to drink much and didn't want any difficulty about it. He was here to eavesdrop. Over the years he'd found that the gossip most useful to a man of his interests tended to be found in the roughest taverns. It was certainly proving true tonight.

The tables along the wall were separated by board partitions that didn't run all the way to the rafters and lathes above. He could follow a very interesting conversation from the next one, given his training and a focused mind. The knotholes and gaps in the boards were helpful as well, giving him an occasional glimpse of the talkers.

'Bring 'em here, take 'em there. I tell ye I don't like this,' a heavy-set man was saying to his companion. 'It's gettin' worse there all the time! I don't want to go there any more, I tell ye!'

'Easy, Rox,' his skinny companion soothed. 'We've never been paid so well.' He hoisted his goblet. 'Drinkin' the best wine, ain't we?'

Which at The Cockerel, Coe thought, must be a whole two steps above vinegar.

Rox leaned in close to his companion, his glance nervously darting around the room. 'It's not right, what we're doin', not right at all!'

Skinny whooped with laughter. 'Well, of course it's not!' he said.

'That's not what I mean,' Rox snarled.

Skinny looked away impatiently.

Rox gave his shoulder a shove. 'You know what I mean,' he said. 'That place, there's somethin' about it.' Rox rubbed his lower lip with a dirty thumb. 'It's not right.'

Skinny shook his head and then the rest of himself, like a dog flicking off water.

Rox grabbed his arm. 'You know what I mean!'

'What I know is it's the best money I've ever seen,' Skinny said stubbornly. 'And that's all I need to know, or want to know, and if you're smart, you'll be like me.'

Rox subsided for a moment, scowling darkly. 'What's he want with all them kids, then?' he demanded suddenly.

Skinny started to snicker. 'Maybe he, hee-hee, maybe he's running an orphanage!' He smacked his thigh and whooped with laughter. 'Out of the goodness of his heart, like.'

Even Rox grinned for a moment, smiling as he took a sip from his cup. But when he lowered it his frown was back. 'I don't want to go there any more,' he grumbled. 'Why can't he get somebody else to take 'em?'

'I think he's keepin' it secret,' Skinny said. 'We know about it, so,' he shrugged, 'he uses us instead of tellin' someone else. Keeps it more secret, see?'

Rox sat growling quietly for a few moments. 'I want to quit,' he said suddenly.

'We can't quit!' Skinny snapped. 'We need the money, best money we ever got. And beside . . .' He stopped and rubbed his face with his hands, then looked over his shoulder. He leaned toward Rox and whispered, 'I don't think we can quit.'

'Whaddaya mean?' Rox sat up straight, looking worried.

Skinny leaned closer still. 'He's important.' He looked over his shoulder. 'He can do things to us.'

Rox just stared at him, shaking his head slightly, confused.

'You know what I mean. When people like us annoy people

like him we don't stay healthy.'

Rox's eyes widened. 'Ohhh!' he said.

'So just hang on, all right?'

'I suppose so,' Rox conceded. He picked up his mug and drained it, then smacked it down loudly. 'Hey!' he shouted. 'Innkeeper! More!'

'So we'll just deliver the boy to the manse, take our money and go. Easy. Just hold on. Maybe this will be the last time we have to make a trip out into the country.'

The bigger man didn't answer but he made the innkeeper leave the pitcher of wine he brought to refill their goblets and then proceeded to get very drunk.

Coe listened to all of it and decided that he, too, might just make a trip out into the country. It might be very interesting to see this place that 'wasn't right'.

Jimmy led the girl down toward the warehouse district on the wharves. In his experience he'd discovered that one could usually find an abandoned space or two or more there. Besides, a lot of these places were sparsely patrolled; one or two watchmen to a row and those weren't usually the most alert of men. Or the most curious.

He kept them to the shadows, which resulted in a lot of tripping on Lorrie's part. At first he'd been sympathetic, then amused, but now she was beginning to curse and he was worried that she'd attract attention. The watchmen probably would not come looking, but if he and Lorrie forced themselves on them they wouldn't turn a blind eye.

'Lorrie,' he whispered, 'we have to be quiet.'

'I can't see where I'm going!' she said between her teeth.

Jimmy stuck his tongue in his cheek and took a long, deep breath. He knew better than to get involved with ordinary citizens, they were nothing but trouble, yet here he was dragging one around by the hand. 'I understand, but could you at least stop swearing? Out loud, I mean.'

'Oh. Sorry.'

They moved on. He was looking for somewhere run-down, preferably abandoned. But all the warehouses they'd passed so far seemed tightly locked and well tended. Land's End seemed to be a busy port, for all it was a smaller one than Krondor. *This close to Kesh I suppose it would be*, Jimmy thought. Then he spotted a likely-looking place. He led the girl to a dark recess between two buildings. 'I'm going to scout around,' he said. 'Why don't you take a bit of a rest?'

She didn't say anything for a moment, then, in a highly suspicious voice she asked, 'Why?'

Nothing but trouble, he thought. 'Because I think I've seen a place where you can sleep for free. But I've got better night-sight than you do and I don't want to drag you over there for nothing. I'll be right back. I promise.'

'Oh!' she said, sounding as if the idea of *free* lodging had never occurred to her. 'All right.'

Jimmy gave her shoulder a pat and moved off. The place had stairs to the second storey and he put one foot on the bottom step very lightly, only to have it squeak even when he kept his weight to the inner side of the riser. Going up there would probably make enough noise to wake the dead; he was going to have to find another way up.

After looking around he found a shorter building that backed up to his chosen site; the peak of its roof was just below a single window, and the shorter building was eminently climbable. He tested the route and found the window unlocked. Slipping inside . . .

A nice, long-deserted attic room over the main warehouse. Probably used to store occasional high-value cargo – brandy, say, or spices. It held very little now, a keg or two of what was probably nails, one or two bolts of cheap sacking cloth, some broken furniture and a wealth of dust. Jimmy walked carefully, but the floor was solid oak planks which were neatly pegged and made no noise: that sort of construction lasted forever if it was kept dry, and the roof seemed very sound. The door to the main loft opened inward – but there were crates stacked in front of it, almost touching his chest when he stepped into the doorframe. He gave an experimental shove and found he couldn't move them. At least not without more noise and effort than he wanted to make. He pushed his knife gently through a crack between two slats, and it chinked dully when it hit the cargo within, but straw and willow-withy padding showed too.

Crockery of some sort, he thought. *Damned heavy. Good as having a fortress wall in front of you – you could hear them hours before they cleared the door – and the only other way in is the window.*

Doubtless others before him had found the building below to be the perfect route into this warehouse and the owner had moved to block them.

'Perfect,' he said, rubbing his hands together.

Lorrie was exactly where he'd left her, sitting with her back against the building.

'C'mon,' he said. 'I've found a place to stay.'

She was a game little thing, he had to admit, if far too trusting. *I could be a slave-taker, or a brothel agent, or just a freelance rape-and-murder artist. This one is a little lamb far from home.*

Once he'd described their route to the window and started to climb she followed him without question or complaint. Once they were in the room he began unrolling one of the bolts of cloth.

'What are you doing?' she asked, sneezing at the dust he was raising.

As he'd thought, once you got through the first few layers the cloth was clean and dust-free, though still smelling sour from long storage. 'Making you a bed,' he said with a grin.

'I can't use that,' she said, sounding honestly horrified.

'Of course you can,' he reassured her. 'You're only borrowing it. What harm can you do it by sleeping on it? Besides it's obviously been here for years, so no one's missing it.' When she still hesitated he rolled his eyes and continued, 'And if you leave it the way we found it no one will ever know.'

'I suppose you're right,' Lorrie said. She grabbed the other bolt. 'Perhaps one day I'll be able to do a good turn for the man who owns it.'

Jimmy kept unrolling cloth, looking toward her shape in the darkness. Honest people never failed to amaze him.

Together they arranged the cloth into a reasonably comfortable bed and Lorrie thanked him. Jimmy considered trying to steal a kiss from her, then decided that might complicate things too much.

Then she decided to complicate things by asking, 'Will I see you again?'

'I'll check here tomorrow,' he said. 'If you're still here I'll see you then.'

'Thank you,' she said. Reaching out, she found his hand and shook it.

She had calluses on her hands, he noted, but the hand felt small and shapely, her teeth were good, and she was tall for her age: working folk, but not poor. 'You're welcome.' He felt suddenly awkward. 'Good night.'

'Good night.'

Jimmy climbed out the window and down the other building, then headed back to Aunt Cleora's house.

That was strange, he thought. He wondered what had brought the country girl into the big city. Especially disguised as a boy.

He'd like to see her in daylight, see if that glimpse he'd had of her had told the truth. Did she really resemble the Princess as much as he'd thought? Maybe he would return tomorrow. Time permitting.

TEN

The Baron

The sleeper tossed and moaned.

Outside the room the guards ignored the sounds, for they had heard them before; it was a rare night the Baron slept the night through without the dreams. The guards were hard men, picked for their ability to ignore the strange goings-on inside the baronial home as much as for their ability to defend their liege. They were all former mercenaries, men whose loyalty was to gold, not tradition, and they were content to be oblivious to the screaming that often came from their master's quarters, or other parts of the mansion.

Bernarr ap Lorthorn, Baron of Land's End, vassal to Lord Sutherland, Duke of the Southern Marches, writhed in troubled sleep. He knotted his fine linen sheets in clutching fists and struggling limbs, the fabric already damp with perspiration. In his dreams he was not the scrawny, ageing man with limp grey hair of his waking hours, but young and strong and deeply in love with his beautiful wife Elaine.

Please, no, he thought. The lips of his aged body whimpered the words. *Please, no.*

The dreams were wonderful, and hateful, beyond description. They were always the same, as if he were riding in the mind of his younger self, seeing and smelling, tasting and feeling as he had – but in some lost corner of his mind he knew how the story ended. Disaster loomed on the horizon, rearing like some ghastly fortress of demons beyond the edge of time, casting a shadow that made all the beauty and glory a sickness. Yet he was doomed to relive the past in his dreams, to endure the joy and wonder, only to find, at the last . . .

He'd met her in Rillanon.

It was early summer when he first visited Rillanon, a time of flowers, blossoms everywhere. Wherever his glance fell a riot of nature's favourite colours gladdened the eye. Even the wharfside taverns bore window-boxes or were wrapped in some flowering vine.

As he left the docks, on horse, to ride to the King's palace, the sheer magnificence of the Kingdom's capital took his breath away. He hated even to blink for fear of missing some new and even more beautiful sight; only a lifetime's practice enabled him to ride the unfamiliar horse through the crowded streets without being thrown off, while his eyes were captivated and his mind beguiled.

The city was built upon hills wound round with silver ribbons of rivers and canals. It seemed that Rillanon had no top, but kept reaching up to the clouds forever. Graceful bridges arched over the waterways. Countless spires and slender, crenellated towers bore colourful banners and pennons, all fluttering in the breeze as though applauding the wind.

His heart, so heavy since his father's death during the winter, lifted at the sight. Bernarr's eyes teared with pride and his heart swelled at the great honour of being a part of the Kingdom of the Isles.

Thank the gods duty delayed me, he thought. *This must be the most beautiful of seasons in the most beautiful of cities. I have seen her at her best, and the image shall be in my heart always.*

He'd come to offer his fealty to the King and be installed as the new Baron of Land's End. Traditionally, his demesne was part of the Western Realm, and his master, Lord Sutherland, was vassal to the Prince of Krondor, but it was traditional that every noble of the Kingdom, no matter from how distant a province, made a journey within as short a time as possible to kneel before the King in the ancient birthplace of the nation.

Then came a whirl of images: settling into his guest quarters, touring the city and its environs, meeting the many scholars he'd corresponded with, visiting booksellers with as many as a hundred volumes in their collections.

Then a moment of clarity from that time returned: *I'm happier than I've ever been in my life,* he had realized suddenly one day, letting a heavy volume in his lap fall closed. *I don't want to go home, to settle suits over cows and count the arrows in the store-rooms and talk of crops and hunting and weather, pointless patrols along a border Kesh rarely troubles, instructing captains to set to sea to chase pirates out of Durbin. I wish I could stay here, for all my days, among the learned and wise, among those who understand the value of knowledge . . .!*

Stop, the old man's lips said silently, as his hands plucked at the coverlets. Tears squeezed out from beneath the thin wrinkled lids of his eyes. *Oh, please, stop now.*

Bernarr took his hands from between his liege's and rose, looking up into the careworn face. He was close enough to smell the cinnamon-and-cloves scent of spiced wine on the older man's breath, and to see the slight dark circles of worry beneath his eyes. The court was a blaze of colour around them.

The ceremony was quickly over. King Rodric the Third, a tired, anxious-looking man, offered a few words to the new baron, then Bernarr was hustled quickly away by court functionaries: there were others behind him and the King had many men to greet. Somehow he knew he would never again see this king, and that soon after leaving Rillanon, Bernarr would receive word that the King had died, and his son, likewise named Rodric, would assume the crown.

Receptions and audiences, a brief encounter with Prince Rodric, and the days flew. The provincial baron was viewed with indifference by most of the resident courtiers, though a few showed envy at the Prince's interest in the scholarly young noble from the west. Alone of those in court only Lady Lisabeth, one of the Queen's ladies-in-waiting, showed a personal interest in Bernarr, but her stout figure and lecherous demeanour repulsed him. She didn't want him; she wanted any man with a title; even a country noble like Bernarr could see that.

The memory that was a dream was vivid. Bernarr almost jumped a foot when Lisabeth popped out of the bushes as he made his way to the centre of the maze, intending to read in solitude amid the pleasant smell of green and growing things. The tinkle of the fountain would be his only company. He quickly adjusted his expression to an indifferent mask. 'My lady,' he said coolly, with a slight bow. Then, clutching his book, he moved on.

She begged his attention, and balancing between being polite and curt, he attempted to disengage from her grasp as he explained he sought solitude, not company. He saw her lips move and remembered fragments of the conversation, but it blurred a moment, then came suddenly into focus as a peal of merry laughter was followed by a voice: 'Oh, Lisabeth, let the gentleman get on with his studies and come away with me, do. We need another to play at cards and we would welcome your company.' Bernarr turned his attention away from the unpleasant visage of Lady Lisabeth to find himself confronted by a vision in a plain green gown.

No! The old man's voice keened through the dark closeness of his bedchamber. *Not this! Please, not this! Let me wake, let me wake!*

It was as though someone had taken his book and clubbed him over the head with it. All he could see was the young woman's sparkling green eyes and the lush fall of her dark hair, the white column of her throat and that sweet, sweet smile. Birds with plumed tails and rings of silver on their claws walked about her, and the trumpet-vines behind her trembled purple and crimson in the breeze that moved wisps of her hair. His heart leapt at sight of her.

The Lady Lisabeth appeared momentarily annoyed at the interruption. Then she glanced at Bernarr and threw up her hands. 'I see that you are right, Elaine,' she said and moved toward her friend. 'The Baron has no time for me.'

As they prepared to move away, Bernarr came to life again, feeling a wrenching sorrow he could not name, one that squeezed his heart and chest like the shadow of future grief. 'My Lady Lisabeth,' he said breathlessly, 'will you not introduce me to your friend?'

Although an angry flush appeared in her cheek, Lisabeth was not in a position to refuse an introduction to a baron. 'My lord, may I present the Lady Elaine du Benton.' Her tone and manner were perfunctory. 'Her family has a small estate outside Timons.' Lisabeth took evil delight in stressing the word small.

'Enchanted,' he said, softly, his voice barely above a whisper.

It is no courtly flattery, he thought, *for she has cast a spell over me with but one smile.*

Elaine curtseyed, her eyes downcast, she did not rise.

Lisabeth rolled her eyes impatiently. 'My lady Elaine, I have the honour to present Lord Bernarr, Baron of Land's End.'

Elaine rose with a radiant smile and offered her hand to him. He took it gently and kissed it, suddenly, painfully aware of the ink-stains on his long fingers.

'I am delighted, Baron,' Elaine said.

She had dimples. For the first time he could see why they were considered pretty.

'Please excuse us,' Elaine said, 'our friends are waiting.'

'Of course. I hope to see you again soon, my lady.' He bowed, and it took every shred of willpower he possessed to release her delicate fingers from his grip.

They were already moving away, arm in arm. Just before they turned the crisp corner of the hedge Elaine turned and gave him a shy smile and a little wave of her hand. That easily she made him her slave.

The dream burred, and bits of memory flashed through his mind. Days and weeks passed and their acquaintance hardly progressed. He contrived reasons to be near her, yet he never seemed to find the opportunity to speak to her alone. She always had a previous engagement, or her duties to the Queen prevented any meeting. He found himself intruding on groups of younger courtiers when she was allowed away from duties and was with her friends. They regarded him as an interloper, but his rank provided him a great shield against their youthful disdain, and his blindness to others when Elaine was near prevented him from seeing their mocking amusement at his obvious infatuation. The more she eluded him, the more he desired her. Despite his nearly thirty years of age, despite his responsibility as Baron and his years of running the barony while his father lingered ill, he was unprepared for a girl barely more than half his age. Knowing next to nothing about Elaine, he found himself falling deeper and deeper in love with her.

Longingly, he thought of her during every waking moment and in his dreams: for she seemed to him everything that was lovely and feminine and sweet. It was impossible that he could love her this deeply and she could feel nothing for him; she must just be hiding her feelings, waiting for a time when they were alone.

The part of Bernarr that was an old man in a lonely bed no longer begged. It panted slightly, like a beaten dog lying in the dust, scarcely flinching as the whip fell.

Baron Hamil de Raise was a nobleman who exercised considerably more court influence than Bernarr, and had some real wealth as well: there were ancestral banners and weapons on the panelled walls of his chambers, but also instruments and books. It had been his scholarly interests that had caused him and Bernarr to gravitate to one another.

Their early meetings flickered through Bernarr's mind without sound, glimpses of a glass of wine shared, a banquet where they sat nearby and exchanged pleasantries, then suddenly the dream became vivid, as if reliving a memory.

Hamil was leading Bernarr down a dark street in a seedier part of the city. The stench of garbage in the alley they passed before reaching their destination was vivid, as was the sound of bootheels grinding in the damp gravel and mud. Hamil said, 'Hers is a very minor family, of no particular consequence, fine old name, originally a line of court barons from Bas-Tyra, but now reduced to the one lone estate in the south. Her father is an active embarrassment to the proud name. What remains of it. He's been stripped of every hereditary title his forebears gained, and clings with near desperation to the rank of "Squire", which the Crown permits as an act of courtesy. She is merely "Lady du Benton". He's a most intemperate gambler who has squandered considerable wealth over the years. With no male heir, the line dies with him and I'd wager the Crown forecloses on the estate.'

The gambling house was of a low sort and it was set into the basement of what was probably a brothel, with ancient smoke-marked beams barely a tall man's height overhead once you had gone down the six worn stone steps. The two men kept their long cloaks close about them as they entered, but the very fabric of the dark cloth marked them out. Eyes shifted toward them; hard, feral eyes in scarred faces; bodies shifted, clad in rags or raggedy-gaudy finery. The guilty drew away in fear while the predatory moved closer.

Hamil smiled thinly and let the hilt of his sword show. The worn shagreen of the grip sent a stronger message than the inlay-work on the guard; the various toughs and bravos stepped away.

'Not the sort of place to find a gentleman,' Hamil murmured, echoing Bernarr's thought.

'And we haven't,' the younger man said, equally quietly.

Du Benton was unmistakable, leaning forward on a bench and ignoring the newcomers; he was thin and dirty and his clothing, once of good quality, was stained and torn. His pale eyes held a frantic light as they watched the play of the dice. As du Benton placed his bet he licked his thin lips with naked lust.

Bernarr turned his head away; this was more than he'd wanted to know about any man, least of all the father of the one he loved.

Yes, loved!

Hamil was right: the man was a disgrace. That a flower like Elaine had blossomed from such slime defied belief. *I must save her*, he thought, *before her beast of a father defiles her*. For he could see that a man like du Benton would drag her down with him in some foul way if she wasn't freed of him. The desperation in the man's face as he lost the wager told Bernarr that du Benton would gladly offer his daughter's hand to any man with a pouch of gold. He must obtain leave to wed her. He must save her from her father offering her hand to some fat old merchant or wastrel son of an idle eastern noble. 'Let's go,' he said to his friend. 'I've seen enough.'

'I hope you have,' said Hamil, though from his tone it was apparent he knew Bernarr mistook his meaning. As they returned towards Hamil's apartment near the palace, the older baron knew this lesson was lost on his young friend.

There were formalities to be observed. Bernarr quietly petitioned the Crown for permission to marry and after a contentious meeting with the court official who was responsible for recommendations to the Crown, permission was grudgingly given.

Having the King's permission, if not blessing, armoured Bernarr and he set out to woo and win the lady of his dreams. He found that love was a glorious feeling: dizzying, intoxicating, delightful past all measure.

At first he hadn't been sure that Elaine shared the feeling and he'd been in an agony of uncertainty, all the more painful because of his overwhelming love for her. Her declining of his invitations and her duties to the Queen made her seem unreachable. He began to find ways to be with her, even if it meant contriving invitations to social events where she was in attendance. But it was so difficult to get her attention. She was always surrounded by a butterfly cloud of her fashionable friends. There was one fellow in particular who usurped her time, a handsome but dissolute young fellow named Zakry, the third son of a minor court squire. He wore the latest court fashions and carried himself with a swagger born of arrogance, not battle-won confidence.

His mouth was almost feminine as he pursed his lips in disapproval over some imagined flaw in Bernarr's attire, and his smile was constantly mocking. It was obvious to Bernarr that his intentions toward Elaine were not honourable, but it was equally clear that she was infatuated with the boy. He would need to act soon or her generous nature and naïveté would lead her into disgrace. Bernarr was certain once Elaine was sure of his true love for her, her childish attraction to a dissolute boy like Zakry would be swept away.

Had his father been still alive he might never have dared to ask for her hand. The old baron would have demanded a more politically advantageous match for his son, and future grandsons. But Bernarr was free to act for his own happiness and so he did.

Soon he began ignoring social conventions and seeking ways to be with her. He would simply put himself at her side whenever possible, ignoring dark looks from Zakry and her other friends as he used his rank to force them aside.

Elaine was always gracious, but always correct. Her smiles were cordial and she laughed politely at his quips. After a while, he realized that she was shy and pure and didn't know how to show him her deeper feelings. She was a true lady, despite her awful father. She hid behind a mask, for it was impossible for him to imagine she could not return his feelings. She must love him!

Being loved by a goddess like Elaine made him feel special and powerful, capable of accomplishing anything. Even winning her hand and heart, despite her modesty. Suddenly he had new insight into the romantic poets and the fixations of men who had gone to war for the love of a woman. After less than a month of seeing her briefly at the palace, he resolved to put an end to this matter and sought out her father.

*   *   *

Elaine's father had agreed with shocking alacrity. A baron sought the hand of his daughter, and moreover, one unconcerned with his inability to provide even a token dowry. He had agreed to every one of Bernarr's suggestions, including a modest annual allowance to provide for the squire's apartment in Rillanon. Bernarr was not being generous; he wished the man as far from them as possible. Had he agreed, Bernarr would have found him an apartment in Roldem or the one of the eastern kingdoms. The squire promised Bernarr that his daughter would be in the royal maze the next day at one, to receive Bernarr's proposal. The old man had been positively beside himself with joy as Bernarr left the seedy inn where he had negotiated the hand of the woman he loved.

Bernarr found her on one of the benches at the centre of the maze, looking pale and as nervous as a startled fawn. Instantly he went down on one knee and took one of her hands in his. Today his fingers were clean and the slight tan of his skin made a pleasing contrast to the delicate white of hers. 'I have spoken to your father and he has consented to our marriage,' he said, his heart virtually leaping into his throat as he watched her reaction.

'You do not know me,' she said, her voice soft and breathless. 'How could you possibly love me?'

With a smile he kissed her fingers. 'To see you is to love you,' he assured her. 'I know you better than you think. But, you do not know me, which is my fault.' Bernarr bowed his head over her hand and stroked her fingers with his thumb, lost for a moment in the wonder of her touch. Then he looked up at her. 'I do love you, my lady. I promise to be a good and gentle husband to you. I beg you to make me the happiest man alive by honouring me with your hand. My love will awaken your heart and you will come to know what I do, that I could not love you so deeply, so passionately, without your loving me in equal measure. We will be happy, I promise you.'

She was staring at him as if in wonder, then she closed her eyes and caught her breath, catching her lower lip in her teeth. After a moment she let out her breath in a gasp and lowered her head. 'Of course I will marry you, my lord. I could never refuse such an honour.'

He reached out and lifted her chin, waiting until her eyes met his. 'You would marry me of your own free will?' he asked. 'Because you love me?'

A single tear traced a path down her pale cheek. 'Of course I do,' she said, her voice choked. 'Of course.' Then she leapt to her feet and said, 'Forgive me, my lord, I am overwhelmed and must collect myself.' So saying, she fled, leaving him puzzled by the behaviour of women, but thrilled and delighted, his blood dancing with joy.

She loved him!

The next time he saw her, Elaine insisted that the ceremony be held as quickly as possible. Her boldness had taken his breath away and sent his heart's blood rushing. For a moment it was hard for him to think and this time he took her in his arms in wonder and delight. When he lifted her head and looked down into her lovely face he thought he would melt with the heat of his passion. He realized at that moment, she would give herself to him without hesitation. Pushing aside his passion, he whispered, 'I would not so dishonour you.' Elaine blinked, looking up at him in astonishment. 'But we will be married as soon as it can be arranged.'

The wedding was an intimate affair in the chapel of Ruthia – the Goddess of Luck – at the palace, witnessed by more of Bernarr's friends than Elaine's.

'It is nothing,' she said, making light of it. 'It's the way of things here. I have moved on and so have they.'

He thought that she was hurt by their desertion for all she dismissed their peculiar absence so carelessly. He tried to make it up to her by being extra attentive through their small but elegant wedding feast. Later, when they were alone, he presented her with his personal wedding gift, a magnificent emerald necklace. 'To match your eyes,' he told her.

Elaine was enchanted and stared into the mirror for a full minute without saying a word. She touched each stone, then looked up, and into his eyes in the mirror. Her lips parted and she pulled at the bow that held her nightgown closed. With a shrug the fine gown dropped to her feet and she turned, smiling, and went to him, naked save for the emeralds.

That night, that passionate, wonderful night, had been the happiest of his life.

In his sleep, the tormented old man cried, tears emerging from closed eyelids. *No!* he shouted in his mind, knowing that he had once again visited and left behind the single most joyous night he had known, and knowing what pain and suffering was to come.

The trip home had been as comfortable as he could make it, but Elaine was not a good traveller. His relief as they came into the harbour of Land's End was enormous, for he had begun to fear for her health. She had been sick at almost every stage of their journey and he was resolved that she should see a chirurgeon as soon as possible.

As he stood beside her at the ship's rail, his arm curled protectively around her slender shoulders, Bernarr could sense the disappointment that her smile hid. For the first time in his life he saw Land's End in comparison with Rillanon, Salador, and Krondor, and it did not compare well. It was a small, work-a-day place, shabby, plain and ordinary.

'You will make it beautiful just by being here. My people will love you,' he promised.

Elaine smiled dazzlingly and embraced him and his heart lifted. She was wonderful, everything he had thought she would be and more. If only she were not so often ill.

He took her to his estate in the country, thinking the air would be more pure there. Elaine seemed bored and listless, but her colour was better and he thought she seemed stronger.

They had been home less than three weeks when a ship came to port carrying a number of Elaine's friends. And they came carrying evil tidings. Her father had been murdered in a tavern brawl. To his horror, Elaine fainted dead away. Bernarr ordered the servants to carry her to her room and then turned his fury on her friends.

Zakry, the squire's third son of whom Elaine was once so fond, seemed overcome with astonishment. His handsome features slowly turned from amazement to anger under the Baron's blistering attack. 'I would never try to hurt the Lady Elaine!' he exploded. 'She is very dear to me.' For a moment Bernarr was certain the boy would draw his sword, and found himself anticipating the confrontation with pleasure. Then, Zakry seemed to come to himself and gestured behind him to where his friends stood. 'To all of us. I apologize for being insensitive to your lady's delicate nature. We should have anticipated what a shock the news would be.'

They all nodded and curtsyed and murmured their agreement.

Bernarr looked at them, his nostrils pinched with disapproval and his face white with rage. 'Because my wife has such regard for you, and because you meant well by coming here I will, of course, extend to you the hospitality of my house. But I warn you, at the slightest hint that you are upsetting her, I will order you to leave.' With that, Bernarr spun on his heel and followed the servants to his lady's quarters, to sit by her bed until she woke.

*   *   *

Indeed, it seemed to Bernarr that Zakry's estimation of Elaine's feelings for her father was correct. For, although she should have been in deep mourning, after recovering from her faint, she showed no signs of distress: rather, she spent all of her time with her old friends, laughing and gossiping and even dancing and singing. Bernarr didn't approve; it was unseemly. And yet, he could deny her nothing. Especially since he'd met her wretched father and could well understand her lack of concern. It must have been a horror being raised alone by such as he. Still, after several social galas Elaine organized and many forays into the city to shop, the local squires and rich merchants could barely hide their disapproval of her frivolous manner. He felt embarrassed. Yet he forgave her everything, accounting her actions to her youth and the influence of her callow friends.

He wanted to stay by her side every moment, but the duties he'd left behind had piled up over the months he'd been away and there was always work to be done. Often he was called away to the city, or away at nearby villages, conducting the business of the barony, and was gone for two or three days. The old castle overlooking the city was garrisoned, but it was otherwise empty, lacking even a pretence of occupation. Other than soldiers and his personal secretary and the city officials who visited, Bernarr was alone. On those occasions, he burned with jealousy and hated himself for it.

He knew her friends were leading her into unseemly behaviour. Elaine meant well, but she was so innocent that she truly saw no harm in their silly play that in this time of mourning bordered on the debauched. Not in Rillanon, perhaps, but certainly in Land's End.

He must do something! At the very least he must do something about Zakry. He was the instigator, the one who led them all astray. Get rid of him and the problem was all but solved.

Yes, something must be done, and soon.

*　　*　　*

The old man's pain did not lessen in his sleep, but the thin lips with their deep vertical grooves pulled back from yellow teeth. There was little strength left in his face, but for a moment an observer might have seen him as he had been in youth and anger, a cold pale rage the deadlier for coming from the mind as much as the heart.

But there was nobody to see; no one at all. Outside the door stood two members of the household guard. Hand-picked, they followed orders, and the orders were the same tonight as they had been every night since they had taken duty with the Baron: no matter what they heard or thought they heard from within the Baron's chamber after he retired for the night, they were never to enter unless called for by name by the Baron. Both men on duty were used to cries and moans and curses. Both men ignored the piteous weeping they heard at that moment.

Images cascaded, one on top of the next, and Bernarr gripped the sheets as a drowning man would a lifeline.

He was hunting, and Elaine's friends were with him. An arrow flew, killing a boar, and Bernarr turned in rage. The impudent whelp had robbed Bernarr of his kill!

Suddenly he was near the cliffs, the pounding surf on the rocks below, as he sat listening to Zakry shout, 'Sir! You will listen to me!'

But Bernarr could hear nothing over the pounding of the waves on the rocks, and while Zakry's lips moved, Bernarr could not make out the meaning of his words. Bernarr pulled up, waved his boar-spear in rage, and Zakry's horse shied, and suddenly Bernarr sat alone on his horse.

A ride, and suddenly he was back in the castle, his guests dismounting as a chirurgeon hurried forward, glad tidings on his lips. He was to be a father!

Then he was at Elaine's side, and she wept, her shoulders

shaking and he couldn't remember why. Was it the news of Zakry's disappearance? Or tears of joy?

Then he saw carriages as her friends from Rillanon left, eager to depart by ship before the winter storms prevented them.

Now the old man lay still, the only motion the rapid rise and fall of his chest, and the movement of his eyes behind the closed lids.

For a brief moment, he remembered peace. He remembered the quiet joy he felt in anticipating fatherhood. Elaine was quiet in her confinement, saying little to him or the maids who attended her. Occasionally a woman of the barony, a squire's wife or the wife of one of the more prominent merchants, would visit and she would brighten for a bit in the company of another woman while sipping tea or strolling through the gardens, but mostly she seemed sad in a way he didn't understand.

Then came the night Elaine went into labour. A storm had sprung up out of the sea: hills and walls of purple-black cloud piled along the western horizon, flickering with lightning but touched gold by the sun as it set behind them. The surge came before the storm, mountain-high waves that set fishermen dragging their craft higher and lashing them to trees and boulders, and to praying as the thrust of air came shrieking about their thatch. When the rain followed it came nearly level, blown before the monster winds.

Whips of rain lashed the manor too, and lightning forked the sky while thunder rattled the windows. Bernarr had bribed the midwife to stay at the manse the last two weeks and given the dreadful weather was glad he'd done so.

The storm blew in a traveller and his servants who begged shelter, which Bernarr granted gladly – hospitality brought luck, and at this moment he wanted his full share. The house was so still these days he welcomed the company and was delighted to discover that his guest was a scholar who cared far more for the books in his coach than for either his horses, his servants or himself.

'Lyman,' the old man said in his sleep, his lips barely speaking the name.

Bernarr could not see the man's face. He stood in shadows and no matter how hard Bernarr tried, the memory of the man's face eluded him. In his fever-dream, the old man remembered, he had shared wine with this man, he had seen him in daylight, yet at this moment, reliving this terrible night, he could not see the man's face in the shadow.

Then the scream came, and he could hear Lyman's voice, as if coming to him from a great distance, carried by the storm, 'You should go to her, my lord.'

Bernarr rushed from the room even as another cry rent the air, terror lending wings to his feet. Yet as he hurried, his feet refused to carry him. The hall was impossibly long and each step was a struggle. He felt as if his body was encased in armour, lead boots clasped around his feet, and terror rose up within as he fought to reach his chambers. Then he was at Elaine's door in moments, throwing it open—

The midwife stood there, her face at once showing joy and fear. The baby was coming, but Elaine was in distress.

'You have a son, my lady!' the midwife said a moment later. She handed the babe to one of the maids and that one rushed the child over to another who tended a bath.

In his dream Bernarr stood unable to move, and then he watched himself approach the bed, stand at its foot and stare in horror at Elaine. Bernarr saw himself look down at his pale, lovely wife, her face drenched in perspiration, her dark hair plastered to her head. Her night clothing was hitched up over her stomach, and everywhere below he could see blood.

Elaine's eyes sought his, and in them was a silent pleading, and suddenly there was a presence at his side.

'My lord,' said a quiet voice at his elbow.

Bernarr saw himself turn to stare at his guest. 'What are you doing here?' he asked Lyman.

'There may be something I can do.'

Then came a rush of images. Lyman raised his hands and the room plunged into darkness.

The midwife tried to hand him his son, but one look at the child and Bernarr shouted, 'Get rid of it! I never want to see it again.'

Suddenly a monk was in the room, a healing priest from the order of Dala, and then he was accompanied by the chirurgeon. Then he heard the monk's voice. 'I am sorry, my lord. She is moments from death, there is nothing I can do.'

Now he was outside her room, and Lyman was chanting. Bernarr again stared at the figure, but could see no face under the broad-brimmed hat.

At last he saw the face of his wife, lying in agony on her bed, her face white and her eyes filled with blood. 'Let me go!' she pleaded.

Bernarr woke with a gasp, his heart pounding and tears in his eyes, his head lifted painfully from his pillow. He fell back with a sigh and closed his burning eyes.

He'd had this dream before. Too often in fact. But the ending was new; he'd only dreamed that she spoke to him once before.

'I won't let you die,' he whispered to no one.

He turned his head toward the doorway to her room. The candles had burned down. Even though time moved slowly in her room, it did pass. Seventeen years had come and gone since that dreadful night. Each day Lyman had renewed the spell and every day he tried to find a spell that would save Elaine.

At first they had tried only white magic: seeking healers from across the land, even once, at great expense, sending to Great Kesh for one they'd heard could work miracles. Then they'd tried healing spells, none of which seemed to affect her in even the slightest way.

Each time they lowered the spell that preserved her he feared she would slip away, but each time she'd lived long enough for them to fail and then renew the spell.

Of late, they had turned to darker magic, a spell found in an ancient tome Lyman had secured from a trader from Kesh. There was something evil about that book, but Bernarr had exhausted all other options. He must try this terrible and bloody thing, or he would finally go mad.

Lyman assured him that soon they would succeed. They must succeed; or Elaine would be lost forever.

ELEVEN

Discovery

Lorrie awoke with a start.

There were the usual morning sounds; cockerels crowing, birds singing, but the smell was wrong; dusty emptiness around her, and under that too much smoke and too much dung and nothing green. And the floor beneath her was hard board, not the straw-stuffed tick she slept on.

Where—? she thought.

It crashed in on her, dazing, like a horse's kick in the gut: *I'm in Land's End. I'm here looking for Rip. Mother and Father are dead.*

It was late morning, by the look of the yellow light that filtered in through the shuttered window, a column full of dancing motes of dust. She was alone, alone enough to lie still for a moment with the tears leaking down her cheeks.

Mother! she thought. *I need you, Mother!*

But she would never see her mother again, and their last words had been a quarrel. Never again would she see her father coming in from the fields to smile and rumple her hair, or sit by the hearth on winter evenings and tell the old stories in his slow deep voice.

She felt like crying, but tears wouldn't come. Instead there was a dull, aching void. She sat, scrubbing at her face. *Rip is alive*, she scolded herself. She had to concentrate on that. *And I will find him!*

But when she concentrated, she sensed something else: that Rip was no longer in Land's End. She flung aside the cloth she'd been using for a blanket, jammed her shoes on her feet, then rose and went to the window.

She couldn't see anyone below and though there were windows in the surrounding warehouses she couldn't see anyone moving behind them. She'd just have to take the chance that they wouldn't see her either. She gave one glance at the rumpled cloth she'd meant to rewind onto the bolt and shook her head regretfully. There wasn't time to do that. Rip came first. She put one leg on the window-sill, turned and felt for the roof behind her with her free leg. The window was offset the shed roof below. She remembered Jimmy cautioning her to reach up with her left hand while using her right to steady herself on the wall, the swing to the left a little, and pull up. She determined to reverse the procedure and get to the shed roof. From there it was a short leap to the alley below.

'What the hell do you think you're doing!'

The man's shout seemed to come from directly behind her. Lorrie gasped and almost lost her grip. She slipped down and grabbed hard on the window-sill. For a long moment, she held motionless, her chin barely above the still, clutching the window, for her life in fact, because there was nothing below her but hard cobbles, twenty feet down. Glancing fearfully over her shoulder she saw no one. No one was looking out of one of the windows opposite either.

'What do ye mean?'

The voices came from the main street, just beyond where the alley below joined it. Right about where the main doors of the warehouse were.

'I mean those crates are due on the dock in less than an hour if the *Crab* isn't to lose the tide. Why aren't they on the wagons? What have you been doing all morning, standing there with a thumb up your arse?'

'I just got the order a few minutes ago! 'S not my fault!'

Her relief that the shout hadn't been directed at her caused Lorrie to drop a few inches. She was going to try to swing a few feet to her right and reach the tile roof. As she tried to swing a little to the left, she felt the pain; a sudden, violent burn that was colder than winter ice at the same time, and beneath it all the ugly slicing feeling of being cut.

She'd had accidents with tools and sharp branches before. Not like this. Something very sharp was digging deep into her leg. The hot trickle of her own blood down her leg made her shiver and she gasped at the increased pain even that small movement caused.

That made her want to scream and twist around to grab her leg at the same time; but either of those would mean that she would die.

And Rip will have nobody.

Her head swam a moment, but she fought down dizziness and panted through her mouth. *Don't let go!* she commanded herself. She glanced down and saw a seemingly innocuous shard of glass wedged in between the stones. Some glazier had been sloppy in his work and the long piece had fallen from a broken window to wedge hard between stones. Like a crystal dagger it had cut up into Lorrie's leg. She forced herself to take a deep breath and knew she would have to use every ounce of will and strength to regain the window.

Her hands firmed on the ledge, driving her fingers painfully into the splintery wood. But she couldn't stay like this: the fall from this height would be a lot more painful than what she was feeling now. Lorrie took a deep breath and hoisted herself up on the window frame. The shrill of agony as her wound was savaged further almost made her lose her grip, rendering her too shocked to even cry out. Once the surprise was over she kept herself from crying out by gritting her teeth and remembering Rip.

If she was caught she might be gaoled, and if she was gaoled she couldn't help him. *I can't let them catch me*, she thought. *I have to be strong.*

The argument in the street below continued unabated, growing louder, if anything. It was to be hoped it was loud enough to cover the sound of her panting and of her movements as she struggled back into the hidden room. But she needed to move fast, before the yelling attracted people to the windows around her. Lorrie pulled her wounded leg back as far as it would go, but when she hoisted herself up again found it wasn't quite far enough. She gave one sob of pain and frustration, then continued her progress, even as it tore her leg.

Now she was halfway into the room, hanging from the window at her waist. She breathed in and out through her teeth, fast and desperate, then gave one jerk that almost made her scream and she was free of the protruding glass. As quietly as she could Lorrie scrambled back into the room, sliding down onto the dusty floor, biting the base of her right thumb to keep the screams that forced their way up her throat muffled.

Once she got her breath back she sat up to check the damage.

The sight almost made her faint as the pain had not. A long, deep and jagged cut started just above her knee and ended at her upper thigh. Blood poured from the ripped flesh, already pooling on the floor; the only good thing about it was that it didn't jet and spurt. The leg moved when she jerked it in horror, so the tendon wasn't cut. The shard had dug straight into the centre of the muscle. But bleeding that bad could kill her in an hour. A country girl knew about cuts – and how much blood a pig had, which was about the same as a man's.

Do something! she shouted at herself.

With trembling hands she loosed her water bottle from her belt and poured some onto her leg. It burned like fire and she greyed out for a moment, dropping the bottle. She caught it up quickly, listening to see if someone had noticed the sound. Nothing happened and she looked down at her leg again.

When the blood had been washed away Lorrie was able to see that it needed stitching. She'd once watched her mother sew up Emmet, their man of all work, when his axe had slipped and had listened carefully to her instructions. But this looked a lot worse and she had nothing to use for a needle. And she didn't have her mother. Lorrie pressed her hand against her mouth, hard. She didn't have time to cry, she was bleeding, and badly.

Dragging herself over to the bolt of cloth she cut a clean length of it; then she pulled down her trousers and bandaged the leg as tightly as she could, strips around the leg holding a thick pad on the wound. If she couldn't stitch it up, then she could at least press it together. Maybe that would be enough. Then she pulled up the trousers and lay back down on her makeshift bed.

What am I going to do? she thought. She could feel Rip getting further and further away. But she couldn't even climb down from this place with the wound in her leg, even if no one was down there, let alone follow two men on horseback. *I shouldn't have sold Horace.*

But she'd been so certain that Land's End was their final destination. Why else would they steal her brother but to sell him to slavers? Yet he was being moved inland; the feeling was like an inner weathervane, shifting slowly and pointing the way. *Why?* she repeated to herself, over and over again.

She'd begun the internal shout in despair and ended it in anger. Why Rip, why her parents, why her, why now? Who were these people, what were they doing? And beyond all and above everything, and forever, why?

Lorrie closed her eyes. Blackness fell like a crashing wave.

It was just past dawn when Flora slipped into Jimmy's room; a quiet dawn, by Krondor standards.

'Where were you last night?' she demanded in a very loud whisper.

Jimmy, caught by surprise, yanked his pants up so hard he hurt himself. He glared at her over his shoulder, fighting an urge to clutch the painful parts.

'You . . .' His voice came out so high he coughed and started again. 'You're supposed to knock first, remember?'

'Tsk! You haven't got anything I haven't seen before,' she said scornfully.

Jimmy arched his brows. 'Does your aunt know that?' he said sweetly.

Flora's lips twitched down at the corners as she looked away and brushed her hair back, blushing. 'No. And maybe you were right. Maybe I should just keep it to myself.'

'I honestly think that would be for the best,' he said, not without sympathy. 'Best all round, I mean.'

She gave an unladylike snort. 'Yeah, I mustn't forget you're in there, too.' Then she looked at him through narrowed eyes. 'So, where were you last night?'

'I went out for a walk,' he said, frowning. 'Just taking in the town and I felt I needed the exercise.'

Flora pressed her lips together anxiously and moved over to him, putting a hand on his arm. 'You mustn't do anything wrong while you're staying here,' she whispered. 'Please, Jimmy. It's important.'

'I didn't do anything wrong,' he protested.

'Well,' she waved her hands in exasperation. 'Don't!'

'What, as in, never again? I can't promise that, Flora. I'm a Mocker, not a priest.'

'At least not while you're here,' she said, her eyes pleading. 'If you do something wrong it will reflect on me and on them, and the disgrace would be dreadful.'

'By "anything wrong" I suspect you mean more than simply, "don't steal",' he said. 'I bet you mean don't go to taverns, or get drunk, or get into brawls, or gamble . . .' She shook her head, her eyes wide.

'Or . . .' He stroked a finger gently down her cheek.

Flora reared back as if she'd never taunted a sailor in her life. 'Especially not that!' she said.

Jimmy stared at her. *It wasn't that long ago* we *were doing that. Now look at her!* It hadn't taken any time at all for Flora to become officiously respectable. He put his hands on his hips and laughed at her.

She shushed him, glancing at the closed door of his room.

'Flora,' he said, shaking his head, 'I can't imagine how you're going to survive this degree of self-restraint.' Though of course ample meals, comfort, and no worries about the future would help mightily. 'But if it's what you want, then that's what you should have; I was worried about you when all this started, you'll remember.'

She still looked anxious, so he took pity on her. Placing a hand on his heart he said: 'I have no intention of disgracing you, or your relatives.'

With quiet determination she asked, 'Then, please, tell me what you did last night.'

Jimmy gave a deep sigh and hung his head. 'All right. If you must know I saved a girl.'

Flora made a strangled sound and when he looked at her saw an almost comical expression of surprise on her face. 'Who? And from what?'

'Really!' he said. 'She was a country girl disguised as a boy and she'd fallen in with some very corrupt thief-takers. Y'remember Gerem Benton?'

She nodded. 'Gerem the Snake? Confidence grifter used to work the dodge on farmers looking to get rich quick with the Pigeon Drop and the Fake Diamond cons? Yeah, what about him? He's dead, isn't he?'

'He's alive and running a gang of thief-takers here. Looks like he's set himself up with the local constables; at least that's what it looks to me. He almost had this girl but I got her away. He didn't know she was a girl, else he might have tried harder to hang on to her.' Jimmy shook his head. 'Y'know, this town would be a lot better off if they had an Upright Man of their own,' he added wisely.

'A country girl disguised as a boy?' Flora said, wrinkling her nose dubiously. 'Why was she in disguise?'

Jimmy thought about it. 'She didn't say. But she definitely was honest; she didn't want to use some old cloth for a blanket in case she damaged it.'

Flora nodded, apparently seeing the truth in that observation. 'So where is she now?'

'I found her a place to sleep in an abandoned room in a warehouse,' he said. 'If she keeps her wits about her she should be fine.'

'Take me to her,' Flora said suddenly.

'What? Why?'

'Maybe I can help her,' she said.

'Well, aren't you Lady Bountiful? Don't you believe me?' Hurt, he let a little of his resentment show in the tone.

'Maybe if someone had offered to help me when I was first orphaned,' Flora said with some heat, 'I wouldn't have had to become a whore!'

'Oh,' Jimmy said. *Ouch.* 'All right. But she might not still be there,' he warned.

'Well, at least we'll have tried.' Flora gave him a hard look. 'I'll go and get my shawl and tell Aunt Cleora we're off shopping, so remind me to buy something on the way back.' As she moved through the door, she added, 'We should pitch in with chores when we get back, like respectable youngsters. I want to make a good impression before Aunt Cleora takes me to meet Grandfather.'

Jimmy looked at the closed door. *Chores,* he thought. *Wonderful.*

Exile was looking worse all the time.

Flora pulled the back of her skirt up through her legs and tucked it into her waistband, forming a baggy equivalent of trousers which would allow her to climb.

Looks like nothing is going to discourage her, Jimmy thought, casually glancing to either side. There were people down at the end of the alley who could see them if they looked . . . but they probably wouldn't. And even if they did, they probably wouldn't care. The men – the ones loading crates of pottery on a mule-drawn wagon – were busy, and Jimmy's experience with teamsters was that they didn't go looking for trouble, unless it was after work and they'd been drinking.

Jimmy turned his attention to the climb. At least the bright light of morning showed the handholds well and they started to climb the low building beneath the window of the abandoned room in a workmanlike fashion. Flora had insisted on bringing along a bag of food she tied up in her skirt, and a small wine-skin which Jimmy had tied to his belt. *If anyone stops us I guess I could say we're here to wash the windows,* Jimmy thought as Flora moved up.

Then Flora said, in a hoarse whisper, 'Jimmy! There's blood!'

Flora looked down and showed Jimmy her hand, the palm of which was now smeared with a sticky brownish stain; the blood was nearly dried, so it had been there for a while. Jimmy took out his belt-knife and transferred it to his teeth; there were a few situations in which that was useful, and hostile entry into a room was one. He motioned for Flora to move to the side so he could pass.

Maintaining careful track of his tongue – he kept his knife sharp – he crouched below the window, then threw himself in with a roll, dropping the blade and catching the hilt as eyes and knife-point probed all around.

'Shit,' he said calmly, sheathing the knife, turning and extending a hand. 'She's hurt. Come on.'

Flora pulled herself up to the window and gasped at the sight of the blood on the floor – she knew almost as well as he did what constituted a serious wound – and when she saw Lorrie's pale form lying amid the bloodstained cloth she put her hand over her mouth and plastered herself against the wall.

'Banath protect us,' she whispered. 'She's been murdered!'

Jimmy went to one knee beside Lorrie's pallet.

'No, she's breathing,' he said in relief. But there was still a lot of blood around. 'Lorrie,' he called quietly. He touched her shoulder. 'Lorrie,' he whispered.

The girl woke with a start and gasped as though drawing breath to scream. Jimmy hastily put his hand over her mouth. 'It's Jimmy,' he said. 'It's all right. I've brought some food.'

'*We've* brought you some food,' Flora said, elbowing him aside. From her tone she had no intention of forgetting how much he'd protested when she'd asked him to buy the bread, cheese and wine they'd brought.

'What happened?' Jimmy asked. 'Who did this?'

Astonishingly, she smiled: 'Me,' she said. Even then, the resemblance to the Princess gave him a jolt. 'I was climbing out of the window and somebody yelled.' She pulled herself up on her elbows and looked at him groggily. 'I was surprised and I slipped.

My leg got caught on something.' She lay back down again. 'I put a bandage on it, but it hurts.'

I'll bet it does, he thought, looking at the tight sodden bandages. *Gods but she's clumsy!* That brought a stab of guilt: *Well, she's not a Mocker. Just a farm-girl.*

'There's a lot of blood,' Flora said. 'You'd better let me take a look.'

Lorrie blinked at her, then turned to Jimmy.

'This is my friend Flora,' he said. 'She's all right.'

Lorrie nodded and struggled to sit upright, untying the string at her waist, then looked at Jimmy. 'It's on my leg,' she said.

Jimmy nodded. 'Do you need help?'

The girl stared at him, dumbfounded.

'Jimmy,' Flora said between her teeth, 'turn around.'

'Oh!' he said and did so. *As if I care*, he thought. He heard Flora suck in her breath. 'What?'

'It's bad,' she said. 'A really deep, nasty cut. I need you to go and get some things.'

'Now wait a minute,' he said, starting to turn around. The two girls immediately made such a fuss he stopped and kept his back to them. 'What do you need?' he asked, his tone surly.

'Some powdered woundwort, some powdered yarrow and yarrow leaf tea, tincture of lady's mantle, some willow bark tea, and –' he could tell she hesitated, '– some poppy juice. And a fine needle and thread. Catgut, if you can get it. Waxed linen, if you can't.'

'What,' he said after a moment, 'nothing else? No dancing girls, no elephants, no . . .'

'No poppy juice,' Lorrie murmured. 'I have to find my brother.'

'You're not going anywhere with that wound on your leg,' Flora said. 'Not today. Go!' she snapped at Jimmy.

He went, considerably annoyed. He'd already bought this Lorrie wine and bread, now he had to buy out an apothecary for her? What else was he going to be expected to do? Poppy juice! Did Flora know what poppy juice cost? Although Lorrie had said she didn't want any. He thought about that as he walked along. No, better get it. With all that blood she must be hurting badly. Jimmy sighed. Why did good deeds always turn out to be so expensive?

When he returned Lorrie was asleep again and Flora was looking thoughtful; she glanced up as Jimmy swung easily through the window.

'Thank you,' she said, taking the medicines. Then after a pause: 'Thank you a lot, Jimmy. Nobody's ever been as kind to me.'

'Nothing,' he said gruffly, shrugging.

Princess Anita, what have you done to me? he asked himself, feeling that it was only half a joke. *I was never one to stint help to a friend, but this is ridiculous! Flora doesn't need help, she's landed in the honey pot, and I barely know this bumpkin! Even if she does look like you – like you would if you'd been born a bumpkin, that is.*

He noticed that Flora had made an effort to mop up the blood: there was a pile of soaked cloth in one corner, and the bandages on Lorrie's leg were fresh. The smell was still there, faint against the musty mildew and dust of the warehouse, but at least now they didn't have to worry about someone noticing it dripping through the floorboards. She'd also gone for water, which was essential to someone who'd lost a lot of blood.

Flora laid out the medicines and the needle and thread. Lorrie woke, though she seemed muddle-headed; Flora had probably given her the whole bottle of wine for the pain.

'Help me turn her over,' she said.

He did, wincing as she uncovered the wound and went to work; he supposed modesty was less important when all that was bared was a section of thigh that looked as if it were on the way to a butcher's shop. But he looked aside anyway.

In a way it was less grit-your-teeth to have a wound of your own sewn up than to watch it done to someone else, unless you could just think of them as meat.

Lorrie bore it well, not having to be held, just shivering and panting, and his initial good opinion of the girl went up several notches. Besides, he reflected, it would go on hurting her a lot longer than it would him.

Flora's doing a good job of work there, too, he thought: she wasn't quite digit-agile enough to make a pickpocket, but she had neat hands for needle and thread.

'We have something we have to ask you, Jimmy,' Flora said, not looking up, as she tied off the last running stitch and cut the catgut with a small sharp knife.

'No,' he said to the wall. 'I was thinking on my way back that you'd ask me for something else and the answer is no.'

Lorrie opened her eyes and looked at him.

'No!' he said, looking away. Lorrie's sad eyes were far too much like the Princess's for comfort. It was hard to believe that he might be susceptible to a girl's eyes, but he was very much afraid that he was.

'My brother has been kidnapped,' Lorrie said, her voice husky. 'He's only six years old.' She took a deep breath, obviously trying to stop herself from crying. 'They killed my parents and burned down our house and barn. There isn't much left, but the land has value, and there's still some stock and a wagon. I'll give it all to you if you'll help him.'

'Do I look like the Constable to you?' Jimmy asked. 'And isn't this something the constable should be doing?' He gave Flora a look that said, *Yes, this is something the Constable should do and you know it.*

'No one would believe me,' Lorrie wailed. Flora shushed her. 'I'm sorry,' she whispered. 'All our neighbours thought my parents were killed by wild dogs or something and that my baby brother was dragged off by them. But he wasn't. There were two men. One big, the other skinny. They rode off on horseback and came here. Now they've moved on, going inland, and they've taken Rip with them. I can feel them getting further and further away.' She broke down, weeping as though her heart would break. 'Please find him. Please.'

Jimmy looked at the two young women with astonishment. 'How can I do that?' he asked. *Even if I wanted to, which I don't.* 'I don't know what these men look like, or where they've gone, I don't know your brother, I don't have a horse, and even if I did, I can't ride. You're asking the impossible!'

'Be quiet!' Flora hissed. 'Go and think about it while I clean Lorrie up.'

Thus dismissed, Jimmy sat looking out of the window. *Why am I suddenly a villain?* he thought, reminding himself not to pout. *I already rescued her! Twice!*

After what seemed like a very long time – and one or two small, smothered sounds of pain, somehow more disturbing than the many he'd heard before – Flora said, 'You can turn around now.'

'Look,' he said, noting how pale both girls were, 'I'm not trying to be mean-spirited. It's just that . . .'

'That you'd rather not get involved any further,' Flora finished for him.

He raised a protesting finger. 'I didn't say that.'

'You don't have to,' she said scornfully. 'I know you, Jimmy. But . . .'

Flora stopped and sighed, letting her shoulders droop. 'Helping Lorrie's not something you would have done in Krondor. I can't help but be disappointed; I thought you'd changed.'

Jimmy raised one eyebrow and tightened a corner of his mouth. He most certainly would have helped Lorrie, even in Krondor. But that wasn't something that Flora would know; she'd never met the Princess and knew nothing about his feelings for her. And maybe it wasn't something he wanted her to know. He glanced at Lorrie, who really did look very much like the Princess Anita, even to the haunted look the Princess had worn when thinking about her imprisoned father.

Lorrie's eyes shifted and met his. As he watched one crystal tear rolled silently down her cheek. Jimmy heaved a sigh. He was undone: there was no way he could walk away from those eyes and not feel less of a man.

'All right, I'll try,' he said. He rose, every move speaking his reluctance. 'I'm not making any promises, and I don't know when I'll be back.' To Flora he said, 'You'll have to come up with a story to tell your aunt about why I'm gone.'

'I'll tell her you're travelling for a bit . . .'

'Tell her it's an employment opportunity. Apprentice to a trader or something. Be vague; I didn't tell you details – I'll have a completely cooked-up story when I get back.'

Flora nodded. 'I think they're moving northeast along the coast road,' Lorrie said. 'Try going that way first. And be careful. Those two killed my mother and father and Emmet handily enough and none of them were soft or weak. You watch yourself.'

'Thanks,' he said, 'I will.' He looked at Flora who was rolling up a bandage looking proud enough to pop. 'Give my regards to your aunt, in case this takes a while.'

She was up and giving him a fierce hug before he could say anything else. Then she released him and gave him a little push.

'Go on then, and be careful.' She crossed her arms beneath her breasts, looking grave. 'You know where to find me.'

Jimmy smiled at her and shook his head. She was changing so fast he hardly knew her. Then he turned away and climbed out of the window. First thing he should do, probably, would be to get a horse.

* * *

'No,' the innkeeper said indifferently. 'Left just after dawn, they did. Same as always.'

Jarvis Coe dropped a couple of coins on the bar. *Surprising,* he thought. *From the way they were talking yesterday, I'd be expecting them to drink a long breakfast.* Low-priced thugs rarely had much discipline or sense of purpose. If they did, they'd be in another line of work . . . or charging higher prices, at least.

The innkeeper ignored the copper, polishing around it. His eyebrow twitched when silver rang beside the duller metal.

'Which road did they take?'

The coins vanished into the innkeeper's big hand. 'North on the coast road, same as always.'

You couldn't rent a horse at a stable, but you could buy one with the understanding that eventually the stable-owner would buy it back. Coe walked briskly through the North Gate, cursing the delay; it was a mildly warm late-season day, perfect for travelling – for his quarry, too, worse luck. Even then his trained eye caught details – the casual way the guards leaned on their spears and halberds, offset by the relaxed alertness of their captain's eyes; and the state of their gear, which was worn but serviceable. From everything he heard, the lord of Land's End had taken an unusual position on the care of his barony's main town; he had garrisoned the bulk of his army – some two hundred men-at-arms – in the old fortification on the edge of the city, and had kept only a small honour-guard in his household estates many miles away. But he had no heir, so perhaps he felt the safety of the citizens outweighed his own.

Administration seemed to be left to the one royal magistrate in the district, the leaders of the town's guilds and the harbour-master. It was probably a fair enough system as long as war didn't break out, or the Duke call up a levy. But the local garrison had come to neglect the countryside: there was not even so much as a regular patrol between the old castle and the Baron's country estates up the coast.

That had left the countryside in disarray. It didn't take much by way of neglect for bandits to move in. Or for a dozen local bullies to decide they'd rather rape women and steal sheep than work. And the local constable had neither the time nor resources to really enforce the law, short of a baronial order or a writ from the magistrate.

Coe reflected on this odd state of affairs as he walked through the gate. Land's End was still more of a large town than a small city, comprised of the usual gaggle of trades and workshops impractical or illegal inside a walled city, so no true foulbourg had been allowed to spring up outside the walls, but a thriving open market had been established beyond the clearing under the wall. He headed for the unmistakable smell of a dealer in horses, and slowed as he drew near.

'Master Jimmy!' he said. 'This is a pleasant surprise. How's your young foster-sister?'

If Jimmy was equally surprised he made a masterful job of hiding it. In fact, his dark eyes were level, coolly considering, beyond his years, even if he had grown up rough and quickly, which Coe would wager he had.

Looking him up and down, Coe revisited a judgment he had formed aboard ship about Jimmy: *barely a boy, well short of fifteen summers. But a very unusual and gifted boy. Inside that egg of boyhood is a man tapping at the shell, and a dangerous one, too, from all appearances.* Curly brown hair – badly cut, likely with a knife – contrasted with carefully respectable but not showy tunic and trousers; Coe suspected that the boots hadn't acquired their wear on Jimmy's feet.

But here was the thing, Coe thought, *he carries himself without a trace of adolescent awkwardness. He moves like an acrobat, as fluid as a cat sensing everything around him; he has the trick of avoiding people without needing to watch for them, deftly slipping through crowds without jostling them.* Coe smiled. Perhaps that wasn't entirely true, but should Jimmy bump into someone on the street, Coe suspected it would be intentional.

The sword at his side was enough to catch the interest: it was a tall man's blade, far too richly hilted for the part the boy was playing, of someone on the ragged edge of gentility. But Coe suspected that the blade was of equal quality to the guard and scabbard, which would make it worth the rent of a dozen farms. And more to the point of how it had come into his hands, the boy could use it with enough skill to make challenging him a very hazardous choice. *Even now, a wise man will be careful. This one is quick as a ferret, I'll wager, and would give as little warning when he went for the throat.*

'Flora? She's making Aunt Cleora very happy,' Jimmy said. 'Nice to see you again, sir.'

'And you, my lad. Are you looking for work as a stablehand?'

'Gods no, sir!' Jimmy grinned. 'I know nothing of horses. But I've got to take the coast road a way and I guess I'll need one.'

'In which direction?' Coe asked.

Jimmy gave him a suspicious look. 'Uh, north, east.' He shrugged.

'The very way that I'm going,' Jarvis said cheerfully. 'Why don't we ride together?'

Without waiting for an answer, he called to the stable-master to saddle another mount and before Jimmy could object, tossed a gold coin to the man, saying, 'We'll wish to sell them back when we return.'

Catching the coin, the stable-master said, 'If you bring them back sound, I'll buy them.'

Turning to look at Jimmy, Coe smiled and said, 'There. It's done.'

If the boy resented such highhandedness, he hid it well. All he said was: 'I'm not experienced.'

'Make it a gentle one,' Coe called to the stable-master.

'I don't want to hold you up, sir,' Jimmy said.

'I'm sure you won't, Jimmy. I'm not planning to gallop – like a man, a horse can walk further than it can run. Do you have any supplies?' *Or anything more than the clothes on your back, that absurdly grand blade, and a suspiciously large amount of hard cash?*

'Uh, no. I thought I'd arrange a horse, then buy what I need in the market,' Jimmy said. 'As I said, sir, I don't want to delay you.'

'Not at all, not at all,' Jarvis said, giving the lad a hearty slap on the back. 'And as I said, I'm in no mad rush. Where are you bound?'

There was something about the boy that didn't ring true. He couldn't put his finger on it. But he and his so-called foster-sister, young as they were, struck him as rather more experienced and less benign than they were trying to seem. He was intrigued and wanted to know more. *I always do. It's one thing that makes me good at my job,* he thought with flat realism. And it was something of a bonus that he could indulge his curiosity without going out of his way. This time. On other occasions, that curiosity had led him into situations in which someone ended up dead.

Still smarting from that hearty slap, Jimmy grinned falsely. He would probably be wise to get away from this fellow. Generally he didn't trust back-slappers, thinking them bullies who didn't quite dare to show it. But bullies took things from you and yet Coe was falling over himself in his eagerness to be helpful. It was disconcerting.

'I'm just catching up with some friends,' he said. 'They left at dawn.'

'Ah,' said Coe, his interest visibly sharpening. 'I wonder if I know them. I, too, am late in following a pair of fellows I must speak with. We'll share my supplies, my young friend.' The stable-man brought the two horses over, saddled and ready. 'Mount up.'

I'm in his debt now, Jimmy thought. *And look to be more so. I hate debts, but it's stupid to turn down help when you need it. What do I know of chasing men through field and wood?* Alleys and sewers and even Radburn's dungeons he could manage. In the countryside he'd be as lost as ... well, as Lorrie had been here in town, where even a complete stranger like Jimmy could land on his feet.

Jimmy considered the situation. *I could simply run away, but that would attract attention. Besides, you're never out of options until you're dead,* he thought. He could take the chance of trav-elling with Coe and see what happened. If things looked dicey he could stop somewhere with people in sight and say they were his friends. Or, if worst came to worst, he could make for the woods and hide. He was good at hiding and climbing.

How much harder could it be to hide in a thicket of trees than in an alley?

He was suspicious of the man, but then again, suspicion was his response to every new face. Coe had helped him, with the wristband that had stopped Jimmy's seasickness, and had given them good advice on where to stay in Land's End. One of the things he'd learned in last night's ramble was that The Cockerel was indeed as bad a place as any in Krondor. He and Flora hadn't needed the warning, but Jarvis Coe wouldn't know that. In fact, the man had nothing to gain from either act, because he had no reason to expect to ever see Jimmy again.

And I'm curious about him. Curiosity is one of the very things that makes me a good thief and, damnit, it'll make this chase after Lorrie's little brother less boring. After all, he'd been wondering what he would do if he did catch up with the kidnappers.

Well, he'd told himself, *I'm a thief. I'll steal the boy back.*

But that was bravado and he knew it. One of the things Jimmy was learning of late was that he really couldn't do everything he imagined, just most of it. Facing one hardened man with sword in hand was worrisome. Facing two, well, that was just plain stupid. If he could enlist Coe then maybe he might actually stand a chance of saving Rip.

There was something about the man that didn't quite ring true, but Jimmy's instincts told him that Coe was all right. Secretive, perhaps, even hiding his true reasons as much as Jimmy was, but not bad. Living as he had in Krondor, bad was something the young thief could sense without thinking and nine times out of ten, he'd be right. His bump of trouble just didn't react to Coe.

What really worried him was who Jarvis Coe was trying to catch up with. For a brief instant Jimmy considered that he might be a colleague of the two who had kidnapped Rip. Then he shoved the thought aside: had that been the case, Jimmy's bump of trouble would be positively throbbing.

The stableman cleared his throat; Coe was looking at him with a cocked eyebrow.

'Sorry,' he said. 'Thinking.'

One of the stable's lackeys linked his hands. Jimmy looked at them, then at the tall horse, and put his foot into them. Not that he needed a step up, but he'd observed that ordinary folk got a little disturbed when you exhibited excessive agility.

The stablehand was thick-armed. He also surprised Jimmy by the strength he employed giving him a leg up, almost tossing him right over the horse. Had the thief been less agile that's exactly what would have happened. He glared at the man, who shrugged and grinned, almost looking disappointed.

Jarvis shook his head. 'They're all like that,' he said to Jimmy. 'Everyone thinks it's fun to play practical jokes on a beginner.'

The fellow shrugged again, and showed strong yellow teeth

much like those of his charges. 'Life's dull,' he said, 'y'have to make your entertainment when ye can.'

Jimmy glared at him. 'Do you like gratuities?' he asked, pulling a silver piece out of his belt.

'Huh?' asked the lackey.

Switching to street vernacular, Jimmy said, 'You like tips?'

The man's grin broadened. 'Certs!'

Putting the coin away, Jimmy said, 'Then find your entertainment somewhere else.'

Coe laughed. 'Let's go,' he said and turned his horse.

But Jimmy could tell, even before they left the yard, that his horse had a sense of humour much like the lackey.

Suddenly, he thought, *everyone I meet is a character. Gods, when will I be able to go home to Krondor?* By the time they passed the last booth at the edge of the market, his arse was already sore. *It can't be soon enough*, he thought.

They still weren't out of traffic – everything from a herd of sheep being driven in toward town, to wagons heading out, and more pedestrians trudging along beside the dusty white ribbon of highway that snaked off to the north; a faint hint of the ocean came on the breeze, and the occasional trees showed the direction of the prevailing wind by the way they leaned to the right. Dust got into his teeth, kicked up by feet and hooves and wheels. The deep ruts showed that mud was probably worse.

Jimmy coughed and shifted uncomfortably and the horse decided that meant it should take off at a trot, and nothing he could do or say thereafter would change its mind. Coe came up beside him, obviously trying not to laugh. 'Sit back,' he said. 'Don't yank on the reins, as that will only irritate it. Tug once as you sit back, then release the pressure. If it doesn't stop, tug again.'

Jimmy sat back, shifting his weight to the rear of the saddle.

The horse hesitated, as if uncertain what its rider wanted, but after a couple of steps, it slowed, then stopped.

Coe's horse made as if to nip it and Coe handily yanked the beast's head away.

Jimmy gasped out: 'Thank you.' *It's stupid to be afraid of falling off this thing!* he thought, rubbing at a rib where the hilt of his sword had thumped him painfully. *I've jumped down from far higher roofs!*

'You really don't know how to ride, do you?' Coe said.

The young thief shook his head. 'I've never left Krondor before,' he said. 'And there I had no need of riding.' He made a wry face. 'I've seen it done often enough and it looked so easy. I was sure I could manage it.'

Coe gave a cough that sounded suspiciously like a muffled laugh. 'Well, for starters, you see that loop in front of your left knee? You can slide the scabbard of your sword through it. Until you've ridden a little more, having it loose at your side can be dangerous.'

Jimmy slid Prince Arutha's gift from his belt-sling and through the loop and the sheath settled firmly.

'Riding's more like dancing than just sitting down on the animal. You're quick and strong, though, it shouldn't be too hard. Just remember that the horse's back is going up and down whenever it's moving. The faster it goes, the faster the movement. That's why you grip – so you don't bounce up and down even harder. Use your knees like springs – as if you were jumping down from a height . . .'

All right, I'll try that, Jimmy thought: he was reminded of the way Prince Arutha had shown him the sword. He was immediately aware that the mare was more relaxed. *Which makes one of us,* he thought bitterly.

'Now remember that the horse can feel what you want it to do. If you squeeze tighter with your thighs and lean forward, it knows you want to go faster. If you lean back, it knows you want to stop. Try turning it by pressing one knee, touching the rein to the same side of its neck, and leaning a little forward and in the way you want to go – just a little, more a matter of shifting your balance than moving – you only pull on the bit when you need to shout. Right, that's good. Now –'

'This is pretty tiring,' Jimmy said after a few minutes.

'That's probably because you're too tense,' Coe said. 'And you're using muscles you haven't used before. Don't worry, it gets easier with experience.'

'I hope we don't have far to go,' Jimmy muttered.

Coe did laugh at that. 'Look at the bright side; you'll cover more ground on horseback.'

'I just won't be able to walk at the end of it.'

'You're young and fit, Jimmy; it'll pass quickly.' Coe moved a little ahead and said nothing else for a time, leaving Jimmy to sort himself out. After he and the horse had come to an understanding Jimmy rode forward until he was by the older man's side.

Jimmy felt discomfort in his legs, but nothing compared to the discomfort he felt about Coe and his relationship to the men they were following. Acting casual, he asked, 'These men you're looking for, they're friends of yours?'

Coe shook his head. 'No. I just think they might have some information I need.' He turned to look at Jimmy. 'And you?'

The young Mocker distinctly remembered telling him that he was going to meet some friends. Evidently he hadn't been believed. *I was going to have to tell him the truth sooner or later. Might as well tell him now.* 'Truth is,' he said cautiously, 'I've never even seen them.'

'Correspondents are you?' Coe asked, grinning.

Jimmy didn't even smile. Instead, he shook his head. 'No, sir. It's like this: Flora and I met this girl, a farm-girl just come into the city looking for her brother. She's hurt and can't go anywhere and she says these men took her brother from her family's steading. She asked me to go get him back.'

'Just like that?' Coe asked. He looked genuinely astonished. 'It's very generous of you, Master Jimmy, but how were you planning to persuade them to give the boy up?'

'First I needed a horse,' the young thief replied, 'so I was concentrating on that problem when you appeared. And the horse problem got resolved so quickly, well . . .' Jimmy hesitated. 'Truth is, I hadn't actually planned that far ahead.'

Coe chuckled. 'Well, isn't this something?' He shook his head, then said, 'We seem to be following the same two men. They are very, very dangerous.'

Jimmy tried to sound confident. 'I've had dealings with dangerous men before.'

Coe looked at Jimmy and there was no humour in his expression. 'This is no lark, boy. So if you've any notions of doing heroic deeds with no one getting hurt I suggest you turn that beast around right now and hie yourself back to Land's End. Because that's not the way things will happen. These two have information I need, and they will probably be disinclined to give it freely. I expect blood will flow before we're through. And since I don't want you disturbing my plans I must insist that I be in charge. Because I do have a plan and I'm going to assume I'm also more experienced in this sort of thing. Follow my instructions, and we'll try very hard to ensure that the blood which flows isn't ours. Are we agreed?'

Jimmy sat silently, then he laughed. 'I can't begin to tell you how relieved I am to be with someone who has a plan. Because I was talked into this much against my better judgment and have no idea of what I'm doing.' He let out a theatrical sigh of relief. 'So what are we going to do?'

If the older man was taken aback by Jimmy's practical enthusiasm he hid it behind an unmistakable expression of pure doubt. Then he sighed and picked up the pace.

'First,' he said, 'we must find them.'

TWELVE

Escape

Two men crested the rise.

They rode into sight as they reached the summit of the next hill. Jimmy pointed them out, then turned to see Coe's reaction. His companion wore a startled, unhappy expression, as though someone had just dumped something cold and slimy down between his collar and his skin.

Jimmy frowned, forgetting the areas he felt like rubbing at the moment. Which were many. 'What's wrong?'

Jarvis rubbed a spot on his chest, then grabbed something beneath the cloth of his shirt and pulled it away from his body. They'd been riding since mid-morning, about five hours or so as well as Jimmy could judge; he didn't realize how used he was to the shadows of the city telling him what time it was. They hadn't stopped to rest the horses either, and the animals appeared to Jimmy's untrained eye to be no less fatigued than his legs and backside were. Moreover, Jarvis Coe hadn't proven talkative along the way, and Jimmy was still a little vague on what it was they were going to accomplish once they got wherever they were going. He returned his attention to Coe, who still stared at the two men on the next rise.

'Master Coe?' Jimmy prompted.

The man's eyes moved and he stared at Jimmy's face, but it was a moment before they seemed to actually see him. 'There's a wicked feeling about this place,' he said.

Jimmy looked around: there was a copse of trees to the right, fields to the left and up ahead, a slight rise in the land with a jut of rock around which the road wound and which now hid their quarry. A peasant was working in the field, taking something out of a sack and throwing it on the lumpy ploughed land. He shook his head. 'Seems ordinary enough to me.'

Coe looked at him sideways, still clutching whatever it was he wore beneath his shirt. Then he shrugged. 'Perhaps I'm mistaken. Just a feeling after all.' He gave his head a hard shake and blinked his eyes. 'Was there something you wanted?'

All right, Jimmy thought. He'd had 'feelings' of his own a time or two. *Time to get careful. Maybe my bump of trouble doesn't work outside the city, and Jarvis Coe's does.* 'I saw two men riding up ahead,' he said aloud.

'Then let's try to catch up to them.' Coe trotted ahead. When Jimmy caught up to him the older man looked over at him. 'Do you have a weapon besides the sword?' he asked.

'My knife,' Jimmy said, his voice implying a shrug he couldn't manage at a trot.

'Lag behind me as I catch them up. I'll tell them I need directions to Land's End. When they tell me it's behind us I'll berate you for getting the innkeeper's directions wrong.'

Jimmy grimaced and Coe said, 'What's wrong?'

'It's a little hard to miss Land's End from the road if you think about it.'

Coe tried not to laugh. 'I was never very good at subterfuge on my feet. What do you suggest?'

'Just ask if they mind if we travel along, in case of highwaymen. That should distract them, even if they say "no".'

'Very well. We ride up together. I'll hale them and start talking while you look for the boy, if you can get close enough, grab him and run. I'll take care of the rest. Understood?'

'Yes,' the young Mocker said. It seemed a reasonable enough plan. 'If it's them they must have been dragging their heels for us to catch up to them when they left so long before us.'

Coe didn't answer, but then he didn't need to: Jimmy was self-evidently correct. When they made the turn around the low hill they found the two men, their horses at a standstill, apparently having an argument. The smaller man had a bulky sack tied onto his horse behind the saddle, but there was no sign of a child. The two men looked back at them and their horses began to prance nervously.

'Excuse me, sirs,' Jarvis called out. 'Could you spare a moment, please?'

The two men looked at one another and shortened their reins; then, before Jimmy could catch up to Coe, they set heels hard to their horses' sides and took off down the road as though pursued by demons.

'Well that certainly looks guilty,' Jimmy muttered.

Coe didn't hear him; he'd whipped his horse after the two men as soon as they'd started off. It was a chase they had no hope of winning, for their horses were hardly as fresh as the kidnappers'. They'd been riding steady, while the two men had apparently dawdled along with many a rest, for Jarvis and Jimmy to have overtaken them so soon.

Still, we have to try, and we might get lucky.

Jimmy clapped his heels into the horse's sides. It took off after the other man's mount: horses were obviously gang-minded, Jimmy decided. He could feel the power of the gait, the thunder of hooves and the rushing speed, faster than anything he'd experienced before – and the hammering of the saddle against his abused hams. Jimmy flapped his elbows like a chicken, but he had almost supernatural balance, and managed to get into the rhythm of the horse's gait without difficulty. He had the odd notion that he had no idea what to do if the horse decided to stop suddenly; Jarvis hadn't mentioned how to ride at a gallop and he genuinely had no idea of what to do to slow the animal. The saddle was slamming him hard in the arse and his teeth were rattling. He put his heels down, as Coe had reminded him several times during the day, and stood up in the stirrups. Suddenly, his teeth stopped rattling and his head stopped bouncing enough to have a clear view ahead. *Ah ha!* he said silently, *that's how you do it!* He let his knees flex and his legs and hips rolled with the horse's gait, while his upper body remained relatively level with the road.

For a giddy moment, Jimmy thought, *this riding business isn't so bad if you keep your wits about you.* Then the horse decided it was tired of running, and it was only Jimmy's uncanny reflexes and superior sense of balance that kept him from launching from the horse's back, landing on the hardpan road with painful consequences. As it was, he ended up in front of the saddle, hugging the animal's neck. The horse seemed irritated by the unexpected display of affection and with a snort began to trot, returning Jimmy to the teeth-rattling again.

Jimmy pushed himself back into the saddle, and started his rocking motion for a trot. He was about to try another gallop, when the horse crested a rise.

Beyond the next hill was a large, fortified manor house – practically a castle – with a moat around it; it lay among rather neglected-looking gardens and there was a low wall around those with a wrought-iron gate at the end of a lane that gave off from the main road. The two men headed for it like lost chicks to a mother hen.

Jimmy pulled up suddenly, or perhaps his horse did. He could feel a wrongness, almost exactly as if something very dead and very cold had drawn a hand down his spine and then pushed the hand inside him to clutch at his gut. He yelped without volition and the horse whinnied in protest, then suddenly he found himself headed back towards Land's End at a gallop without any instructions he could remember. It was only with difficulty that he managed to pull up, leaning back in the saddle, bracing his feet in the stirrups and hauling down until the horse's mouth nearly touched its chest.

He looked around, panting, and Coe was right on his heels, looking pale and grim, if more in command of his mount.

'What was that?' the young thief asked. 'Ruthia, what *was* that?'

It was a long moment before the older man answered. 'I don't know,' he said. He gave Jimmy a quick look. 'It's good to know I wasn't the only one to feel it, though.' He took a deep breath and let it out slowly. 'We should get out of here in case they send someone out looking for us. I'm fairly certain I could handle those two brigands, but I'm not willing to take on a dozen household guardsmen.' He started down the road, then looked over his shoulder. 'You staying?'

Jimmy looked at him, then back toward the manor house. 'No sir,' he said and followed.

'Where have you been? I wanted him here last night!'

Rip didn't recognize the voice. It sounded like a very crabby old man. He felt funny, like when he had been sick last winter and slept all the time. He felt too warm and too wrapped up but when he thought to move, he discovered he was too tired to do anything about it. He couldn't be bothered even to open his eyes. Besides, his hands wouldn't move, and his feet were tucked under him and he just couldn't seem to think of what to do next. But he could listen.

'Sorry, m'lord. But the boy's place was a long way away. We left Land's End at dawn this morning, sir.' This was the growly voice he'd been hearing lately. He'd never heard him sounding so nice before.

'Dawn you say! And it took you half a day to get here! Did you carry your horse on your back? Did you walk on your hands like a mountebank? Five hours!'

'Well but, sir, if we was too late by not 'aving 'im 'ere last night wot does it matter if we babied the 'orses this mornin'? The poor creatures is that tired, me lord.'

That last was the weasel voice, or so Rip thought of it. And even now he didn't sound nice, but wheedling and whining and nasty.

'Impudence!' cried the old man. There was the muffled sound of someone being clouted. 'Take your money and go!'

There was a clinking sound muffled somewhat, like coins in a sack dropping to the ground. Then there was a silence that went on too long. Rip shifted uncomfortably and wished everyone would shut up and go away.

'Thank ye, sir,' the growly voice said at last.

Rip felt himself lifted, and sensed he was being carried. It wasn't uncomfortable and this person wasn't talking, which was a relief. He heard the click of a lock being undone, then a door being opened. Then more walking, followed after a while by the sound of another door being unlocked. Then he felt himself being lowered onto something soft. He relaxed and settled down to sleep at last.

Rip woke as if swimming up from a dark place. He blinked and stirred, not knowing where he was. Then he felt a presence and sat up, rubbing his eyes.

'He's awake!'

Rip's eyes opened in surprise. A girl with dark eyes and curly brown hair was in front of him. She seemed a year or two older than Rip, though she was petite enough she wasn't a half-head taller. She grinned. 'I'm Neesa,' she said. 'Who are you?'

He was in a room – a big room, bigger than his family's whole house! And the bed was big too, bigger than Ma and Da's bed, with smooth sheets. There were hangings on the wall, cloth with pictures in them, pictures like old stories.

He was taken completely by surprise when a boy roughly his own age hopped up on the bed and began jumping up and down.

'What's yer name? What's yer name? What's yer *name?*' the boy shouted gleefully.

'Stop that, Kay!' an older girl said, giving the boy a shove that knocked him onto his back. 'You know what it feels like when you wake up.'

Kay giggled, ignoring the girl's glare. She offered Rip a clay cup. 'Thirsty?' she asked.

Rip nodded, took the cup and upended it, drinking its contents down in a few big gulps. It was some sort of fruit juice, but not like apple cider; more like berries.

He gasped for air and said, 'Thanks.'

'I was thirsty it seemed like forever,' the girl said. 'I'm Amanda. My family calls me Mandy.' She was older than Rip, looking to be almost as old as Lorrie, but unlike his sister, Mandy was a solemn-looking girl, with bright blonde hair and pale blue eyes.

'Rip,' he said by way of introduction. 'Where am I?'

The room he was in had stone walls under the cloth; he felt a moment's awe at how much of the fancy cloth there was. He knew how long Ma and Lorrie had to work to make even enough for a new shirt.

The stones neatly shaped into blocks, not like the stones in the fireplace at home. People in funny clothes riding horses rippled in a draught; it wasn't really very warm, and there was a queer musty smell to the air he didn't much like. The bed, he looked around – no, beds – had lots of covers. His even had a roof on it, like a fancy tent.

'You're in my bed,' Mandy said. Not that she was going to kick him out of it immediately, but like she was just letting him know he couldn't stay forever.

'Are we in a castle?' Rip asked. He couldn't think of anywhere else that had stone walls. *And – that word Emmet told me in the story of King Akter – tapestries! Yes, those are tapestries! And kings live in castles of stone.*

Mandy shrugged. 'I suppose it's a castle.'

'We can't go out,' Neesa said. She glanced around and put her arms around herself, as if cold.

'Sometimes they come and take someone,' Kay said. He lowered his voice to a whisper, 'And they never come back.'

Rip looked around. He didn't know what had happened, why he wasn't safe at home with his parents. He was frightened. 'Maybe their mothers and fathers come and take them home,' he said hopefully.

Kay's face screwed up into a mean little knot. 'You just got here! You don't know anything!' He hopped off the bed and ran over to one of the other beds, flopping down and turning his back to them. Rip could hear sobbing as Kay cried into the covers.

Rip softly said, 'I want my mummy and daddy.' Tears welled up in his eyes. Mandy watched him for a moment, then leaned close to him and put her arm around his shoulders. 'He's just scared. They take more boys. I've been here a long time and they've taken away four boys.' Lowering her voice even more, she tapped the side of her head with a finger. 'Kay's not quite right. He's Neesa's age, ten, but he acts like he's five.' She lowered her voice even more. 'Neesa's not right either. She sees things and hears things.' Rip was surprised to learn Kay was ten years old. He didn't look it, or act it.

Rip was sturdy and tough for seven. He had been around when his father had butchered animals and had helped his sister dress out rabbits she hunted. His nature was to get quiet and withdrawn rather than to cry or complain; softly he said, 'I'm scared.'

Mandy patted him on the shoulder. 'We're all scared, boy. Are you hungry?' she asked.

'Food will help,' Neesa said. Her eyes were bright and she nodded.

Rip sat all the way up and scrunched forward until he was able to put his feet over the edge of the bed, where he swayed dizzily before flopping over onto his back.

Mandy sighed and got up. 'Stay there. I'll bring you something.'

'Maybe I shouldn't,' he said, feeling queasy again.

'Did you eat today?' she asked him.

'I don't know.' He frowned. He couldn't remember anything except an occasional comment in the dark by Growly or Weasel. Where were his father and mother? He couldn't feel Mother at all, that was strange. It was like when he lost a tooth and there was a space there before the new tooth came in. Maybe this time there wouldn't be a new thing coming. Lorrie? He reached for her and felt, very faint and far away, an echo of her presence. Maybe he was just too far away from his mother to feel her. But something told him that wasn't the case. It felt like memory, but without the pictures and sounds that came with remembering.

'Where's your mother?' he asked Mandy.

She dropped the plate of smoked meat, cheese and apples into his lap, giving him a cold look. 'We don't talk about them,' she said.

'Why not?' he asked, reasonably enough, he thought.

'That's your bed,' she said, pointing to a bed in the corner.

Rip knew that she was telling him to get lost. He slid off the edge of the tall bed carefully and stood, unsure for a moment if he was going to fall down. 'Don't be angry,' he said. 'I don't understand.' He shook his head. 'Why are we here? Where are we? I just want to know what's going on.'

'Go sit on your own bed and eat,' Mandy snapped. She hopped onto her bed and sat hugging her knees, glaring at him over them. Rip could see her eyes shine, as if she was trying not to cry.

Puzzled, and a little hurt, Rip went over to the bed in the corner and sat down. He hung his head over the plate so that they couldn't see the tears running down his cheeks and stuffed a hunk of meat into his mouth. He didn't want to cry, but he couldn't help it. Even when Lorrie was mad at him, she didn't treat him like this, like he just didn't matter.

'We don't know anything,' Kay said into the heavy silence, his crying fit over. 'Nobody will talk to us. They bring us food, but they don't say a word. They only come to bring us food and water and to clean up.'

'Or to bring someone or to take someone away,' Mandy added. 'That's all we know.'

'But we think . . .' Kay began.

'We think our parents are dead,' Mandy said.

'No!' Neesa shouted, her face red with anger as she slapped Mandy's arm.

'Ow! Get off my bed, right now!' Mandy said and gave the younger girl a shove.

Neesa fell to the floor and began to cry. Kay rolled his eyes and pulled the pillow over his head, while Mandy crossed her arms and ignored them. Rip put his plate aside. He went over and put his arms around the girl and she clung to him, weeping as if her heart would break.

'I don't want my daddy and mummy to be dead,' she wailed.

'Maybe they're all right,' Rip said, trying to reassure her. 'We don't know.'

She sniffed and looked up at him, then nodded. 'Yes, maybe they're all right.' She pushed herself up to her feet. She gave him a brief smile and crossed over to her bed, where she gathered up a roll of cloth and brought it back with her. She sat beside him and began vigorously rocking the bundle in her arms while singing loudly.

At least she's singing, Rip thought. It was tuneless and word-less, but he thought it was supposed to be a lullaby and the roll of cloth a baby. He stood up and went back to his bed and his meal.

The cheese was wonderful: soft and mild in flavour, with a slightly nutty taste. He'd never tasted anything like it before and he looked around the plate greedily for another piece.

Two days later Rip woke up determined to escape his luxurious prison. He was too young to recognize that he had been drugged, but he knew something had changed since he woke. He was scared, and missed his family, but sensing Lorrie out there some-where reassured him. But he knew, somehow, that his only hope of ever seeing his family again was to run away.

He didn't like any of the other children. Well, he didn't dislike Neesa, but she was very annoying most of the time. She was always singing. The first night he'd been unable to sleep because she never stopped. So he went over to her and asked her to shut up. Then he realized that she was sound asleep and still singing!

Mandy had rolled over and said, 'She does that all the time. You'll get used to it.'

But he did not think he would. And he absolutely hated Kay. He might be bigger and older, but like Mandy said, he acted like half his age. If he didn't get out of here soon, Rip was sure he was going to try to kill Kay. He was a biter and a pincher and he liked to sneak up on you and do one or both. Rip had punched Kay in the stomach once, already, so hard Kay had almost thrown up, and had sat on the floor gasping for breath for a long time. Still, it didn't seem to matter. Kay would stay away for a while, maybe an hour, then he'd pinch and run, trying to hide under the bed. He didn't bother Mandy or Neesa the way he did Rip, so Mandy must have taught him to leave them alone. But now Rip knew he was going to have to beat Kay to get him to stop, and Rip didn't want to beat anyone; he just wanted to go home. Besides, he didn't know if he could beat Kay up, unless he somehow got on top of him.

He was also frightened by the feeling that someone was watching him. He'd wakened the morning before with a feeling that someone was leaning over him. But when he opened his eyes there was no one there. But the feeling didn't go away until he reached out. Since then he'd felt as though someone was standing behind him, staring, or holding something over his head. Sometimes it felt as if more than one person was watching him.

'Mandy,' he whispered.

She looked up at him and he went over to perch on the side of her bed.

'What?' she whispered back.

'Do you ever feel like . . . like someone you can't see is watching you?'

Reaching out, Mandy grabbed him by the neck and drew him close. 'Shut up!' she said through her teeth. 'Talking about it, or thinking about it, just makes it worse.' She smacked him, then said out loud, 'Now get off my bed.'

Mandy spent the rest of the day glaring at him and refusing to talk, and he couldn't really blame her. She'd been right, things had gotten worse.

All that day he'd felt as if people were standing close to him, leaning over him and staring. He tried to ignore it, but it was so unpleasant that he'd hardly been able to eat supper. Then later that night he'd been wakened by the sense that someone had touched him. He opened his eyes to see the black silhouette of a man standing before him. And then the man was gone, just like that. Rip lay still, absolutely still, feeling as though the man was still standing there and that he meant no good, and that he had no face but what Rip had seen, a blackness like a shadow made solid.

Rip was so scared he could hear his own heartbeat and he wanted to cry but he didn't dare, so his throat ached and it was hard to breathe and his mouth was as dry as cotton and he had to use the pot but couldn't. He wanted to wake one of the others so that he wouldn't be alone in the dark, but he was afraid to speak out loud. Rip was so wide awake it never occurred to him that he might go back to sleep. But somehow he did. And when he woke, it was with the feeling that someone unseen was leaning over him. He lay there thinking, I've got to get out of here.

Twice a day a fat man with a mean face and a bad smell came to bring them food and take away the slops bucket, replacing it with an empty one. Other than that the door was locked and there were bars on the windows and they were up high anyway. So Rip would have to get out when the door opened.

'I'm going to get out of here,' he told the others.

The girls just looked at him; Mandy in scorn, Neesa with eyes wide. Rip didn't think she knew what he was talking about.

'Oh, they'll come and get you really soon now,' Kay teased. 'And they'll chop off your head, whoosh!' He pretended to be waving a sword.

'They'll probably come for you first,' Rip snapped. 'You've been here longer than me!'

Kay gasped, taken by surprise by Rip's vehemence and the truth of what he had said. Then he got mad and made to run at Rip.

'Stop it, Kay!' Mandy snapped.

By the way the other boy stopped in his tracks Rip knew he'd been right about Mandy teaching Kay a thing or two about behaving himself. Kay still glared, but he did it from a safe distance.

'How do you think you can get out?' Mandy said.

'I don't know,' Rip said. 'Maybe we throw a sheet over his head and while he's trying to get it off we run out of the door.'

Kay made a farting sound and laughed. 'That's so stupid! He's twice as big as you. All you'd be able to do is throw a sheet over his bum and his brains may be there, but his eyes and hands are what you have to worry about.' He laughed and pointed at Rip. 'Stupid!'

'Shut up, Kay!' Mandy snapped. 'It's what we've all got to worry about. We've been lucky so far, but that's not going to last.' She glowered at him, then lowered her voice. 'Besides . . . it's getting worse.'

Kay's eyes widened and he cast a quick look around. Clearly he was startled that she would even hint at the presences that haunted them.

'Yeah. So stop pretending that you're not just as scared as the rest of us and help us think up how we're going to do this,' Rip yelled.

Kay looked resentful and mulish, but then he suddenly brightened. 'Hey! I know, we can trip him! Then we can throw a sheet over him.'

Mandy looked thoughtful. 'And we could maybe tie it around him so he couldn't get loose.'

'We could take his keys,' Rip said, 'and lock him in.'

'We could whack him on the head!' Neesa cried gleefully. 'Bonk! Bonk, on the head!'

The others laughed. 'Good idea!' Rip said and patted the little girl on the back. 'That's just what we'll do.'

*   *   *

When their burly caretaker came with their breakfast Rip and Kay were on opposite sides of the room playing catch with an apple. The man turned to put the tray of food on the table that was usually by the door only to find it had been moved to the centre of the room and shrouded in a sheet that trailed out onto the floor.

'What's that doin' there?' he growled.

Neesa raised the sheet on one side and said haughtily, 'It's my house and this is where it's s'posed to be.' She dropped the sheet.

'You two,' the man said to the boys, 'move that back over here.'

'No!' Neesa shouted. It was amazing that so much angry sound could come from such a petite source.

'Please,' Mandy said, looking pained, 'can we wait until she's finished playing with it? If we move it, she'll yell the house down.'

'No! No!' Neesa screamed, startling even her friends with the increase in volume.

'All right!' the guard shouted. He shut the door by kicking it with his foot, but couldn't lock it because of the heavy tray. He glared at the children and the two boys slumped down and sat on the floor, Mandy continued to lie upon her bed with her eyes wide and Neesa was crooning to her doll under the table. Satisfied that no one would move, the guard marched toward the table.

Which was when Rip and Kay yanked the satin rope that had tied back the bed-curtains from its hiding place under the rug to about ankle height and the big man went down, the tray and the food on it going flying with a colossal crash.

The guard tried to break his fall with his hands, but the explosion of breath from him when he hit the floor and a quick, deep groan of pain as something – wrist, or arm – broke, was followed a moment later by the loud crack of his chin hitting the stones.

The man's eyes rolled up into his head and he lost consciousness. The two boys traded places, winding the rope around the guard's legs. Mandy leapt off the bed and pulled the sheet off the table and dropped it over the guard's head; then she and Neesa gathered the points on either side of him and Mandy tied them in a knot, encasing him in a bag.

'Let's go!' Rip said.

The children gathered up the spilled bread, cheese and fruit in pillowcases and ran from the room. To Rip, it was like leaving warm water for frigid air and his teeth gave an involuntary chatter. He looked at the others uneasily and they looked back, pale and obviously frightened. Mandy glanced back into the room behind them.

'No!' Rip said and slammed the door, turning the key he was happy to find still in the lock. 'We can't go back. Let's get out of here.'

Their heads swung left and right and they found they were in the middle of a corridor which looked identical at either end; stone walls, high small windows on one side, tiled floors, huge blackened beams high overhead.

'This way,' Neesa said, pointing to the right.

'Why?' asked Mandy.

Neesa said, 'Because that's the right way.'

Mandy glanced at Rip and ignored Kay, then shrugged, heading off to the right. It might be the wrong choice, but at least it was a choice. Judging from the view from their narrow window they must be at the top of the house. 'Look for stairs,' Neesa whispered.

Mandy gave Neesa a look, but didn't say anything.

Rip felt awkward, because he had been the one to force the idea of escape on the others, but someone had to do it. He didn't know why the older children were content to let whatever horrible things happened to the children who had gone before continue, but he wasn't going to endure it. He didn't know if he could act like a leader, no matter how many times he had played one in his imagination, but someone had to do things. If he hadn't locked the door they all might have bolted back inside. It wasn't safe in there, but out here felt really dangerous. It seemed to be getting colder for one thing and he felt as though a lot of people were crowding the hallway, or were about to.

Stairs, Rip thought desperately. *Where are the stairs?*

Neesa was crying, quietly in a tired and really frightened way. Tears poured down her face and she was struggling not to make much noise, but still gave out a high-pitched moaning that didn't seem to involve breathing since it was continuous. She clutched Rip's hand like a hot vice, tugging him along, one way, then another. No one else had an idea where they were going, so they just let her lead.

Rip thought she was too scared to complain. He knew he was. He held her hand as much to reassure himself as to keep her close. Otherwise all he'd have to think about was the invisible something that always seemed just about to pounce on them. Or the biting cold that let him see his own breath even though it wasn't even close to autumn yet.

They'd been creeping about this huge house for what seemed like hours and they were all exhausted. They'd found stairs, but when they'd gone down two flights they'd had to turn around to avoid someone coming up the stairs. Whoever that was had them running up three flights before they took off down the corridor to the next turning. They'd ducked into a room while footsteps paraded up and down outside the door and something seemed to hover just above their heads. At least it had been rest of a sort or by this time they wouldn't be able to move. After the footsteps had stopped they'd sneaked out and managed to get down two flights but until now they'd still been trapped on the same floor they'd started on.

And all the rooms were empty and full of dust and unseen watching eyes.

Rip released Neesa's hand and tiptoed to the staircase.

Crouching down, he looked over the edge and watched, straining his ears to hear any motion on any of the floors below. Satisfied at last, he waved the others on and they crept down the stairs. Before they could get to the next staircase they heard footsteps and went racing down the corridor in front of them, hearts pounding.

The sense of an invisible pursuer sharpened as a feeling of anger reaching out to smash them began to build. The children ran faster and found it hard going, the air here seemed thinner somehow and the cold bit deeper causing them to stumble and to sob.

We've got to hide, Rip thought.

Down the corridor before them a door seemed to beckon. He grabbed the handle and pulled, only to find it locked. Yanking out the guard's key he tried to fit it into the lock, but his hands were shaking too much. It was like a live thing struggling to get away and he let out a frustrated sob. Mandy grabbed his shoulder and he gasped in surprise.

'Let's go!' she said in a shrill whisper. She tugged on his shirt.

But Rip grabbed onto the door handle, not meaning to be dragged away, and by a miracle it turned. It had only been stuck! Now he grabbed Mandy's skirt and opening the door dragged her in after him; the two other children followed. He and Mandy together shut the door and leaned their weight against it. Something on the outside hit it hard, rocking the door in its frame and causing a trickle of plaster dust to hiss to the floor.

Rip had a sense of something foul striking the door and then recoiling in hurt or fear. But it hadn't gone far; he could feel that too. Still, for the moment he felt safe. Safer even than in their prison up above. He turned to look at the room they were in. Kay and Neesa stared at him, pale and frightened. Beside him Mandy gave a sigh and slid to the floor, huddling in on herself, her eyes staring at nothing.

Rip looked around. They were in a bedroom. It was furnished with stark simplicity, and yet the furnishings themselves were finely made, like more of old Emmet's stories, or the ones Ma had told him about palaces in the sky. The furniture was all carved delicately out of dark wood, and polished, and there was cloth on the seats, fine weave with a pattern in it. There were no mirrors or pictures on the walls, or the large cloth hangings like in the other room, but Rip knew this room was used by gentlefolk. Then he noticed Neesa was staring and he turned to see where her eyes looked; opposite where he stood was a doorway.

Neesa pointed and said, in soft tones, 'She's in there.'

As though drawn, he went toward it, but when he got there he hesitated. Something bad was behind this door. Not something wicked in itself, like what waited for them out in the corridor. It was as if something bad was happening in the room behind the door.

But Rip had to see and fear didn't hold him long. He opened the door. The room was dim, as though some of the shades of night still lingered there and candles brightened it only slightly. There was a bed in the middle of the room and on the bed was a beautiful young woman. Asleep? No, she wasn't breathing. The woman was dead. He took an involuntary step backward, then stopped.

Rip looked closer at her, fascinated and appalled. He took in a long, slow breath of horror, having realized somehow that though she should be dead, she wasn't. Then he slammed the door and leaned against it, feeling sick. When he looked up he saw that the others had also seen what he had. *Did you feel it?* he wondered, but didn't dare say anything out loud. It was like the presences: for some reason he didn't think it would be wise to acknowledge what he'd felt.

'That's a dead lady,' Kay said, whiter than ever.

Neesa whispered, 'No. She's not dead.'

'But she's not moving,' Rip said. 'She's not breathing.'

'She's not dead,' Neesa repeated. 'She talks to me.'

'We can't stay here!' Rip sounded accusing and panicked.

The others looked at him in surprise. Mandy said, 'Where else can we go?'

Rip insisted. 'We can't stay here!'

Kay sat on a chair nearest the door and said, 'I can't move.'

Neesa came and put her hand on Rip's shoulder. 'It's all right. We'll be safe here . . . for a little while.'

Rip didn't know what to say. He had no idea where else they could hide, so he sat on the floor. He was tired and hungry and scared. Right now, despite the lady in the other room, this place felt safer than any place he had been since waking up.

Rip looked around the room; there was a decanter on a table beside the bed and a goblet. He went over to it and took a sniff. Wine. He wrinkled his nose – he didn't like wine unless it was well watered. But he was thirsty enough not to really care. He poured himself a draught and he took a swallow.

His eyes flew open. It was good! It spread a fragrant warmth through his mouth and down his throat all the way to his belly. From there it sped to warm his skin. He looked uncertainly at Neesa, then decided that she wouldn't be harmed by just a little. No doubt she was as thirsty as he'd been.

'Let's eat,' he said. Then bringing the decanter and cup with him, he sat down in the middle of the floor.

Mandy licked her lips, then nodded and fetched out the bread and cheese from her pillowcase. Neesa gnawed a chunk off the loaf with a look of fierce concentration that almost made Rip laugh.

'We can't eat here!' Kay said, barely containing his whisper. 'There's a dead woman in there. We'll die!'

Mandy snorted. She took the loaf from Neesa and broke herself off a piece. 'We will not!' she said. 'That's the stupidest thing I've ever heard. You always eat when someone dies. Gran died, and we all ate these pastries and things; even Mother, and she was crying.'

'Drink this,' Rip said and offered Kay a goblet of the wine.

Kay recoiled, his face full of disgust. 'I'm not going to drink that! It's probably poisoned.'

Rip rolled his eyes. 'It's not poisoned. I just drank some, do I look like I've been poisoned?'

'Besides,' Mandy said, offering Kay a piece of bread and a chunk of cheese, 'who would keep poison on their night table?'

'I'll take some!' Neesa said, reaching out for the goblet.

Rip gave it to her. After she swallowed three times, Mandy forced her hand down and said, 'Just another sip. Can't have you passing out on us.' Rip nodded. Like any farm-boy, he had witnessed the effects of too much wine on his father and the other men in the area during festivals and he knew it wouldn't take much to get the small girl completely drunk.

Neesa seemed on the verge of complaint when Rip pulled the cup away, but kept her objections to herself. Kay reached, shame-faced, for the goblet.

'Wait your turn,' Mandy said and took it for herself.

Kay gave her a weak smile and backed off. He went to the window and looked out. 'Could we get down from here if we knotted the sheets together?' he asked.

Rip went over and looked out of the window. It was a sheer drop of perhaps forty feet onto a flagstone courtyard. He just looked at Kay and walked back to the others.

Kay turned from the window, pouting, and slid down the wall to sit in a crouch and eat his bread. After a moment, he began to sob, then to cry in earnest. He made a sad and unattractive sight, his face bright red, his mouth wide open, revealing half-chewed gobbets of bread.

Rip and Mandy looked at one another uncomfortably, uncertain how to react. This was so unlike Kay, who would have laughed unmercifully if one of them had broken down so completely. Neesa looked at Kay for a moment, then pushed herself up from the floor and went over to pat him on the shoulder. 'Don't be sad,' she said.

After a moment Kay looked up at Rip, tears pouring down his face. 'I'm sorry,' he said, his voice hoarse. 'I'm sorry. But I am so scared.' He leaned over, putting his cheek against Neesa's head, and continued to weep.

Neesa frowned, then put her hand up to the top of her head. 'You're getting my hair wet,' she accused.

'Sorry,' Kay said and lifted his head. He got his crying under control.

'We're all scared,' Rip assured him. 'I don't like saying it, but I am.'

'But what are we going to do?' Kay asked, tears threatening to break loose again. He pointed to the inner door. 'There's a dead woman behind there.' Then he pointed to the outer door, 'And there's a ghost in the hall. We can't get out of the window. What are we going to do?'

Mandy pushed the goblet at him before he could go off again. 'Drink,' she said with ferocious emphasis. Kay did so and it seemed to help.

Rip stared glumly at the opposite wall. It was decorated with a carving of a plant in an urn. It was very elaborate, with all kinds of curlicues, not very pretty, but well done. As he stared, it seemed to him that something was wrong with that wall. From the way it projected into the room there should be a closet in it, but there wasn't. And now that he thought about it, the wall in the corridor was straight and smooth. So why was the wall on the inside bent like that? *Can it be a secret passage like King Akter used to escape the wicked uncle?* he thought.

Suddenly Neesa said, 'Yes!' She stood and walked right to where Rip was looking, and went to the wall as if hypnotized and began pressing every berry and flower centre, tracing every curve of every frond, looking for something that might press in.

He hadn't been too sure just what a secret passage was or how it worked when Emmet had told him the story, but he hadn't seen a real castle then. They were so big. Could he actually be looking at one right now?

'What are you doing?' Mandy asked.

Neesa pressed one last projection. It sank beneath her finger and something clicked. The wall swung open with a soft creak. Rip approached and stared at it breathlessly for a long moment then Kay and Mandy came to stand beside him.

'Open it,' Kay said, looking pale and dazed.

Rip did. The opening revealed a set of steps leading into pitch blackness.

'Dark,' Neesa said, taking hold of Mandy's hand.

'We'll need candles,' Mandy said, ever practical. 'There's some in that woman's room . . .'

'No!' Kay said and grabbed her arm. 'Don't go in there!'

Rip silently agreed.

'Well what are we supposed to do?' she demanded. 'If we take that one,' she pointed to the night table, 'they'll know someone was here.'

'They'll know someone was here anyway,' Rip said. 'We drank most of the wine, remember?'

'But if we take the candle they might guess we went this way.' Mandy's face had a stubborn look.

'They won't know!' insisted Rip. 'They'd have to find the passage like Neesa did.' Then he looked at Neesa. 'I was thinking about a passage, from a story my pa told me. How did you know?'

'I didn't,' answered Neesa. 'She told me.' With a nod of her head she indicated the next room.

Rip couldn't repress a shudder. 'Look, they might think we were here, but they'll think we left by the door.' He marched over and unlocked it, suddenly certain that whatever had tried to follow them into the room was not there. He didn't know why he knew, just that it felt right. 'So, they'll look all over the place, and even if they come back and find this passage, we'll have been gone a long time,' Rip explained.

He went to the night table, checked the bedside drawer and found two more candles and a striker. Handing one to Mandy, he stuffed the other into his shirt, then lit the one in her hand and took it from her. They were very good candles – wax, not tallow dips – Ma had three like them for special times. Then he put the striker in his shirt next to the other candle.

He and Mandy looked at one another for a long moment, then Mandy's eyes flickered toward the corridor. She took a deep breath. 'You go first,' she said. 'I'll follow.'

Rip took a deep breath to steady himself and hoped it didn't show. He was afraid of that dark hole between the walls too. But since they had no other way to go he supposed they might as well get it over with.

A timid knock on the door of Lyman Malachy's laboratory brought his head up from his work table. A glance at the Baron who sat beside him was met with a frown.

'Come in,' Malachy said. He wiped his hands and stepped toward the door. The Baron rose from his chair and put aside his book.

A very nervous and greasy-looking mercenary opened the door and advanced a half pace into the room. His posture was absurdly deferential.

'Sorry to interrupt yer worships,' the man said, bobbing in an almost continuous bow, eyes flickering to the geometric shapes on parchments pinned to the walls, to things chalked on the floor, to books and instruments.

'The, uh, the children . . .'

Lyman closed his eyes; he'd known it was going to be bad, but if something had happened to those children heads would roll. 'Ye-sss?' he said aloud.

'They've, uh, the little brats have escaped, yer worships.'

The Baron shifted his stance and Lyman knew without looking that he was giving the messenger a look that might cause a strong man to faint. This fool was not a strong man. The wizard moved to defuse the situation.

'You mean they're out of their room,' Lyman said calmly. 'In point of fact they cannot get out of the house.' Speaking over his shoulder to the Baron he said, 'I've made arrangements.' He turned back to the mercenary. 'So they'll be somewhere in the house.' Flicking his hand in a gesture of dismissal he said, 'Go and find them. And, mind you don't harm them. I very much doubt you'd like the consequences if you so much as scratch one of them. Do you understand?'

The man nodded and backed out, bowing, pulling the door closed after him.

Lyman shrugged. 'Damned nuisance!'

Bernarr frowned. 'Indeed,' he said coldly. He sat down again. 'Why do you have so many at one time? We won't need another one for at least a week.'

The wizard bit his lips and looked thoughtfully at the Baron. Then he went over and pulled a chair close to the one in which Bernarr was sitting. 'I've been collecting them for several reasons,' he admitted. 'One, it's not that easy to find a child born on the day your lady . . . entered her present state. And though the spell we found to extend her life by using the life-energy of these children has at least kept her condition from deteriorating, well,' he extended his hands palms up and shrugged, 'it hasn't improved it at all.'

'I thought that I saw something the last time,' Bernarr said. He stared into the distance as though remembering. 'A twitch of her mouth, and a finger, I'm sure I saw one finger move, ever so slightly.'

'Mmm, mm, yes, just possibly,' Lyman agreed. 'But we need more, much more, my lord. After all, our goal is to free her completely, is it not?'

Bernarr's eyes shifted toward the wizard and narrowed. 'What is in your mind?' he asked in a slow, quiet voice.

Lyman rubbed his hands excitedly. 'The very book that you're reading gave me the idea,' he said. 'If we can raise a life-force powerful enough we may well succeed in curing and waking your lady.'

Furious, the Baron lunged forward, grasping the front of the wizard's robe in his gnarled hand. 'Why have you not told me this before?'

'Because I did not know about it,' Lyman said with a sick smile. 'We only just acquired that book, you know.'

The Baron let him go and leaned back in his chair. 'Show me!'

Nervously, the wizard took the book, sped through the pages and presented it to the Baron once he'd found what he was looking for.

Bernarr studied the text, frowning over the curious antique phrasing. Then his eyebrows rose and his mouth opened.

'Seven times seven,' the wizard babbled. 'A mystical number, you see.'

'Forty-nine?' Bernarr said in disbelief. 'Forty-nine! Are you mad? Why not nine times nine? That, too, is a mystical number.'

'Unnecessary,' Lyman said with a wave of his hand. 'The effect isn't increased if the number of sacrifices is larger.'

'It sickens me to murder these children one at a time!' the Baron exclaimed. 'But . . . forty-nine? We will be awash in blood.'

'What I think will increase the effect,' Lyman said as if he hadn't heard the Baron's objections, 'is to sacrifice them all at once.'

Bernarr stared at him. 'Forty-nine at once? Is that what you said?'

'Yes. You see we'll create a means to collect all the life-force at once and direct it to your lady. Such a large jolt is sure to do the trick.'

'Are you suggesting that we recruit forty-seven helpers in such a bloody act?' Bernarr looked at him warily, as though uncertain about the wizard's sanity.

'Gods forbid!' Lyman exclaimed. 'No, no, that wouldn't do at all. The blow must be struck absolutely simultaneously in all forty-nine cases. One could never co-ordinate that, even if your helpers practised for weeks.'

Interested in spite of his disgust, the Baron asked, 'Then how do you propose to accomplish such a thing?'

'I've designed a machine.' The wizard jumped to his feet and went to the work table. He returned with a roll of parchment and spread it on his knees. 'You see,' he indicated several points on the drawing, 'when the original blow is struck all the other knives descend as well.'

Bernarr leaned over the drawing, studying its particulars. 'But how can you be sure you'll have enough pressure?'

'That's what these cylinders are,' Lyman said, indicating them on the drawing. 'They're twenty-pound weights and, of course, the knives will be extremely sharp. So?' He looked at his patron. 'What do you think?'

'Fascinating,' Bernarr murmured. Then he shook his head. 'But I cannot like it. Bad enough to take them one by one, but this many at once will draw attention.' He thought for a moment, then shook his head again. 'No. I don't see how we can do it.'

The wizard drew back, affronted. 'Well, of course, the ideal solution would be to use a child born at the exact instant that your lady was endangered. That would have been your son.' He looked at the Baron with a stiff-lipped frown. 'But, unfortunately you impulsively made that impossible. Didn't you?'

Bernarr glared at him. 'Well you might have said something at the time,' he pointed out.

Lyman sniffed. 'Perhaps,' he said. 'But you didn't trust me then and might not have listened. And you were understandably distraught; another man might have succumbed to a paternal impulse and kept the child while letting his beloved go, but you saw the boy as the cause of her death –' a black look from Bernarr caused him to amend his statement, '– her unfortunate condition, and had him disposed of.'

Something flickered across the Baron's face and not for the first time Lyman wondered if there was more involved in that choice than he understood, even after all these years. He said, 'Still, a terrible waste.' He thought for a moment. 'Hmm. Do you know where they buried him? Perhaps I can do something with the bones.'

Bernarr thought about that. 'I don't know,' he said at last. 'I wasn't interested at the time. And you've never mentioned it before.' He frowned. 'I will ask the midwife. She still lives in a nearby village. She will know what was done with the creature.'

'Excellent, my lord,' Lyman said, smiling. 'And do keep the plan and think about my other suggestion. I fear that without your son it may be the only way to bring your lady back.'

Baroness Elaine woke with the feeling that someone had been calling her name. But now there was no sound and the call, if there had been one, was not repeated. Her thoughts were slow: even the breaths that she took seemed unnaturally spaced and Elaine wondered if she were dreaming.

She felt weak: that was the first physical sensation she was aware of, then the pain. It tore into her like a furious cat, digging into her vitals with sharp claws and teeth that ripped and chewed. Elaine wanted to writhe, wanted to scream in agony, but she couldn't. She couldn't even open her eyes, or so much as twitch. Trapped in the darkness behind her eyes, she screamed in her mind, begging for something to ease the pain, for someone to come and help.

This wasn't like the terrible birth-pangs, which came in waves of agony cresting higher and higher; they were over. Elaine was sure of that: she had heard the crying of her child. *I saw his face,* she thought. The memory brought comfort, or at least took her mind from the pain. But not for long – the pain wouldn't be denied and she wanted to weep, but she couldn't.

She could feel her life flowing away slowly but irresistibly. It terrified her. She struggled to hold on: she wanted to live! She wanted to see her son grow to manhood. She wanted Zakry!

Elaine imagined him holding her hand and telling her to be strong. His touch seemed so real that in spite of everything she was briefly happy. Then the pain bit deeper and in her mind she screamed, and screamed, and screamed. Soon she was begging for death.

But death never came. After a while Elaine lapsed into darkness until at last both she and the pain were gone.

THIRTEEN

Hiding

The magician looked up.

'It's not a complicated spell,' Lyman Malachy said, when the preparations were complete. 'But it's tricky. The degrees of similarity must be delicately balanced.'

He looked aside at his . . . employer? Host? Friend? Benefactor? Someone who'd given him shelter for seventeen years, and let him carry on researches which would be . . . frowned upon . . . in most places, at least. No, he amended, it would get him hanged or burned alive in most places.

They were alone together in the room, with only the candle's flame for company; certainly, the remaining castle staff were used to that. They were probably the best-paid domestics outside the great cities and the households of the greatest lords; and they weren't much as far as quality went. But, like the household guards, they were paid as much to ignore what they heard and saw as they were to render service.

The magician's mouth quirked slightly as he drew his robe more tightly about him – the spring rains were heavy tonight, a thrush-thrush-thrush sound on the shutters and the streaked diamond-pane glass of the windows; he would have liked a cheery fire himself, but Bernarr cared nothing for the damp chill of this stone pile.

Gold can do many things, he thought. Even overcome superstitious fear among servants and soldiers. But it cannot make a fortress a comfortable place to live.

Bernarr waved a hand that trembled ever so slightly. 'Yes, yes. The brat must bear a similarity to both me and my lady Elaine, and your spell will find it,' he said. 'Damn the midwife! I gave orders that the brat be disposed of!'

Lyman nodded downward at the three shallow gold disks with their thin crystal covers, each about the size of the circle made by a man's thumb and forefinger. Silver and turquoise, platinum and jet made complex inlays on the inner surface of the gold. Above that was a thin film of water, and on that floated a needle. Each of the three needles was wound about with a hair – for the needle of the central disk two hairs were twined around it, crossing each other; the crystal covers kept the whole undisturbed.

'However, it may be fortunate that she disobeyed,' Lyman said. 'A pity that we could not get more details from her, but this will do as well – better, for the knowledge it brings will not be seventeen years stale.'

Lyman rose and shook back his sleeves. His eyes closed, his lips moved, and his hands traced intricate, precise patterns over the central casing.

While the man Bernarr still thought of as a 'scholar', rather than 'wizard', conjured, he remembered the first night they had met.

It had been the night of the big storm, hills and walls of purple-black cloud piled along the western horizon, flickering with lightning but touched gold by the sun as it set behind them. The surge came before the storm, mountain-high waves that sent fishermen dragging their craft higher and lashing them to trees and boulders, and to praying as the thrust of air came shrieking about their thatch. When the rain followed it came nearly level, blown before the powerful winds. The onslaught accompanied his beloved going into labour with the little monster they were now trying to find. His joy at the impending birth of a son caused him to be generous in offering hospitality to the stranger, an odd-looking man with protruding brown eyes and a large nose, made to seem enormous by a very weak chin. He appeared a few years older than Bernarr, in his middle to late thirties, but Bernarr was uncertain about his true age, for he appeared much the same as he had when he had first arrived some seventeen years before.

Lyman had introduced himself as a friend of Bernarr's father, a correspondent who had never met the old Baron in person, but who had been consulted by Bernarr's father occasionally on matters of scholarship. Most specifically, the purchasing of old tomes and manuscripts. He had come to enquire as to Bernarr's intent with the library, not knowing if the son shared the father's enthusiasm for scholarship and wishing to purchase several works should the son not wish to continue caring for the collection. He had been pleased to discover that Bernarr shared his love for learning.

And then had come the news that the Baroness was having trouble with her delivery, Bernarr remembered.

His memory brought Bernarr's remembered pain. He leaned back, swearing. Then he saw the two hairs twined about the central needle were writhing, like snakes – snakes which disliked each other's company. They wriggled away from the floating needle, pressed to opposite sides of the casing, and then went limp again.

That's about the most emphatic case of non-similarity I've ever seen, the magician thought, his face impassive. *If there's one thing certain, this pair did not make a child together.*

'What does this mean, Lyman?' Bernarr snapped. His eyes glinted with suspicion: when it came to matters concerning his wife, the Baron of Land's End was rather less than sane.

As I of all men know, Lyman thought. Aloud he continued: 'Ah ... my lord Baron ... could it possibly be that you have another child? One fathered before you met the lady Elaine?'

That stopped Bernarr's anger; instead he shifted a little in his chair, and reached for his mug of hot, spiced wine. 'Well,' he said, his eyes shifting. 'I was a man grown before I wed ... thirty summers ... a wench now and then ... and of course, for all I know –'

'Of course, my lord, of course; we're men of the world, you and I,' Lyman soothed. 'But it would make the twined hairs incompatible with the nature of the spell, you see. That is why I begged another of your lady's hairs. The spell will not be quite so sharp, nor function over quite so great a distance, but it should still function.'

He stood, moving his hands over the left-hand casing. *And I'm not going to use the one with only your hair, my lord Baron, because I suspect it would be quite useless for our purposes.*

Bram halted as he came to the crest of the hills and looked down on Land's End. The city was familiar enough: he'd made several visits. He tried to see it as Lorrie would.

The first thing she'll need is money, he thought.

He grinned, despite his anxiety, and the ache in his legs. He hadn't wasted any time on the journey, and he was more than ready for sleep, not to mention ale and food. She wouldn't get far on the few coppers he'd hidden under the mattress of his bed. While Bram's life savings, he had a short life so far, and by city standards it wasn't much. He suppressed an idle thought: he'd had daydreams about her lying in his bed, right enough, but not in quite that fashion.

He shifted the bow, quiver and rucksack into a slightly less uncomfortable position and strode through the usual throngs to be found on a road so close to the city gate. If he remembered rightly, there were a couple of horse dealers not too far outside the north gate.

'Help you, lad?' the horse-trader said, looking up.

He was standing with a cob's forefoot brought up between his legs, examining the hoof. The sturdy little horse shifted a little when it thought he was distracted, and began to turn its head – probably thinking of taking a nip at the man's rump. The trader elbowed the flank beside him, and Bram reached out with the stave of his yew bow, rapping it slightly on the nose.

It gave a huge sigh and subsided, and the trader let the hoof down with a dull clomp. 'Thrush,' he said over his shoulder to the cob's owner. 'You should know better than thinking a dip in tar will hide an unsound hoof from me, Ullet Omson. I'll not have him, not even if you treat the thrush and bring him back; not at any price. He's vicious.' The disappointed seller led his animal off and the man turned to Bram. 'And how can I help you?'

'I'm looking for a girl,' Bram said, and then blushed under his ruddy tan as the horse-dealer roared with laughter, looking him up and down.

'Well, I'd say you won't have much trouble, even if your purse is flat,' the man wheezed after a minute, 'for you're a fair-looking lad. But that's not my stock-in-trade. Fillies and mares, but only the hoofed sort. M'name's Kerson, by the way.'

Bram gave his own and shook his hand, and to no surprise found it as strong as his own, or a little more.

'She'll have sold a gelding,' he said. 'Not more than three days since. A farm horse, saddle-broke but more used for plough work, and well past mark of mouth.'

He went on to describe Horace, whose markings he knew like

his own: the two families had swapped working stock back and forth all his life.

'Wait a minute!' the trader said. 'Why, yes, I bought the beast – but from a young lad, not a girl. Could he have stolen it?' He frowned.

Well, of course she's passing for a boy, idiot! he thought. *She can't be going about countryside and town in your old breeches as a girl in boy's clothing, now can she?* 'No, I know that lad,' Bram said.

The trader shrugged. 'He seemed a nice enough young sprig; pretty as a girl, though, and a few years younger than yourself. Friend of his came out to enquire about the horse just today.'

Friend? Bram thought, cursing himself.

'Overheard the lad who bought the horse talking to a gent who purchased another. Seems the boy is foster-brother to Yardley Heywood's granddaughter and they're staying with her aunt. Anyway, the two of them rode out together about midday, heading north. The lad mentioned that his friend had sold the animal to me . . .' The trader received a puzzled look from Bram but continued, 'He said the girl who owned the beast originally was also staying with the Heywood girl.' Fixing Bram with a narrow gaze, he asked, 'Are you sure that horse wasn't stolen?'

'Hmm, pretty sure,' answered Bram.

He wondered at who that lad might be and why he'd buy Horace to go riding north, but decided to focus instead on where Lorrie might be. 'Where would I find this young lady, Yardley Heywood's granddaughter?'

The trader gave directions. Bram hurried on into Land's End, his head whirling. He'd expected to find Lorrie lost, or hiding in some cheap inn. And she'd made a friend? A wealthy one, too, from the sound of it. And what of Rip?

Elaine stirred. She was still uncertain of the state in which she dreamed, for she knew she must be dreaming. There had been pain in the dreams at first, but after many awakenings Elaine was able to distance herself from the pain. Never easily; it demanded attention and refused to be tamed, but for a time she could go beyond it and feel it as a distant thing. She endured these times, straining to hear if anyone was nearby. Sometimes she'd make out the croak of a night-bird, or perhaps a distant shout. But otherwise she seemed to be alone.

It puzzled her. She was the Baron's lady and she had just given birth. Where was everyone? Why didn't someone help her? How long had she been like this? And most horrible, was this how she was going to be for the rest of her life?

She knew her body lay unmoving, or at least she suspected that much. So she assumed she had become trapped in some sort of elaborate dream, but one which had a connection to the waking world.

The pain had been her first conquest, and then had come the terrible thing that had tormented her. Time was difficult to measure: she was certain many hours, even days, had passed since she had given birth to her child. Perhaps she was struggling with an illness contacted in childbirth, or a fever that had come after delivery.

Whatever the cause, she had struggled, surfacing to something that resembled consciousness then lapsing into periods of vagueness in which memories floated. Sometimes she experienced images so strong she wondered if they were real, perhaps the sort of prophetic visions some witches or holy women were reputed to have; or perhaps echoes of a distant past, or someone else's memory. Then came the blackness again. Two things were constant, the blackness and the pain.

Between the periods of blackness, Elaine called for help in her mind, raging and shouting and wishing evil things to happen to her husband who had abandoned her like this. Once she felt something touch her body. The cold touch, the sense of something slimy gliding across her skin, beneath her gown: a violating intimacy, uninvited and repulsive. Yet she could do nothing about it. Was that horrible touch real, or a memory? The fear and outrage that accompanied the sensation was real, for she remembered crying out in silent revulsion, *Leave me alone!* And the touch had gone away. Had it returned, or had the next merely been the memory of the first touch? She couldn't tell.

Over time, her mind grew stronger and the fear and revulsion turned to anger and calculation. Occasionally she remembered a conflict, a moment of defiance when she had rejected something that had oppressed her, but she couldn't recall the details. Vile things had been tormenting her and she had somehow attacked them; she conjured up images in her mind of the vile things having bodies and with hands formed by her mind she reached out and gripped them. They tried to flee but she tore at their substance, rending and tearing until they were but shreds and strands that seemed to evaporate into nothingness, leaving behind a lingering cry of pain and fear.

She had sought for something beyond the pain and the cold intruder, as she thought of the evil, slimy touch. Then she had found them, things lurking in the corners of the estate.

She sensed their presence, shocked, fearful, indignant that anything could harm them; they were hiding from her. Soon she would sleep again for she was very tired. But she wanted another, wanted very badly to destroy them all. Yet though they lurked nearby she could find none of them. She must make them come to her. Between periods of darkness, she plotted in her dreams. Lucidity came infrequently, but she realized that if she was dreaming, she could dictate the rules of this dream, and she would have it out with these lurking shadows in her mind.

Elaine pretended to sleep; suppressing all thought, she waited. Eventually one of her enemies came forward to test her and Elaine grabbed it.

She squeezed it and it howled, yanking her this way and that as it tried to flee. Finally it came to some sort of barrier and began to drag itself through. Elaine held on, trying to drag it back so that she could get a better grip on it. But this one was stronger than the first had been and persisted in its struggles. Finally it dragged her right up to the barrier, leaving very little of itself in her imaginary hands.

It was like being pressed against something hot and hard, yet she could feel herself slipping through and gripped the thing in her hands tighter. If she lost her grip she didn't know where she might find herself, but she didn't want to be in worse case than she already was so she held on for dear life.

Suddenly she could see! Elaine was so startled that she released the thing she'd been clinging to. It was daylight, but there were candles all around her bed. Then she felt herself rising, light as dandelion fluff and with no more control; she struggled to stop her ascent and succeeded only in turning over so that she could see below her.

Elaine found herself staring at her own body lying on the bed. *Am I dead?* she wondered. She had heard tales of people floating over their bodies, seeing mourners or visions of their homes before being taken to Lims-Kragma's Hall of the Dead. Such tales were told by those whom the healing priests had recalled the instant before their transition from life to death.

Then she saw her chest rise, ever so slowly: but she was breathing! She examined herself closely. She didn't look at all well. *Am I dying?* She panicked and tried to bring herself closer to her body, waving her arms as though swimming, then realized that she had no physical arms. She had no body around her! The shock of that realization caused an instinctive reaching out, as if trying to grip her own physical being with her spiritual hands. Suddenly, she was back inside her body, back with the pain and the long, slow silence. Her tormentors were gone:

she could feel that she was alone again. Then, suddenly, like a candle being snuffed out, awareness was gone.

When awareness returned she understood; the 'dreams' as she had thought of them were her mind leaving her body, while the waking stages had been her mind being trapped within. She must learn to control this ability, to set her mind free, she decided.

How long it took she did not know but with much concentration, Elaine found that she could leave her body behind and float from room to room, going through walls and floors as though they were made of water.

The manse was dirty and nearly deserted. The few people she found were the kind of mercenary scum that even her father wouldn't have hired, yet many wore the garb of the household guard.

Her enemies still lingered, but they never came near her any more. Sometimes she seethed at the thought of what they had done to her and hunted for them. At other times she was almost grateful to them, for they had shown her the way out of the darkness and the pain. Mostly she wanted to see them, to find out what they were. Then she'd decide what to do about them. Were they supernatural beings? Or ghosts? Or agents of some other power?

Where is my baby? she wondered suddenly. Then was amazed that the thought hadn't occurred to her before. How could she forget her only child? Her little boy. She must find him.

But it was too late, she could feel herself being pulled back. Elaine didn't even fight any more, she knew there was nothing she could do to stop it. At least she didn't have to be there all the time. Before she was sucked back into her ailing body, she saw that the candles had burned down quite a bit.

*   *   *

When next she woke she heard the voices of children! A girl's voice echoed in the distance, calling to her. At once Elaine found herself in the corridor and for the first time in a long time sensed the presence of those horrors who had abused her so. She called out, *This way!* Round the corner of the hallway came a small group of children, two girls and two boys. They looked exhausted as well as frightened.

Hovering over them, Elaine saw her enemies for the first time. They looked like tendrils of black smoke, writhing and twining in and out of a central blackness, and they projected fear and an icy cold.

This way, she called again, pointing toward the door of her chambers. Over and over she shouted to them. At last one of the girls seemed to understand, leading them to her door. They piled into her room and slammed the door shut behind them.

Elaine swept toward the black cloud furiously, snatching at one of its tendrils. It pulled back, retreating slightly, keeping just close enough to tease. Rather than waste her energy, Elaine went back to her room and hovered protectively over the children, pleased by their presence, delighted by the littlest one; he was perhaps seven or eight years of age, and despite being very frightened, he carried himself well.

She sensed her enemy lurking in the corridor, but it did not attempt to enter. It was only then that she saw the warding on her walls, traceries of light, of command, of this-shall-not-change. Perhaps someone had heard her pleas for aid after all.

As she listened to the children talk she found that they were desperate to escape. It saddened her that they found her as terrifying as the entity in the corridor, but she supposed she couldn't blame them. *If only I could help the poor little things.* Elaine peered into the corridor; the thing snickered at her and she withdrew.

As she looked around her room she sensed an older warding and sought it out. She went through the wall and rediscovered the hidden passageway there. Her husband had shown it to her the day he installed her in these rooms. 'They go all through the manse,' he'd said.

She saw the youngest boy staring at that wall, and something in his eyes told her he was on the verge of understanding. She spoke to the girl who had led the others to her rooms, telling her about the passageway, telling her the key was in the sculpture on the wall. Soon she could see that she was listening. She got up and went to the carving, testing all the little projections until she found the right one. *Oh, bright child!* she thought.

Then she was out of time again, being drawn back to her body. She might never find out how this ended and was frustrated indeed. She wished she could wake up for good.

When she next awoke, Elaine wondered about the children, especially the girl who seemed to hear her. As she pictured her she suddenly found herself beside her. This had happened before, but she had no control over it. She would think of some person or place and find herself there, but only within the confines of the manse. She'd never yet been able to even enter the rose garden. But she did have access to everywhere and everyone inside the house. Except for Bernarr. When she thought of him she found herself in the presence of a much older man. An uncle or cousin, she'd assumed, since she knew his father was deceased.

She didn't really mind that he never came here any more; she hadn't loved him and she didn't miss him. But she did want to see her baby and her little one must surely be with the Baron. She sighed and the candle one of the boys was holding flickered.

'Be careful!' the oldest girl almost cried, her voice sounding very loud in the passage.

The younger girl, the one who sometimes could hear Elaine, whimpered, but was bravely holding back her tears.

Elaine's heart melted for her. They were all covered with streaks of dust and looked exhausted and the food-sack tied to the older girl's belt looked sadly empty. *Poor little things*, she thought. They needed a refuge, but *her rooms* wouldn't do. She frightened them, and the old man who looked like Bernarr slept there.

''S'not my fault! There's draughts,' the boy holding the candle said, his youthful anger at being blamed for something he didn't do overriding caution and the need for quiet.

The others said nothing but watched the stub of the candle anxiously. It was plain they were afraid of being left in the dark.

Elaine remembered a place they could hide that should do very well. Bernarr had brought her there just after she'd arrived. 'It is warded so that when you wish to be private no one will bother you here.' He'd smiled proudly. 'It shall be your own sanc-tuary.' She'd felt no need at all for such a place, but he'd been so proud of his gift that she'd smiled and leaned up to kiss his cheek, a kiss he'd claimed with his lips.

'Come with me,' she whispered to the girl who seemed to hear her. 'I know a place where you'll be safe.'

Neesa stood up, looking down the dark passageway. Her crying stopped and she smiled.

'What is it?' Mandy hissed; her eyes glittered in the candle-light as she tried to look in every direction at once.

'Let's go this way,' Neesa said like someone in a dream. 'It's the right way.' She walked off.

Kay and Mandy looked at one another, but Rip pushed himself to his feet and started after Neesa. 'C'mon,' he said impatiently.

Mandy got up and followed. 'You coming?' she threw over her shoulder at Kay.

Rip was moving carefully so as not to put out the candle, their only source of light. 'Wait!' he said to Neesa and his breath blew it out.

Mandy gasped and Kay cried out in fear.

'Don't make noise!' Rip admonished. 'I'm in front of you. Hold hands! We've got to stay together.'

'It's your fault!' Kay snapped.

'It doesn't matter,' Rip said tiredly, 'it was going out anyway. Be careful! Right, everybody here?'

'Yeah,' Kay muttered, fear reducing his voice to a hoarse whisper.

'Then let's go,' Rip said. 'Every time Neesa's had this feeling it's led us somewhere safe.'

'I wouldn't call this safe,' Kay sneered.

'It's safer than the halls,' Rip reminded him, 'or the room we were locked in.'

'We can't get out!' the other boy shouted.

'Shhh!' Mandy said. 'We couldn't get out before either. Unless you've got a better idea put a stopper in it, Kay.'

They were silent then, moving carefully in the pitch-darkness. They slipped down corridors so narrow they had to turn sideways and went up and down stairs both narrow and creaky until at last Neesa brought them to a halt.

'Here,' she said softly.

The others stood still and listened to the sound of her apparently patting the walls. There was a muffled click and they all flinched as a narrow crack let in a blinding light. Then Neesa impulsively pushed open the panel and led them through. She squealed with delight at what she found.

Though everything was covered with dust and the air was stale from long disuse, the room was undeniably cosy, and well lit from a high window.

'We won't run out of candles here,' Mandy said, smiling.

Everywhere they looked there were candlestands with branches of candles in them. There was a full scuttle of sea-coal as well. Plumply cushioned chairs and sofas abounded and there was a feeling of peace about the place.

'Now all we need is something to eat,' Kay said. 'And water. Got any feelings about that?'

Rip raised one eyebrow and was immediately pleased with himself for having done so for the first time. So instead of getting annoyed at the other boy's attitude he thought about the question. 'Yes,' he decided. He picked up the empty sack and looked at Kay. 'Want to come?'

For an answer Kay plucked two candles from a stand and lit them from the strikebox. He wasn't about to refuse to do something the younger boy was willing to try.

Rip peered out through the hole in the carving. *This is fun!* he thought. His young mind had a problem understanding all the terrors that were around him since he had awakened in this place, but spying on people from a hidden location was something he could finally grasp, and it felt like a game to him.

The secret passages turned out to have a lot of doors and peepholes. The narrow corridors felt a lot safer than the old room had. He shuddered, turned and put his finger to his lips, and then put his eye back to the hole.

He saw a really big room again; but then, most of the rooms were. This one had windows open, and he spared them a longing look. There was a long table set for a meal with fancy metal tableware, not wood and crockery, not even pewter, but real silver. An old-looking man was sitting at the head of the table, talking to two other men who stood with their caps in their hands.

Rip's lips pursed. Those were the men who'd taken him and brought him here. He could tell by their voices. They looked cruel, and scary, too. A third man sat with his back to the hole, silent.

'Take this,' he said, pushing something across the table at them.

One of the men reached out, then pulled his hand back as if the little thing had burned it. 'Magic!' he blurted.

'Of course it's magic, you fool,' the old man said. 'The needle points at the man you are to take for me.'

The other seated man spoke, his voice smooth and soothing and somehow reminding Rip of the stuff his mother sometimes smeared on burns, or when you got stung by poison-oak or nettles. 'It's entirely harmless, I assure you,' he said. 'You need merely follow the needle's point. It may lead you on a long chase – the man in question may be as much as fifty miles away – but it shouldn't be too difficult.'

'And the pay is good,' the older man snapped. 'More than for all the others.'

One of the standing men nudged his companion; he picked up the small thing from the table reluctantly and wrapped it in a rag, tucking it into his belt.

'It's a man this time?' he asked. 'Not a boy?'

'He should be just seventeen,' the old man said, turning his head aside. For a moment Rip saw how sad he looked, and felt a little sorry for him. His voice sank, so that the boy could barely follow it. 'Just seventeen . . . he should be tall, perhaps fair-haired, perhaps brown.'

'We're yer men,' the standing man said. 'For six hundred, we're yer hands and fingers, m'lord.'

'And when you bring him in, put a bag over his head. I have no wish to see his face. None!'

'Then how'll ye know it's 'im, sir?'

The smooth-talking man said, 'That needle will only point at one person in this entire world. That is who you will bring here. Now go!'

They both bowed low; after a moment the old man and his companion followed them, talking.

'Oh, good,' Rip whispered, and opened the door a crack. It

was set into the panelling, and even Mandy would have to stoop to get out of it. 'All right – come on – they're all gone!'

The four children scampered out into the room. Rip almost stopped as he felt them again, the bad ones, but he was hungry. Mandy and Neesa ran straight to the table and began to gather food up in handkerchiefs; bread, cooked chicken, pastries stuffed with vegetables. Rip and Kay didn't stop for that, although it smelled very good; instead they raced over to the door.

They cracked the door and peered through, waiting while the girls grabbed up as much food as they could carry. Rip wanted to stick his head out into the hall, but resisted the urge.

Kay grabbed his arm. 'I can feel something coming,' he whispered.

'Me too,' Rip said. He had a sick feeling in his stomach, as he had in the room they'd been locked up in; and it was getting worse.

Without a word, they stuffed the candles back in their pockets and bolted for the secret door; the girls were already through, eyes wide, and all of them gave a sigh of relief as the panel clicked closed.

Immediately they all felt better too; the sense of peering malice went away as if the stuffy darkness of the secret passage was part of another world.

I wonder why it's always like this when we come out of the passageways? Rip thought.

Then Mandy started unfolding one of the napkins. 'What did you get?' he asked eagerly as they started their trek back to their safe room.

FOURTEEN

Abduction

Jimmy reined in.

He'd followed Jarvis Coe all the way around the lands belonging to the great house they'd seen, from sea-cliff edge to sea-cliff edge, a long ride in a rising wind that reminded you with every step that spring was young.

A long trip and an unpleasant one. The only way to find out if they'd gone beyond that skin-crawling feeling was by testing; one step in – run away! – one step back – perfectly normal.

'What is it?' Jimmy asked, struggling to keep his old nag from bolting like a racehorse.

'Nothing good,' Coe answered.

Jimmy snorted. Brilliant! How fortunate that he had someone along to tell him that. The awful feeling seemed to have no end. He certainly wasn't going to try climbing up the cliff face to see if the way to the manse was clear from that direction because it probably wasn't. He'd long ago learned not to squander his energy.

'Ever felt anything like it before?' he asked.

Coe turned to look at him. 'Ever been in a haunted house?'

Jimmy grinned. 'Not that I've noticed.'

'Oh, you'd notice,' the older man said. 'As I recall, it feels a great deal like this.'

After a moment of contemplating his companion's broad back Jimmy asked, 'When were you in a haunted house?'

'Long story,' Coe said without turning his head and then lapsed into silence.

Jimmy grunted in irritation. This seemed to him to be a perfect time for a long story. Because, except for those soul-curdling moments when they went too close to the manse, he was bored stiff. If they kept on like this he was going to be grateful for the distraction of his aching arse.

They reached the edge of the cliff and Coe sniffed the wind, looking out over the white line of snarling surf where sea clashed white-green on rocks and the blue-grey waves topped with foam beyond. 'There'll be weather tonight,' he said. 'We need to find ourselves some shelter.'

'I guess asking at the manse is out,' the young thief muttered.

Coe gave him a wry look and turned his horse, heading off across the ring of forest and through it, into the cleared fields beyond. The line of . . . unpleasantness . . . nowhere reached the cultivated land, but it had little embayments well into the woods and rough moor kept as barrier and hunting grounds for the manor.

Jimmy sighed and followed, feeling the oppression on his spirits lift as they came back into land that bore the sign of man, not to mention sheep, goats and cattle. All he could see from this lane – it was too narrow and irregular to be called a road – was a rising field of something green, probably young grain, and a ridge lined with tall trees.

'I don't think that was even your typical haunted house,' he muttered.

'Not quite,' Jarvis Coe said grimly.

Even then, Jimmy felt a little startled at his tone. Coe was looking back towards the fortified manor, and his mouth was a hard line; his right hand kept straying to his breast, and the young thief thought that there must be something beneath the cloth – an amulet, perhaps.

'In the meantime, the day's mostly gone and if we're to find out what's happening, we need shelter,' Coe said. He cocked an eyebrow. 'Unless you'd rather ride back to Land's End?'

'If you're staying, I am,' Jimmy said, flushing. 'I gave my word.'

Coe smiled, then more broadly at Jimmy's scowl. 'No, lad, I'm not laughing at your keeping a debt of honour,' he said. 'I'm just remembering some situations I got myself into with promises, once. The more credit to you.'

He reined his horse about and Jimmy followed. The setting sun made it hard to look west – not something that was often a problem in Krondor, where tall buildings were more common. Despite that, Coe led them to the junction of two lanes in that direction, and cocked his head to one side.

'Ah, I thought so,' he said. 'There's a brook there. Hear it?'

Jimmy tried; all he could make out was rustling, whooshing, crackly sounds of wind through vegetation, birdsong, and a lot of insects. But . . .

'That tinkling sound?'

'You've a good ear, Jimmy.'

'Thank you, Jarvis,' he said.

'Well, in the country, where a road or path crosses water, chances are you'll find folk living,' the older man said.

They rode down the lane through a belt of trees that arched over the road; it reminded Jimmy of an alleyway, in that you wanted to look seven ways at once to make sure nobody was sneaking up on you. The trees all seemed of the same size, and most were in rings around thicker stumps.

'Coppicing,' Coe said, noticing his puzzlement. 'If you cut an oak or beech, a ring of saplings comes up from the stump. Leave them ten years, and they're good firewood, or the right size for charcoal, or for poles, and when you cut them you get more coppice shoots – think of it as farming trees. Another sign we're near some dwellings.'

Ah, rural mysteries, Jimmy thought a little snidely.

Jarvis pulled up near the footpath that led to a small cottage. 'That's a farmstead off that way,' he said, pointing to a haze of smoke. 'But we'll stop here. A cottager will be more glad of a few coins, and more likely to be gossipy.'

He rose in the stirrups. 'Hello the house!' he called.

The cottage lay a hundred yards or so to their right, in the direction of the manor; a huge oak overshadowed it.

Which isn't hard, Jimmy thought. *A small bush would overshadow it.*

The building was a single storey of wattle-and-daub, white-washed mud plastered over interlaced branches and poles; the steep roof was thatch, with an unglazed dormer window coming through it above the doorway like a nose. Smoke trickled out of a stone-and-mud chimney, and a shed of the same construction stood not far off. The large vegetable garden beside it was newly planted, the dark soil as neatly turned as a snake's scales, and a nanny-goat stood in a small rail-fenced pasture beside a young sow; a few chickens scratched around the plank door of the modest home.

'Hello, strangers,' a man said, as he turned from latching the wicker garden gate with a twist of willow-twig.

He had a spade in his hand, oak with an iron rim; he smiled as he set it down against the fence, but that put his hand within reach of a billhook leaning against the same barrier. That was a six-foot hickory shaft with a heavy hooked knife-blade socketed to the end, a common countryman's tool but also a weapon at need; some soldiers carried them, although military models added a hook on the back of the blade for pulling mounted men out of the saddle.

The man himself was in patched and faded homespun breeches and shirt, barefoot, and no longer young, but tough as an old root from his looks.

Jarvis Coe bowed slightly in the saddle. 'We're travellers,' he said, and gave their names. 'We'd appreciate a place to stop for the night, for we've seen no inn, and would be glad to repay hospitality with a silver or so.'

The cottager's eyes went wide, then narrowed: that was a great deal of money for an overnight stay. Jarvis flipped the coin, and the man caught it, examined it and tucked it away.

'That's generous of you, sir,' the man said.

Jimmy found his accent thicker than Lorrie's had been, a yokel burr that swallowed the last syllable of every word.

'And it will help pay the tax on my cot. We've room for two on the floor – my sons are living out, working for Farmer Swidden – and I've some comforters with clean straw, and there's the paddock for your horses. My Meg has some bean soup on the hob, and she baked today.'

The top half of the cottage's door opened, and a woman looked out – late in middle age, as brown and nondescript as her husband, with lips fallen in on a mouth mostly toothless, and shrewd dark eyes. She nodded and went back inside as the men unsaddled, watered and rubbed down their mounts – Jimmy carefully copying what his companion did – and turned the horses into the small paddock.

The cottager came up with a big load of hay on the end of a wooden-tined pitchfork and tossed it to the horses, giving the nanny-goat a thump in the ribs when she tried to snatch some.

'I've oats,' he said. 'Get some from Farmer Settin over there for helping with the reaping.'

Jimmy looked around as they ducked into the cottage. It was a single room, not overly large, with a tick bed on a frame of lashed poles in one corner, the hearth in the other, and a floor of beaten earth – which Jimmy would have minded less if there hadn't been evidence that his hosts neither wore shoes nor scraped their feet before coming in from the yard. A ladder ran up into the loft, where the vanished sons had probably slept.

For the rest, there were a few tools on pegs – a sickle, two hoes, a scythe – and a few garments, along with the iron pot that bubbled over the low fire in the hearth. It was warm enough, and not so small they'd feel cramped. It was better than sleeping outside, Jimmy decided, even if the food didn't look particularly inviting.

The cottager leaned the billhook against the inside wall beside the door; Jarvis and the young thief took the hint, and propped their swords beside it.

'Let me see if I understand,' Bram said uncertainly.

He felt intimidated by the tall stone house in town, and by the two – well, ladies – who were sitting across from him.

Mind you, they look friendly enough, he thought.

One, who everyone seemed to call Aunt Cleora, was dressed as finely as a lord's wife, although not in quite the same style; she was probably about the same age as his mother, but looked a decade younger to peasant eyes. Miss Flora, her niece – newly arrived from Krondor – was a pretty enough lass, although not a patch on Lorrie. Lorrie looked strange herself, in one of Miss Flora's dresses, with her bandaged leg up on a settle.

Even the cook, who looked to be right brutal when she wanted, had been sweet as candy to him; but then, he supposed she felt motherly.

Serenely unconscious of his tall, fresh-faced blond good looks, brought out by a bath and clean clothes, Bram finished the last pastry and wiped his hand on the napkin provided, remembering not to lick his fingers. Which seemed a pity, since they were covered with fine clover honey. The kitchen was about the size of the ground floor of his parents' farmhouse, but more homely than the rest of the fine house: flagstone floor, copper pots and pans on the walls, a long board table, and sacks of onions and hams and strings of sausage and bundles of garlic and herbs hanging from the rafters.

He could eat in comfort here, and was glad that Miss Flora had suggested it. He was still overwhelmed by the reaction he had received upon presenting himself at the house; Lorrie had nearly cried for joy at seeing him – which had caused his chest almost to burst at the feelings he was just beginning to confront – and that had caused Flora to treat him as a long lost-friend. Her aunt had instantly taken the young man under her wing, insisting he bathe and refresh himself, providing clothing belonging to one of her male kinsmen – he was vague as to who, exactly – and then set to feeding him. Apparently Aunt Cleora liked to see a man eat.

'So Miss Flora's brother here –' he said around a mouth full of food.

'Jimmy,' Flora said helpfully.

'Rescued you from thief-takers, and found you a place to stay, and then he and she bound up your leg, and he's gone to look for Rip?'

Lorrie nodded vigorously. 'And then you came after me. Thank you, Bram!'

Bram felt himself blush, and at the same time swell with pride; he was as ready as the next man to bask in feminine admiration.

'Well, I couldn't leave you to sort this out alone,' he said. 'Whatever that bunch of greybeards back home thinks. Wild beasts don't burn down farms, or attack men in the light of day. Why they couldn't believe you, Astalon alone knows,' he observed, invoking the God of Justice. 'Lorrie's no bubblehead, like some I could name but won't, like Merrybet Glidden.'

Lorrie's eyes filled with tears, which made him feel bad and good at the same time. Flora sighed at him, and Aunt Cleora clasped her hands together beneath her slight double chin.

'This is as good as a minstrel's tale!' said the older woman. 'Young men setting out to rescue folks! Why, it's downright heroic!'

Bram blushed even more. 'I'm no hero,' he said softly. 'Only a farmer's son. But I'm still going to head after Rip, to help your brother, Miss Flora.' He yawned enormously. 'Best start early, too. On foot, it's going to be a fair old chase, they being mounted.'

Flora nodded decisively. 'You'll have to get a horse, then,' she said.

Bram laughed. 'Miss Flora, I'd like nothing better. But I can no more afford a horse than I could dance north on my hands.'

Lorrie reached into the pocket of her borrowed skirt. 'But Bram, I've got the price I got for Horace!' she said. 'Surely you can get something for that.'

Bram fixed Lorrie with a wry look, and both knew he was intentionally ignoring the coins she had filched from his room. It wasn't much, but it was all he had.

'And if you can't, I'll top it up,' Flora said.

'And you can take what you need from the kitchen for supplies on the way,' Aunt Cleora said. 'Best take my cousin Josh's rain gear, too, by the look of things.'

Overwhelmed, Bram looked down at his toes in their home-cobbled shoes. That reminded him of something. 'At least I'll be able to track your foster-brother, Miss Flora,' he said. At their wide-eyed look: 'Well, seems he bought Lorrie's Horace. And there's a nick in his left off shoe that I'd know anywhere.' Then softly he added, 'If the rain doesn't wash away everything, that is.'

*　　*　　*

Jimmy looked out at the pouring rain and sighed. Why Jarvis couldn't just ask what he wanted to know was beyond him. But by now he knew a great deal more about the family who had agreed to give them shelter than he did about some of his friends.

'I was midwife to the Baroness,' the old woman said proudly. 'A tiny thing she was, poor lass.' She shook her head. 'Bled to death I'm sorry to say. The Baron was never the same after,' she confided.

'T'Baron was never the same as anyone else his best day,' her husband said sourly.

Jimmy turned around and went back to the fire. This was more like it.

'Used to be if a tenant had a complaint he could go up t' the house when the lord was there and get the thing straightened out. Even cottars like us! Not no more ye can't.'

'The Baron sent all the servants and guards away after his lady's death,' his wife said. 'The very day after she died.'

'And hired those, those . . .'

'Mercenaries,' his wife said firmly, giving her husband a stiff-lipped warning glare.

'Mercenaries,' the old man said, pulling his lips away from the word as though it was filthy. 'Neighbour went up t' see the lord one time he was there and those . . .' he gave his wife a look, 'fellows near beat the poor man t' death. I ask you, is that any way for a lord t' behave?'

From what Jimmy had seen and heard in his life that was the way a lot of lords behaved. Wisely, he didn't say so.

'There's a strange feeling about the place,' Coe observed.

Husband and wife glanced at one another.

'Aye,' the old man agreed. 'Year by year it's got worse. Nobody goes there now 'cept those bully-boys he hires now and again, and they don't stay long if they can help it.'

Coe raised his brows and said, 'Mmph.' He puffed his pipe

for a contemplative moment or two. 'Must have been a grand funeral,' he said.

Once again the old couple exchanged glances.

'I believe she was buried in Land's End,' the old woman said.

'Mebbe even got shipped back to the court she came from,' her husband suggested.

'What about the baby?' Jimmy asked. 'What ever happened to it?'

The old couple looked at him in surprise as though they'd forgotten his presence. Jarvis looked enquiringly at them.

'Well,' the old woman spluttered, 'we've, uh, we've never seen him.'

'Did the child survive?' Coe asked quietly.

'We never heard that he didn't,' the old man snarled, his eyes flickering to his wife.

'He'd be about eighteen now,' his wife said dreamily.

'I ask because no one in Land's End ever mentioned him,' Jarvis said. 'So I'm surprised to hear the Baron had a child.'

'He must have been sent away to be fostered,' the elderly midwife suggested. 'The nobility do that you know.' She gave an authoritative nod.

Coe said, 'Mmph,' again. Then, 'The house looked to be in reasonable repair,' he commented. 'Though I was still on the road when I saw it.'

The old man grunted. 'The lord must be having those bast –' he glanced at his wife, '– mercenaries look after the place. Not one of us has been near there for near eighteen years. And I'll tell ye true,' the old man stood and knocked his pipe out on the fireplace, 'ye couldn't bribe me t' go there now.'

Me neither, Jimmy thought. *But you could threaten to cry and wheedle and appeal to my better nature.* He wondered bitterly if he would always be so susceptible to the blandishments of women. Or was it that he enjoyed making the occasional grand gesture?

*I just hate it when said grand gesture turns out to be bloody incon-
venient and more like suicide than heroism.*

Rescuing the Prince and his lady would have been a wonderful
grand gesture, and a bonus besides since his real purpose had
been to rescue his friends. But rescuing some sprat he'd never
met because Flora expected him to felt like being put upon and
he didn't like it a bit.

And yet, as soon as he was certain his hosts and Coe were
asleep he was going out to that house of horrors to see if he
could find the boy and get him out. After all, if a load of low-
life bashers could stand to be in that place then so could he, by
Ruthia.

Then the rain started in earnest, and Jimmy muttered, 'Maybe
I'll go out tomorrow night.'

The Baron tossed in his bed, clutching the soaking sheets as he
did no less than one night in three. The dreams were always the
same, the hunt, the cliff, the laughing face of the youth. The
storm, the dark man arriving, all came and went, in different
order each time. Sometimes it was a fleeting glimpse, sometimes
he watched himself as if standing a short distance away, while
at other times he relived the past. Sometimes he knew he was
dreaming, while at other times it was as if he were young, and
trying to grapple again with the love and hate which gripped
his soul.

For days Bernarr had sought an opportunity to deal with the
young man privately. The laughing jackanapes had preoccupied
a disproportionate amount of Elaine's time. She seemed willing
to suffer the fool's attentions, but not only was she shirking her
responsibility to her other guests, she had virtually ignored
Bernarr since Zakry's arrival.

The opportunity had finally presented itself in an unexpected fashion. He had organized a hunt to entertain his guests, and all but Elaine joined in with pleasure. She was once again ill. This time he sent the chirurgeon to her with stern instructions to examine her and not take 'no' for an answer.

The rest of them were quickly swept up in the excitement of the chase, the cool crisp air of autumn, the raucous note of the horn. Beaters and hounds flushed a magnificent buck and they tore through the woods with a will. The hounds baying, the beaters sounding their ram's-horn instruments, the stylish riders dressed in every colour and flashing with gold and jewels even brighter than the leaf-cloak of vineyard and tree. It was a magnificent sight.

As they rode Bernarr's quick eye caught sight of a thrashing in a thicket.

Boar! he thought, catching a glimpse of the low-slung body, the massive bristly shoulders and long curved tusks. And wily, too, to be heading away at right-angles rather than attracting the attention of the hounds by running.

The pack hadn't scented it; the wind was blowing in his direction. Bernarr knew the forest pig's ill-temper required little to turn it aggressive, and only the presence of so many hounds and riders was causing it to flee.

And I feel like boar-meat tonight. It would be a prideful moment, the head borne in on a platter, the tusks gilded, and Elaine glowing with delight at her husband's deed.

Bernarr slung the bow over his back and yanked his broadbladed boar-spear from its socket, plunging past trees and leaping his horse over rocks, never letting his prey from his sight. By its size and the sharp, unblunted outline of its tusks the creature was young, in its full strength but still reckless, giving the Baron reason to think this would be an easy kill. An older, more aggressive male would have turned to fight already.

Suddenly the boar faced a thicket too dense to crash through.

It turned first left, then spun right, then came to bay, facing Bernarr in a flurry of dead leaves, its little hind legs stamping as it set itself to charge, to rip at the horse's belly or the rider's legs.

The Baron slowed only a little, to adjust the aim of his spear for the over-arm thrust that would split the beast's heart or spine from above. He would give the inexperienced boar no time to charge and endanger the horse.

Before he could make the thrust an arrow came from behind and to his right. The thick bone and gristle of the boar's shoulders would have stopped it, but the shaft struck right behind the shoulder, the broad-bladed hunting head slicing like knives through the beast's heart and lungs.

It collapsed, spewed blood, kicked, voided itself and died.

Bernarr pulled his horse up hard, causing it to rear and almost fall back on its haunches. He turned to find that Zakry had followed him; the younger man was just lowering his horn-backed hunting bow.

Zakry, his mocking grin in place, spoke, but the words seemed indistinct to Bernarr, and then the youthful rider was gone.

Bernarr was now riding with his wife's other friends from Rillanon, a stag carried proudly behind him by bearers. Then the images faded.

Well, it's not all that different from being a sneak-thief in Krondor, Jimmy the Hand thought. *Just be sensible and don't try to walk too quickly.*

It had been a day and a night since they'd bedded down in the cottage; the old couple didn't seem to find it odd that they chose to stay and spend their days mooching about the woods.

Or perhaps friend Jarvis's silver contains their curiosity, Jimmy thought, stifling a sneeze. He was watching the manor from behind a sheltering belt of bushes, and something in the bushes made his nose and eyes itch. Plus the musty green freshness of it all was disconcerting; Krondor smelled bad, right enough and often enough. But the stink was what he was used to, not this meadow-sweet greenness. At least spring had decided to be spring, with blue sky and warmth and some fleecy-white clouds above, instead of cold rain.

Their curiosity but not mine! his thoughts went on. *Something very nasty is going on at old Baron Bernarr's house, and unless my bump of trouble has lost its cunning, Mr Coe is looking into it – looking into it for someone.*

'Find anything?' Jimmy asked casually, conscious of Coe coming up behind him. *I may not be able to identify every rustle and squeak in the woods, but I know a man's footsteps well enough,* he thought with some satisfaction. It was just a matter of filtering out what didn't matter, same as in town.

'There's an odd absence of bigger game towards the house,' Coe said. 'Plenty of insects, plenty of lizards and birds and even squirrels, but anything near a man's size evidently feels a man's unease about the place. You keep watch on the gate; I'm going to circle around the other side.'

'Yessir, right, sir,' Jimmy muttered under his breath as the older man ghosted across the road and into the brush on the other side. 'Why don't we just get in there?' Coe's caution was beginning to make him itch, almost as much as these damned bushes. Jimmy wanted something to happen.

Something did. A pair of figures came around the central block of the fortified manor house; he knew the stables and sheds were there, so as not to spoil the view from the road, he supposed. They were leading horses; soon enough they mounted, and began to canter towards the outer wall and the gate.

Ah-ha! Jimmy thought, as they came closer.

In their twenties, but looking older; one slight and wiry, the other like something a smith had pounded out of an ingot. A weasel and a mean pit-fighting dog, Jimmy thought, as he got a good look at them. In Krondor he'd have picked them for Bashers – or Sheriff's Crushers. They wore rough leather and wadmal, travelling clothes, and buff-leather jerkins; but their swords were good, if plain, and they had a noteworthy array of fighting knives in belts and tucked into boot-tops. One of them also had a short horn-bow in a case by his right knee.

Let's follow them, he thought. *But carefully.*

As they passed through the wrought-iron gate the thicker-built one reined in.

'Come on, Skinny,' the bigger one called. 'You heard the man – he may be sixty leagues away.'

'The more reason not to get lost in the first league, Rox,' the weasel-faced man replied, looking down at something in one hamlike fist. 'Ah, straight south.'

'Why don't you set up for a prophet, then?' Rox gibed. His friend rumbled something that sounded like obscene instructions, and they both laughed.

Jimmy waited until they were half out of sight along the road southward before he brought his horse out and mounted it. *Jarvis Coe made a big point about how he could track horses and tell them apart, he thought. He can track mine if he wonders where I am.*

After two days, most of the aches of his first ride had simmered down to occasional shooting pains: he was young and supple and strong. Coe still made an occasional mocking comment about his form; especially his flapping arms, but he could usually keep the mild-mannered old horse going in the direction he wanted, even if it seemed determined to amble; the two bashers' mounts weren't exactly fiery, snorting steeds either.

This section of road didn't have much traffic, but it did have enough that one horseman wasn't conspicuous; Jimmy kept the two he was following at the limit of vision for most of two hours, before they halted at a stream to water their mounts. He ducked aside from the road in a dip that hid him from them and vice versa, found a convenient tree to tether his mount – you had to do that at head-level, he'd learned, or they could step over the reins and do dreadful things – and slipped forward on foot for the next hundred yards. If he could get within earshot without their noticing, he might pick up something interesting about their employer and goings-on in the household of the Baron.

A murmur of voices came from the road ahead. Skinny and Rox were there, standing on the stepping-stones of the ford while their horses stood fetlock-deep in the water, muzzles down and slurping. Jimmy eeled along the ground behind a fallen hemlock that was sprouting a fair assortment of bushes from its rotting trunk and listened.

'S'odd,' the bigger man, Rox, said. 'Look how the needle points straight no matter how you turn it.'

It was evidently something Skinny held in his hand; he extended it towards Rox, and the thick pug-faced man shied back as if being offered a scorpion. 'It's magic!' he said, his voice going shrill. 'Of course it's odd. It's bloody cursed!' A pause. 'That house is cursed, too. And that magician – that demon's lover the Baron keeps around – he fair drips with curses.'

'This is cursed, that is cursed, you're not happy unless you've a good curse going,' Skinny jeered. 'It's six hundred gold if we bring him in, you fool. With that much, we can retire – buy that bawdy-house you're always talking about.'

Well, there's an ambition, Jimmy thought. *Six hundred gold. That's serious money, even for a baron with a town and a farm income. You could buy a modest whorehouse with that, and stock it too – if the girls weren't too pretty. Who's this 'he' they're talking about? And a magician? Friend Jarvis will be very interested.*

The two hired swords led their horses out of the water and

prepared to mount; Skinny stopped them with a soft oath as Rox put his foot into the stirrup.

'Wait,' he said. 'The needle quivered, like. See, it moves if I put it left or right, always towards right ahead of us! And I hear sumthin'.'

Jimmy did too, over the purling rush of the stream against its own bed and the flat rocks set in the ford. The familiar hollow clop-clop-clop of a horse ridden at a fast walk.

He looked up, squinting between ferns sprouting from the dead tree-trunk that sheltered him. The ground beneath him was damp; he was down nearly to the river-level, and it took him a minute to make out the rider coming down the low slope toward the water. The horse was nondescript and the tack cheap; the man on it . . .

Well, the lad on it, Jimmy thought. He didn't think the rider was much more than two or three years older than himself. Rough-cut golden hair, face saved from prettiness by a strong jaw and straight nose, frank blue eyes, an outdoorsman's tan. His clothes were rough and serviceable, a farmer or hunter's, perhaps; he had a long yew bow slung over his back, along with a quiver of arrows, and a long knife at his belt as well as the usual shorter all-purpose tool.

'Greetings, friend!' Skinny called.

He looked over his shoulder at his friend. Skinny still had the whatever-it-was in his hand; he moved it from left to right at full extension, then nodded with a pleased smile.

'He's the one,' he said. 'And right into our arms, too! Easy money!'

Skinny sauntered up the rutted roadway toward the newcomer. 'Good place to water your horse,' he said, in a voice dripping with a bad imitation of goodwill.

Evidently the handsome stranger thought so too; Jimmy could see him frown, and touch his bow. Evidently he wasn't used to

being on horseback – the longbow was a footman's weapon –
and a bit uncertain with it.

A better rider than I am, but not by much, Jimmy thought.

'I'll pass by, friend, if it's all the same to you,' the young man
said. He had a rustic accent a lot like Lorrie's.

Am I always to be rescuing farmers' children? Jimmy thought
with irritation along with a healthy hint of fear.

Taking on two grown men, and experienced killers if he'd ever
seen any, was no joke – no alley scuffle, either. He couldn't count
on being better at running and hiding in the woods than either
of the mercenaries.

What to do, what to do?

Skinny didn't appear to have any doubts. He waited by the
side of the road until the traveller was by him, then darted in
with a yell and grabbed for the young man's ankle, plainly
intending to heave him out of the saddle, leaving him stunned
and helpless on the ground.

The young man kicked instead, and Skinny staggered back
with another yell, clutching at his face. The traveller clapped his
heels to his horse and went through the water at a plunging
gallop.

'No, you fool!' Rox yelled, as Skinny pulled the short thick
bow from its case on his saddle and drew a shaft to the ear.

The big man's shout went to wordless rage as Skinny loosed,
nocked another shaft, drew and loosed again. The first arrow
passed so close to the blond rider that Jimmy thought it had
struck him. Then he was close by, and Jimmy could see that it
had – just along the lobe of one ear, the razor edge of the head
slicing it open into the sort of wound that bled freely but didn't
slow you. The second went into the cantle of the saddle with a
thunk!

'You kill six hundred gold and I'll kill you!' Rox bellowed.

He pulled something of his own from his saddlebow, then

began whirling it around his head; Jimmy had just enough time to recognize three smooth pear-shaped iron weights connected by strong cords before it turned into a blur over the big man's head. He cast it when the young rider was twenty yards away and moving fast; cast it at the horse, not the horseman.

It moved fast too, whirling through the air like a horizontal disk. The young man's horse gave a terrified shrieking whinny and crashed kicking to the ground; where it lay writhing and struggling with the weight wound around its hind legs at the hock. The golden-haired bowman lay immobile for a moment, then began to stir. Rox and Skinny bellowed triumph, drawing their swords and dashing through the ford towards the fallen horse and youth.

I could just steal their horses, Jimmy thought. *No, let's get close and see what we can do.*

None of them were looking at the roadside woods, and the growth there was thicker; because the edge got more sunlight, Coe had told him. Jimmy trotted quietly along, trailing the two mercenaries by a few paces, close enough to hear their eager breathing and curses.

By the time they reached the spot both man and horse were back on their feet; the horse had evidently kicked the bola free, for the iron weights lay scattered in the deep dust of the roadway. The blond youth was still woozy, his side and shoulder spattered with the drops that rained from his slit earlobe. He tried to get his bow off his shoulder, but by then the two mercenaries were close, and he tossed it aside rather than trying to nock a shaft, drawing his long knife instead.

'You tried to kill me!' he cried – as much in surprise as indignation, Jimmy thought.

'Na, na, yer worth too much alive,' Skinny said, grinning and showing bad teeth. 'Put the slicer down and come peaceful, and y'll not get hurt.'

The two bravos parted to go around the blond youth's horse; they advanced with professional caution, swords up. The youth backed away, moving his knife between the two; it was ten inches in the blade and good sharp steel, but theirs were each three times longer, and they had leather jerkins and arm-guards to boot.

You haven't got a prayer, farm boy, Jimmy thought regretfully. He looked around and found a couple of nicely fist-sized rocks. *Have to do something to alter the odds.*

The same calculation seemed to occur to the blond youth. With a shout, he leapt forward to attack Skinny, trying to drive him aside. If he got past him he might be able to get to the ford and leap on one of the mercenaries' horses.

Skinny grinned, feinted, and then swept the sword around. The flat of it slammed into the youth's knife-hand, and the blade spun away, its honed edge glinting in the sunlight. A second later Skinny screamed; with admirable presence of mind, the youth had kicked him in the crotch. He staggered backwards, clutching at himself.

'Hey!' Jimmy shouted, pelting forward.

Rox turned at the sound. Jimmy threw the first rock as he ran. Rox took it in the gut; the stiff leather of his jerkin took most of the force, but he still went *ooof* and staggered back two steps.

'No!' Jimmy shouted. 'Run, curse you! Run for the ford!'

With more courage than sense, the blond youth was trying to pick up his knife despite the pained numbness of his well-whacked wrist. Skinny had recovered a little by the time Jimmy arrived on the scene. He dodged the second rock, even at point-blank range, and the young thief dropped with a yell beneath a vicious backhand sword-cut; Skinny didn't have any reason to keep a chance-met stranger alive, and was probably still feeling the effects of the kick. He had to be wearing a boiled-leather cup under those greasy calfskin breeches, to be able to move at all.

Jimmy landed on his back in the dust, hands spread; one palm came down on something cool and metallic, and closed over it in reflex. Skinny's sword glittered above a snarling face; the blond youth barrelled into him before it could come down, and Jimmy rolled and flicked himself back to his feet.

Skinny was coming at him, sword ready and malign intent plain. Behind him Rox grappled with the youth; he hit him on the point of his shoulder with the pommel of his sword, bringing a muffled grunt of pain, then grasped the back of his neck with one spade-sized hand and ran him forward four steps. The youth's face made brutal contact with his own saddle; he bounced back and fell limp. The horse turned and bolted for the ford; Jimmy did likewise, diving aside into cover as something when past him with an unpleasant whistle.

It was a knife; the point thunked into a sapling and the blade quivered with a nerve-racking hum; but there were no sounds of pursuit once he'd made a hundred yards or so. Panting, he stopped and examined the thing he'd caught. It was like a locket, but with only a hair-wrapped needle on a card inside the crystal cover. Shrugging, he tucked it away.

A twig cracked under a foot nearby. Up! was his immediate impulse; and a big beech looked as scalable as a wall. He swarmed up it, and lay along a branch thicker than his body.

Weasel and pit-dog paused beneath him. 'I say we should find him, and scrag him proper,' Skinny said. 'I don't want any witnesses.'

The bigger man guffawed. 'Who's he going to take his story to?' he laughed. 'The Baron? Good luck to him! If he heads back to Land's End to talk to the Constable, all the better, for it'll be days before he sends anyone out here to poke around, assuming he does anything at all. Come on, let's get out of here.'

Jimmy lay motionless on a large branch, catching glimpses of the two men through the foliage. They hoisted the unconscious young man to his feet, and Rox held him up while Skinny lashed his ankles and wrists, then they heaved him over the neck of Skinny's horse. Jimmy saw them ride off, and waited until he was certain the two men were gone. He let himself down, dropping the last six feet to land lightly on his toes. 'What do I do now?' he muttered to no one.

FIFTEEN

Discovery

Bernarr lay dreaming.

Sweat beaded on his forehead and he moaned as he clawed at the sheets. The dream was vivid: he could hear the breeze rustling in the trees, the sound of the surf against the cliffs. The colours were vibrant and even the scent of the woods, the horse's sweat, and the oiled leathers filled his nostrils.

'How dare you take my kill from me?' the Baron demanded furiously. 'Have you no manners at all?' The boar lay twitching at the feet of the Baron's mount, while Bernarr resisted the urge to draw steel and attack the youth.

The younger man bowed in his saddle. 'I am sorry, my lord. I feared that you would miss and endanger yourself.' Zakry's tone was dripping with sincerity, but the slight lift of his lip offered mockery.

Bernarr stared at him coldly. 'I have been hunting boar in these woods of mine since you were soiling your swaddling-clout,' he said. 'And I am hardly in my dotage now. I assure you, I am capable of taking down one of my own boars.'

Zakry inclined his head. 'Sorry, my lord. I will have the

huntsmen gather it up,' he said, sounding apologetic.

'You will leave it where it lies,' Bernarr said abruptly. 'I will not have it on my table.' He touched the rein to the neck of his mount and turned back toward the hunt.

'My lord,' Zakry called out behind him. 'I would speak with you in private.'

Bernarr stopped his horse, clenching his teeth. Such impudence! Even so, he turned and rode back to where the young lord sat fiddling nervously with the reins. 'Follow me then,' he said. 'Let us get out of these woods and go somewhere no one can listen to this "private conversation".'

He broke from the woods into meadowland starred with yellow flowers, drying slightly to a golden shade as the summer grew late, and rode up a hill. Birds broke out of the tall grass before them as the horses' hooves threw up clods of earth. Bernarr kept the pace to a hard gallop until he came to the top of the rise. They stopped just short of the cliffs, the sea below a glorious vista. Gulls wheeled overhead.

Zakry pulled up past him, patting his horse's neck. 'Magnificent,' he proclaimed, taking a deep breath.

'What do you want?' Bernarr asked impatiently.

'My lord,' Zakry said, 'the Lady Elaine should never have left Rillanon: she pines for it, and even you can see that she is thin and pale. She should return to the capital. This is not the life for her! She needs excitement and the glamour of the court. I would ask you, for her sake, my lord, to put her aside.'

Bernarr stared at him in disbelief. 'I beg your pardon?' he said. 'Would you repeat yourself, sir?'

Zakry looked surprised. 'My lord, I assumed you to be a man of the world. You must have known that Elaine and I were lovers.' He laughed nervously. 'Certainly you knew she wasn't a virgin.'

'Stop!' Bernarr shouted. His knuckles were white on the reins and his eyes were wide, his breath whistling through his teeth as he tried to contain his fury.

'I love her,' Zakry said, as if the older man hadn't spoken. 'I never should have let her go. But it isn't too late, you could have the marriage annulled. She would thank you for it.'

'Put her aside? Are you mad? Elaine would die of shame if I were to do such a thing!'

'It is what she wants, sir! She loves me, my lord. And I know she wishes to be with me. Please, have pity on us and let us be together.'

Bernarr made no attempt to hide his rage. 'You will return to the castle now! Pack and leave my house and take the first ship from Land's End you find, or I will not answer for your life beyond sunset.' Turning to ride away, he wrenched at the rein with a strength that brought a squeal of protest from the horse.

'Sir!' Zakry shouted. 'You will listen to me!' He dug his spurs into his horse's flanks and nearly collided with the Baron's bay.

Will he lay hands on me, on my own land? Bernarr wondered. But he said nothing. With a whistle of effort, he turned and struck the other man hard with the back of his fisted gauntlet, iron studs ripping into flesh. Zakry fell back with a cry of pain. His cheek was laid open to the bone within a fraction of an inch of one eye. He dropped his reins and raised both hands in a protective gesture.

Zakry's horse backed, confused and frightened, and flung up its head. Bernarr's horse, sensing its rider's anger and knowing the reins had gone slack, became excited. It laid back its ears, spun and kicked. Zakry's horse, struck hard in the chest, reared. Making a single protesting whinny – almost like the cry of a giant child – it stepped backwards and to the side: one, two, then a third step.

And suddenly they were both gone.

Bernarr pulled hard on the reins, forcing his fractious mount into a tight circle. When he had finally re-established command, he slowly guided the horse to the edge of the cliff and stood up in his stirrups to look over the edge.

Both man and horse had disappeared. Below him, the wild waves crashed around fanged rocks, the spray tossing up forty or fifty feet at each great surge and making the solid granite of the cliffs tremble. Then, briefly, he saw the barrel of the dead horse amidst the breakers, the retreating tide pulling the animal out to sea. Of Zakry there was no sign.

Zakry's disappearance was explained away by a contrived excuse: a message from the east, the need for him to return home by the first ship; and the willingness of those who listened not to offend their host by showing disbelief. Zakry's luggage was sent to town the next day, to follow him to Rillanon, and Elaine's friends continued to enjoy her husband's hospitality. Elaine seemed distant and withdrawn.

Days later Bernarr had to send for a chirurgeon to examine Elaine, for she had taken to bed and complained of being ill.

'I have the most happy news for you, my lord,' the man gushed.

'My lady is not ill,' Bernarr said, his lips lifting in a smile.

'Even better, my lord!' The man preened as though he'd worked a marvel. 'The Baroness is with child! Quick work, my lord, eh?'

The Baron stared at him, his face an unreadable mask. He remained motionless, until the chirurgeon bowed again. 'My steward will see to your fee,' Bernarr said coldly and went into the house. Yet even the chirurgeon's vulgarity could not destroy his delight at the news, or his relief that Elaine was not truly ill. He went directly to her rooms.

She looked up, startled at his entrance, her green eyes wide. Bernarr knelt at her side, taking her hand in his and kissing it.

In his dream he could still feel the fragile fingers, the soft skin, still see the pulse beating in her neck as she lay pale against the white pillows and cushions.

Tears gathered in her eyes, yet her expression was not joyous. They spoke in broken sentences, and he remembered nothing of what they said, save that when he left her chamber, she was quietly weeping.

The guests observed the obligatory feigned joy at the news of her condition, used it as an excuse to organize a feast, and drank a large portion of the baronial wine cellar.

But soon they were forced to leave. By ship to Krondor, then overland to Salador and on to Rillanon was a trip of more than a month. Once the Straits of Darkness were in the grip of winter storms, the only passage was around the southern tip of Great Kesh, a travel of three months beset with storms, pirates and Keshian raiders. When it became clear the Baron would not invite them to spend the winter in Land's End, they bid their host and hostess a polite farewell, and departed.

The Baron twisted in the damp sheets, his eyes fluttering as he moaned. The storm . . .

On the night on which the Baroness Elaine went into labour a storm sprang up out of the sea; hills and walls of purple-black cloud piled along the western horizon, flickering with lightning but touched gold by the sun as it set behind them. The surge came before the storm: mountain-high waves that set fishermen dragging their craft higher and lashing them to trees and boulders; then to praying as the thrust of air came shrieking about their thatch. When the rain followed it came in nearly horizontal, blown before the monster winds.

Whips of rain lashed the manor, too. Lightning forked the sky and thunder rattled the windows. Bernarr had bribed the midwife to stay at the manse for the last two weeks and now he was very glad he'd done so.

As he got ready to dine, a servant announced a traveller and his servants at the gate, begging shelter. This Bernarr granted gladly – hospitality brought luck, and at this moment he wanted his full share. The house was so still these days he would also welcome the company and he was delighted to discover that his guest was a scholar who cared far more for the books in his coach than for either his horses, his servants or himself.

He was a tall, imposing man, with large eyes and a penetrating gaze, a few years older than Bernarr. His name was Lyman Malachy.

'Yes,' said Malachy, 'when I heard of the sudden death of your father, I began my journey from a great distance. With many distractions and delays behind me, I arrive tonight.' He shook his sleeve as if to dispatch the remaining drops of rainwater on the cuff. 'I had exchanged missives with your father, but I had no knowledge of his heirs. I feared you wouldn't know what you had in his books and might sell them to someone else before I could possibly make an offer.'

The Baron smiled and shook his head. He was about to speak when he noticed that Lyman's eyes had gone distant, which surprised him. Up until this moment the little fellow had been an excellent and most attentive guest. But almost immediately Lyman's eyes cleared and he looked gravely at the Baron.

'A child will be born in this house tonight,' he said. 'A boy.'

'How could you know that?' Bernarr asked in wonder. 'The Baroness is with child, but she isn't due so soon.'

Lyman smiled tersely. 'I would not trust everyone with this knowledge,' he said. 'But, as you are an educated man, beyond crude peasant superstition, and so generous a host, I will confess. I am a magician.'

'Ah,' was all Bernarr said. But he wondered what to do. He'd taken an instant liking to his mysterious guest, and like most citizens of the Kingdom he had his doubts about those who dabbled in magic; yet he felt a curious kinship with Malachy. He chose to be delicate; after all, the man would be gone in the morning. 'That must cause you some . . . difficulty.'

'It has at times,' Lyman admitted. 'There is prejudice against those of us who follow the art, who have the gift . . . But fortunately for me my family was well off and I was sent far from home to study. As a result, no one who knew me as a child knows of my talents, and as my parents left me with a handsome legacy, I am able to support myself quite comfortably. Which means I can afford to buy books!'

They both grinned at that. Then came a sharp rap on the door.

'Come,' Bernarr called.

A servant appeared, his face drawn and his eyes wide. 'My lord! The Lady Elaine's time has come!'

Bernarr rose to his feet, his heart leaping to his throat. As he passed his guest, he saw a small smile raise the corner of the magician's mouth.

Images sped by.

The midwife standing by the door, a worried expression on her face. 'The baby is coming . . .' and then her words faded.

Then the face of Elaine, pale and drenched in perspiration as the midwife commanded her to push. The screaming and the blood.

The crying baby, held out proudly by the midwife, who said, 'You have a son, my lady' to the fading Baroness, who was in too much pain even to recognize the baby for what it was.

Blood was everywhere.

Blood.

Bernarr turned in bed, moaning and crying, *No!* he tried to say, but only another low groan escaped his lips.

Then Lyman was at his shoulder. His manner was calm and commanding. 'Everyone leave the room,' he said simply.

Then the screaming stopped.

Bernarr sat up in bed. He was panting as if he had run for hours, and his still-fit body was taut and drenched with perspiration as if he had fought a battle. He rolled out of bed, pulled off his soaked night shirt, and threw it across the floor. Through the window he could see the morning sun had just crested the mountains, and another day had started. *Only hours*, he thought, as he sat naked on the bed, reaching for a mug and the pitcher of water left on the night table. He drank and refilled the mug to drink again.

But the other thirst – the thirst to end this nightmare that had plagued him for seventeen years, to see his Elaine restored and free of the endless pain – still lingered.

Standing up, he moved to the tub of water awaiting his morning wash. He didn't mind the cold water: he had grown used to it. He needed to cleanse himself of the foul feeling on his skin, and would not don clothing until he did. He stepped into the small copper tub, squatted and grabbed the sponge upon the table next to it, ignoring the chilly bite of the water. *If only I could clean away my pain*, he thought, as he had every morning for seventeen years.

But soon . . .

Aunt Cleora went pale. 'Oh, Ruthia!' she gasped, a hand pressed to her throat.

The horse-dealer prodded the saddle where it lay on the flag-stones of the kitchen floor. A black-and-white kitten came up to it, sniffing at the fascinating scents of horse-sweat, leather and blood.

'Aye, it's blood, right enough,' Kerson said. 'And this —' his toe touched the stub of an arrow that jutted up from the rear of the saddle, '— isn't no hunting shaft, either.'

He produced a pair of pliers from a loop at his waist and bent, putting one foot on the saddle and pinching the tool closed on the glint of metal where arrow shaft joined leather.

'Come up there!' he grunted, heaving backward, the muscles in his arms and shoulders bunching.

It came free, and he stuck it under their noses. 'See? Bodkin point, not a broad head. None use that, except for hunting men — it's meant to pierce armour or jerkin.'

Lorrie stared at the saddle with a sick dread in her heart, worse even than the cold feeling that had held her since her family died. She knew they were dead; she knew Rip was still alive for the feeling was there in distant flashes. But she didn't know whether Bram was alive or dead.

'The horse come in at first light,' Kerson said. It was an hour after sunrise, and the family had just been finishing the morning meal when the horse-trader had arrived at the door of the house. 'Poor beast had its ribs beat raw by the stirrups, and dried foam caked halfway to its tail. Looks like it was trotting all night. Took a bad fright, and I thought seeing's it was that tall blond lad, your young niece's friend, that bought it, and he was on his way chasing after your niece's other friend, the lad I sold . . .' he pointed to Lorrie, '. . . your old horse to, well, anyway, seeing as it sort of all fit together, I thought you should know.'

Aunt Cleora looked around. 'The Constable?' she said.

Kerson snorted. 'For an affray in the town bounds, certainly,' he said. 'Although he uses those two-a-penny thief-takers, more than his own men. No, out on the road it would be the Baron's men-at-arms who'd be the ones to see, except he doesn't pay no mind to common folks' problems these fifteen year and more.

The soldiers might turn out if Kesh attacked the city, but for a lost lad, taken by bandits or slavers, no. They'll not stir.'

He looked at Lorrie and Flora, where they sat side by side on the bench. 'It's all that I can do, Miss Flora. I've my own family and kin and business to look after. I just thought you should know, like.'

When the man had gone, silence lay heavy for a moment. Cleora came over to put an arm around Lorrie's shoulders.

'He went to look for Rip, and he may be dead,' Lorrie whispered. 'And all because of me.'

Surprisingly, Flora shook her head. 'No,' she said. 'He would have looked for your brother anyway. He was that sort of man – I could tell.'

Lorrie nodded dumbly, fighting back tears and wiping at her eyes with the back of her hand.

'And Jimmy's my . . . foster-brother, and he went looking for Rip, too, and he may be dead,' Flora said decisively. 'Or they may both be hurt. I have to go and look.'

'That's impossible!' Aunt Cleora squeaked. 'A young girl, on her own in the country?'

Even then, Lorrie had to smile; Aunt Cleora seemed to think goblins and bandits lurked behind every bush. *Or maybe they do*, she thought, looking at the saddle again, her eyes drawn to it with unwilling fascination.

'She won't be going alone. I'm going too!' Lorrie said.

It's my baby brother and my intended. And I can't let Flora go alone, after all she's done for me!

Both the other women looked at her. 'But you can barely walk!' Flora said.

'I can use a stick,' Lorrie said stoutly. *True, it's healing fast, but how far will I get?* she thought, more honestly. 'I can ride, maybe. Or crawl, if needs must.'

Aunt Cleora looked from one to the other. 'I wish Karl were

here with his men,' she said unhappily. 'It'll only be a couple of weeks until his ship's back from Krondor.' She looked at them again; Lorrie could tell Flora wore the same mutinous expression as herself. 'I don't like it. I don't like it at all,' Cleora said again. 'But if you must go, you'll take my dog-cart.'

Flora sprang up and hugged her aunt. The dog-cart was a vehicle with two tall spoked wheels and a body slung on leather rests, with a folding cover, drawn by a single horse. It would hold two easily, and on a good road wouldn't be too hard on a healing leg.

'Thank you, Aunt Flora!' she said, and Lorrie nodded enthusiastically.

The pretty, middle-aged features of the older woman creased in worry, but Flora was already up and about, stuffing things in bags.

'What is it?' Jimmy asked, prodding with his finger at the locket-sized device that lay on the table.

The old couple whose cottage it was huddled back by the hearth, unconsciously gripping hands as they stared at the thing. They had just finished supper, happy to provide porridge, eggs, a pair of apples and a very bitter brew that almost passed for ale for another of Jarvis's silver pieces.

Jimmy thought that on another occasion, his entire focus would be upon Jarvis Coe's purse, for it seemed to possess an endless supply of silver. But that was then, and this was now, and there were mysteries to unravel and boys to save.

Jarvis Coe sat on a stool, hands on his knees as he leaned forward. His craggy face was set, and the low flames from the hearth cast restless red lights across the lines and planes of it. 'It's magic,' he said softly. Jimmy felt the small hairs bristle down his spine at the word. 'Forbidden magic. It's a man-finder, bound by blood and bone and seed.' His finger traced the needle. 'See, here? The needle is bone from a dead baby harvested in the dark of the moons –'

The old woman moaned and shivered, huddling closer into her husband's protective arm.

'– and the hair is of the man you wish to seek, or from his close kin. Mother or father, or both, if you wish to find their child. I'd say that was the case this time: you said the boy was fair-haired, and this tress is brown. Not necromancy; not quite, but related to it. Dark enough magic to be troubling, in any event.'

'Who are you, that you know this?' Jimmy asked.

Jarvis looked up quickly, his eyes hooded. After a long moment he nodded. 'Well, you've a right to know, I suppose, if you're to be involved in this affair. I'm an agent for the High Priestess of Lims-Kragma in Krondor.'

The young thief bounded backward, hand going to his knife. The old midwife made signs with her hands, and her husband rose too and sidled towards the door, where his billhook was propped.

Astonishingly, Jarvis Coe laughed. 'No, no, my friends, you needn't worry. She is the Mistress of Death, not murder. We're all coming home to Her, eventually, so she doesn't need anyone hurried along.' His lips quirked, and he quoted in an archaic dialect:

> 'Under her sway gois all estatis;
> Princes, prelatis, poetasis;
> She sparis na prince, for his presence
> Na clerk, for his intelligence;
> Her awful straik may no man flee . . .'

Jimmy who had no time for such fripperies, nodded stiffly, still alert and poised. 'And what are you doing on the trail of men who kidnap children?' he asked.

'The Temple particularly doesn't like people who make death-magic,' Coe said.

'Why not?' Jimmy said, thinking of rumours he'd heard of those priestesses.

'Because it gives the Goddess a bad reputation,' Coe said. 'And that endangers the temples. In ages past, before the temples reached accord with the Crown and agreed to allow the Temple of Ishap to settle disputes, there was more than one riot in which an angry mob sacked a temple and killed all the worshippers. Even with a hundred years and more of peace between the temples, there's still a strong potential for mayhem if word of something like this gets out, and if people think the Temple of Lims-Kragma had a hand in it.

'Moreover, it's stealing from Lims-Kragma: the life energies which should be returned to Her hall for judging are denied their proper placement on the next turn of the Wheel of Life. Those souls are tortured, tormented and eventually vanish as if they had never existed. It's an abomination and heresy of the worst stripe.

'No good ever comes from these practices, and only those who are truly evil or truly fools undertake such.' He showed his teeth. 'I am the particular "no good" that will come to the necromancer who's working in the vicinity. I'm no magician myself,' he went on. 'But I do have some . . . talent in these areas . . . and I have resources from my employers, which will help me deal with him.'

'But not necessarily mercenaries, stone walls and iron bars?' Jimmy said sardonically.

I'm really not happy, he thought. *I'd almost rather he was one of Jocko's spies. On the other hand, he's likely to be much more useful than one of the secret police, and if I'm to undertake hero-of-legend deeds against an evil enchanter, no less, I could do with some help.*

He didn't want to go back to Lorrie and tell her he couldn't find Rip: after all, he'd promised. On the other hand, he didn't want to be chained to a red-hot metal plate in a dungeon for the next thousand years, either; or have his death-essence used to power a spell. Risk was one thing, doom another.

Besides, I suspect that ducking out on friend Coe would be unlucky. I do not want the hatred of a goddess dogging my steps. Her favour, on the other hand, and the favour of her priestesses . . .

'All right,' he said at last. 'What does this necromancer want with our blond-haired friend?'

'In just four days the three moons will be dark,' Jarvis said, his fingers toying idly with a crust of barley-bread. 'And certain stars will be in conjunction. At that time . . . well, let's say that the wayfarer they picked up and brought back to the manor would be useful for certain dark arts. Useful in a terminal sense. As would young Rip, your friend's brother.'

Jimmy winced. He was used to beatings, stabbings and affrays: he'd taken part in them himself. But human sacrifice was another matter altogether. 'This is getting beyond belief,' he said. 'Children, then wayfarers –'

'One specific wayfarer,' Jarvis said carefully as if reflecting on that fact.

The old woman made a noise and her husband tried to shush her, but she pushed him aside. 'Four days, you say, priestess's servant?'

Jarvis bowed. 'Goodwife.'

'That would be seventeen years to the day from the time Mistress Elaine died in childbed,' she said. 'Seventeen years to the very hour, at midnight.'

Jarvis's face changed. A shadow of fear – and maybe disgust – passed over it. *Uh-oh*, Jimmy thought. *This is bad news.*

'Did you . . . were you sure she died?' Jarvis held up his hand. 'Did you see the body laid out?'

The midwife shook her head. 'He thrust us all out of the room, and later word was sent that things had been done,' she said softly. 'Thrust us all out, but kept with him a chance-met guest he'd been hosting that night, a scholar.'

'Ah. I doubt that it was entirely chance, not on that night – certain happenings cast their own shadows, forward and back-ward in time.' Jarvis looked down at the talisman. 'Have you anything of the lady's?' he said. 'Anything that touched her body?'

The old woman rose and went over to her pole-frame bed and dragged out a cedarwood chest that looked incongruously fine in the wattle cottage. Prodding around inside it, she brought out a small bundle wrapped in silk stained with old, dried blood. 'She were fond of me, and a kind lady,' the midwife said. 'She knew she could trust old Meg; many a secret a midwife hears. This she gave me, for safekeeping. It would have been as much as her life were worth, did the Baron find it.'

Jimmy came close as Jarvis took the bundle from the old woman and swept the rough wooden surface of the table clean of crusts and crockery before he laid it down and began to unfold it.

'Should the talisman be doing that?' Jimmy asked.

The needle beneath the crystal lid was jerking; first it pointed southwest, toward Baron Bernarr's manor; then it swung towards the bundle.

'No, it should not,' Jarvis said. Inside the silken handkerchief was a true locket, a delicate shell of electrum. 'Even if this is the lady's blood from the birthing –'

'It is,' the old woman said.

'– or hair, or nail clippings,' he went on. 'The spell is linked to the similarity of essences. It should be pointing toward the son.' Jarvis opened the locket, his fingers probing delicately for the catch. Within one half was a miniature portrait, a tiny thing no bigger than Jimmy's thumb. The other held a love-knot, a twining of hair braided together, one strand blond, the other brown. 'Could you bring me some light, Jimmy?' he asked.

Jimmy went to the hearth. A tube of birch-bark stood on the bare earth beside it, containing long splints of lightwood from resinous pine, ready to kindle. He took one and held it to the low flames of the fire. It hissed and spat as it caught, giving off a resinous, medicinal scent. Jimmy brought it back to the table, holding it higher and to one side so that no driblets of hot sap would fall on the table, careful that none struck him, either.

The light was wavering and none too bright compared to a candle, but the old couple had none of those, or even tallow dips, but it was still bright enough for him to see the handsome blond young man in the portrait.

'Ruthia!' Jimmy blurted. 'That's the one they took!'

'No,' the old woman said. 'That's young lord Kethry, by the name of Zakry, who were Lady Elaine's friend from Krondor. From before she met the Baron. Him who disappeared.'

'Oh-ho,' Jimmy said. 'Well, from his looks –'

'And from the behaviour of this needle –'

'I'd say that while the Lady Elaine may have had a son seventeen years ago, the Baron surely didn't,' Jimmy said.

Jarvis gave a lopsided grin. 'You can see further than most, Jimmy,' he said.

The cottager sighed. 'You'll have to tell them now,' he said wearily. 'No helping it.'

Meg the midwife nodded. 'The Baron would have none of his son . . . well, of the baby. For a moment he was overjoyed to have an heir, but when he saw his wife at the edge of death, he became a man possessed. He blamed the baby and told me to get rid of it, so that he would never see it again. Set it out for the wolves, he meant, but I couldn't. So I took it to a farmer I knew – name of Ossrey – near Relling, whose wife had lost her babe but still had milk. They were glad to take it in and raise it as their own.'

'Relling's not far south of here, and somewhat east. Still on the Baron's land, of course,' her husband added. 'He promised never to speak of it, and to give him credit, I've never heard the rumour come back. Like as not they've forgotten the babe wasn't theirs; all they knew was the mother died birthing it, and likely they thought it some serving-girl's by-blow.'

'This makes a good deal of unpleasant sense,' Jarvis Coe said. 'The Baron obviously loved his wife very much.'

'To madness,' Meg said, sitting down on her bed and sighing as she looked at the cedarwood box. 'And I never thought she wasn't fond of him – even when she took sick after Kethry disappeared.'

'Disappeared?'

'In a hunt. Rode off to Krondor, the Baron said, leaving his servants and traps to be sent on, but nobody saw hide nor hair of him again. Young Lord Kethry never reached Rillanon.'

Jimmy snorted. *I know that sort of sudden leave-taking*, he thought. *Bet if you asked, nobody saw him arrive anywhere else, either. The sea hides a good many sins.*

'Well . . .' Jarvis said, looking at the three of them and obviously thinking how much to tell. Jimmy raised an ironic eyebrow: it was a bit late to be cautious about things.

Unless he plans to leave no witnesses, and I doubt he's quite that ruthless.

Jarvis confirmed his guess by going on: 'If a magician of the . . . right sort . . . were at hand, as the lady lay dying, he could . . . not keep her alive, exactly. Suspend her, between life and death, so that someone could attempt to heal her entirely later.' He reached for a wooden mug of the old couple's ale. 'Let me wash out my mouth! She'd be suspended between life and death . . . for . . . by the Goddess! Seventeen years, dying every second!'

Jimmy felt the coarse bread and eternal bean soup turn into a heavy lump under his breastbone. 'Lims-Kragma rest her!' Another thought struck him. 'And why do they want her son?'

Remind me never to get involved with wizards again, he thought. Looking back on it, he felt a touch of fear at how lightly he'd dealt with old Alban Asher, even.

'Well, the force of life is released at death. They could try to revive her with anyone's, but the more like to like, the easier. Children, because her life was lost birthing a child. The child himself, best of all – it's the natural order that the lives of parents run on in their children, but it can be forced into reverse.'

The old man spat into the fire, which hissed.

Jarvis looked up. 'We have four days,' he said. 'And so does young –' He looked down at the locket.

'Bram,' Meg said.

'– Bram,' Jarvis echoed.

Jimmy sighed. 'I suppose, if he loved her that much . . . it's evil and mad, but there's a sort of grandeur to it.'

'Less than he thinks,' Jarvis said. 'You can get someone back, in a way, but they're often . . . changed. Unsealing the boundaries of life and death lets . . . other things . . . in.' He closed his eyes. 'Things that once in our world are most difficult to cast out.' Coe let out a long sigh, as he contemplated what that meant.

Jimmy felt the hair on the back of his neck and arms rise up, and wished more than ever he had just lain low in Krondor and not tried to be so heroic.

SIXTEEN

Developments

Rip tried to peer through the hole.

'Chain him well,' the old man's voice said. 'And keep that bag on his head, I told you!'

Rip slid back down with a muffled gasp. The problem with the peepholes in the secret passages was that they were made for grown-ups.

Another voice sounded – the weasel voice.

'As you wish, my lord. Ah, my lord –'

'You'll get the rest of your money, oaf. I don't keep that much cash here: my man of business in Land's End will bring it up next week. I have need of you anyway, until then. Be silent, and go.'

Chains clanked. 'Your son is waking, my lord,' said the oily man's voice. 'Perhaps we should leave. I have examined him, and apart from a few scrapes and bruises, he is healthy enough. More than healthy enough to last three days.'

'Do not call him my son, ever again,' the old man's voice said, softly menacing. 'He murdered my lady Elaine.'

Steps faded away, and the lantern-light through the peephole went out as the outer door of the room thudded shut; they could hear the key turn in the lock.

'They caught someone else?' Mandy said. 'And chained him up?'

Rip nodded, and made an affirmative sound in his throat.

'That's cruel,' Neesa said. 'I mean, even more cruel.'

'But the old man said he was his son,' Rip said, frowning.

'You mean he chained up his own son?' Kay asked, sounding horrified and delighted at once. 'Like the Wicked King and the Good Prince?'

'Let's go and look,' Rip said.

He felt for the catches of the secret door, and they stepped into the room. It was bare and empty, with a stone floor and stone walls, and was lit dimly by one barred window high up on the far side. It was not large, as rooms went in the big manor. Rip thought it might have been used to store things once: it was on the ground level near the kitchens, which made it chilly and damp.

'That's a grown-up!' Neesa said, her whisper carrying too clearly.

The figure chained to the opposite wall raised his head. He was a tall young man with a burlap sack over his head; for the rest he wore only breeches and shirt. There were manacles on his wrists, running down to an iron ring that also held the ones that joined his ankles: if he'd been standing he'd have had to stoop, and take small steps. Another chain ran from one ankle to an iron bolt driven deep into the stone of one wall. There was a basin of water and a slop bucket within reach, but otherwise he couldn't go beyond a semicircle six feet in circumference.

'Who's there?' he asked groggily.

Hope blazed up in Rip, and he felt giddy with excitement. He dashed across the stone, making shushing sounds, and fumbled

310

at the drawstring that held the bag over the young man's head. Hands closed on him, strong but not hurtful.

'Bram!' Rip squealed, remembering to be quiet at the last minute.

'Rip! Rip, lad!' Bram said, and hugged him.

Rip hugged him back; it felt so good to see a familiar face.

'I came to rescue you!' Bram said, laughing, as he held the boy at arms' length.

'And now I can rescue you!' Rip said, delighted. 'I've got keys.'

Bram laughed ruefully and held up his manacled wrists, turning them so that Rip could see them in the dim, fading light. There were no keyholes, just an overlapping joint with a thin rod of soft wrought iron pushed through it and peened over with a hammer.

'Did that on an anvil, and the feet are the same,' Bram said ruefully. 'I remember that much, and the two who caught me – folk'd pay to see that fight, and laugh themselves silly, I've no doubt.'

'A big strong one and a skinny one who talks like a weasel?' Rip said.

'The same,' Bram replied. 'And so unless you've a cold chisel and a hammer, Rip lad, you're not setting me free.'

He looked beyond the boy at the children, who stood looking back big-eyed; Neesa hugged her doll to her side, and stuck her thumb in her mouth. Bram's expression softened.

'Well, but you're not kept close here, then?' he said.

'We were,' Rip said. 'We got out.'

'It was Rip's idea,' Mandy said. 'We tripped the man who came with our food.'

'And tied him up!' Kay said, grinning.

'And then we pulled a sheet over him and tied that up,' Mandy put in, shyly touching her white-blonde hair.

'And I hit him with a candlestick,' Neesa put in with a grin.

'Well done, the lot of you,' Bram said. 'Though I should have known Rip was up to it, after he put that itchweed powder in my breeches while I was swimming, last year.'

Rip blushed and others looked at him with awed respect.

'Did Ma and Pa send you?' he asked eagerly.

Bram's face changed. 'Lad –' he said. 'I have grave news, and no time being gentle in telling you.' He explained about Rip's parents, glossing over the details of their death, then rapidly assured him Lorrie was safe in Land's End.

Rip collapsed against him; the tears didn't last long, though. He'd done his fair share of crying since being taken, in the dark where nobody could see. After a moment he felt the children crowding around, and Bram's other arm went around them too, as far as he could reach.

'I want you to kill them!' Rip said after a moment, wiping at his face with his palms. 'They're . . . they're evil!'

'That they are,' Bram said. He clanked his chains a little, ruefully. 'But I'm a bit tied up at the moment.' His smile turned to a frown. 'I still don't know why they've taken you, or me,' he went on. 'Even a baron can't do this sort of thing for long. Stealing children – there'll be rebellion if it gets out. Parents won't wait for the Prince's Magistrate to come down from Krondor. Those who've already lost children will be the first to riot.'

'They had kids before us,' Mandy said in a small voice. 'After a while they'd come and take them away and they didn't come back.'

Rip swallowed. 'I think . . . I think one of them is a magician,' he said.

Bram frowned. 'And the old man –'

'The Baron? I don't know. Everyone does what he says, though.'

'The Baron,' Bram confirmed. 'Baron Bernarr of Land's End.'

'And . . . Bram, there are . . . things here.' Rip looked around at the shadows; he could feel them. 'Wrong things.'

Bram nodded, and his voice went hard and grim. 'So now we know what he's been doing with the silver we sweated to give him all these years, bought with the good bread we didn't eat and the cloth we didn't wear come winter; not paying men-at-arms to keep us safe, or to hold court and give justice, or patch the roads. Yes, I felt it too. Even the cut-throats who brought me here did. There's something bad here, something rotten.'

He looked up, almost bristling, bruised lips curling back from his teeth. A breeze they could all feel cuffed at their heads, stirred the dark air.

'What was that? Who calls?'

Impressions blurred and memories returned.

The children!

They were not where she had seen them last. She didn't understand the cycles she endured, pain, blackness, being in her body, being out. Forces tugged at her and sometimes she ached just to remain in oblivion. There were times she raged in frustration at her inability to interact with those around her, and she often felt confused by the sudden jumps from night to day and back, and the rapidly changing light outside the windows, sometimes the cold and foggy skies of winter common to this coast, other times the brilliant golden sun of summer. It confounded her senses as much as anything else, not knowing how long she had lingered in this state since the baby was born. She floated away from her body, looking for the children.

The girl, the one the others called Neesa, she was almost able to talk to Elaine, and Elaine hungered for some human contact. No matter how long it had been since the birth of her son, it felt as if she had not known the touch of a hand or the sound of a voice in a very long time. She sensed the children had moved to another room, and she hastened there. As she entered, she saw the black cloud, the spirit presence of some unnamed evil that had avoided her for so long. It hovered over the children.

Elaine swept toward the black cloud furiously, snatching at one of its tendrils. It pulled back, retreating slightly, then it fled. Rather than waste her energy chasing it, Elaine hovered protectively over the children, pleased by their presence, delighted with the littlest one, the boy, and feeling a connection with the girl.

Then she realized something had changed. There was a new presence! It was . . .

Zakry! Elaine called.

They had brought Zakry – chained him, beaten him. Her rage swirled about the man she loved, and they retreated before it, afraid, drawing back their looming presence like the fading of the stench of rotten meat.

Her anger was palpable, enough to ruffle their hair and stir the burlap sack on the floor beside him. Beaten! Chained!

Then she heard what the children called him. Bram. She looked – somehow, like this, she could look deeper into a man than she'd been able to do before, see the links between things.

Not Zakry. Although the image of him; but he was younger, ten years younger, and different. Features softened a little, and hair a deeper yellow, not quite so fair. Eyes a darker blue. Shoulders broader and arms thicker.

My son! The knowledge hit her, impossible to deny. *My baby, Zakry's son!* Despair threatened to overwhelm her. *How many years! How long have I lingered in this place between life and death?* Clarity arrived and she understood now; those darknesses, those times when she thought she had slept for minutes, those had been days, weeks even. The changing light had been the passing of seasons. She had been trapped in this horrible state of not-living, not-dying, for years. Years when she had thought it but days! Rage rose up. *Who has done this thing to me?* She wailed a soundless cry of pain, and Neesa seemed to sense she was near. She looked right at where Elaine floated, and there was sadness in the girl's eyes. She inclined her head toward Bram, as if saying, See, this is what you came for. Elaine looked again at her son and a soft yearning began to replace the anger. She wanted to hold him in her arms, to comfort him, to tell him of her love. And she wanted to protect him, for now she understood the presence of the black tendrils of evil, the need for a child of hers, and she knew without doubt Bram's life was at risk. Someone must warn him.

Tell him, boy! Tell him! Elaine shouted.

'Tell him, boy,' said Neesa, as if listening to another voice. 'Tell him!' she repeated softly.

'Bram . . .' Rip said.

'Mmm?' Bram said, his strong white teeth tearing at the bread.

It was stolen from a guard's table while the man went to use the privy, and it was tough and black, made from mixed barley and rye and full of husks. That didn't disturb either Rip or the young man; it was much like what they ate every day.

'Sorry,' Bram said when his mouth was free; he took a long drink of water and a bite of smoked pork. 'Right hungry. Haven't had much to eat today, except hard knocks.'

'Bram, the old man – the Baron – said something really strange.' Rip frowned, remembering. He couldn't stop remembering. It played over and over again in his head. 'And the oily man. He said you were the Baron's son, and the Baron said not to say that, because you'd killed his lady.'

'Me the Baron's son!' Bram laughed. 'Baron Bram of the Barn! My lord of the Muck-heap!' Then his face changed. 'What did he say about a lady?'

'That you'd killed her, and that was why he wanted the bag over your head.'

Kay cut in. 'It is like the Wicked King and the Good Prince!' he said. 'The evil stepmother wants to kill the Prince, and the King hates him 'cause his mother died having him, so she puts him out in the woods, but the woodcutter finds him and fights the wolves and takes him home to raise him as his own!'

'That's just a story, youngster,' Bram said uneasily. 'Right now, we're in the part before the happy ending.'

Rip looked at him. *Bram doesn't think we will have a happy ending*, he thought. *But we will! Bram's a hero!*

'What are they doing?' Flora asked curiously, pointing.

Lorrie goggled at her, and then at the field beside the road. The strong sweet scent of the cut hay drifted over to the two girls in the dog-cart, and the scythes flashed as the mowers moved down the flower-starred field. Birds burst up out of the grass before them and circled above, diving at the buzzing insects that the blades disturbed. The mowers were singing as they worked – that made it go easier, as she well knew, with memories of days at hatchet and churn and spinning wheel and hoe and rake – until one of them called a halt. He unslung a little wooden barrel he wore around his neck on a cloth sling, pulled the bung with his teeth and tilted it back until a stream arched into his upturned mouth; cider, probably.

She could see the worn shirt sticking to his back with sweat; he looked up as he passed the little barrel on and waved at her with a grin. He'd be the farmer, the Lord of the Harvest. She knew she was right when he gave the signal to start work again a moment later.

There were six working with scythes, five men and a woman: swinging a scythe took strong arms and back, much more than harvesting grain with a sickle. Women and girls and youths followed them, raking and turning the cut hay and pushing it into a long roll on the ground, a tad. They'd be back, of course, to keep turning it until it cured, and then to pitch it onto a cart and bring it home to go under cover and feed stock through the next year.

'Why, they're cutting the hay,' Lorrie said, conscious of the long silence of her astonishment. 'First cutting, but a bit late. Haven't you ever seen hay cut before?'

Flora shook her head, and Lorrie almost lost control of the reins as she gaped.

They were going along at a slow trot: Aunt Cleora's carriage-horse was a big glossy gelding, far finer than poor old Horace, but not noticeably faster. Leather slings gave the dog-cart an odd greasy sway too, not like the forthright jouncing and jolting of a farm-cart, but she had to admit it was easy on her leg, which pained her little more than it would have done while she lay on a featherbed in her friend's house.

'Never seen hay cut?' she cried.

'Well, you've never seen the Prince's men parading through the streets of Krondor,' Flora said.

'Oh, I wasn't mocking you,' Lorrie assured her. 'It's just . . . well, I've never met anyone who's not seen haying, before. That's all.' She sighed. 'That's when Bram kissed me first,' she said shyly. 'At a dance at the end of a haying-day, last year.'

'So you're going to marry Bram?' Flora asked, plainly glad to change the subject.

'Well, I think he wants to,' Lorrie said shyly, keeping her attention on the reins and the horse.

'Gods of love, he's handsome enough!' said Flora with a giggle.

Lorrie giggled in return. 'He is, isn't he?'

She felt a spurt of happiness, absurd under the worry. *He isn't dead*, she thought. *He can't be dead!* But if her mother and father could die, the pillars of all her life, what was safe? Resolutely she pushed that aside, enjoying the day. She looked at Flora. 'Flora,' she said suddenly. 'Why are you helping me?' Then, hastily: 'Not that I mind! But you and your foster-brother, you've treated me like your own kin – and I'm just a girl from a farm with four cows and one horse, not a fine lady like you.'

Flora had been frowning, slightly thoughtful. At that she laughed. There was an edge of bitterness to it. 'Fine lady!' she said.

Lorrie blinked at her, confused. 'Well, you are,' she pointed out.

The furnishings in Aunt Cleora's house alone were worth a decade's rent for any ten farms in her home valley, with the inn at Relling ford thrown in, and possibly the gristmill.

'I'm Aunt Cleora's sister's daughter,' Flora said slowly. 'But she ran off with a baker. Ran off to Krondor.'

'Ah!' Lorrie said, understanding. 'And your father's Da cut him off?'

That happened sometimes back home, too. Young men seemed made to quarrel with their fathers about the time their beards sprouted, and sometimes it grew hot. Even Bram, good-hearted and willing, butted heads with Ossrey sometimes, like rams in spring. That was one reason he had hired himself out to merchants' caravans as a guard and wrangler now and then, besides the cash.

'Right. And then the baker . . . my father proved his judgment right and my mother's wrong when he crawled into a brandy-barrel, and stayed there.'

Lorrie nodded. That certainly happened back home, too. 'Ah, you'll have had to work out,' she said. 'Do laundry and sewing and suchlike.'

Vaguely, she knew that was one of the things poor women in towns did; she didn't suppose they could hire themselves out as maids of all work or dairy-hands.

'Yes, suchlike,' Flora said shortly, then chuckled. 'A town can be a hard place for a young girl. All alone, and everyone a stranger.

I ... came back to Land's End, and things worked out for me, but you didn't have anybody.'

They drove on in companionable silence. After a while the land rose; they went through a patch of forest, cool grateful shade that reminded Lorrie painfully of her day hunting. Beyond that there was a man bent nearly double under a load of faggots, his axe on top thrust through the loop of twisted bark that held it together. The woodsman set it down as they passed, rising to rub the small of his back and look – a dog-cart and fine horse with two pretty girls in it wasn't something that he saw every day. He took off his shapeless wool cap. 'Missies,' he said respectfully, bowing slightly.

Lorrie felt embarrassed by that: if she'd been walking by the road in her own clothes and met him back home, he'd have called her 'lass' and waved instead.

'We're looking for a young man,' she said.

At the sound of her voice the man relaxed a bit; they were twenty miles from Relling and his own accent was slightly different from hers, but nobody could hear her speak and doubt she was a commoner too – perhaps a well-to-do farmer's daughter, at most. Just as he would have placed Flora as city-born and gentlefolk, if she'd opened her mouth.

He not only relaxed, but also grinned as he straightened. 'Not a young man any more m'self, miss, but I could wish I were, seein' the two of you pretty as the spring daisies,' he said. 'From over to Relling, are you then?'

Flora laughed, and Lorrie felt herself smiling despite her worry.

'Hard by Relling,' Lorrie agreed. 'We're his kin, and we've a message he'll want to hear, family matters. He would have passed through day before yesterday, riding – on a good grey gelding. A young man, just seventeen, but man-tall and strongly-built, hair the shade of ripe barley and blue eyes, and a yew bow over his shoulder.'

'Ah!' the woodcutter said, rubbing his back again and stretching with both hands pressed to it. 'Yes, I do recall; not seeing him myself, you understand, but Bessa – Bessa at the Holly Bush, just up the high road and off on Willow Creek Lane – mentioned him. No mistaking, from your telling of his looks. Fair mooning over him, she was!'

'That's my Bram!' Lorrie said.

'Ah, kin of yours, this Bram, lass?' the woodcutter teased. 'Lucky man, to have such sisters!'

'Kin by marriage soon, like enough,' she said. 'We'll ask at the inn, then.'

The man frowned. 'Well, I'd not do you an ill turn, so be careful,' he said. 'There are some rough sorts stop there.'

'Drovers? Badgers?' she said. Those who took stock on the road for sale did have a bad reputation – a man didn't feel as restrained outside his own neighbourhood, in a place where he wouldn't be back. Drovers and guards often caused more trouble than the money they brought justified.

'Soldiers, down from the manor,' the woodcutter said, and spat. 'I'll not say anything ill of the lord baron, you understand –'

Not wanting a whipping or the stocks or your ears cropped, Lorrie thought, nodding.

'– but some of the guardsmen he's hired these last years, they're right cut-throat, skirt-lifting bastards, and times they've lifted skirts will-she, nil-she.' He winked and put his finger alongside his nose, as if making a locally recognized gesture. 'Outsiders. Foreigners. No offence,' he went on.

'None taken,' Lorrie said mildly – everyone back home thought of anyone from more than a day's walk as foreign and somewhat suspicious, too.

'Maybe your kinsman was thinking of taking service with the Baron?' the woodcutter said. 'Manor's only a brace of miles further on. It would do the neighbourhood good to have some better-mannered boys wearing the Baron's livery.'

Lorrie shook her head. 'Bram's a farmer's son, and badgers for caravan-masters now and then,' she said. 'Thanks for your time and help, gaffer.'

'No trouble, talking to a pretty girl on a fine spring day. Summat to talk about, this next season!'

Lorrie nodded thanks and they drove on, after she made sure of the directions twice; she knew how hard it could be to give good ones, when you knew your district like your own house and couldn't imagine someone who didn't.

'We're close,' she said to Flora. 'I can . . . feel Rip.' She frowned; the sense wasn't really very directional. 'Back in Land's End, I could say "northward, and a bit east" but here all I can say is "close".'

'And where Rip is, Bram will be, and Jimmy,' Flora said. 'And I know where we'll be, if we want to find out anything.'

Lorrie looked at her, and Flora gave a wry smile, seeming older than her age; she often did, to Lorrie's way of thinking, like a woman grown. 'Where?'

'At the tavern. Where men drink, they talk.' With a flick of her wrists, Flora moved the gelding to a slightly faster pace, anxious to get to the tavern.

SEVENTEEN

Plan

Jimmy fidgeted.

'Why aren't we in there?' Jimmy asked.

Looking at Baron Bernarr's mansion was boring; profoundly, deeply boring even to someone as patient and used to waiting as a thief. The big square building just sat there, amid its frowzy neglected gardens, silent save for an occasional voice or rider coming down the lane from the main road, and the eternal beat of the surf on the cliffs half a mile away. Even the vines growing up the grey granite sides seemed to have died of tedium; for they were brown and sere even though spring was well along.

An occasional glitter of steel showed at the big iron-strapped doors, as a sentry paced. That was it. Jarvis Coe shrugged. 'Three reasons,' he said, holding up a hand and bending down fingers. 'First, what's loose in there makes anyone reluctant to go in; so we've been finding reasons not to.'

He looked serious; Jimmy glanced over from behind the tree that sheltered him and stared at Coe in open-mouthed astonishment. 'You mean we're delaying and making excuses and you know it?' he burst out.

'Yes.' Jarvis held up a hand. 'It's not procrastination. It's magic. Sometimes you can't tell the difference.'

'Oh.' Jimmy had no idea what 'procrastination' meant, but he wasn't about to let on; besides, he thought he understood the gist of what Jarvis was saying. Jimmy shivered a little at the idea of things affecting his mind and emotions without his knowing. 'What are the other reasons?'

'Second, it's difficult to get in – it's a fortress, even if it isn't a very strong one, and it is garrisoned, even if the troops aren't very numerous or very good. There are only two of us.'

'Why can't you get . . . oh.'

'Yes. Right now, Bas-Tyra has other things on his mind. By the time an official complaint went through, all the evidence would be safely buried.'

'Oh.' *As I thought, the sea hides a lot of sins.* 'What's number three?'

'It isn't quite time yet. We'll have to strike when they're distracted – and that means waiting almost until the time for their sacrifice.'

'But –'

'Yes. That means risking them going through with it before I can get inside to stop it.' Jarvis took out a stick of jerky and began chewing it. 'That would be very bad. And the magic – the side-effects of that necromancer's magic – is affecting our judgment.'

I want to go home to Krondor, Jimmy thought. The wrath of the Upright Man and the menace of the secret police was looking more attractive all the time.

'At least Flora and Lorrie are safe,' he said.

The Holly Bush wasn't much of an inn, Flora decided as she jumped down from the dog-cart in the dying hours of the day.

In fact, it was more of a farmhouse, judging by the odours of hay, turned earth, manure and mud. It had two storeys, to be sure, and was sheathed with plank which had weathered silvery-grey from many seasons without paint, but it was a thatched farmhouse just the same, with a barn and sheds behind, a field of young wheat beyond that, and an orchard still bearing drifts of blossom. The only signs of its trade were the branch of holly pegged over the lintel, the benches set outside on either side of the door, and the width of the beaten muddy path that led up from the ruts of the road and a larger-than-usual paddock for stock in which travellers' beasts might be accommodated.

No, I take it back, Flora thought. *They've put half a dozen flag-stones around the door, and there's a wood scraper. Civilization!*

One of the worksheds was a smithy, not a fully equipped one, but a little farrier's set-up with a small charcoal-fired hearth, a bellows and a single anvil: just right for shoeing horses, or doing minor repairs. A man was at work there, tapping a shoe-blank into shape with the ring of iron on iron; a youth worked the leather bellows. She waved, and he dipped the blank into a tub of water and set it aside. Then he came striding through the barnyard, the wooden pattens on his shoes keeping the valuable leather out of the mud. He went to take hold of their horse's bridle, looking at it with respect.

'Will you be staying, then, missies?' he asked, in a burr much like the woodcutter's.

'If you've room,' Flora said, and saw him perk his ears up at her Krondor speech.

'Room and to spare,' the innkeeper-cum-farmer said. 'No merchants or travellers by right now.'

He was a man of medium height and build, already getting summer's tan, and knotty with the muscle of hard work. The only thing unusual about him was the tint of red in his hair, and the freckles that stood out on his face.

'I'm Tael, and I keep this inn and farm. Bessa!' he went on, turning his head to shout. 'Bessa! Come on, take the ladies' trap. Davy, get out here!'

Flora moved to help Lorrie down from the dog-cart, as Tael clucked at the sight of the stick she used to spare her leg. 'Here, lean on me, miss,' he said. 'Bit mucky here, with the rain.'

'Thank you,' Lorrie said shyly. 'My name's Lorrie.'

A brow raised at the accent, so similar to the local's, and quite different from Flora's. He glanced back and forth between them; they didn't look like kin either, though he had probably assumed they were.

'We're looking for Lorrie's friend Bram,' Flora said, and Tael's face changed briefly, for an instant.

'Later,' he said crisply. 'Come inside. Room's three a night, and that includes the evening meal.'

Two youngsters came bustling up; a boy like the man with fifteen years cropped off and an amazing scatter of pimples with purple rims, and a buxom young girl with freckles of her own, who took the wicker box that held their luggage.

The innkeeper led them respectfully to a table in the main taproom, and Flora realized that she was enjoying herself. It was nice to be treated with respect – not chased out, or shaken down for a share of her earnings or personal favours on the side.

With sunset coming on, the interior of the inn was dim and a middle-aged woman made her way around it and lit bundles of oil-soaked rag in clay dishes. These added a smoky tang of linseed oil to the cooking smells in the room; the floor had good fresh rushes on it, though, and the hearth was cheery.

'Bean soup with ham,' the woman said, calling from where she ladled two bowls full from a big iron pot hanging over the coals. 'There's sweet cider, hard cider, ale and small beer. Cider mulled, if you want it. You'll be hungry, travelling far. From Land's End?' She set the crockery bowls down before them, and rounds of bread, butter, cheese and onions with them, and a wooden dish of sea-salt.

'Yes,' Flora said. 'I . . . live with my Aunt Cleora, in Land's End. Mulled cider for me.'

Tael came back in, stepping out of his pattens, his feet crunching on the cut river-reeds that covered the floor which gave a pleasant green scent, for they'd been mixed with pungent herbs and flowers that gave off a scent of dried memory, like hay.

'Cleora Winsley, that would be,' he said, catching what she said. 'Karl Winsley's wife, and Yardley Heywood's daughter?'

'Yes,' Flora said, a little surprised. *It's nice to have a family people know, too*, she thought.

'I've done business with Karl Winsley,' Tael said. 'Buying hops.' He looked at Lorrie. 'And Bram is your friend?'

'We're neighbours,' Lorrie said. 'His . . . his horse came back to Land's End, saddle empty and an arrow in it. I'm staying with Mistress Winsley. We came to see if he's all right.'

'I can't tell you,' Tael said.

His wife returned with mugs made of turned maple, and an iron rod with a wooden handle; the tip of the metal glowed white-red.

'Thanks, pet,' Tael said.

He took the mulling iron from her and plunged it into Flora's cider. The drink bubbled and seethed, hissing as the metal quenched; the iron had gone dark when he removed it a moment later, but it was still hot enough to make him cautious as he returned it to the hearth. A pleasant smell of apples and spices rose; Flora sipped cautiously.

Tael took a long drink of his beer as he came back, and wiped the back of his hand across his mouth, taking the last of the foam from his moustache, thinking hard. Flora spooned up some of her soup – she was hungry, and it smelled good – and ripped apart one of the small loaves for dunking. It was hot enough to steam slightly, and good wheat bread, nearly white.

'Well, as to young Bram, he stopped here for food about noon couple o' days ago,' Tael said abruptly, like a man who'd been ordering his thoughts. 'Nice lad, polite, for all he's from Relling way. Sorry.'

'No offence,' Lorrie said; a small smile quirked at the corner of her mouth.

'And he came looking for a young lad named Rip, who he thought would have been in the company of two men, and maybe not happy about it.'

Flora and Lorrie nodded. The innkeeper hesitated and drank again, then nodded as if to himself after some internal dialogue.

'Well, I'd seen no such boy,' he said. 'But I had seen two men who might have been the ones he were looking for, you see.' Another hesitation, then: 'Men-at-arms from the manor; men of the Baron's. Skinny and Rox, they're called; gallows-bait. I soldiered a bit myself when I was younger, and I met enough like them; ready-for-aughts, if aught were somethin' that meant money for no work, but not the sorts a good captain would have in his troop, or ones that a wise comrade would trust with his purse or back, if you takes me meaning?' They nodded. 'I told your Bram that much, for he seemed a good enough sort, and they're no friends of mine, for all they spend their pay here. Then he thanked me, polite-like, and rode up north toward the lord's hall. The next we see is his horse running south; we tried to catch it and couldn't. Didn't think to lure it with grain until it was half-way down the road to Land's End. Glad it got back to you; I'd have sent word had I caught the beast.'

Lorrie had no doubt he meant that, but she knew country ways and 'sending word' would be to mention to a passing wagon driver heading towards the city that he'd found a horse, just in case someone came looking.

'And next evening, in come Rox and Skinny, laughing, and

spending free – a roast goose between them, and everything of the best. Wine and beer and spirits, and I had to send Bessa to bed early.'

Flora looked at Lorrie, and their hearts sank. Lorrie leaned close and whispered, 'Rip's here . . . not far at all. Close.'

'And if Rip is, and these two men are, maybe Bram is too.' *Unless he's dead*, Flora thought. *And that would be a pity. He's sweet, and pretty as a picture. And Lorrie's a friend, I wouldn't want her to lose her man before she's even had him.*

Tael observed the byplay, crunching an onion between strong yellow teeth. 'Thing is . . .' he said when they looked at him.

'Yes?' Lorrie said eagerly.

'Lass, they both looked as if they'd been in a fight, not a bad one, but bruises and such. And that Skinny, he carries a bow in a case at his saddle. Short bow, horn-backed and double curved, Great Kesh style.'

With that he nodded to them and went about his work. Flora looked around as the two girls ate. 'I've got an idea,' she said, glancing up at the roof.

It wasn't very high – seven feet at most, likely kept low to make the main room easier to heat. The rafters were roughly-adzed pine-trunks, and the planks pegged over them had generous cracks, probably to save expensive sawn lumber; bits of straw stuck through them.

The singing below their room had died away. Flora and Lorrie lay prone on the boards; Lorrie had her eye to a crack, and they'd carefully picked out a clear place between two of the planks. Loud voices came up from the table below them, harsh and slurred. Flora shivered a little.

Jimmy was right, she thought, remembering the quick hot glint in the eyes of the sergeant who'd flung her into the cart in the sweep of Mockers in Krondor. *I'm well out of the trade.*

'*It's them,*' Lorrie whispered.

She was white-faced; Flora realized suddenly it was anger, not fear. Killing anger.

'It's the two who took Rip,' she said, her voice like ice crackling on a winter puddle when you stepped onto it, crackling and letting things ooze through. 'And burned my home and killed my parents.' Flora patted her shoulder awkwardly; she'd lost hers early, and from what she remembered they were no prizes anyway.

Then she pressed her eye to the crack again. There were four of them sitting around the table and the picked remains of several chickens; she could recognize Skinny and Rox from Lorrie's description. *Bad ones*, she thought, wrinkling her nose; she could smell the stale beer in their sweat, and the jerkins that had never been cleaned, with old blood on them and worse, and the neat's-foot oil on weapons. *Badder than most.*

Skinny smiled too often, and Rox not at all. They did look as if they'd been in a fight lately; Skinny had a fading shiner, and Rox a set of puffy knuckles on his right hand. The other two were nondescript men, nothing out of the ordinary about them except an unusual number of scars, hard feral eyes that showed occasionally when they tilted back their flagons and greasy dark hair that swirled back from their foreheads.

One of them took something out of a belt-pouch and shook it in his closed hand – dice, probably. 'Come on, you two,' he said. 'Let's see some of that gold you were boasting about. I can feel it calling to me – wants to rest in my purse, it does.'

'Sure it would if I were fool enough to use your dice, Forten.'

Forten's fist closed on the knuckle bones he had produced; perhaps he would have made something of it, if Rox had not been hulking on the other side of the table. From where she lay, Flora could see Skinny's right hand, where the fingers brushed the hilt of the knife tucked into his boot.

'And we haven't got all of it, yet, not the fee for the new one,' Skinny said.

Forten grunted as he put away his dice, then poured more wine from a pitcher into his mug. 'Bad enough those little 'uns hiding and skulking in the walls. Fair near broke my head, where they'd rubbed grease on them stairs by the main gate. That new one, he could be real trouble if he got loose, big as a grown man. Bugger him anyway. The Baron and that wizard'll sort him out soon enough.'

The mercenaries fell silent for an instant, looking uneasy; one or two made signs against evil with their hands, and they all drank.

Flora turned her head. Lorrie's face was blazing with hope. They drew back to the other corner of the room, speaking quietly. 'That's them!' Lorrie said. 'The new one – big as a man – that must be Bram. And the little ones, they must be Rip, and some other children!'

Bram yes, Flora thought. *And maybe it's your little brother. More likely than not, yes.*

She nodded, and Lorrie went on, her smile fading: 'They must be in the manor, though. How could we get in? It's like a fort, and guarded, and . . . you know what the innkeeper said about the castle.'

Flora shivered. 'That it feels wrong? Yes. But –'

'But we've got to get them out,' Lorrie said. 'And soon. You heard. Something special planned for Bram!'

The girl from Krondor nodded, tempted to shiver again. Then she thought rapidly; things she'd heard from other girls, and from other Mockers. 'Wait a minute,' she breathed. 'I think we can get in! And those hired swords will be the way we can.' She felt in her skirt pocket; the little sack of 'something special' was still there. *Jimmy knew what he was doing when he left me some of this!* she thought. 'Here's how we'll do it.'

*　　*　　*

Flora rearranged her bodice, unlacing it so she could turn under the cloth, giving her as plunging a neckline as any she had worn while walking the streets of Krondor. She removed the kerchief she had worn while riding in the cart, and shook her hair out, letting it fall loose over her shoulders. She tugged at her bodice one more time, ensuring it showed enough to make acceptable working clothes. The night had gone cool and overcast, with the smell of rain on the wind from the sea. That raised goose-bumps; it did nothing to dim her wide smile as the two troopers stumbled out of the door of the Holly Bush. A backdrop of red firelight silhouetted them for a moment, and then their weaving steps were in the muck.

'Well, hel-lo,' Flora crooned.

The mercenaries stopped and goggled; it was Forten and Sonnart. Their companions had headed home earlier, and not quite as drunk.

'Who're you?' one of them asked.

'Not the innkeeper's daughter with the big teats,' the other observed owlishly.

'I'm the new girl in these parts, boys,' she said cheerfully, rolled a hip and winked, mustering up every trick she had learned to overcome revulsion; she had lain with more repulsive men in her day, but that was before she had come to think of herself as having more to her life than surviving from day to day. Choking down an urge to gag, she asked, 'You walking home, or do you want to come to the stables and ride, first?'

Negotiations went quickly; the men were practically lowing as they panted after her, bumping into each other and huffing as they staggered in her wake around the rear of the inn.

'This's far enough,' one of them grunted, clutching at her.

'It's muddy and it's going to rain,' Flora cast back over her shoulder. 'There's a roof and nice straw and horse-blankets in the stables. Only a few more steps!'

For all they'd taken aboard, the mercenaries had a well-developed sense of self-preservation; they made her go first through the doors into the darkened stables, and their hands went to their hilts when they saw Lorrie standing there.

They relaxed again, grinning, as they saw it was another girl. 'Ruthia!' one blurted. 'This is our lucky day!'

Lorrie held her hand forward, palm up. As Forten reached for her, she took in a sharp breath and blew across the hand into his face.

Flora was already dodging sideways, holding her breath. The stable was a dim cavern, with only a little light filtering in through the door and the slits under the eaves, but she'd placed the hickory axe-handle precisely where it needed to be, and her hand fell on it.

Forten was already down, falling limp and face-forward in the packed manure and straw of the stable floor. Sonnart behind him hadn't got much of the dust in his face; he gave a strangled shout and managed to half-draw his sword, a glitter of bright metal in the darkness. Flora took a firm two-handed grip on the smooth length of dense springy hardwood.

Thock!

The yard-long axe-handle landed on his right kneecap with the sound of a maul hitting a block of wood. The mercenary gave a high shrill scream that died away to a gurgle as Flora collected herself and smacked her weapon down again, this time on the back of his head.

Light flared as Lorrie took a bucket off the lamp they'd brought out. Horses stamped uneasily in the stalls, and one snorted as he caught the scent of blood. Both mercenaries were alive, but Sonnart wouldn't be feeling well when he woke up.

Lorrie drew her belt knife, teeth showing in what was most definitely not a smile. Flora hurried over and caught her arm.

'No!' she said.

Lorrie turned on her. 'Why not?' she said fiercely. 'They work for the man who had my brother kidnapped and my parents killed!'

'But they're not the ones who did it,' Flora said. 'I wouldn't stop you if it was. But if we kill these two Tael will get into a lot of trouble – hanging trouble – swine they may be, but they're a baron's men-at-arms, Lorrie!'

'And you heard what they said about Bram!' Lorrie went on, but the wild look was dying out of her eyes, and she stopped trying to tug her arm free of Flora's grip.

'Ah,' Flora said. 'Well, I had a thought about that.' She held up two dried pinecones from the tinder-box of the smithy. 'You see how all the leaves on the pinecones run one way?'

'Yes?' Lorrie said, puzzled.

Half an hour later, two cloaked and hooded figures rode down the highway from the Holly Bush towards Baron Bernarr's manor. One of them scratched disgustedly.

'Didn't they ever boil these to get the nits out?' she said.

'It could be worse,' the other replied.

'How?'

'Let me tell you about Noxious Neville, some day,' she replied.

The Baron groaned, and again clutched at his sheets. But now dream and memory were blurred, as were waking and sleeping. He drifted from knowing what night it was, lying in his bed, to thinking he was a younger man, facing terrible choices.

He stood looking in horror at his wife's pale form, life draining from her as blood pooled in the bed, the midwife clutching the crying baby.

A voice at his elbow. 'I can help.'

Without looking he knew it was Lyman. 'What can you do?'

'Cover the lady, and leave the room,' commanded the visitor and it was done.

Then he was outside the room, the midwife already gone with the child to give it up to the wolves. But . . .

Bernarr's eyes fluttered, and he realized it was night and he was alone, and the baby was now a youth, chained away in a secret room. He groaned and rolled over, clutching the pillow as he shut his eyes.

Lyman said, 'An hour is but an instant, and a day but seconds within that room. She will abide while we seek a way to keep her from Death's Hall.'

Healers came, chirurgeons and a priest of Dala, and another from a sect down in the desert of Great Kesh, but none could revive the lady of the house when Lyman lowered the time spell. Each time he failed, he vowed to redouble his efforts to find a way. And each time Bernarr accepted his vow, he felt more darkness seize his mind and heart.

Soon, Lyman had become a permanent member of the house, given his own rooms and places for his servants. Books were purchased and scrolls and tomes sent by collectors across the breadth of civilization. No matter what the price, Bernarr paid, but no solution was found.

Then the books of dark magic appeared, and blood was needed. First animal, but then . . .

Bernarr sat up, a scream torn from his chest, a man tormented beyond endurance. He forced his eyes open, willed himself awake and pushed himself to the glassed doors leading to his balcony. Throwing aside the sash, he opened the doors and stepped out into the cold night darkness. Only two more nights. He took a deep, cold breath of air. Then he whispered, 'In two nights, it will be over.'

EIGHTEEN

Magic

The storm raged.

'Meg!' a voice bawled outside the cottage.

Thunder rumbled outside, and flashes of lightning filtered through the boards of the shutters. Rain hissed down on the thatch, but it was tight and showed no leaks as yet.

Jimmy looked up from putting a final edge on his dagger; Jarvis was already throwing his cloak around his shoulders.

'Meg!' the voice shouted again, and this time it cracked in an adolescent squeak.

Jarvis opened the door; a boy blundered in. Jimmy put his age at about two years older than himself, with a revolting crop of pimples that he'd been spared himself so far, praise be to Banath, God of Thieves. The lad was dripping from the steady rain outside, and panting as if he'd run several miles – which the rich spatter of mud that coated him to waist-height also bore out.

'Come in, boy,' the cottager growled; Meg brought a cup of something hot and herbal from the small pot she kept on the side of the hearth.

'Why, Davy, what are you doing out on a night like this?'

The boy paused at the sight of the two strangers; Jimmy gave him a smile and snicked the dagger home in its sheath at his belt; the firelight caught the fretwork on the guard of his rapier.

'Travellers,' the cottager said. 'Now, Davy-boy, why'd you come calling for Meg? Someone ill, or come to their time?'

Aside to Jarvis and the young thief: 'This un's Davy, son to Tael at the Holly Bush. Not the first time Meg's been called out on a filthy night.'

'Two of the Baron's armsmen,' Davy said, sipping at the herbal drink and calming. 'Beaten! Naked and beaten in the stable.'

'Serves them right,' his host growled. 'Let 'em fester, I say.'

'Your mother could handle bruises, or setting a bone broken in a brawl,' Meg said. As she spoke she went to the bed and hauled out another box, this one of boards covered in rawhide. 'What else is wrong with them?'

Davy looked at the men, shuffled from one foot to the other, and then blurted, 'They walked out of the door and claimed that a . . . a whore lured them to the stables, and her pimp beat them!'

The cottager scowled more deeply. 'A likely story. There aren't no loose women at the Holly Bush.'

'That's what they say,' Davy claimed. His pimply face looked more hideous as he blushed. 'And . . . well, their clothes and weapons and all were gone, and they had their hair and beards cut off, and they were all rolled and slobbered with dung, and . . . and –'

'Out with it, boy!'

'And someone shoved a pinecone up their arses! Both of them!'

Meg began to cackle with laughter as she sorted through her herbs and simples and tools. After a moment of blank incredulity, so did her husband, howling until he had to bend nearly double and hug his ribs, staggering across the cottage and bumping into the walls.

'Ah, many's the time I've wanted to do that to one of the toplofty cut-throat bastards myself,' the old man wheezed. 'Hee, hee, hee! They'll be sittin' down careful for months, they will – and squatting cautious-like at the jakes. Hee, hee!'

Davy gave an uneasy grin, but by the way he was standing he was also tightening his buttocks.

Jimmy chuckled, too. *Probably funnier to hear about than to see,* he thought. *Still, I wouldn't mind hearing the same news about Jocko Radburn, or del Garza, or their master either.*

'And them girls is gone,' Davy went on.

'Girls?' Jimmy said sharply.

'Them girls that came in the dog-cart from Land's End yesterday 'bout suppertime,' he said. 'Pretty as pictures, they was.' He gave an enthusiastic description.

'Flora!' Jimmy and Jarvis said at the same time.

'– for all one had a limp,' the boy finished.

'Lorrie!' Jimmy said.

The bottom dropped out of Jimmy's stomach, and Jarvis Coe cursed quietly in a language Jimmy didn't recognize. They looked at each other.

'That's torn it,' Jarvis said grimly.

Jimmy nodded, pulling on his oil-treated wool cloak. He yanked the hood forward, reflecting bitterly that this was what came of Flora's newfound sense of responsibility. She'd got him poking his head into a sewer rats' den again.

'No time for subtlety,' he said.

'No time at all,' Coe replied.

The rain blew cold into their faces as they left the cosy, smoky warmth of the cottage.

The skin wrinkled on the back of Jimmy's neck, and he didn't think it was down to the trickle of cold water; rather it was due to the thought of Flora and Lorrie in that place.

*   *   *

Bram looked up sharply, startled out of an uneasy doze. Thunder crashed, and lightning glared through the high small window – far too small for a man to squeeze through, and barred with iron, even if he hadn't been chained.

It wasn't time for the meagre ration of bread he got; he'd be weak with hunger by now, if it weren't for the food the children brought him. It wasn't time to empty the slop bucket either. But he could hear the rasp of a key in the lock. A moment later, he was squinting against the yellow light of a lantern held high in the turnkey's fist, a tin cylinder pierced to let the candle-shine out.

Then it went out, a freak gust turning it into a wisp of bitter-smelling smoke gusting out through the metal. The turnkey cursed, and so did the mercenaries crowding behind him.

'Well, get another'n lit: we need light for this,' one of them said to a man behind him.

Bram grinned. He didn't feel the cold fear that sometimes blew through this chamber. Instead he felt something that radiated anger – but it wasn't aimed at him, and somehow it made him feel warm and safer, however mad that was. It reminded him of his mother.

Another lamp came, and went out; the third guttered wildly but didn't extinguish, since the holder shielded the flame with his hand. With the light, the armed men advanced on Bram. One carried a singlejack, a light blacksmith's hammer, and a chisel.

'No games,' a big mercenary said; Bram recognized him from the fight at the ford, and scowled. The big man grinned at him, and went on: 'Lord Bernarr says we can't kill you. But we can mess you up, eh? Nothin' says you have to have sound legs or unbroken arms, right?'

He shoved another burlap bag over Bram's head, and drew the drawstring painfully tight. The young man gasped, drawing in the sweetish scent of the oats that had filled the bag not long ago, and sneezed helplessly.

'Foolishness,' someone said – Bram couldn't see a thing now, just feel the rough hands pushing and shoving him. 'Why not leave the chains on?'

'Sump'n about cold iron, the magicker said,' another voice replied – the weasel-like skinny man's.

The hammer peened musically on the back of a cold chisel, and the manacles fell away so that Bram gave a grunt of relief. Then he bit his lips against a yell, as rough rope bit into his wrists where the iron had rubbed them raw. His feet were still free, though, and he was direly tempted to kick out.

Better not. Just get a beating, he thought. *Wait for the moment. Wherever they're taking me, it can't be worse than being chained in this room with invisible spirits running loose through it.*

As the men hustled him out, he heard an incongruous sound: the whistle of a poorwit, one of the little birds that haunted hedgerows back at home in the valley.

Beneath the rough cloth, Bram grinned. He'd taught young Rip how to whistle that way just last summer. He had more friends here than his captors suspected.

Lorrie looked around, restraining the impulse to rub at her leg. It was itching and hurting; the itching indicated that it was healing, but it was a long way from healed, and if she pushed it too far she could rip it open again.

Bram, she thought. *Rip.* She could do anything she had to do.

'I wish Jimmy were here,' Flora said nervously.

'Nobody's seen hide nor hair of him,' Lorrie said.

'They wouldn't, if he didn't want them to,' Flora said. 'But *we've* got to do something now.'

Lightning rolled again, showing the grim bulk of the manor ahead, outlined against the night sky; rain hissed down unceasingly. She squinted. 'That's a light!' she said. 'Look, there, in the tower at the corner.'

A wavering yellow glow came from the narrow windows there; narrow enough to double as arrow-slits.

'Maybe they won't notice us, then,' Flora said.

As they approached the grounds, a vague uneasy feeling visited them. It seemed to get stronger with every second as they neared the entrance. 'Something's wrong,' whispered Flora.

Lorrie said, 'Maybe we should go look for Jimmy?'

Flora said, 'I think you're right.' She was verging on turning around the dog cart, when she said, 'Wait a minute!'

'What?'

'Do you really want to abandon looking for Bram?' Flora asked.

'Well, we wouldn't be really abandoning him, but we'd be . . .'

'Putting it off just a little?'

'Yes, that would be exactly what we'd be doing,' Lorrie agreed. 'And, besides, maybe the weather will be nicer tomorrow and I think we'd do better looking . . .' She stopped when she saw Flora get a strange expression on her face.

Flora's forehead was lined in concentration, and she set her jaw as if she were trying not to yell out. She narrowed her gaze and said, 'Damn it!' and flicked the reins. Flora urged the horse forward until they came to the wrought-iron gates; there was a small room beside them, built into the wall that circled the garden. It was only six feet tall, although topped with spikes; built long after the manor, and to keep out game and livestock rather than enemies. As if willing the words out, Flora asked, 'What is it you'd rather be doing than going in there right now?'

Lorrie pressed herself back into the leather of the seat as if trying to put as much distance as she could between herself and the gate. 'Anything, actually. Just about anything you could name.'

Flora nodded emphatically. 'Yup. I'm thinking we just ran into one of those wards rich people sometimes pay old Alban for.'

'Who's Alban?'

'Magician I knew once,' was all Flora said. 'You put this thing called a ward around something you don't want people to bother, and they come up with reasons why they don't want to bother with it, just like they thought it up all on their own.'

'I think I understand,' said Lorrie, 'but wouldn't this be better if we found Jimmy first?'

'It would,' said Flora as handed the reins to Lorrie. She got down from the dog-cart, one hand in the pocket under her cloak which held more of the powder that hit men like a fist, and walked over to the gatekeeper's room. Over her shoulder she said, 'But if we did find him, we'd find other reasons not to come here. Right now I want to be anywhere else more than I want to be here, so that tells me that this is where I need to be.'

Lorrie didn't fully understand, but she said, 'So we go anyway?'

'Having Jimmy here would be better, but we go anyway.' She stuck her head into the window that was the only opening on this side and looked around. 'Nobody here,' she said, pulling her head out. 'But it stinks: someone's been living here.'

'How do we get through?' Lorrie asked, looking at the tall iron gates with a worried look. *I might be able to climb that with both legs working proper,* she thought unhappily. *With this, I'd have trouble getting on a horse again, once I'm down on the ground. Maybe we should wait until my leg is better . . .*

'Not a problem,' Flora said, interrupting Lorrie's next reason for not going inside.

She took off her cloak and pushed it through the gate's grille, then unbuckled her borrowed – stolen – swordbelt and did likewise with that, fitting it through carefully.

Then she backed up half a dozen steps, ran forward lightly, and jumped like a cat. That put her nearly head-high on the iron; she swarmed up the rest of the slippery metal as if it were a ladder, and flipped herself neatly over the top before clambering down on the other side. She jumped free when still higher than her own height, and landed lightly, perfectly in control as she took the force with bent knees.

Lorrie goggled. What was it she did for a living in Krondor? she wondered. Set up for a mountebank and tumbler?

Flora was grinning as she heaved at the long bolt that kept the gates fastened from the inside. 'No lock!' she said. 'Just this bolt, and a chain looped through it.'

The chain clattered free, and Flora retrieved her cloak and weapons before they rode up toward the gates of the manor.

'I'm coming, Bram, Rip!' Lorrie said grimly. Once spoken, those words seem to vanquish the terrible feeling she had that they should do more before attempting to enter the grounds.

'Who are you?' Bram said.

'Silence,' the oily voice replied, and a brief stabbing pain came from everywhere and nowhere.

Breath hissed out between his teeth. The room smelled wrong, like a sickroom: old rotten blood and malevolence. There was cold stone under his back, and the mercenaries were fastening him down with leather ties. Oddly, they went around his knees and elbows, not his wrists and ankles.

Oh, gods, he thought sickly. *It's sized for children! This is where they sacrificed the children they stole.* Even then, his belly twisted with nausea.

The mercenaries went about their business as briskly as if they'd been trussing a hog for slaughter. It left him stretched out like a starfish, painfully so since the ties were at a slightly lower level than the ridged surface on which he rested. Cold air flowed across his skin as his breeches and shirt were cut away and pulled off. Then fingers fumbled at the drawstring of the bag that covered his head. He could already see a diffuse glow of light through the coarse weave of the cloth. When it was pulled away, he had a brief glimpse of a large richly-furnished room with windows, two doors, and through one a bed on which rested a beautiful, pale-faced woman, apparently asleep.

'Cover his face!' a man barked. The voice sounded old and weary, but the command carried authority.

Of him, Bram could only see the back and his clasped hands; there were jewelled rings on the fingers, and his jacket was of rich dark velvet.

'It is done, my lord,' the nondescript middle-aged man standing by Bram's head said.

Nondescript, that is, until you saw his eyes. They were like windows into . . . not emptiness, but a void where even darkness would be snuffed out. Like nothing Bram had seen in his life, they caused fear to visit the pit of his stomach, ice to run up his back, and his arm hair to stand on end. The man's eyes were windows into less-than-nothing.

He smiled and dropped a long silk scarf over Bram's features.

'Wouldn't want to leave you out of the festivities, boy,' he murmured as he went about his work.

The silk would hide him from anyone looking, but Bram could see through the gauzy cloth himself – dimly.

During the brief moment his eyes were clear, he'd also seen the inscribed figures drawn around the stone-topped table to which he was bound, and the black candles that guttered at the points; a rug rolled back against one wall showed that they were usually covered. Bram had his letters. He didn't know what those writhing glyphs were, and had no wish to know. Looking at them made his eyes hurt, and he wrenched his gaze away. At the edges of his consciousness, something giggled and tittered.

'Let me loose, you bastard!' Bram yelled.

'Silence,' the man said again; and the pain returned, shooting spikes into his gut and groin and joints.

Silence it is, Bram thought, testing the bindings. Strong leather, from the feel of them, far stronger than needed for children, and he couldn't even rock the stone table; it would take six strong men to lift, or two with a dolly.

Bad, he thought. *Very bad. Help!*

Astonishingly, something touched his face for an instant – something like a woman's hand, warm and tender.

Off in the distance something fell with a crash and a clatter. He could hear a distant voice howl in pain, and then: 'It's the little bastards again! Get sand, get water, put out the god-damned fire!'

The unimpressive man with the terrible eyes shrugged.

'Time to commence, my lord,' he said. 'It's only an hour and –' he looked at a sand-timer, '– perhaps five minutes to the time.'

'Elaine,' the older man said.

It was more of a croon; there was a longing in the word that made the young man take notice despite the hammering of blood in his temples and the dryness of his mouth.

Bram could see the one with the evil eyes, the magician as Bram now thought of him, pick up a small tool and a pot and he steeled himself for more pain, but there was only a brief wet coolness, touching him just up from where his pubic hair began. The magician was chanting under his breath, in a quick-rising, slow-falling tongue Bram didn't recognize.

Another touch, just a little higher than the first. Bram craned his head up until his neck creaked, trying to glimpse over the muscled arch of his chest and see what the man was doing. It took a moment to realize what was happening; then he began to tug at the restraints again.

A neat line of red dashes was being painted up the centre of his body, heading for the breastbone.

'Why isn't there anyone here?' Flora said, looking around the entrance hall of the manor.

The great building should have had someone on duty at the front door, even though it was just before midnight. Instead there was only the clear blue flame of an expensive lamp filled with imported scented oil.

'Just be glad there isn't,' Lorrie said.

They both shed their wet cloaks – the greasy wool didn't smell any better for being soaked through and it just made them chillier now that they were out of the rain – letting them drop to the floor.

Then: 'Rip is here. He's close – he's thinking about me!'

'Where do we –' Flora began.

Then she jumped and squeaked. Beside the great fireplace a section of wood panelling was swinging outward on smooth, noiseless hinges.

Lorrie's hand went to her knife. Then she caught her breath and collapsed onto one knee despite the twinge in her leg, holding out her arms.

'Lorrie!' Rip squealed.

He ran to her so fast he skidded and didn't quite bowl her over. Three other children followed him out. Lorrie gasped.

'Oh, I'm sorry,' Rip said, drawing back. 'I forgot. Bram told me you hurt your leg.'

'Bram!' Lorrie said. 'Where is he?'

'He's up there.' That came from a blonde girl about Lorrie's age, in a dust-stained frock. She pointed to one corner of the room, where a stone staircase curled upwards. 'They took him away,' she said and her great blue eyes looked haunted. 'People don't come back, when they take them away.'

The other two children nodded. These two were younger – a boy with a defiant yet frightened look about him, and a girl who desperately clutched a doll.

'We watched but we couldn't do anything,' the little girl said, taking her thumb out of her mouth. 'They're big.'

'They've got swords!' the boy said, trying to sound brave, yet revealing how frightened he truly was.

The younger girl pointed at Lorrie. 'She's got a sword.' The chubby finger shifted to Flora. 'She's got a sword too.'

'But they're just girls,' the boy answered, refusing to be reassured.

'You shut up, Kay!' said the older girl.

Lorrie forced herself back erect. 'We do have swords,' she said, patting the unused weapon at her side. *Even if neither of us can use them much. But I'm a dab hand with an axe-handle!*

Flora spoke, leaning down a little. 'We have something better than swords,' she said, patting her pocket. 'Magic!'

The children's eyes grew round. 'There's magic here,' Rip said. 'Bad magic.'

'Take us to Bram, then,' Flora said decisively.

Lorrie went along; after a moment Flora gave her a shoulder, to help her hop up the stairs without putting too much strain on the wounded limb. It seemed to go on forever; she'd never been in a building this large, or imagined one until she saw Land's End. That was intimidating enough, but there was something else that made her teeth want to chatter, and it wasn't the lingering chill of her damp borrowed clothing. Things kept moving out of the corners of her eyes, things that she couldn't see but that seemed to be made out of black wire, things that tittered and gibed and made little lunges toward her.

And there was a tension in the air, like before a storm – yet the very walls of the castle shook to the violence outside, so it couldn't be that. Her head felt tight, as if something were stretching it from the inside, and it would be a relief if it exploded.

'There,' Rip whispered at last. 'I . . . I can tell it's down there.'

He pointed down a long corridor. It was dark with a stone floor, heavy carved wooden tables along the walls and tapestries that fluttered slightly in the draught. At the end was a corner, and from beyond that a faint glow of lamplight.

'You go,' Rip said – his head was turned to one side, as if he was listening to someone. 'We'll get ready. They're going to hurt Bram really soon now.'

Lorrie nodded, a little puzzled but trying to focus on the task ahead.

They walked down the corridor, their boots making thumping sounds on the carpeted floor. The light grew stronger as they neared the corner; closer, and she could see it was T-shaped, and she was walking down the long bar. Light to their right, darkness to their left.

'That you, Forten, Sonnart?' a voice called. 'You lazy swine, it's nearly midnight! You knew you should have been back an hour ago!'

Flora made some muffled sound, trying to make her voice hoarse, and Lorrie did likewise. From the sound of the voices, it wasn't much more than six feet or so from the corner to where the speaker stood.

Thinking inarticulate prayers to half a dozen deities, Lorrie dropped back slightly and ducked her head, taking a deep breath and working her fingers.

Bram. Think of Bram.

They turned the corner; lamps were burning in metal brackets on either side. Four men lounged in front of a tall closed door of polished wood. Two sat on benches; the other two stood together, leaning on halberds.

Jarvis Coe gasped as he drew rein before the wrought iron gate. It was open, but only a sliver; they had to slow almost to a halt from their pounding gallop to get through it.

Particularly since it's as dark as a yard up a sewer rats' nest, Jimmy thought. The saddle had pounded his hams back into pain, and the rapier had caught him under the ribs with a couple of good whacks as well; he hadn't wanted it out of reach if he had to dismount in a hurry. 'Something wrong?' he asked the older man, peering through the gate at the manor; distance and rain hid everything but a wavering light from a high window.

'Very,' Coe said tightly. 'We're late. We're very late. Things have already begun.'

They threaded their way through the entrance and booted the tired horses into an unwilling canter. They pulled up at the entrance to the manor, next to a dog cart with a horse patiently enduring the rain. 'That's Flora's aunt's horse!' said Jimmy. 'I've seen him in the little shed behind the house. Flora and Lorrie must have come here looking for us!'

'Or looking for the young man you encountered,' said Coe.

The main doors of the manor were slightly ajar, and Jimmy felt an unwilling grin curve his lips – Flora hadn't wasted time, or forgotten all she'd picked up as a thief before she went into the mattress trade. They swung down from their saddles, looping the reins over rings in the low wall that flanked the bridge across the moat.

Might have to get away in a hurry, he thought.

'I'll go first,' Coe said, alighting and drawing his blade.

'You go first,' Jimmy agreed, doing likewise.

A muffled shout came through the outer door of the sacrificial chamber. Bram heard a man shout in alarm, and the clash of steel on steel, and a high shriek that could have come only from a woman's throat, and then a cry of pain that could have been made by anyone.

The man in the velvet jacket spoke a sharp command. Skinny and Rox were standing by the door; one opened an eyehole cover set into it and peered out cautiously – not wanting to be stabbed through it, probably.

'Probably the little rats again, my lord,' Rox said. 'Otto's down – not bleeding, that I can see. Looks like the others have taken off after them.'

'Get out there, but stay close to the door,' Baron Bernarr said. 'Let no one by, on your life.' He turned back towards the magician.

'Timing is very crucial now, my lord,' the man with empty eyes said. 'We must strike at precisely the right moment; and we will have only a few seconds while your lady lies between life and death. If you would take your position?'

Baron Bernarr came closer; the magician offered him a long curved knife, and he took it with a disturbing familiarity. The blade was also inscribed with symbols and, like the ones on the floor the young man could no longer see, they were somehow obscurely repulsive and unnerving.

'Be careful,' the magician said. 'The best symbolic representation of a sharp knife is a sharp knife.'

The other man chuckled a little, in a perfunctory manner. The way a man laughed at a joke he'd heard often before.

The room was cold, but Bram could smell his own sweat, and feel the prickling itch of it as drops ran gelid down his face and flanks. He'd always thought himself a brave man – he'd faced dangers before, fire, flood, a few fights working for caravan-masters – but right now he suspected he'd be begging and pleading if it wasn't so obviously useless.

Lorrie saw the guard's eyes go wide as they turned the corner.

'Hey, you aren't Forten and Sonnart,' the man with the polearm said. He had a bandage on one hand, from what was probably a burn.

'Damn me!' the other halberdier said. 'It's a girl!'

Flora blew across her palm.

The halberdier collapsed with a limp finality. The two men on the bench sprang up with yells of alarm, reaching for their swords. Lorrie already had hers out, both her small hands clenched on the long leather-wrapped hilt. She managed to get it around in time to hit the head of the polearm as it stabbed at Flora. Steel clanged on steel, a harsh unmusical shriek; then her sword slid down the spike on top of the halberd until it caught in the notch between that and the axe. The man grinned and twisted his weapon with all the strength of his heavy arms and shoulders and the sword flew out of Lorrie's hands and over his head; his comrades danced aside to let it clatter against the door behind them.

Then the man yelled and leapt: Flora had stabbed him in the thigh with her belt-knife.

'Run!' she shouted.

Lorrie did, half-noticing that Flora had taken the other arm of the T, and that the two swordsmen were after her – and not catching up, from their swearing. She ran as fast as she could, gasping every time her left foot hit the ground. The mercenary behind her was calling out a mixture of threats and obscenity. A brief glimpse behind showed he was limping nearly as badly as her.

Race of the cripples, she thought, almost grinning.

This is like being Hotfingers Flora again, she thought as she ran down the corridor, glancing from side to side for places to hide. *But I can't keep this up.* Booted feet pounded behind her. *They know the building; I don't. They'll trap me.* Breath was harsh in her throat, and she could feel the acid taste of fear. *I could be back in Land's End, eating blueberry tarts and cream with Aunt Cleora!*

Then the booted feet stopped and she turned to see her pursuers go hurtling face-forward on the floor. One gashed his left arm on his own sword as he fell, and howled as they floundered on the carpet. Behind them a dark cord lay across the corridor. One end was tied to the leg of a heavy oak sideboard. A panel popped out of the wall, and four small figures emerged, throwing things – Flora caught the flash of a silver candlestick. Then pottery crashed, and she could smell the cooking oil in the jars.

Run! she told herself: the children were already ducking back into the wall, and the mercenaries heaving themselves up. She did; careered off a wall, and then down a shorter corridor and down a flight of stairs.

'This way!' Jarvis Coe cried, charging up a curling stairway.

'Right behind you,' Jimmy panted. Running through a lord's house at night wasn't anything particularly new to him, but the feeling of tension behind his eyes was getting worse. 'You can deal with this magician, I hope?'

'I have bindings,' Coe replied. 'Leave him to me.'

'Oh, no argument.'

'I can feel what he's doing. By the Goddess! There isn't much time.'

They ran down a long corridor and whisperings seemed to follow them. Now Jimmy could hear a voice rising, muffled as if by a door, but harsh and commanding, the words dropping like syllables of burning ash.

Oh, I really don't want to meet this man, Jimmy thought, and kept running. Except for Alban Asher, every encounter with a magician recounted by members of the Mockers had ended badly – if anyone distrusted and feared magicians more than thieves, Jimmy couldn't imagine who they might be.

They turned right. A door stood a dozen feet in from the turning, and two men stood before it, swords drawn: a big dark man and a slight skinny one; they both moved forward a little.

Jarvis Coe didn't waste any time; he went straight at them in a lunge, point extended. The big dark man beat the sword aside, then tried to kick Coe in the knee as the blades locked. Coe let the kick glance off the side of his leg, and rammed the big man in the pit of his stomach with his shoulder, throwing him back against the door and stumbling into the room beyond.

'Hurry up!' a young man shouted from the room. 'For the love of the gods, hurry up!'

Jimmy didn't bother to watch any more than that: the thin mercenary was coming at him, sword in his right hand, a long knife in the other, knife-hand advanced over the same foot. The young thief frantically tried to remember everything Prince Arutha had told him, all at once and without using words.

'Skinny's gonna carve you up proper, me good son,' the scrawny mercenary said. 'Come to poppa, yer little bastard, an' get a spankin'!'

'Help!' the young man's voice in the room beyond shouted. Steel clashed in the room. 'Get me out of this!'

Skinny made a walking thrust – stepping forward and lunging at the same time which gave him tremendous reach. Jimmy didn't try to back up: instead, he used his shorter stature to lift the other man's sword-thrust and went in under it, trying to run him through the throat. That didn't work: the rapier went up over the mercenary's shoulder, and the hilts locked. Jimmy twisted desperately as the dagger in the soldier's other hand stabbed, and then they were chest-to-chest, with the knife-arm trapped against Jimmy's side by his own.

Not good, Jimmy thought, as he tried to knee the older man in the groin, and hit his thigh instead. *He's a lot stronger than I am.*

They circled for an instant, with breath nearly as bad as Foul ol' Ron's issuing from the mercenary, and then Jimmy managed to stamp downward and land his heel on the other man's instep. Skinny howled and pushed. Jimmy bounded backward – and found himself inside the room beyond the door; they'd got turned completely around without his noticing.

The room was brighter than the corridor outside. Jimmy took the situation in with a single flashing glance even as he gave more ground and then lunged with a stop-thrust that nearly spitted the eager Skinny. He backed off in turn and they circled, Skinny on the outside, Jimmy turning on his back leg, left hand on hip, point presented from a turned wrist as the Prince had taught him.

There was a man in a rich coat and breeches standing with a curved knife above a naked young man – who must be Bram. Bram had a red line painted down his centre, shouted too. 'Five thousand gold crowns if you can keep them off!' the man screamed. 'Five thousand – a free pardon, and five thousand!'

Even then, Jimmy felt his eyes grow wider. *I could buy this manor house with five thousand.*

Skinny thought the same. He bounced forward again, grinning even wider, and a trickle of saliva ran down from one corner of his mouth.

Through it all, the chanting ran like millstones grinding at the foundations of the world.

Flora turned a corner, and shrieked. Lorrie was at the other end of it, limping toward her – and the guard she'd stabbed in the leg was limping after Lorrie!

What to do, what to do? Flora thought. Then she shouted, 'Lorrie! Turn right at the door in the middle of the corridor!'

They sped toward each other, and the cries of the pursuers rose to a baying eagerness. The two girls almost collided; then they threw their shoulders against the door together, swung through, slammed it closed again.

The room was a sleeping chamber, with four double bunk beds, empty except for a clay lamp burning on a table and a single wooden chair. Flora's eyes searched frantically. 'Get me that chair! We can prop it against the door!'

Lorrie tried to dash for it, nearly fell as her leg buckled, grabbed the chair and came back dragging it. Flora was reaching for the chair as the door slammed open and together she and Lorrie tried to hold it closed, but the weight of the guardsmen threw them back with brutal force.

The door swung open, and two men crowded each other as they tried to push through at the same time. Flora staggered back until the table struck her buttocks. She threw her hands back on either side to keep from falling and splinters bit painfully at her palms. The men were raving: mouths spewing hate and frustration, their beards glistening with the flaxseed oil from the jars the children had thrown . . .

Flora's mind moved quickly, but everything else seemed very slow. She half-turned and picked up the clay lamp, careful not to douse the wick by grabbing it too hard. Then she took two steps forward and threw it, watching as it turned to spray the spirits of wine from its reservoir into the men's faces.

The oil caught at once: not a flare of flame like pine resin, but quick enough, the flames yellow and thick in their hair and beards. Both men seemed to dance in place, screaming as they beat at their own faces and the fire spread to the oil-soaked cloth and leather on their bodies. Flora stood stock-still, watching with wide eyes.

Lorrie took a step past her, stooped to lift one of the swords the men had dropped, grabbed it in a clumsy two-handed grip and swung it over and over again. Her aim was sure, though.

I suppose she's helped butcher a lot of pigs, Flora thought.

The men went down, twitching and moaning. Lorrie stood panting, the bloody sword in her hand.

The last mercenary stood watching his friends burn, and the

sword dropped from his hand. His mouth worked as he backed away from the two women; then he turned to run.

His shins hit Kay's back at precisely the right height, and he catapulted forward and struck the flagstones with his face. From behind Kay, Mandy stepped forward, a poker in her hand; behind her Neesa came with a candlestick, and Rip with another, heavier one.

I'm getting tired of this, Jimmy thought.

The twin points glittered as they moved. Skinny had a slight bleeding cut over one knee, but it just seemed to make him madder. 'My gold,' he wheezed, as he came forward again.

'I'll handle him,' Jarvis Coe said, stepping in beside him.

Skinny and Jimmy both glanced aside. Rox lay slumped against the wall, legs straight out in front of him, looking down as he clutched at his belly with both hands. Blood flowed out between his fingers.

'You get the sacrifice free!' Coe barked. 'Goddess, this is like trying to block four holes with one plug!'

Skinny screamed something and attacked; Jimmy skipped aside willingly.

It was a big room, and the one beyond it was even bigger. Jimmy needed six paces to reach the magician who stood at the foot of the table, hands raised. There was a crawling nimbus about him, more like darkness in a man's shape than anything else. He leapt forward in an immaculate long-lunge.

Can't chant with two feet of steel through his lungs, he reasoned.

One of the upraised hands moved. Light exploded behind Jimmy's eyes, and he screamed in anguish.

'No!' Bram howled, as the lad with the rapier staggered backward. 'No, no, no!'

The old man raised his curved knife, and the magician chanted.

Bram could feel a wind blowing – a wind of rage, and suddenly of air as well. There was a rushing, a woman's scream that came from everywhere and nowhere.

'Now!' the magician thundered. 'Now! Strike!'

And the silk flew from Bram's face. He looked up into the wrinkled face of the man who would kill him, and snarled defiance.

The knife dropped, despite the magician's howls. 'Zakry?' he whispered.

Who? Bram wondered, suddenly shocked out of his fear and anger. He'd never seen such pain as that on the age-scored face above him: the man's features writhed, and tears trickled down the cheeks.

'Zakry! Zakry's son. It was true! Elaine, you whore! You bitch!'

'She's dead,' another voice sighed. 'Oh, damnation. You waited too long.'

I am dead!

That rang through Bram's head like the tocsin of a great bronze bell. There was a figure standing before the lord now. He could hear its voice, not so loud, but echoing as if it made his bones vibrate in sympathy.

Seventeen years dying! Seventeen years, dying every minute. You killed me! You killed my Zakry, my darling, the father of my son! You tried to kill my child, too, but I stopped you, you monster!

'Whore,' the old man wheezed. 'Seventeen years I lived for nothing save to bring you back, and now I see Zakry told me the truth. You were his lover and this was his child! How I hate you!' He raised the dagger and struck at the insubstantial figure before him.

Its mouth gaped, emitting an endless dolorous wail that made Bram want to smash his own head against the stone table beneath him, if only that would stop it. The knife flashed again, and again.

*   *   *

Jimmy the Hand wheezed with a pain so great that he couldn't even scream. There was a scream going on, and it blew through him like a wind, like the agony of death stretched out to years. His vision had cleared a little, though, and he knew that he'd feel no more pain – or anything else, ever again – if he didn't move in the next moment.

There. The glitter of steel. He turned and lunged.

The effort hurt, but it cleared his head. He saw Baron Bernarr dodge, leaping backward to avoid the point of the rapier. That took him nearly to the window.

The window had been made as an archer's position: the man-width slit at the outer edge of the wall had sloping sides on all edges of the inner, so that the bowman could shoot to either side. The sill caught at his heels and he toppled backward, the knife glittering as he dropped it so that it landed point-down in the floorboards. But that allowed him to grip the smooth slanted stone and hold himself there with the friction of his palms. Then he struggled to get a leg behind himself and push his body upright.

Something came between the Baron and Jimmy. Jimmy thought it was a woman, but his head was still hurting too much to be sure; and he also thought he could see the Baron through it.

It screamed, and Jimmy dropped his sword to clutch at his head. He saw the older man's hands fly up likewise, and the O of his mouth as he fell backward and out of the window with a long scream, smashing through the fragile, costly glass and tumbling away into the lightning-shot night.

'Fifty feet down, onto stone,' Jimmy wheezed, bending and scrambling for the hilt of his rapier.

A huge weight seemed to have been lifted from his shoulders – or from the inside of his head. The night blew in through the shattered glass, and the black candles flickered out. Ten feet away Skinny goggled at him, and then slipped backward. Blood spurted as he pulled his throat off the point of Jarvis Coe's sword.

A sigh cut through the silence.

The magician at Bram's feet shook his head, and tucked his hands into the sleeves of his robe. 'It seems I must seek another patron for my . . . art,' he said, his voice whimsical and light. He raised his hand and suddenly he was gone.

Coe looked at the space the magician had occupied a moment before and swore. Jimmy didn't recognize the language, but the tone was unmistakable.

Behind him, Flora came into the room, supporting Lorrie; but the farmer's daughter shook herself free and hobbled toward Bram with her brother dancing behind her.

Bram raised his head and looked at all of them. 'Will someone please cut me loose?' he asked plaintively. 'And get me some breeches!'

Jimmy the Hand reined in and looked back down the road. There were enough people around the doors of the manor for the buzz of their voices to be audible even half a mile away. He shook his head ruefully and patted the hilt of the rapier slung at his saddlebow. 'So much for minstrels,' he said, taking a deep breath of the cool spring air.

Gulls flew through the air above, reminding him of home with an ache whose pain surprised him.

He and Coe rode, while Flora drove the dog-cart. Lorrie had elected to stay with Bram and the children, who were going to travel to Land's End in an old wagon from the Baron's stable. They had taken enough time for Jimmy to explain to Flora who Coe really was, while hiding the truth from the others. Jimmy felt Flora needed to know the whole truth, but decided against mentioning Coe's real identity to Bram, Lorrie and the others.

He didn't know why, except it seemed the Mocker's way to keep things from outsiders.

'Minstrels?' Flora said.

Jimmy cocked an eye: evidently she'd watched how Lorrie handled the reins, because she was managing the dog-cart with easy competence.

Jarvis Coe chuckled. 'I think young Jimmy is thinking of how the hero gets the girl, the gold and half the kingdom,' he said.

'Instead of which, Bram Blockhead does,' Jimmy said. Flora sighed, and he rolled an eye at her. 'What sort of baron do you think he'll make?' he asked Coe.

Coe shrugged. 'Better than the last, if the court and the Duke find for him. There are plenty of witnesses that he's Baroness Elaine's lost son – and it'll be convenient to have a local man, after the way Bernarr ran the holding into the ground and neglected his duty. Duke Sutherland paid no heed because he spends most of his days in Rillanon, rather than the western court, and the Baron paid his taxes on time. I think with Guy du Bas-Tyra in Krondor, a more critical gaze will settle on Land's End. Great Kesh is close: a strong man's needed here. Young Bram might have the makings of a hero.'

Jimmy shrugged. 'Some hero,' he said. 'Oh, he looks the part – but what did he do? Get knocked on the head, get tied up, and get rescued by . . .'

'By a pair of boys, four girls, a thief, and a witch-finder who officially doesn't exist,' Flora said tartly. 'Still, I think Bram's sweet.'

'Girls,' Jimmy said, and then laughed. 'Maybe I'm a hero-in-training, then.'

'Or a witch-finder,' Coe suggested. 'You show a lot of talent, Jimmy. I could use an apprentice . . .'

Jimmy shuddered and raised a hand. 'Oh, thank you, but that's far too much of an honour. I respect your goddess – and look forward to meeting her, *many* years from now.'

'Well, if you change your mind, send word to the Temple. I have to go looking for that magician, and could use some help.'

'Where do you think he is?'

'Out there somewhere,' answered Coe. 'Getting ready to cause trouble.' He glanced at Flora, who was watching Jimmy, then said to the boy, 'There are things in the world, my young friend, you may never appreciate. Like the distant war with the Tsurani in the west. You might hear about them, and they may have some bearing on your life, but you may remain blissfully ignorant of most of what occurs. But you also may find yourself confronting some aspect of a struggle that I can't begin to imagine myself, let alone tell you about.

'That magician, that Lyman Malachy, was no chance visitor to the manor on the night Bram was born. Why he was here, at this place, on that night, may forever be a mystery, but I can tell you this much.

'He or someone else like him will return to cause more evil. At the end, I sensed dark spirits in that house. Whatever the Baron thought would happen, I fear something else far more dire would have occurred. I think perhaps there was another agent of evil waiting to possess the Lady Elaine's body at the critical moment.

'There are dark forces loose in the world, my friend; dark forces which benefit from blood, murder and chaos. We could use a bright lad such as yourself in facing that evil.'

Jimmy laughed ruefully. 'Thanks, but I think I'll stick to something a little less dangerous, like stealing gold from under the nose of sleeping dragons.'

'You could stay with m— with us, Jimmy,' Flora said.

The young thief cocked an eyebrow, and she blushed.

'I don't think I'm cut out to be your . . . foster-brother,' he said cheerfully. 'And if I stayed, you'd have me helping old ladies across the street, and slaying demons, and Ruthia knows what else! Besides, what would your aunt's Captain Karl find for me to do? Cabin-boy, puking up my guts watch after watch?'

Flora and Coe laughed at that.

'What will you do, then?' Jarvis asked curiously.

'Go back to Krondor – and by land!' Jimmy said.

Coe laughed. 'Then turn your horse around, my friend, because you're heading in the wrong direction.'

Jimmy blinked like an owl caught in lantern-light. Then he laughed. 'I knew that!' he shouted, and clapped his heels to the horse as he turned it around. 'Fare well, friends! If you ever get back to Krondor, Flora, you know where to find me!'

She halted the dog-cart and stood up, waving. 'That I do, Jimmy the Hand!'

'And no offence, Master Coe, but I will sleep better if we never cross paths again!'

Coe laughed. 'Fare thee well, youngster!'

They both stared after him for a long time, as the hooves faded into the distance, beating a tune that echoed back from cliffs to sea. 'Do you think he'll get home safely?' asked Coe.

Flora laughed. 'And with gold in his pockets, too, I'll guarantee.'

'Gold?'

Urging the horse forward, she grinned. 'He'll dodge Bram and Lorrie and the kids in the wagon, circle around through the woods, then revisit the manor on his way back home. If Bram returns to find a silver candlestick or any of Lady Elaine's jewels still there, then I don't know Jimmy.'

Jarvis Coe laughed and moved his horse in beside the cart. 'I hope that boy finds a different calling in life. It would be a shame to see him end his days at the end of a rope.'

Flora laughed again. 'That'll never happen, Master Coe. I don't know what will happen to him, but I'll wager my life that no hangman will ever get his rope around the neck of Jimmy the Hand!'

They rode on.

EPILOGUE

Krondor

The Daymaster looked up.

A half-sized door – one which most members of the Mockers didn't know about – swung open. It was hidden in the stonework, disguised by the dark edges and the dim light, one had to know it was there to find it.

A small figure loomed up out of the darkness. The corner of the huge basement under the brothel known as Mother's or Mocker's Rest was reserved for the Daymaster or Nightmaster and their immediate subordinates and given wide berth by most other Mockers until they were called in.

The Daymaster suppressed a chuckle. 'Well, young Jimmy the Hand,' he observed, 'back so soon?'

'I had cause,' Jimmy said. 'Enough time has passed, hasn't it?' he added, taking a wooden chair across the table from the Daymaster.

'That depends,' said the Daymaster. 'There's still a swarm of crushers out and about looking to find out who did what over at the castle. Duke Guy is back in triumph from routing the Keshians in the Vale of Dreams, and no one has heard of the crew of the *Royal Griffin,* so must be thinking ol' Jocko Radburn got himself drowned, if that's not a pipe-dream. Del Garza has managed to shift most of the blame for everything on to Radburn.' He lowered his voice, as if not wishing to be overheard, which was somewhat theatrical, since they were alone deep in the bowels of Mother's. 'Rumour is Prince Erland lies dying and Guy was fit to be tied learning that the Prince had been tossed in the dungeon, but del Garza laid that one at Jocko's feet, too, so it looks as if no one will suffer much for it. Except the Prince, of course. So, things are a bit quieter, but you'd still better have something for the Upright Man to salve his anger, given all the trouble you caused at the castle.'

Jimmy reached into his tunic and pulled out a small pouch. 'Two hundred gold sovereigns,' he said nonchalantly. 'Will that help?'

The Daymaster nodded so that his jowls jiggled as he spoke. 'That's a right good start. It'll keep him from tossing you in the bay, I suspect, but you'd better have something more to add to the kitty else you're still going to the Bashers for coming back early.'

Jimmy sat back in the wooden chair and beamed.

The Daymaster couldn't help but return the infectious grin. 'There's something up that sleeve of yours, young Jimmy, I have no doubt. Let's have it.'

'Remember Gerem the Snake?'

'Gerem Benton? For certs. What about him?'

'He was running a gang of thief-catchers for the old Baron of Land's End.'

The Daymaster sat back. 'Thought old Gerem was dead.'

Jimmy said, 'I think he wanted it that way when he left Krondor. Had his own little operation down there, and his thief-catchers were pretty much running things. They arrested anyone dodgy who came to Land's End, but ran their own dodges on the side, so the Baron's men thought they needed to keep Gerem around. I tumbled the new Baron to the scam and he rewarded me with the gold. So, I just put him and his mob out of business.'

Jimmy thought it best not to mention that the 'new Baron' was a farm boy who hadn't yet been approved by the King's court in Rillanon, and that the 'reward' had come without Bram's knowledge as Jimmy had pilfered quite a number of valuables from the unguarded manor house the night after everyone thought he had left Land's End. He had taken what he could carry and easily dispose of; a brace of silver candlesticks and a handsome dagger owned by one of Bernarr's ancestors; and he had agonized for a long time over which pieces of Lady Elaine's jewels to lift and which to leave behind for Bram to give to Lorrie. He was still puzzled by what Coe had told him about the dead lady's part in the events of that last night, but his sense of debt to her outweighed his greed and so he had stolen only a little from her. He had found eager buyers before reaching Krondor for the valuables, so by the time he entered the city he hadn't had to deal with any of the local fences.

He had ridden in wearing a fancy coat and clean shirt, and the guards at the gate were far more interested in ruffians and thieves trying to leave the city than in a well-to-do lad from Land's End arriving for a visit. He had sold the horse and saddle, so now all he had to show for his adventure was a fancy hat, coat, and another bag of gold he wasn't sharing with the Upright Man.

The Daymaster studied Jimmy for a long moment, then said, 'So what you're saying is Land's End is ripe for a well-spotted gang to move in?'

'Exactly,' said Jimmy, trying hard not to look too smug and failing miserably.

The Daymaster chuckled. 'Well, I'll speak to the Upright Man about it. Seems a good enough price for forgiveness if you brought us an entire town to run. Nicely situated, too, right there near the border with Kesh. You head out for your crib and lie low for a couple of days and if he says no, I'll send you word on how much longer you have to hide out. Another month or two, I reckon. But if he says "good enough", do you want to head back to Land's End with the gang and help set it up?'

Jimmy got up out of the chair swiftly. 'No, thanks,' he answered. 'I'll stick to Krondor. Here, there are only crushers, guardsmen, soldiers and the occasional merchant with a knife to concern myself with. Child's play. Country life is just a little too dangerous for my liking.'

With that, the boy thief turned his back on the Daymaster and returned to the sewers. Jimmy took a deep breath as he slogged down the filthy brick tunnel, and felt safely back in the place he counted as home. He knew the Upright Man would make him lay up for another week or so, just to ensure Jimmy didn't mistake who was running the city, but he knew that there were purses to cut, and rooms to burgle and the Guild always was hungry for its cut. Sooner or later the word would arrive and Jimmy the Hand would return to his trade. He'd had enough of aiding princesses and farm girls, battling dark agents of some unknowable horror.

As he vanished into the murk, he started to whistle.

AFTERWORD

'Why collaborate?' I'm often asked.

This is the third book in the *Legends of the Riftwar* series. For the next few years I'm going to be concentrating on my solo works, but I plan on doing more collaborations in the future if I can. My reason for wanting to do them is twofold.

First, for me, Midkemia has always been about 'other voices'. To understand what I mean, you have to remember that the world of Midkemia was developed as a role-playing campaign by a number of very bright people over a number of years while we were students at the University of California, San Diego, in the late 1970s.

To me, the personalities of those involved in creating the world had a profound effect on how I see Midkemia, its diversity and its unique qualities. When I choose a location in the world to place my work, the nature of that locale is often something that was decided by someone else years ago.

So working with other authors is a chance to bring 'other voices' into play. The first three, William R Forstchen, Joel Rosenberg, and the co-author of this book, Steve Stirling, are writers whose work I admire and enjoy. Their styles differ from mine in significant ways, but we all worked together easily.

The way we worked was remarkably similar, and very different from the way in which I worked with Janny Wurts on the *Empire Trilogy*. With Janny, we would pass chapters back and forth, rewriting several times until there were places I can't tell you who wrote what.

With Bill, Joel and Steve, we agreed upon a general storyline, then I'd turn them loose. When I got their rough draft, I'd rewrite it, trying to keep their 'voices' intact, while I made sure the work remained consistent with the world in which we were writing. We'd e-mail one another or talk on the phone, and along the way a blended voice would emerge.

For this book, *Jimmy the Hand*, Steve Stirling chose this character as one of his favourites, and I was happy to do a story about Jimmy's 'first' solo adventure, long before he saved Arutha from the assassin on the rooftops of Krondor. I think it safe to say that after having written many books about Jimmy/Lord James, I would have been unable to return to that character without being burdened by what I knew lay before him. Steve managed to find the boy who perked up the last four chapters of the first half of *Magician* and remind me who he was.

In *Murder in LaMut*, Joel and I got to 'clone' three of my favourite characters from his universe, changing them just a little bit to make them Midkemian, yet echoing their well-chronicled history in Joel's *Guardian of the Flames* series. My original idea for that story went back years ago to a notion I once had of doing a solo book about Roald, the mercenary friend of Laurie, who was featured in *Silverthorn*, set in a blizzard-strangled city where murder was done. This worked out better, I think.

Bill wanted to write Xenophon's retreat through Persia as a fantasy and I wanted to write a *Sharpe's Rifles*-style story, so we came up with *Honoured Enemy*. Bill's strong background in military history and his familiarity with historical figures gave me strong characters that I cherish along with those I've developed; but I could never have imagined them on my own.

All three authors were fun to work with, and as always I learned from getting to peek inside another author's head. I hope my readers find these books as much of a treat as I do. I look forward to working with other talented writers in the future.

Raymond E. Feist
San Diego, CA 2003